Heralded for his collaborations with filmmakers Andy Warhol and Jack Smith and his inspired coinage "theatre of the ridiculous," RONALD TAVEL is the author of such Off-Off-Broadway classics as "Gorilla Queen" and "Bigfoot," as well as the novel "Street of Stairs" (Olympia Press, 1968). He was artist-in-residence at the Yale University Divinity School and Cornell University in the 1970s and the recipient of many awards and fellowships. Born in New York in 1936, he first visited Bangkok in 1981-82, returned briefly in 1995, and lived there continuously from 1997 until his death in 2009.

RONALD TAVEL

CHAIN
A NOVEL

FAST BOOKS

Designed by Michael Smith
Cover photograph by Daniel Montero

ISBN 978-0-9794736-8-5

FAST BOOKS, P. O. Box 1268, Silverton, Oregon 97381
http://fastbookspress.com

CHAIN

THE FIRST DAY

"CHAIN WAS BORN during the postwar ethnic riots in dire poverty in the shadow of the Oriental, a building that would become Asia's most expensive hotel. A stone's throw away, he pilfered the trash tanks behind the French Embassy; and swam in the Chao Phya River, which winds through the city like a Naga—that Buddhist dragon humped with crested arches—down to the Bight of Bangkok: the fist of the South China Sea. These facts determined his life."

Cory Simon glanced at me for approval of his prepared opening. Then he pulled back the drape in his furnished room and called me over to the casements. Nearly six foot and powerfully put together, he pointed to the eloquent Oriental Hotel. The day before, he had claimed it leans landward like a wind-blown palm or a mandarin lowering his head to a Peking potentate.

Of course, it does not. What is more, a high-rise frenzy surrounding it has dwarfed the famous accommodation.

"Here we go," he insisted. "It is urging its fateful silhouette directly across that lane to our left. That lane is Soi 36, otherwise Soi Rongphasi Kao. In the squat, whitewashed wood house there, Chain was born."

I asked, "Did you pick this studio for your current stay so you could see it?"

"That is correct," Cory said, impatiently hopping in place.

"Do dragons come to mind because Chain was Sino-Thai?"

"'Sino' is an umbrella term, similar to 'Euro.' His family had fled Yunnan, the Chinese province on the border of Laos, at the onset of World War II. But Chain lived with his exact lineage as men do a shameful secret."

"He didn't look Chinese?"

"His skin was blue tint—and on some days a mellow lion. He was short and had a muscular, proportioned body I would have associated then with Malay ports of call or Micronesia. Yet who, after all, populated the Pacific isles? Later I saw how he vivified the cormorant fishermen in Ching dynasty paintings—or a sentry in photos of Kunming. Because several inadvertent reactions had regionalized his remarkable appearance. I learned his particular pedigree through investigation."

"Why did he think you would care what he really was?"

"In laid-back Siam, those Mainland migrants and workaholic refugees had the 'genetic advantage,' as we say now. The Hainanese and Teochew, who'd come earlier as professionals and merchants, were, if not the capital's lawful movers and shakers, then at least its power brokers. A precarious position for a minority, no? Still, Chain was Chinese only by territorial claim. His actual origin was anathema to him, hidden in the zealotry of his westernization and buried in his hatred—for Thailand. What *I* thought didn't matter."

I said, "So his beauty was like the cormorant-keepers in a Manchu scroll..."

"With limestone cliffs soaring out of pure white space, and pagodas and bridges suspended in a swab of fog. With sampans on unpainted lakes. It was like the wilderness after rain, and a wall of monsoon water crushing outcrops east of Nicobar. And like many more extravagant things I'll think of as we stumble along," Cory offered playfully. "You are turning this into an inquisition!"

"That's my job," I protested.

"No! An interview is an intellectual crime. So let me speak uninterrupted and report the contest between Chain and me as it naturally volunteers itself. Questions can be counterproductive. You know what I mean? Off-center, or alien and parochial, they'll throw me clear of the mark."

"I'm adding angles. My reservations prompt unusual angles. I seldom get complaints. Most subjects are not as articulate as you."

He hung a straw broom on an outside hook, pulled-to the casement, and let the drape fall back, which dropped the glare and heat that defeated his narrow balcony's weather-shield. He settled on the sofa. Other than the double bed and breakfast counter, that is all the World Inn itself provides. His fairly large studio is disorganized. Under the windows and running the length of them, Cory Simon has planted a jungle. That thicket of shoots, spiraling vines, giant flowers, and airborne parasites cannot be called houseplants, or even a garden: it is a space-eating indoor rain forest, a *tableau vivant* that must require daily cultivating. A desk, fridge, two garment racks, framed pulp-fiction cover art, eight shelves of books, videos, and DVD classics (but no TV), and next to them a gimcrackery of bizarre, incongruous curios, in addition to the wingback I took and the coffee table separating us, round out the clutter.

"But *I am* articulate," he announced without the faintest trace of irony. "Singha?"

"Oh—not now. A little later, O.K.?"

"You don't object if I…?" He stomped a bottle of beer onto the coffee table, inches from my miniature mike, and instantly shot off its cap with his thumb.

"Cory, you'll topple the mike-stand!" I warned. What fingers! I steadied the fragile clasp.

"Never!"—downing a third of the liter. "I know the balance on—and danger in—that ear to hell. Even if that ear's a gimmick-generation wanna-be doctor in Cultural History and Queer Theory. *You* take care you brought enough tapes."

"I'm fixed fine." I was wondering if he had started sloshing before I arrived. I decided I would have to know him better in order to tell. His sober—or tipsy—articulation comes from Mr. Simon's ability to think farther ahead through his sentences than average talkers can or try to. He can phrase his thoughts, with multiple and complex subordinates, up to a minute in advance of reaching them. I believe it is this that erases any gap between his extemporaneous speech and writing. But as he had not been interviewed before, no one has pointed this out. Also, there are no published photos of him. Filling in, then:

3

Cory Simon is appealing, his body chiseled, his age indeterminable. He could easily pass for forty. He moves in paced streaks like a startled—or stalking—cat; called on this, he turns actorly, as if phoning-in a performance. He sports a close black beard. His hair, dark, lustrous, and heavy, is worn differently on successive days for no apparent reason. The part might be dead center, in the fashion favored by Thais, or carefully drawn on the left or right. Or that mane could be gelled and hauled back from his short brow. This beard and changing hairstyle stumped me at first from pinning down just what his face was reminding me of. The knobbed chin and always gnawing, square jaw, his broken nose which veers right, and a deep scar dividing his left eyebrow add up to the look of a sensitive boxer—like one that was all the rage when Cory was young. More disorienting still than such a face on a writer are his eyes, which are small and appear to have epicanthic folds: they slant radically toward a trio of suntanned wrinkles. What frustrates your coming to a quick decision on which race or races they and his sharp cheekbones represent is their color, a poised robin's-egg blue: when they are not feline-lemon, storm gray, or splintered green. They respond to his position in relation to the source of light, the hour, how long he has been awake, and the number of beers that man puts away.

I said, "Got twenty gay artists I wanna rout in Beijing, Nam, and Bangkok. Columbia's Division of Oral History pays poop for each. Zero for travel. You pull three Franklins. –Is that a kick-back I'm starting to feel?"

"Yeah, stand up: you'll feel it real fast," he snapped. Cory wears a large gold ring carved in the shape of two Thai mermen. He worked it, sliding it up and down his thick wedding finger. He would go on, in general, to fidget with some toy, if not the ring then a nail clip, the bottle caps or a pen, a comb or a toothpick, even a sheet of paper that he creases into a shut fan and twists like worry beads. When his hands are not occupied, he tends to raise them and block his face.

I think he liked me. There is this foreplay, like quibbling about honoraries, with anyone I record. People jockey for alpha. I take it in stride.

Cory Simon did not consider his private life to be public domain. Gayness was a subject he felt conflicted writing about—and never had. He could write a novel, of course, if that were not unfair. He distrusts art and questions its legitimacy, and respecting this caution, confines his output to non-fiction: articles on architecture and film, serious voyage journals, gulls' guides, and quirky takes on a hot political scene. *I* tracked him through reviewers who ballyhoo his haut style, a style to be admired—and, conceivably, emulated.

But at his age now, like so many of his contemporaries, he thought there was little to lose, being honest: that it arguably was his duty to gay-ambivalent adolescents. He remembered his own youthful torment all too well. Since he loved to drink and spin a yarn, here was the carpe diem, providentially delivered, so to speak, to make a positive statement. And assisting *me*, a college gay, he could help himself to a physical audience, that tangible return denied the lonely writer. So the agreement we had made in a café the day before was this: rather than invest in a scattershot sketch of his whole life, invariably misleading, we would spend several sessions together, the number it took him to relate one comprehensive episode in it. I would rearrange my schedule to accommodate Cory's (patronizing) generosity with his time.

Of a sudden, Cory knuckled his hand with the ringed finger and jabbed the ring at me. In a gravelly voice, he reprimanded: "I need to tell you one story before we start. Early in our relationship, Chain mentioned that an acquaintance from Hat Yai had passed him a pair of plane tickets for the upcoming weekend down there. He said a 'disciplinary action' was preventing that man from using them himself. Hat Yai is the nominal capital of the Islamic south. Chain knew I'd no desire to visit a town yet more cancerous than Bangkok: we'd get from its outskirts to the Tarutao archipelago, a national marine preserve that reaches into the legendary Straits of Malacca off the southwestern-most coast of Thailand—the tip of Tarutao Island is within swimming distance of Malaysian waters. He gave me no practical reason for wanting to go to this preserve, referring to it only as a scenic diversion and break from the stress of city life. And my own flaky self."

"Now when exactly was this?"

"Before the May monsoons in '82: they close that area to outsiders from the end of April to November. This was when he still had to chastise me for stepping directly on thresholds—a defense of moody indoor spirits stands on the raised threshold to a room; if you step on their heads, chances are they'll retaliate. Naturally, as we left my apartment for the airport, I stomped my worn tennis shoe right on one of their top-knots."

I suggested, "Well, you can't see them."

"*We* can't. But Chain could.

"Immediate we landed in Hat Yai, he made a phone call at the nearest booth. An ordinary truck for transporting produce or animals shortly picked us up, and we sat in the open hold with a few other passengers wearing headscarves and fezzes who stared me down and sometimes blinked at Chain. After a couple of hours along scrub country roads, we arrived at a skeletal port I now assume was Pak Bara; there we boarded a tramp steamer and sailed to Tarutao. Diving dolphins swam with us; visible from the gunwales, they turned silver when they'd bullet under the boat over chimneys of coral or platters of pastel beehive. At Tarutao we transferred to a motor scow. Chain appeared edgy on that warped, deserted dock and eager not to linger.

"Our destination was an islet farther out: I've never been sure if it was Ko Ah-dang, Ko Dong, or Ko Rawi. He evaded identifying it, responding to my need to know names with one of those indrawn smiles Asians utilize to warn, 'Halt here: don't push this.' However, when we ate at a government installation fronting the beach, after memorizing my face for the hundredth time, he was happy to draw me a simple map of this castaway's haven, with arrows pointing a path to a waterfall; and to satisfy my curiosity as to why he'd acted so unreservedly uncomfortable back on Tarutao. Tarutao had been a penal colony. It was set up in the 1930s, and by 1941 three thousand common criminals and politicos were therein conveniently incarcerated, dis-

6

couraged from escaping by a surround of crocodiles and sharks. During World War II a Japanese blockade cut off their food provisions and malaria medicine, and seven hundred guards and convicts died. The survivors found the ingenuity to raid passing merchant ships, thrived beyond their desperation, and enjoyed the salt-air thrills of piracy straight through 1946—when a disgusted British fleet rounded them up and burnt down the prisons. The ghosts of those who'd perished still roam the mountain range there. Tarutao concedes no ground in remaining, for its unfortunate visitors, and for all time, *the* most palpable Thai Island of Terror.

"After lunch Chain wanted to nap in one of the development's collapsing shacks. Thrown out of sorts by this use of a tale to scare little children to distract from not accounting for his accelerating shifty behavior (including his insistence that our present whereabouts be labeled nameless), I said I'd go swimming: white sharks and reptiles no more troublesome to me than the phantoms of left-wing dissenters or their brutal guards. Of course, once having paraded my devil-may-care, I'd no intention of disturbing the amphibious infestation, let alone breaker-scouting man-eaters, and wandered instead, his map in hand, amongst the nautilus strew and coral-piece piles on the beach. The sun was so fireball that I could feel my exposed skin turning scarlet and had constantly to rub a moisturizer on every spot my T-shirt and shorts didn't cover.

"I'd gone some distance—it was at least an hour since I could see the point from which I'd started off—when I came upon a shelter of dense, inter-clutching casuarina trees and heard what I recognized to be a substantial waterfall. I worked my way carefully atop the slippery maze of roots until I stood within sight of the cascade and paused there to admire it for so long that I began to feel rooted myself. The water broke over sparkling granite boulders fifty feet high and spilled into a glass lagoon.

"Then, as if I were hallucinating, or somehow watching an old Flaherty classic—but I assure you I was neither—Chain, growing piecemeal apparent from behind it, parted the curtain of the cascade and waded into the shallows of the lagoon until the brackish water reached nearly to his knees. He wore only a dripping *jongkraben,* the Siamese wraparound of wat murals and period films, its tail taken through the legs and pulled up to tuck in at the waist. It was bleached-cream, brocaded with five twin-rows of brown, nine-inch double X's with dark brown shoes or gloves at their points. He carried a small cyan canister, removing its lid before placing it on a jutting rock. Then he drew a blade of burgundy soap from the circular canister and lathered himself: caressing his neck, underarms, shoulder clefts, and nips with a serene yet lubricious, unhurried approximation of self-arousal, splashing seductively at the suds and directing their semen-like rivulets into his navel. He loosened the waist of the wrap, slipped both fists inside, and for almost a minute massaged his fullness, vacantly and deliberately, before scooping water with the container's lid and washing the foam through his pouch. He raked his nails into his slack, indigo hair; then raised as much of the garment as would give, and in a kouros curve squeezed the soak from its gather. This final position, his vision adrift but shut in itself, his lake-rinsed, cobalt torso and the crystal-winking cavity of hip, his nates all the more naked for the clinging loincloth outlining them, was so reminiscent of Paul Chabas's *September Morn* that I—like the Americans who first saw that oil—literally gasped. Chain did not hear me; but the leaves and lianas in the maritime tangle visibly shuddered at my response.

Then he looked up and to the left of him, where the pool funneled into an estuary: some thing or other sound caught his attention. And presently it came into sight, a deeply chiseled palm-stem canoe with ballast barrels or wickers secured to a frame overreaching either side. Four fierce-looking Malay indigenes were standing in it and paddling countercurrent. Far from jarred, Chain openly grinned; and the lead paddler, statuesque, iron-limbed, and patrician, held forth a friendly salute. They drove the canoe to the stream's embankment, where all four paused to *wai* him from their brows. Jumping out, they steadied the pirogue in the silt as Chain, leaving his soap and container on the rock, excitedly plowed the water toward them.

These are Malay aborigines, I thought: their bodies black, their eyes huge, gleaming, and round. When he reached their craft, the three subsidiary men had undone the hindmost wicker and partially extracted what appeared to be a sizable stone head: by its four faces and four-tiered crown, I assumed a Brahma. They pointed to the remaining wickers with satisfaction, and Chain warmly embraced the leader. Then Chain got into the dugout and squatted cross-legged in its center. The others shoved it into the stream, resumed their original standing positions, and paddled with the current swiftly out of view.

"At that moment, the wider tree barks nearest to me in the coastal heath came away from their trunks: and morphed into graceful men wearing bark-colored kerchiefs, brow-bands, and lungis. They darted a look at me and, crouching with fear, slipped into the evergreen and thoroughly vanished. Clearly perceived as an intruder, I froze where I was, imagining, despite my map, I'd already created a disturbance dangerous enough. Only a barely perceptible rippling told me that these men, nearly a dozen of them, were rowing away on several rafts in the direction opposite to the one Chain and his confreres had taken. I managed a glimpse of this coven through a deciduous crack in the forest, fixing them in my mind's eye: spare, mountolive, and muscled.

"When the surrounding area became as quiet as it would, I swam over to the rock and retrieved the deserted soap container. It was glazed clay, a celadon jewel box, minimally carved with fish and flora: possibly from the shipwreck discovered in the Gulf of Thailand some eight years prior, I guessed by the design; and so to date back to AD 1450.

"I retreated to the beach, found a knoll to scale, and scanned the horizon. I identified Chain's dwindling canoe hugging the shore along the farthest outcrop to my left and, when it reached its sea-most extension, circle that short, sloping cliff and disappear. For the next three hours I stared at the industrious fiddler crabs and freckled mudskipper fish. 'These creatures have an active afternoon,' I mused, 'but not nearly as eventful as a certain person's afternoon nap.'

"I returned to the installation at sundown and had a few beers on its canteen's tropical verandah. There'd be little profit in visiting the shack to which Chain had repaired…like a worrywart, hound, or spy…whether or not he was there now. I was naïvely hopeful that whatever he did in the Straits of Malacca was none of my business. We were not on the Island of Terror, but what to put money on right then was that he unaccountably (as yet) counted on me to be above the indiscretion of a clumsy attempt at escape. –And that he'd shortly order snow fish.

"So, circa 8:00 p.m., dressed in a snow-white shirt and snow-white slacks, Chain appeared and ordered grilled snow fish; and, looking angelic, listened to the neap tide. When he finished his meal and caught the Pall Mall I flicked at him, I asked about the lean, bark-colored, secretive men one might come across on the island. Oh, he nonchalantly informed me, those are Sea Gypsies: a tribe he called the Seabo, who house on nearby Ko L'peh and wander from islet to islet. They are Indo-Malaysians, collectors of shellfish and lobsters: they speak their own language and worship the fickle Spirits of the Deep.

"Then I enquired about the curious design on his *jongkraben*; he offered, 'Make like this Yunnan. Before: 7,000 years. Use human backstrap loom…'

"His voice softened and trailed off on the last words as he absorbed the fact that I'd seen it. Along with the Gypsies. And must, therefore, have also seen the smugglers. I produced his bluish-green antique jewel box and set it on the table, expecting him to fake surprise. But he lowered his gaze with deliberation; and, after a pause, intoned: 'Can have diamond design also, the *jongkraben*…' Without raising his lids, he eased into a wide, collegial smile."

Cory waited; then reached for his beer.
I said, "Why did you have to tell me this now?"
He clicked his teeth on the bottle's rim. "Because you need to know that as long as you record, or listen to, the story of Chain, it will always be at three removes: hearing and watching a man

watching the nomads watching Chain. It took me some time to realize that with him, certainties would forever defer as on that initiative isle. I surmised that Chain's performance in the lagoon—and how else could you applaud the calculated poses of that public bath but as a performance?—was for the benefit of the Seabos: so that superstitiously detained—either puzzled or mesmerized by his demi-deity—they must then watch the four fierce indigenes carry along their quarry. And that I myself would never see more than just what he permitted the Gypsies to. If they were habitually to slip so furtively away, speaking only their own language, I'd not be invited to paydirt more direct."

"Meaning?"

"Were the aborigines actual smugglers? Was their quarry vintage and authentic? The Gypsies oversee the border—every border crossing. Why force the Gypsies to witness if it weren't? And was I really intended to discover this apparent double-cross? How could Chain know I'd reach that scene in time? He couldn't. I speculated that, as a Thai, he gambled. He believed that the sprawl of spilled temple joss sticks read as infallible prediction. Or predestination. So watching is guessing. It's not weighing in with the jackpot."

"But?"

"Talking, as we are now, sometimes is... I did not feel safe with him. I don't think I ever would. –You *can* interrupt me when I say anything alcohol renders...inexcusably vague."

"I'm hip."

"Be no stopping you, anyhow..." All at once, his bolstered shoulders sank. "This is like being subpoenaed," he chortled, a fast, short snort through a single nostril. Cory Simon had let go.

I asked, "Would you ever crack who had been subjected to 'disciplinary action,' and why? –If some dude actually was."

Cory nodded. "To that question, Chain had one word: 'Nok.' It means 'bird.' A young man named Bird. I'll get to him by and by."

I frowned when he lined up two more Singhas. He said, "No sweat. In those days I used these to wash down gin and vodka tonics."

11

"Yes?—what about those days? With respect now to chronology, please."

"O.K. Let's see...

"Chain's father screamed in his sleep. He'd be back in Guangxi or Kunming, where Japanese strafing tagged him and explosives fell on his tarpaper lean-to. His cries kept the family on edge for years, especially when he'd leap out of bed as if it were his catafalque and shriek at one and all to take cover. In time, he could see the bombers even while awake and hear their deadly eggs whistling into the yard of that wood house where his family had established an ice-packing business. He, of course, became extraneous to this enterprise; and when Bangkok *was* finally bombed, by us, he rapidly degenerated, hid in unlit corners, in closets, under cabinets, and down in the low cellar where he panicked, wept, and shook like the mango leaves loosened in handfuls by the winds that batter the warren of Rongphasi Kao minutes before the midyear's endless scalding storms.

"'He die of afraid. I still little then,' Chain told me.

"...Chain is a nickname he himself chose. His given name was Somboon. I, always forgetting that, perplexed his mom when I'd ask for Chain. Somboon was born shortly after the war, when this territory in turmoil was once again called Siam, and he would be his parents' last child. He bitterly remembered his father's collapse: and its legacy in Buddha's inequitable order. He was put to work early, backbreaking work, lifting, strapping, and delivering by bike the heavy blocks of ice. Chain was to let himself feel that yoke for the rest of his life as his father had let the howling airplanes haunt his.

"Young Somboon went through the compulsory four years of grade school. He studied Buddhist ritual and learned to read and write Thai at the wat in his soi. He had a talent for atonal tongues. His monastery did not cater to that, but his house, situated where it was, next to the central post office, foreign restaurants, the French Embassy, and New Road, the initial hub of British activity, allowed him to listen to a number of European languages. He spoke Mandarin, Teochew, and a Tai dialect as well: fluencies he refuted in front of me.

12

"Approaching adolescence, Somboon entered the monkhood for the minimum three months incumbent on boys back then. His head was shaved; he donned the saffron of renunciation; and begged for rice in the mornings, quietly opening his woven basket. His mother, two sisters, and aunt were very proud of him, and merit accrued to them all.

"He remembered his abbot as menacing. He spied on Somboon when he bathed with his fellow novitiates; and would isolate him, claiming he was so incorrigible that he needed individual guidance and correction. A week into this 'correcting,' he undid the boy's holy robes and played with his genitals. 'When he see how big penis me, he take and pull so I come sperm for him,' Chain disclosed. 'First time I very scared. But after make like this many... many.'

"Abject and agitated, I contemplated Chain on the dismal night he related that, fencing it with a feeble, 'What you say him?'

"'What I can say? He priest. I ten then. That nice for priest, yes? This man priest! Same priest.'"

Cory stops here. He rubbed the mermen ring across his upper gum, then pressed his lower lip against that gum: and shifted the lip back and forth. He snapped a matchstick. "Go on," I urged.

"Taking pity on his work situation, neighbors recommended Somboon to staff they knew at the Oriental Hotel, to serve as a menial in its kitchens..." Cory grabbed a full box of matchsticks, to go at one-by-one. Then he mutters: "Abetted by his language skills, he soon became an attractive pubertal arbiter there between disgruntled guests and the overburdened staff..."

At this point I clock a blank of three and a half minutes. Eventually, I injected: "...where it didn't take long for some guests and the management to discover what Somboon's abbot already had?"

Right here, an unbelievably loud and strident screech pierced the room. "What in heck is that?" I yelled, rising in the wing chair. Cory shook.

13

"A black koel. In the courtyard. He loves its huge umbrella tree."

"He must be huge himself," I speculated. "What a whoop!"

"He's one foot five inches. It's a worried whoop, isn't it? Might start any time and carry on for hours: a reveille nobody shoots. At 4:00 a.m., it strikes me as alarmist, yet that bird's cry is at least a clarion call."

I asked, "Can we see Gabriel?"

"Nope. Sorry. Gabriel comes under the umbrella, in a manner of speaking, of those who blow it out only when camouflaged."

"Scout's honor? Then Gabriel's not unique in this nabe… Would you repeat the story of the Japanese food-taster for me?"

"Think my camouflage is thick enough for that?"

"O.K., I'll watch my mouth. You seem totally uncomfortable with Chain at the Oriental right now, and I'm anxious to include the food sampler's reveille."

"Is it that important?" Cory looked annoyed.

"I could kick myself for meeting you yesterday without my tape recorder."

"The tongue stales in twice-told tales! Let me snatch another Singha." He did and returned to his seat "Need a light, Small-change?"

"Thanks." I craned forward, and when he sparked the match with his thumbnail, saw that he was trembling. He read my stare and steadied himself. I wondered if he was going to jar the table, because his left knee was bobbing out of control. I held the mike, I thought inconspicuously, but he caught that as well, and brought his knee into neutral.

"I WAS SIXTEEN. Gay bars were off-limits. But Dry Dock, on West Eighth in the Village, must have been lit with a dying ten-watt bulb. So a kid, once he slipped in unseen, headed straight for the pitch-black meat rack: this bench at the rear wall. When I considered splitting with a possibility, I needed to engineer him toward the glass-pane entrance, where an outside lantern cast a faint glow into the bar, and there make my decision.

"I was on that back bench of an evening, ducking the bouncer with my head in my chest, a stocking-cap a mask to my eyes, and a scarf pulled over my mouth. Can you picture it?—just this nose to sniff at the menu on either thigh of me. I detected by his accent that the shadowy mountain scrubbing one thigh was Asian. –Decidedly *planetary*: a three-seater. I osmotically also knew that he wasn't very attractive. But the China Seas churned in him, and that brought a catch to my pulse. So when he asked me up to his place, right around the corner on Ninth, I didn't need to ease him into the lantern's opinion. I was going, man.

"His apartment crowned five flights in a shabby New York tenement. Venturing in, you came upon a different world. Though he had scattered about his small two rooms artifacts and treasure from Burma, Brunei, and the Philippines, he essentially had done up the space with rice paper partitions to reproduce a Japanese country house; and had lined the walls with them as well. Wicks that burned scented oil in cylindrical rice paper shades were positioned tastefully at levels which enhanced each other, further dividing and varying his miniature universe. There were four low divans and a low Japanese serving table, no chairs, just cushions, a tokonoma, a few huge old woodcarvings, and spare, evocative watercolors on flush and distant screens. I had cast my lot in the dark and flown a Dark-Arts carpet to a contained and tenable Far East. Boy, was I pleased with myself!

"'Aren't *you* firm! This is real muscle,' he said, his fingers sliding through a deftly undone button on my flannel shirt and gripping my upper arm. 'Firm down here as well?' he asked, his other hand combing for that immediate reward so many gays need so immediately. I wasn't. So, patiently, he warmed a vial of plum wine and continually poured refills into a thimble-size server for me. It was called *A Thousand Branches*; a better name would be *Mother's Milk*. Being a former sumo wrestler-in-training (as I was to learn, but could have predicted), he might have constricted me to his will. Instead he became as gentle as a tiger with a cub; and apparently honest in appreciating my own developing strength, contented himself for a while with simply pawing such prominence as already, if only, was evident in my neck, shoulders, and shins. I certainly was going to capitalize on

15

his Eastern brew and patience by delaying the compulsory hop onto his straw-mat sleeper, since—oh, yes!—*I would most rather talk, then*—talk, talk, talk: *talk in the sunrise if I could.*

"He explained that although he was Japanese, he had been raised on Jolly Boy Island, a coconut patch in the Andamans, quite close to the Jarawa people, Stone Age blacks believed to have settled there fifty thousand years ago: and so to be the link to, and proof of, man's pilgrimage from the Kalahari. Detesting his patrimonial grooming in sumo, he stowed away to Macao, where he studied its kitchens and quickly became a food-taster for Hilton, wherever they featured Cantonese cuisine. A skill, then, requiring Asia-trotting: and so his defiance now shot across Chu Klang or hopscotched the mainland to high Sikkim, forbidden Tibet, and the isolation of Uzbek and Turkistan. I demanded he summon these magical lands for me but, before he could, assaulted him with my own stipulations for Cathay, Tartary, Araby, and the Indies, insisting that he contrive whatever his depiction to support the emergency in my rapturous metaphysic. While he sat on a divan, I lay in the talons of a Taoist stork on a weave at his feet; and snarling like the foo dog, needled him to ply me with which of the outposts he visited was the most strange, the most fabulous, the most remote—for there I belong, I shouted at him, there would I be and there *will* I be! So tell me! tell me! leave no tents or city unsaid—which among webs, inside or outside of Ulan Bator, Lhasa, Sanna, or Buru—if *not* Jolly Boy—is the most phantasmagorical—bait me with that goal and its people, and what reward enfables them, but identify this nova and acme of exotic lures—*exotic, exotic, exotic lure!*

"The shadow of that ziggurat on the shelf of Asia moved like a behemoth's over me. Kneeling, he pulled me against his breasts and stopped my furious incantation; then, holding me hard and fathoming my eyes, unsmiling, and almost grimly, warned: 'Inside or outside of Jolly Boy, child—you, YOU are the snare most exotic: and by far most efficient…'"

Cory went to his desk to look for a fresh pack of butts. He glided there as gracefully as Tico, the lovelorn Aquatican in *Tarzan and the Mermaids* (to whom he bears a close resemblance).

I watched him, trying to imagine the tempting treat he must have been when he was sixteen, with those toothsome, brand-new muscles trepidantly coming together. I enjoyed the image of that continent of flesh getting a piece of it.

This was as much of the food-taster story as I had heard the day before and had wanted recorded. I asked Cory if there was more to it. There was, and he let me have it:

"I jerked away and squinted at the dawn drearily struggling to penetrate the screens that blocked the windows. Then the taster asked for a yank of Yank cream—as by 8:00 a.m. was only fair. So we sixty-nined, lying on our sides. Well, can't let someone like that climb on top of you, you'd be permanently decked. A sidewise sixty-nine was not exactly a cherry-boy's sandbox, since an inch of mismaneuver, or an unforeseen realignment on that cradle-snatcher's part, could have made a mashed potato out of me. Erectility wasn't easy, either: those folds of hairless pelvis and his prodigious choppers lumbered one above the other were a looming shoreline that I, a tiny ship, with my prow right in them, had nowhere charted on the various maps of my amorous destination. However, three sheets to the wind or not, I am courteous; and pretended he was Conan, the destructive pulp-fiction giant—or Joe Louis, the Brown Bomber: that secret but received, vital aphrodisiac. Ephebic Don Juans must, and should, be resourceful with simile.

"When we awoke in the afternoon, he said he wanted to leave me with something—an exoticism I could internalize privately, protected, and for breakfast. He opened a can of sardines, dipped them in beaten egg, passed them through flour seasoned with salt and pepper, dipped them in the egg again, and fried them in sesame paste on a fire plate he stored in an antique lacquered chest. Then he sliced an onion, stirred it into the remaining egg and quickly scrambled that, turning the pan over a bowl of steaming rice. He set out a dipping dish of soy and one of Tabasco sauce. He plucked a fat sardine with chopsticks, touched it into the Tabasco, and fed me himself.

"'Good?' he inquired. It definitely was. 'You see,' my taster, my sampler intoned, 'this way the exoticism will be safe inside you, which is the best place to keep it.' That man actually believed he'd flown the coop, being only a taster.

"The *fact* is, the wine and our breakfast were both Japanese—and this not lost on me; nor his replacing, in his Manhattan pied-a-terre, the ancestral privilege denied in his formative years. We were very different people.

"He showed me to the door. Then, as I regressed into the prosaic hallway, he delivered my allocation: 'Goodbye, child. And thank you for sleeping with an Oriental.'"

"Good God!" I deplored.

"Yeah," Cory agreed. "Festering, till right there, as a goal? Jumping six steps at a time to put a quick distance between us, I blistered at being slandered or stabbed: but not naked. Sumos are an acquired taste. Exoticism, which cuts both ways, is feeling embryonic—in our every dead-end pore!"

It is certainly dissatisfaction. I really wanted to learn. "Did you ever see those Stone Age people yourself?"

"No one's allowed to. They have no defense against our bacteria, and would die off. As it is, they don't number too many today."

"Perhaps a DNA-immune individual, walking around in Thailand?"

"I… I'm not sure how to talk about him. Can you wait?"

"I've a choice?"

Cory smiled.

"IN MID '81, STYMIED by a piece on Belle Époque brownstones, I had settled into an artists' colony, the squatter on a deserted artillery base outside Port Townsend, Washington—because I liked its name: Dvaravati. Dvaravati was a sixth-to-ninth-century state in what is now central Thailand, famed for producing the very finest art. Empowered by that name, I figured I'd up a Chinaman's chance on cracking the glossed-over message in that period's baroque defiance. I figured wrong.

"The Dvaravati isolated me in its eerily weathering barracks, where a thunder of raven daily bombarded the lawn I landscaped there, held me in their crosshair reticles, and created a cacophony that scrambled my brains. Nix to writing at any hour. I'd rivet to their tiny TV's news. Pol Pot's killing fields had recently become general knowledge, yet there seemed to be ongoing fracas, attacks, air raids, and further massacres, whose exact partisans and participants, including, if they did, us, were unclear, censored, or wizened down to a petrifying lie.

"Sleeping in those barracks' claustrophobic cubicles was beyond me. So I'd cart two army blankets onto the lawn, spread one on the wet weeds, and hide from the birds under the other. Then I'd summon my favorite soporific: Uncas, the literal Last of the Mohicans. He'd arrive in moccasins and only a loincloth that relied on a reindeer's single gut: five inches wide, it was embossed by the limits of his patch. I really never knew how to proceed with Uncas. He was derived from cinema, a concocted image, and brought no history. Usually this Mohican simply hovered and flexed. However, as I'd battery up on that open field, something inexplicable would happen. Uncas would enlarge, turn insubstantial though distinctly darker, his shoulders grow as broad as tap roots, and his roux-orange hair, mingled with gray, would boundlessly expand—until it tangled into a storm cloud about him, a darkness that had no circumference.

"And every night I said to him, 'You have no circumference.'

"I'd become that old heirloom, a coiled spring.

"Port Townsend was four streets then, and I walked downhill to the wharf. Its hooked trawlers were whipsawed in a steadily strengthening draft, perhaps the durable monsoon winds that gather on the Gobi that time of year and drop a drizzling chill over half the earth.

"This made me think of Rollo Y-z, the very man I might as well say saw Chain—and Thailand—when I couldn't.

"Rollo Y. we called him. Y-z wasn't *his* real moniker either, of course. He had some long Russian one beginning with 'Y' that nobody could pronounce—or remember—so we called him Y., Mr. Y., or Y-z. Also, Rear Admirable Y., in a nod to the fleet he could wear down in a single night.

"A strange one he, and somewhere other-side that ocean. Needing his address. I rang New York from a booth near the telegraph station and got it from a mutual acquaintance—in fact, scored a phone number for Y. as well. He was in Bangkok. Had been there for seventeen years, my informant, Johnny, thought.

"Siam! –'*An Oriental Kingdom of Barbaric Splendor*,' my lobby-cards had it.

"I trilled, 'Can you telephone Siam—just like that?'

"'It's Thailand now,' Johnny moaned.

"'Thailand to you; to me, Siam! Calls go through?'

"'It's the twentieth century' (tetchily), 'whichever one you're in!' That flirt's amoral, sugary guile came back to me instantly, as if I had listened to its serpentine apologies only yesterday, when in truth it had been many, many years. Johnny had been a recent émigré back then. *His* real name was Achille Vitte.

"'Bangkok's fifteen hours ahead of Washington. It's tomorrow there.' Then, hanging up: 'Don't catch him in the middle of fucking—like you did me!'

"Didn't matter what hour, you'd always catch Johnny in the middle of that. It's tomorrow there, is it? Be 1:00 p.m. Sunday. Reversing charges, I put the connection in at once. And true to the bromide, Y-z sounded as if he were just around the corner: which very place I had every intention he shortly would be.

"'Cory!' Rollo cried incredulously. 'A voice out of the past! Where are you?'

"'That's what I wanna know,' I rejoined.

"'Wanna come here and find out?' Rollo is quick: that too came back quickly. I was still politicking an approach. Rollo, age five, ignored those. 'You're stuck, right?' he hastened along, 'can't figure out what to do, who to do, where to go, what to write—and need a gig, right, right, right? Listen, there's a good one here, I'm not the chair, can't be, I'm a foreigner, but if I O.K. you, you're in like Flynn—wear a tie, dress shirt, polish your shoes. Express me your résumé and I'll advance you a flight. Semestre starts November first. Gotta run.'

"I should tell you little bit about Rollo Y-z... He was Valour Dictorian in his high school *and* university. Spoke eight languages when I met him, at... oh, a clinic—an outpatient clinic."

"For what?" I asked Cory.

"Not to crack-wise: Asian flu. We'd both come down with a scary case of it."

"Go on."

"Eight languages: often minus a grammar manual. Linguists can be like that. But any subject, really. The arts, sciences, engineering, or business—picked them up, excelled, outdid everyone in his class, in the whole university, and twelve thousand went to that one. Thing was, Rollo didn't care."

"By which you mean?"

"A casual observation: of a buxom sailor we two shanghaied and treated to a Lucky Pierre. His navy-seat impressed his stern; it caged his larder."

"And patriotism required you to relieve this discomfort," I sympathized.

"I'll drink to that. Anyhow, he said we looked like complementary bookends, a thin blond and a beefed brunette. He assessed me deeper, but Rollo the faster. He said Y-z could dig in as well: the difference was, he didn't care to.

"Such assessments, even from our serviced men, may only skim the surface. Some people are hurt. Hurt when you meet them, no matter how young, and you never know why. I believe they cannot tell you. In 1964 he suffered a paralysis: one day he couldn't get out of bed; or later, be gotten to walk more than a block or two—not alone, at any rate. Doctors were puzzled, test after test. It infuriated his macho dad. Rollo Y.'s dad had been foreman in a factory; of a sudden, excessed. Inconsolably humiliated, he accused Rollo of becoming contemptuous of him; thereinafter, there was to be no peace between them.

"Then a position was posted at NYU: teaching army brats, the disoriented—or Oriented—offspring of our personnel in Kanchanaburi. I brought the bulletin to Rollo. He miraculously sprang out of bed, made it to NYU, swooped up that gig, and was out of Long Island like a bat out of hell. He never came back.

"USA pay: on that, you could live like royalty in Thailand. So we guessed it was the salary that kept Y-z there. What other reason would a scholar have for wasting his time in a grade school?

We were not sure; and in this case, *we* didn't care. No one knew Thailand. And no one ever really knew Rollo Y-z.

"I slept at a cheap motel in town, expressed my CV the next afternoon, and the following morning thought to explore the entire reach of the ghost post. You know how you get when you're dumping an ambivalence: sentimental, like maybe you didn't do it justice. I took the skipping rope I use in gyms, spun it like a lariat to fend off the ravens, and forced myself to break through the coppice that shielded the cliff-top garrison. Thorns tore my khakis; I was pierced on my calves and knees. On a moraine above the pine line, on its sliced verge, was a vista of the suddenly close and cold sea. That's how I stumbled upon the cannons.

"There were at least a score of them, massive, rusted, ominous armory, hooded with briars or sunk in ditches and nearly concealed by years of autumnal decay. All were aimed at the ocean, pantomimicly hollow, their gaping mouths shouting something you could no longer hear at the vast and indifferent Pacific below. Initially baffled, I recalled federally filed info I'd once uncovered when researching U.S. refineries. Early in the war, Japanese submarines had fired twenty-seven rounds on an oil field near Santa Barbara, hitting its storage tanks. They followed that up with nine salvos aimed at Fort Stevens, Oregon. And in 1945, hundreds of jet-stream-borne, bomb-carrying balloons landed near Bly, Oregon, killing six children and their mother. Half of these still lie buried in our forests; and, if and when touched in the future, will explode and kill again. I dredged deeper and reworked the persistent rumors in my youth of Japanese battleships patrolling this beachfront, even putting reconnaissance troops ashore. So these, then, were the cannons that may have checked the advance forces. The maneuver stays murky, being naval hush-hush at the time to prevent panic; today, proof-positive of that Axis infiltration is emphatically dismissed by our War Department.

"The height from the precipice was daunting. Nevertheless, I stood there until the sun went onion, selvaged with purple, on this shunned arsenal's still diligent grave; then, meaning to turn and leave, at first heard only a soft whirring, and from the corner of my vision saw a heavy shadow sweeping to block a quarter of the sky. I confronted what I immediately knew was a great black eagle, biased on the current like an investigating copter, its wingspan, I estimate, an amazing seven feet. It dived with intent, dropping toward me in ferocious attack. I blocked my face and beat the air with the rope in the direction of its uncurling claws. It temporized, arced upward, and rose rapidly. Flapping off with an earsplitting blast, it sailed over a stretch of water and, burrowing through the vapors, diminished in size and glided into the dimness of the wood.

"ROLLO MET ME at the Don Muang International Airport early in October. I was semi-impervious from jet lag and the drugs that folks who project take to kill a trip and the transition between cultures; or between their nomadic mistakes. So seeing him after seventeen years was robbed of the impact this experience might have had, whether to corrode me ethically or not. His lashes were shorter; and though his piscine eyes still knife-gray, that blond hair was ash-blond now. I got cocky with my pill-induced advantage, thinking chemistry can deflate a shameless recourse taken in desperation. Then—fumbling with my passport, hugging him, and letting him heft my valise—I became disenchanted with my feelings. How could I, at a moment like that, be imbuing so abstract a gamble as this reunion with fervent rivalry?—as if time and a wide fork in the road were of no account.

It wasn't until we entered the viscid cloak of the highway, and the punch of that air caught me in the pit, that I snapped out of my retaliatory speculation and settled for the indisputable. My very first words were: 'Hell! It's hot here!'

"Y-z, without hesitation, said: 'Ever look in an atlas? The Land of Smiles is below the Tropic of Cancer. What were you expecting—snow?'

"Sure, my remark was drivel. His counter jab—characteristically—was saturnine. If he confirmed anything with it, it was probably his rationale for living in Southeast Asia. Just so he needn't hear that, and its like, all over the span of human insightfulness and citefulness. –O.K., we *had* played a not-too-in-nocent game, I allowed in the cab. Or do I invent that allowance because you're recording me?"

I had to respond. "Want to stop for a moment? You seem upset."

"I'm not."

"I'm having trouble following you, Cory."

"Sorry. Must need a refill. No, let me plow on. I'll be more careful. So… –You scan the panorama when you get to a new country. The drive from the airport into any city is invariably disheartening; and in the dark…

"Rollo Y-z was reading my take. 'Bangkok's nondescript; its history isn't. Here, I bought you a book: *Alexander the Great Conquers the Orient.*'

"His pad was in a rear two-story off Sri Ayutthaya Road, next to bustling Phayathai. Boring egg-boxes stand there now. Back then, we walked through a flint-chip drive and a garden with a pond that tenanted turtle, swimming spider, catfish, and carp. A colony of frogs, some as large as puppies, explored its rim. A midway platform in a free pine staircase was radically scooped to permit a brace of wild bamboo. Then the steps rose to a gallery at whose avenue-end was his door.

"His bedroom's privacy was cleverly elbowed into the wrap-around-louvered eating, studying, and smoking lounge. Waving at his alcove-kitchen's picture window, he noted that elephants were often stabled on the meadow outside. 'But this wonderful field, which predates the Cambrian Period, will shortly go.'

"He demonstrated the balancing act for the hole-in-the-floor commode and helped me unpack. He felt a sharp stab in his groin when he lifted my forty-pound dumbbells. 'You lugged these?? You can buy these here!'

"'Not *those*,' I said sleepily.

"A corner of his mouth quivered, exposing a prominent, unsightly canine. Three years my senior, he always saw me as his precocial junior—not to mention a *Terry and the Pirates* crippled by urges best left unspoken.

"When his first gig evaporated along with our army back

in the seventies, Rollo Y-z had moved to Bangkok to lecture in Medical English at Mahidol University of Medicine and Science. But *this* job paid native wages: $7,100 per annum, when the city's cost of living matched Baltimore's. He bought and enjoyed the latest high-tech toys, ignoring his taxes to a tune he could not foresee accumulating. 'And, since a tax-clearance certificate is required for an exit permit,' he mourned, 'I'm sentenced to life in Thailand. I'll die here.'

"I was impressed. His apportioning his satang (pennies) in order to spend his life abroad—stripped of his birthright citizenship, his own culture, and family. 'I've debated reenrolling at Albuquerque,' Y-z told me that night, 'and getting my Ph.D., in quantum mechanics. But that's a pipe dream now. I compensate with theoretical linguistics and drawing up new and more accurate grammars for local use. I keep abreast of the breakthroughs. Listen, it's all right. I'm happy here.'

"Rollo Y-z feared a return of his paralysis. It was only because he believed he'd deal sangfroid with my struggle in Thailand that he entertained my coming. Whatever my imposition should prove to be, it would not destabilize him.

"Nor did I, when I arrived, realize how deceived he was.

"–Remorse mends no fences. Most men find one friend when they're young; and none later ever duplicates his closeness. For me, he was Rollo.

"Would it were still so. There is no man I miss, or need more, even now.

"...Our reunion would lead Y-z to roll out a carpet—for Chain's stranglehold.

"But I am getting ahead of myself."

"Can you stop here?" I asked. "I have to change the tape."

"Good, I have to leak. And fill a bowl of fruit." The sound level was super: it was picking up with max clarity, and practically erasing background interference. You hear sirens or a dog yelping. That is atmospheric. Occasionally, a frustrato guns his bike and covers a phrase of Cory's, or a hurried group of thoughts. I hate his habit of skipping final syllables or swallowing his volume toward the end of sentences. In these spots I approximate or surmise what he said. I take it as standard to condense passages whose specifics seem random to his purpose.

I am amenable to brickbats for myopic omissions. I have stored the tapes in Columbia U.'s Oral Archive, should a reader want them unbowdlerized.

After he brought us waterapples, Cory explains how Y-z cuts his "interview." The Department asks why an author like Cory would need or care to teach Medical English. Y. scares up a cock-'n-doodle that will satisfy the hiring report—in effect, all the chair is looking for. That squared away, they have near four weeks to goof before the term begins. In this segment, what make for catchy mise-en-scènes, anthropologically or otherwise, he deliberates elsewhere.

"Rollo had to powwow at Silpakorn University to arrange for a conference there. He suggested I come along and sit in its open-air snack and study area on the bank of the Chao Phya River. He said curtly: 'Silpakorn's dead center in the tourist sites. So you'll know where they are. So far as I'm concerned, *Krung Thep*—Bangkok: literally: "Abode of the Beneficent Spirits"—is a sauna unfit for saunter. Tomorrow we get *you* an abode, and after dinner we'll go to Patpong. Then I'm done. –Tomorrow's Friday: the fish'll be biting.'

"The art pupils studied in cadres; beyond them barges and freighters trafficked the Chao Phya. Slightly north, trucks, cars, and buses poured over a postcard span to the city's west bank. A very tall, deep-shouldered person, standing by the rail fencing the tables, clearly monitored me for almost an hour. With his back to the sun, I could hardly make him out. He was dressed like an alien, low-paid construction worker. A cloth balaclava exposed only his eyes; a brown, loose-fitting polo and baggy trousers concealed his body. When he saw Rollo approaching, he turned and faced the river.

"Rol squired me to an enormous oval ground outside the campus and stated flatly, 'To our right are the walls of Wat Phra

Kaeo. Inside are the jaofao-gabled roofs of the Grand Palace, the Emerald Buddha, and Thailand's most ornate halls. Thai and Chinese mythical creatures punctuate the passages between them. To our left, the National Museum, National Theatre, and National Film Gallery. Ahead of us is a shrine housing the City Pillar. This expanse is called *Sanam Luang*: Royal Field.' It resembled a racetrack, with a double row of benches and tamarind trees lining its periphery, where vendors in their shade were hawking food to drowsy passersby. The field itself was vacant as an African plain: 'Used to host rituals here with the King officiating; plus political rallies, frightening demonstrations, and three massacres of Thammasat students. It's now for kite-flying in the windy months; and whoring after dark. Teenagers pack those benches, as many as can squash into each—seven or eight, I'd say, leering at prospective strollers.'

"'Do you thin their squash on occasion?' I inquired.

"'I don't pick through alley-trash or Mae Sai runaways in borrowed flip-flops. –That wooded streetside park opposite Wat Phra Kaeo? Twenty hustlers *live* in it, lying around in shredded shorts. They nutcracker one knee so you can see some scrotum. And a plucked chicken neck resting against it.'

"'Do you…' I began.

"'I've *seen* their inch-long chicken necks!' Rollo bristled. He stiffened, with what has to be called a clutch purse in the vise of his armpit, swallowed his large Adam's apple, and acrimoniously inspected a savage-looking child with septic hair who was slumped under a tamarind in a torn shirt and mud-caked shorts. He had violet welts and scabs on his throat and legs.

"Suddenly the man who had been watching me was stationed a yard away. I felt a blood-rush: and moved to contend him. He was a true foot taller than I; when I locked-up to his Sherwood-blue, circular eyes and the quite dark skin enveloping them, he, stunned, cut his breath. I traced the suck in his balaclava. He renewed his examination, woefully scrutinizing me; then purred like a mountain cat, and though I could not see it, there was a laugh in his face. He extracted two objects from his polo shirt and put them in my hand. At length, he radically switched his line of sight to the welted boy and waited for me to do the same. Then he gazed regally at the river and walked barefoot toward it.

"'Into brick-layers?' Y-z snickered. 'You do work fast. Who was that?'

"'Like I know?' I shrugged. 'What did he give me these for? Seem to be a cigar and cheap, pebble specs. This wire-rim's bridge is bent out of shape.'

"Rollo laughed: 'All he can afford!' But Rollo Y-z was patently edged. 'The Chinese smoke like chimneys. And every last one wears glasses because they're forced to read by a dim light, starting at age four.'

"'So?'

"'You've taken the sun since you got here, Cory. You look more Chinese than you used to.'

"Rol threw me out of bed at 6:30 the next morning. He crammed his purse with cigs and our IDs. He nervously castigated me for the eons I wasted drinking coffee. Then we dashed across Phayathai Road and into the first lane south of the Hotel Florida, where a high wall enclosed a complex of three-unit houses standing *feng shui* in a multitiered Manchu garden. He spoke to the landlady, a noodle-thin Sino-Thai with a pinched, no-nonsense face.

"'She's a toughie,' Rollo slurred in an aside. 'But I straightened her out with the second-person singular used for inferiors one rung down. I, after all, am an *ajaan* (teacher). She's a landlady! And we're in luck, she's renting a two-room.'

"It was cozy, with a view of the compound's rear wall riotously latticed with hanging plants including the giant moose-antler, which rejects potting and roots in moss. There was a score of healthy specimens; they're what exotically sold me. The bathroom was a plus: ultramodern. A minus: the windowless bed space, which allowed for the downy double, period. There were no single beds here. Thais have no idea why someone would want to sleep alone.

28

"Or how they can. That's not as lusty as it sounds. Rooms accommodate an army of otherworldlies. Every building has a small spirit house outside to convince ghosts they'd be happier there. Still, you never know with the dearly departed. Some are naughty, bored, or downright malintentioned. The latter can vault the threshold brigade, and thick walls pose no problem. A person alone in a room, any room, is asking for it. Flats and restaurants are installed with an overhead perch for a statue of Buddha. 'Put one up,' Y-z cautioned, 'or you'll spook the maid. She won't scrub, mop, or dust in here.'

"'I'd rather Medusa didn't,' I sniffed, indicating said eldritch swab.

"'Not clean the mess you make? You'll drop *your* status with democratic innovation: and tempt feudal fate. Maids moonlight as the owner's FBI.' Rollo returned the menial's pout with a dash of pepper.

"Now, Rol was the only non-missionary white back then who could speak all the Thai dialects fluently. Learned by listening, mind you. But because of that he couldn't read any: and was blind to the lettering by the gate—establishing that this compound was owned by the municipal police.

"So I took possession a babe in the woods. We moved me in exactly an hour. I spent an identical hour dressing for Patpong. Then galloped soigné back to Y-z's to pick him up.

"'You're going like that?' he squealed in dismay.

"'Balls stick out?' I asked. 'I broke my new pad's mirror on this assemblage. Though I must admit I've hardly cracked my wardrobe.'

"'You cracked something. Long sleeves! Boots?? Yes, your jeans—could they get any tighter? It's Bangkok. You can practically shit on the equator.'

"'Cinch I can't shit these.'

"He peeled my neckerchief, rolled my sleeves, pitched me sandals, and hid my boots and socks. 'Best I can do. Let's go,' he urged.

"'Thank you, Versace.' –Or did I say, 'Edith (gives good) Head'?

"*Patpong!!* Red-light district to the world! The most known and notorious Barbary Coast on earth. Six sois of smiles. The Smiles of a Thousand Daggers!

"In those non-promoted days, a far cry from what the horny scrimmage now: a no-budge tourist trap with each slab of sidewalk chaosed by clothing stalls and fake-label Nike, Calvin Klein, and Rolex vendors—contraband souvenir, CD/DVD pushers, touts, pimps, transvestite prossies, and worming, limbless beggars. Just to reach its exorbitant Go-Go Girl and Go-Go Boy bars—read, go-go upstairs to a lice-ridden sack in a hot half-hour coffin.

"So: in less hectic '81 then, the girlie Patpong Streets 1 and 2, and gay Sois 2 and 4, that run between Silom Road and Suriwong, featured bars and brothels comparatively inconspicuous; and further shielded by linebackers and weightlifters put to pasture as humorless doormen or security guards.

"Y-z daddied me to an undisputed institution: Rome Club—which you can bet your bottom dollar locals pronounced 'Lome.' –The 'r' and 'l' are interchangeable in Thai: depends on the vowels they precede. As *the* gay venue in *Krung Thep* (it remained open until 2000), Lome was kitsch-splendiferous, an 'in,' grandiloquent affair. As you stood in the spacious arched vestibule, to your right was a Stork Club copy of smart tables and padded armchairs, to your left a cut-crystal step-up bar. Rear-lit Pre-Raphaelite vitrines created the soi-side wall; and a proscenium faced you, half the length of the faux-marble floor beneath it set aside for dancing. A jade Portuguese balustrade, on the lip of a gallery along the vitrines, separated the drinkers from the dancers; pulse-stopping natives were planted on it next to itinerants intent on reading their knickers-tab.

"Rol squeezed me through a tour of the landmark, his parental grip on my wrist. Shouting above the DJ, he instructed, 'Five ounces of pump is nearly three bucks: a dent in our salary—don't order refills. Falang (white Yanks and Euros) are expected to tip. Profile your jeans to best advantage at the raised bar—see where that group is positioned now, two-thirds along the... Oh, oh! there's a man you'll want to meet. You know who

Jim Thompson is? –Or was?'

"I said, 'How could I not? The Silk King, no? And before that, a building and landscape architect. The wealthiest foreigner in Thailand. And very connected to heads-of-state.'"

"'Actually, the most famous Caucasian in all of Asia. Still is, even though he vanished into thin air fourteen years ago. On a visit to a jungle in Malaysia. That ticket—swilling—is also an architect. *And* he was cheek-by-jowl with Thompson. You two should have a lot to talk about.'

"The gent in question was mismatched in an argyle shirt and pinstripe slacks; yet tall, aristocratic, and bony, with a bonnet of pure white hair you could spot across a soccer field. Y., rusty with the amenities, introduced me as a typist with a passion for landmarks and suspicious politics. 'Right up your alley,' he fumbled.

"'I prefer Thais going there,' the geezer took advantage to respond, offering a spasmodic handshake.

"Y-z shot, 'Who secretly doesn't? But Cory's interested in an article on Jim.'

"'Ah, poor Jim!' the gent warmed to the occasion, lifting his glass in a toast. Rollo, pleased with his success, turned away relieved and surveyed the crowd with critical eye. 'Randolph Wetzel's the handle,' the man pushed, leaning in and smacking his lips, 'but call me Randy cause that I am. –Thompson? I used to work with *Seri Thai*—that's "Free Thai" to you—the underground resistance here. Therefore, I am at odds in 1946 when a gal name of Héloïse—as in, "Abelard and"—de Crescent, hits me up for a $250 shareholder. To invest in renovating the Oriental, it being run-to-ground by '46, billeting first Jap soldiers and then U.S. She's a terminated correspondent for a French newspaper syndicate. –Gal lobbies like a low-ranking buzzard after a corpse her top brass got dibs on. Naturally I resist Héloïse. I can't resist her equally headstrong partner, James H. Thompson.' He burped. His wrinkled, rheumy lids shifted, and he lost his train of thought.

"Rollo helped: 'Jim Thompson was still in the OSS then, wasn't he?'

31

"'Oh, yeah—Rol! that's right… And is the *chief* unofficial political advisor to the American Embassy here. Couldn't say no to *that*. Patriotically, I mean. Can I buy you a brandy?' It was unclear if the offer was to either of us or to a stripling wriggling on the edge of the dance arena: with such deliberate vigor, I thought, so as to earn our admiration.

"The boy was light-skinned, false-lashed, and shapely. He crushed a small red favor and threw it at us. Of a sudden soberly adroit, Randolph reached out and caught it, opened it, and played its legend: 'I love you mostly dearest one.' He said, 'Yer old alkies, randier than me, prefer tight yak to a screw. Comes to age then, I'm seventy now,'—understandable understatement—'therefore I am only thirty-five when I meet Jim, who is already forty. I ignore that. Got mutual interests. So we become buddies.' I looked at Y. to see what he saw in *this* card: he was crossing his eyes so I'd read his lips, clearly mouthing, '*Bed* buddies.'

"'What mutual interests?' I asked.

"Randolph lifted his pour so shakily that it splashed on my rolled cuff. 'Sorry. –Umm, the Office of Selective Services—forerunner to the CIA, savvy?—is ultraliberal-slash-rad pre and throughout the war. Under their influence, my comfortably born Jim switches from being a Delaware Republican to a more than Massachusetts Democrat. Same as me, get it? *That there's* the mutual interest! And why does Jim ask me to come in on the Oriental, huh? 'Cause *I'm* also an architect—didn't Rollo say? Now, Rollovelt, uh, Roosevelt is dead-set on independence for all of Indochina. He schemes to squelch the French colonial empire. Since Héloïse de Crescent's sympathies camp unrepentant with her nation's empirical interests, a super-spy clash between Jim and her is inevitable. Their antique-vase-throwing battles become a choice topic in the expat community on New Road. Some say the fallout is over Jim's plan for the annex to the old wing, too small now for the mob Jim wants to attract. But closer to Jim's heart and industry—including the Oriental Hotel and modern ideas for marketing silk—is his vision of a new world order. Finding no place in that for a lady partner what's a throwback into expansionism, Jim pulls out of the Oriental.'

"I interrupted Randolph to inquire about those guests who had made the old wing the storied equal of Hong Kong's Peninsula Hotel and Singapore's Raffles. People like Maugham, Vidal, Cole Porter, and Coward. Because in the romance department for me then—unfortunately!—they outclassed him *and* Thompson. Right there, the attractive stripling cartwheeled, cut from the fruggers, and ended downing one of our brandies. *This* time, Randolph unzipped, dropped his pinstripe to his pubes, and pulled the boy onto his lap. I jumped when his fingers fanned the narrow chest and tummy. The boy seemed not to know how he got there.

Rol was antsy. I asked him, if he was bored, why he wasn't cruising himself.

"'*Me?*' he snorted. 'I go to a whorehouse once a week. I'm out by eleven. I'm *here* now for you. This sort of scene, putting on the dog, dancing and flirting—and sampling! Pile of crap!' I felt under duress to select rapidly: I knew he'd want to see me home, believing I hadn't the acumen to chisel with a rickshaw pedaler. Buses stopped before midnight. To gain time, I told him he resembled a president disgusted with his cabinet. He said, 'I feel like one. So do you spot a member meets muster? This once, I'll negotiate in Thai for you.'

"The boy was bouncing on Randolph Wetzel's wagging stiff. He saluted Rol and cried, 'Negotiate for *me*.'

"Randolph grabbed at his ear, attempting to turn him back. Rollo scrutinized the boy. 'Oh, he's cute,' I relayed to Y-z. No response. 'Don't you think so?'

"'What?' Rol Y-z had been melded to a quite handsome Thai, haloed in the vitrines, who'd been sharing his detailed appraisal.

"'Think that he's cute.'

"'What's with what *I* think?' Randolph glared at Y. and tickled the boy. The boy giggled and re-snapped a salute. Rollo grizzled, 'O.K. for you?' I nodded. He barely glanced at Randolph, with that chill of precise dismissal he'd made his own, and spoke swiftly to the boy; then, as swiftly, yanked the boy from Wetzel's clutch and pushed him forward, throwing his own chin up at the door in a gesture to me. 'We're out of here,' he ordered. I bobbed my head idiotically at Randolph, who again was spilling his brandy on its misguided route to the apoplectic O of his mouth; and 'putting on the dog' in terms of meekly tailing the two of them, went around the rim of the arena and into the vestibule.

"At the road, I waxed superfluous: 'Randolph Wetzel not your cup of tea?'

"'If somebody told me that under his trousers he was wearing women's panties, I'd have no trouble believing it.'

"'Well tonight he wasn't,' I observed. In the wobbling rickshaw, called a samlor, our teen-in-tow waved at a senior citizen and babbled boisterously.

"'What's he saying?' I inquired.

"'He's advertising himself. The pension that old fogey there is aching to squander, renting him. But he earns too much to stoop to septuagenarians.'

"'Tell him I won't pay a satang.'

"'*You* have to tell him that yourself. In the nicest way possible, I trust.'

"'I'm no john! I'm really interested in this fellow.'

"'That's good,' Rollo pulverized, 'then you have nothing to worry about.'

"He folded his jittery hands over his purse while the well-fixed one slumped in the crush between us. To avoid dealing with this fly in the ointment, I said I'd not known that Jim Thompson was gay. Rol's impatience, if possible, shot up a notch: 'An interior decorator, an antique collector, a silk, set, and costume designer—a ballet-lover—not gay? Thompson's first project was a combination bandstand and public lavatory. You *do* know what those are used for?'

"'To get your ears split on one side and relieve more than that on t'other?'

"'And why a major fantasy with the rundown Oriental? What do you think those famous fairies were up to, converging there?'

"I stared at the coolie with varicose veins, prominent as a nest of garter snakes, who ground our ancient tricycle. A human taxi—I'd see them hauling four heavy passengers. Pedaling from a high saddle, only inches from us, his labor-hardened buttocks were right in my face. Y. read my thoughts and referred to an acquaintance of humongous endowment: 'Olie nurses a boner all the way home. So he tells the coolie he'll double the fare if the guy comes in.'

"'And?'

"'Spreads those muscular flaps for a while.'

"'And?'

"'They always accept. They're dirt-poor, samlor drivers. They feel lucky.'

"'And what do they feel when they feel what *he* drives with?' I asked.

"'Meat! Olie loves that. Their writhing in pain. The *saints* around here!'

"When I got the dandified punk to bed, he proved to be more than twisted: he was succumbing to a severe chest-cold. By morning he was carried away with sneezing fits and scary coughing. Hot compress, aspirins, Vick's rub, a vaporizer. Without qualms, he accepted my care. In becoming at once an obedient patient, as it would turn out in the wash, he varied little from most dally-boys. This scatterbrained commercializer considered himself no different from the next in Asia's huddle. It had fallen to a stranger to meet him when he had fallen ill. This stranger, fearing Buddha, would and should attend to his recuperative needs.

"To be sure, he insisted I poke him, even the first night, but that domesticity dispatched, I otherwise had a sick kid on my hands.

"On the seventh day, somewhat stronger, he asked when we'd go shopping. We walked to the market east of Phayathai; and ambled through shops. The boy tarried at each venue offering inessentials: of the linked and glittering type. He was thinking that my modus operandi must be to surprise a weeklong live-in with purchases rather than money. If I'd a *jai dee* (good heart), this gold—since he was in the neighborhood of a necklace he drooled over there—might come at the pawnshop to more than his usual 'appreciation,' were it in paper bills.

"I'd given him my mother-loving maintenance for one hundred and forty-eight hours and every sign that I saw no reason for an end to more of the same. But cash, no! I've always had a visceral, violent reaction to play-for-pay. Nor had sitting at a sickbed been big on play, anyhow.

"We returned through the elbow-to-elbow alleys. I doubt he troubled himself about why I didn't spring for a cab. By now I was as dysfunctional as the worst foreigner he'd hitherto hit-up, given even that most, as everyone agrees, are *falang key-nok* (cheap-shit outsiders) and *buh-bah'bahbor* (stone nuts).

"He apparently came to a decision as we neared my soi, for he declined to accompany me farther. I must say I was relieved. Standing with his nose in an overused hanky, he claimed to have chores elsewhere and would call me later. With that—and the entire hustler-conscious street glaring censoriously in his wake—he breezed on to wherever it is that floozies go.

"Did you know that Paulette Goddard bought a silk suit from Jim Thompson: right off his back—at a dinner party in Paris?"

"Um, no, I didn't."

"Now: what preceded my getting to Lome one night at the tail of my third week in *Krung Thep* is no longer with me. Nor is anything else immediately after I went in, or early on in the evening. What I do remember is that I'd carried a mug to the table section and had been facing its wall or persons seated against it; whether busied by talk, or just looking at people, has also left me.

"Bored there, I turned about and hopped down to the marble floor, intending to push through the stompers for an opposite view at the crystal bar.

"And that, suddenly, is when I first saw Chain up close.

"He was side-saddling the Portuguese balustrade on my left, his elbows forward and resting on his knees, as studs using that rail made macho-certain they always were: and holding a full beerglass with both hands. On the catwalk directly behind him, level with his head, was a life-size plaster bust of Hermes or Pallas Athena, the reproduction so poor I couldn't tell which; in back of that and slightly to his deltoid nearer me was a pedestaled amphora painted with black figures depicting Theseus slaying the Minotaur. The queer appeal, presumably, was in the Minotaur's nude, muscular body and, though it had modest, even small genitals, cone-pointed penis. It was kneeling in submission to Theseus, its horns harmlessly embracing his waist, with a hose of its blood quietly connecting its slashed throat with its foremost toes and the foremost of Theseus, which were stepping on them. A black bird flew between the Athenian's massive parted legs. It is not unusual to find these camp copies of Greek art, meant to summon the homogamy of antiquity and thus justify ours, in wanna-be elegant gay establishments; but the juxtaposition of this Thai man, the indecisive bust, and the bloodthirsty vase—a *not* fortuitous contingence, each solidly there—wanted a center and was confusing. My eye roamed from the spherical painting to the bust, from beneath whose armored headpiece sprouted a disorder of epaulet-supported, curl-bottomed tendrils, and then to the Thai himself. He was staring straight down at me: and grinning broadly. His own hair was a high, spilling helmet of thick individual strands, shagged and indigo, with sharp indigo highlights. He'd a sweet, low-bridged Thai pug nose; quarter-mushroom nostrils; and penciled orchid lips that his caracal tongue was moistening with victorious effrontery, awaiting my response to his grin.

"'I wonder how long before you talk me,' Chain said.

"Then, discarding the circumspect, he threw up a sandal to the purpose of blocking my progress—actually touched my ear with its mudguard. He lanced the vertex of its sole in my cheek to let me feel the cold metal tap, then tilted it to the heat of his toes. Thais consider using their foot to do or indicate something to be absolutely *hors de ligne*. But those at ease with foreigners often take liberties: often to put the foreigner in his place. That contact with his toes, like Theseus crowning and crushing the Minotaur's with his, accompanied by the mockery in his icebreaking, duplicated the challenge in an open-and-shut fistfight: its foregone conclusion only sham-hedging, if that, in a peacock's violet vest. This much set to fluctuate, Chain shifted the pinch in his presumptive balance on the rail, removed the foot, and modified his temerity with what could be read as an explanation: 'I see you Lome Club before—know friends you.'

"Oh, yeah? Like who? It was my turn to wonder. He was nattily dressed in a fresh Parisian line that stressed off-white, from the waist-gathered slacks to the cinquefoil threads on the lacewing of his costly shirt. His taste defied indifference. It was calculated to insist on his blue-tint gold complexion. Scholars speculate that Siam, or Sayaam, means 'golden,' or 'darker' (e.g., than we Chinese), though no one is certain, or certain why this entire region was called Siam for a thousand years. My frost fixed on his ankles, I was actually wondering, 'How does blue-tint gold skin feel—between your teeth?' To act outraged, or delay socking his leg, I lifted my gaze to the vase again and first noticed that Theseus's penis was also exposed, taking the air from under his battle-skirt: the length and shape of a handheld, just-used condom.

"Trial and error tells me that if I'm en route, I mustn't be sidetracked by a pass. In this case it was the bar, for an overview of the evening's choices. Given Chain's red light, not much in the way of a goal anymore: still, it sufficed for my makeup. If I've a destiny when someone catches my eye, he *always* looks extraordinary: when I'm bent on nailing, ready and in the right mood for it, no man as handsome ever seems to be about. I *have* tested the flirt four or five times: stopped and spoke to him. Sure enough, after chatting, he decided he'd made a mistake; or I decided I had; and the passing ships got a 'pass' on perusal.

"Therefore I was honestly against the impediment of this arrogant marvel, peering over his high cheekbones with the supercilious wink of a fait accompli. I responded to his claim of prior acquaintanceships with, 'Oh, *do* you…?' Then felt that rejoinder lamer and less definitive than I had desired. In fact, it came off as English too arch for Asians. –Perhaps… At any rate, it was not too remote as to be entirely lost on him. He stirred, released his pat solidity, and appeared to check the phrasing or tone of what he'd just heard. He placed the thumb and forefinger of his right hand on a cautious brow and its pinky on the concave bridge of his nose, in effect blocking his right eye, and examined me with his left for what seemed an uncommonly long time. Then he said:

"'*A-lai' nah*? (What's that?)'—an inquiry in Thai, in just this way, to express a quiet double take.

"So I reworded my skepticism: 'You know my friends? From where?'

"'Here. Other place. –Know you, too.'

"'Is that so? From where?'

"Too incisively to be simply a transliterated cliché, and left completely uncolored, he said, 'Life before.'

"Neither of us spoke for a moment. I became embarrassed, and to cover that, and break the tension, summoned a disgruntled pout. I stepped forward, I believed determined to cross the club. Chain took advantage of what any Leander would sense was a consolidation of less than impregnable resolve, and prodded me—those squirming toes again—this time across my chest. I huffed: defiantly. He laughed! 'Want drink?' he asked. '*Dee*! (Good!). I get. You stay.'

"He dropped from his nest like a falcon and disappeared into the crowd. I leaned against the jade small-poles and looked vaguely over hairdos: and through strained shields in a surround of testosterone banter in which few remarks were distinguishable, despite the parley of more Thailish than Thai.

"And did indeed stay.

"Nothing is so seductive as a man's certainty that he's already seduced you. Yet Chain was *not* confident that night. He was disappointed with himself, his true composure thrown by what he was judging to be his bewildering, and perilous, lack of restraint. He morosely scanned the bar when returning with the beers, a quite different person. As he neared, an older, bespectacled, gargantuan falang, standing with his butt toward me in conversation with a companion, moved between us so that I was studying the thick fold on his neck and his back-hair's barbwire under it. I heard him say, in a glass-edge Etonian accent, 'No, the British Society cannot do *Private Lives*. It's too demanding. Blighters live in Bangkok because they don't want to think.' Then he punted a huge, furry arm at Chain—I wasn't sure how serious its intent. Chain set the beers on a Greek pedestal, apparently there for that purpose, turned swiftly, caressed the small cigar that the Englishman was obnoxiously puffing, yanked it out of his mouth, knotted the man's silk shirt in his fist, and shoved him into the catch of his companion, who held him upright and steadied his specs. Chain stabbed the cigarillo into the pedestal, watched its sparks firework to the floor, and vigorously doused them, using his versatile sandal. Then he ran a nail along the cigarillo's betel wrapping, split it, scattered its tobacco, retrieved the beers, and continued on to me. Holding the mugs' handles at his hips, his investigating live-coals shooting across my face to a liberal meter on either side my ears, he said:

"'My boss me. Own many Sea Gypsy.'

"This was the first of his edifications, which, enlightening as he meant them, left me in dappled shade. I resisted the facile, 'You've a great labor relationship,' or the saucier, 'What boosts might entail "owning" Gypsies?'

"–To be brisk: Chain was proud. He was proud of his looks and he was proud period. And while I was ascribing a win in my ego to him, he was actually afraid of me as a familiar, rejoined, and utterly compromising quantity, possibly neither human nor alive. Inescapably, I was an agent of Narok (Buddhist Hell). So he took to debugging his debt. When his lips moved silently in Lome later on, he was telling himself how the stout, by marrying into their ranks, neutralize that oppositional Ever-With-Us. Something not exactly news to him.

"O.K.: one Singha leads to another. A slave to protocol, *I* automatically ordered a second, and then a third and fourth round. That's another reason why little the ignorant should illuminate got illuminated that night. (Lome was empty till eleven and closed at one—you had business, you worked fast.) Working fast, we vamoosed; and thoroughly blitzed, as soon as we hit my mattress, I saw him as too lovely to know what to do with;

then decided I was too smashed to do anything anyhow, and promptly passed out."

"Oh, come on," I objected, "you must have done something: let's have it."

Cory salivated. "Well: he himself was alert, lying supine, guardant and rigid. I sat on his knees. He responded by raising his fists defensively. I grabbed them, forced them down, and soldered his arms to his side. This caused him to bolt and arch his back, his eyes now the lemur's, huge and sick with anxiety. To reassure him, still clamping his arms at his flanks, I rested my head in the cradle of his ribs: whose heaving naturally lulled me. And that's when, a few moments on, I passed out. Presumably joining my fellow latent-spirits."

I put Cory on: "Some lover!"

"Yes, but at least that coaxed him through his ghastly reservations, or so I imagined, because in the morning he agreed to a date at 9:00 p.m. for the day after. I'm always hung over following a pickup on alcohol: hence grateful if the trick has a sunrise clock-in. Chain said he did. And so, on waking, I didn't hassle him: or probe into his huge, Gypsy-owning boss. He was subdued when we awoke, very subdued, that appeared all. He showered and dressed carefully, slowly brushing his long, indigo waves, gave me his number, and left.

"However deliberate that morning, it was easy money compared to the night of the next day. He was prompt to the striking of the chime. The domestic, reprising Charon (I failed to articulate this then), admitted him to my sitting room, where I was having a hair with Mr. Y. Skimping to phone Chain to get his approval, I'd arranged for us three to see a film. When he entered, I was bent over, wiping the puddle I'd made filling our tumblers. As I readjusted myself to greet him, I saw him darting a look at Rollo; and Rollo cocking his head in a sharp herald toward me. Neither noticed me take this in: each seemed comfortable enough when they both, in a turnabout, assumed that open, expectant aspect of two persons about to be introduced. Stung, I introduced them.

"'Attaboy!' Rollo pealed. 'Guy's cool, behaved—he's introspective.' I'll bet, I told myself: wire-jawed is a closer description.

"The Last Ten Seconds in the Lives of People Who Died a Violent Death. That movie's title! Camera-monitored industrial accidents preserved for posterity or the kingdom's barbaric delectation; and racecar wrecks with the soon-to-depart departing straight at the lens through the windshield of a crashing vehicle: these races, of course, were being filmed. Ten-second takes for ninety nonstop minutes. Three-fourths into such a Cassandra-in-spades, I jumped ship; and wandered along a passage at whose far end was an open window. A hurricane lamp revealed the tar terrace of the theatre's marquee. Atop it was perched the reverse side of the two-yard-high, mostly broken-bulbed letters spelling the name of the theatre: THE SIAM: with the 'S,' 'I,' and 'AM' appreciably separated. I vaulted the window's sill and crossed the terrace. Somewhere in my pockets were the pebble specs and small cigar that the construction worker had given to me. I removed them because the rays of the marquee sufficed to inspect these not-coincidental gifts once again. The shadow of a head, then shoulders, gradationally enlarged on the rear of the letters.

"I slipped both items into my left hand, spun on a pin, and swung. Chain caught the blow in a palm thrown against his throat, though he did tumble back several paces. 'What do you want?' I glowered, surprised by the fight in my voice.

"'Want see what you do,' he responded, shook by the blow. In a cautious, non-threatening way, he reached out and undid my left. His eyes widened in fear. He touched the objects. 'Who give you?' he asked.

"'Foreign man. Maybe black. Work make buildings.'

"'*Toe-leh* (Bullshit),' he shot, in a curveball.

"'–So then, you know him! Now tell something else, Chain. You know Rollo just as well?'

"For a hard moment, he stared at me. He smoothed his neckline. He rubbed his palm, exaggerating, or privately confirming, an adumbration in its soreness. Then he closed my fist on the objects, and stepped up between the letters topping the marquee, where, like Samson, he put his arms around the 'I' and

'AM.' After a minute he turned, evading my vivid ire, spoke to the tar, walked to the window, and climbed through it.

"School to commence in a few days, on those initial evenings we spent together, I sat on my carpet fortressed by mimeo'd lessons. Rol had briefed me, and they read like a refresher on my eighth-grade hygiene course. These print-outs were to teach terminology, back then there being no medical texts in Thai; and, merely incidentally, to review the biological data.

"Chain would throne on the sorrowful, mauve-and-fuchsia columned couch; and at the click of an identical period, relax and slouch into its crushed backrest. Then he'd proceed to paint me in as if I were some compelling piece of theatre. He spoke only in direct response to pointed questions, and pondered my tonality before answering—usually with hesitation and always in clipped phrases. I was not flattered, or made self-conscious, by his investigation; nor did I idle hours on what improbable concerns sponsored it. I had no correlatives for them. At times I'd jerk without warning, assured he would jump through hoops.

"He was differently outfitted every evening, always in complimentary and complementary style, which must have cost. So I wasn't being nosy asking—he not volunteering—just *how* he was employed.

"'Business family!' Subtracting his boss now, that was altogether too pat.

"'What kind of business?'

"He swallowed, then struggled for the word. 'I' was what he managed.

"'"I"?'

"'Uh-huh. I business me.'

"'But, not know what "I" is.'

"His pupils galvanized. Frustration registered in a tortured mouth; he stressed this by grinding his molars. Moments later he gesticulated soundlessly, hardened his gaze, and redoubled the inquest in his inspection of me.

"Next afternoon I asked Rol what he could mean. 'Oh, Thais are troubled by consonants with "c" and "e" together. He's saying

43

he cuts, packs, or freezes ice. Or at least delivers it. –He claims he does that for a living?'

"'Yes. Working with his family.'

"Rollo Y-z appeared about to opinionate (I wished he would): then thought better of it. Chain's riposte, excluding his heavy-set boss, abetted by Sea Gypsies, was circumnavigation at best. And why didn't he go to the fridge, simply open the freezer, and point at the ice-cubes? *'I business me'* was an utterance with great sticking power. I said, 'And another thing. After drilling his acuity into my body, minus so much as a murmur for five hours the other night, he suddenly announced: *"Kim hahn' pee sart!"'*

"'*Did* he?' Rollo was dismayed. 'How odd. It's the King's Siamese. *Very* aristocratic. It means, "Devil of the springtime." Why would he have learned that? There's no "devil" or "springtime" in Thailand.'

"He lit a cigarette and went back to his typing. The audience was over.

"Let me return to Chain's conduct: when I'd tire of my dictionaries and his stately judging, I'd yawn, put away the print-outs, and declare, 'Go bed.' Then, detachedly, he'd undress and arrange his garments on the armoire's hangers. I'd watch this procedure with pleasure, because it required his compact height to jump and jiggle or take recourse to line-of-scrimmage spreads in his solid or paisley shorts: and these presented me with fetching, slow-mo views of his rectangular buttocks. That reduced the brain to imbecility. Buttocks such as one could find elsewhere only in the Vatican Collection on statues of Aries, Perseus, or Actaeon. Neither too firm nor too giving, twin-kitten cushions they were, and Blue Roses of Oblivion. Thailand specialized in delightfully inventive low-risers for men long in advance of their popularity in the West; I looked forward night after night to what new and hugging one he'd selected. In addition to the never-disappointing rear view, his ithyphallic jockeys embraced the choicest plums. Seen from beneath, with those briefs teased down, they resembled camels' drooped humps, or small, literally rolling hills: with their frenum standing by to furl the frieze that wrapped his attentive entablature. Yankees invariably seize on the size of organs—size-queens, no?—the form eludes them. But it was the velour and willet in Chain's enormity that enchanted. Innocent of blemish, even to its only vein-vine, in quintessence, the musk… surefire beer, yes?"

"Check! But I need to hear a history, not play pocket ball."

"He never smiled before getting into bed. His face, rather worked over, was blank. He would edge onto the sheets on his right shin, then sink back and open his arms to me. He slept with his right arm around my neck, always, and he never, ever removed it during the night—an insecurity attempting, it would seem, if at all possible, to integrate or consume me. At first I ached, since he barely stirred so long as he remained asleep, and he slept deeply. In the beginning I'd lie awake for hours, memorizing the apex of his left breast, fearing to breathe too heavily lest that movement make him restless. Sometimes we assumed a nesting-spoons, but his right arm would collar me then as firmly as when we were supine. Despite sleeping alone most of my life, I grew used to this, however flawed, graphic proprietary in fewer nights than I'd have thought I could. For it had an inarguable decision about it. Sharing that decision, I slept the way he wished me to within a week, as undisturbed as he.

"Once, after we'd made love and just before dozing off, I asked: 'Why you want me?'

"He responded: 'I want.' That was all.

"MAHIDOL U.'S OPENING was frantic. You're introduced to dozens of deans, chairs, profs, colleagues, T.A.'s, and secretaries. And two hundred Sino students: *they* had the families who drove them to be doctors. The same never spoke up in class, fearing to sound superior; and fearing to sound stupid, never asked questions. The lecture halls had ceiling fans (no air-con): forcing my students to accept my continuous sweating—and my near inaudible voice, with indistinct pronunciation. They would *wai* me (the lifted-prayer-hands greeting) on entering my class; crouch in my proximity (to lower themselves); kneel when next to me if I were sitting; and all but crawl over the threshold when I dismissed them.

"The commissary was the outdoor military mess hall in Service Films. It was perfectly stifling, deafening, and smoky; your dish was stir-fried when you ordered it, and stood by the wok watching its preparation.

"I met Mick Beale there, a bug-eyed British Columbian researcher in tropical disease and forty-year-old closet case, to whom flamboyance was a crucifixion. Desperate to shun Rol's 'out,' he thereinafter made himself scarce at lunch. That obligatory day, Y-z ignored him—until, sitting opposite us, his sallow cheeks still deeply pocked from adolescent acne, Mick Beale couldn't resist the snicker, under his breath, 'So, Cory, do you stiff the *gahlee*?'

"'Gah-lee?' I asked. (That *lee* or *ree* is a falling tone that sounds stressed to us, as do the lion's share of last syllables in Thai nouns.) 'What's that?'

"'*Gahlee* is prostitute,' he winked wickedly. 'Actually, *sopaynee* is how you translate prostitute. *Gahlee* is filthier, *real* dirt, like "whore." "Golden-flower-girl," *e-duct my' see tawn*, is even worse! –Doing O.K. with them?'

"I gagged on my mixed-fish over noodles: 'I do what I can to avoid them!'

"Mick Beale choked, 'So you're living under a rock?'

"'Why? What do you do?' I asked him. 'Is this a big problem here, avoiding *gahlee*? I go to Rome or Har*rie's* (Bangkok's only other queer disco).'

"'I like 'em young! I like to brown 'em and I like to stiff 'em. Kids at Hua'lompong Station. *They're* glad with a glass of milk. Keep 'em for a week or two, throw 'em out, and snatch up new arrivals!'

"'Must take me along one night,' I scholastically said.

"'That's a date! You, Rollo?' Y. pulled his eyelids down with his index tips. 'Don't dig young 'n' tender? Old walruses *fill* your bill better? They're really hung! What *is* your type, Rol? I never knew.'

"'I'm choosy. Urban, suburban, and rice-paddy men.'

"'Who else is there?' Mick giggled.

"'Waifs on the train in-between,' Y. snapped loudly. 'Or when they're kicked off at Hua'lompong and have nothing to sit on next. Except your can-opener!!'

"'*I* have a lab-stool to sit on,' the scientist sputtered, turning scarlet. 'Left a Petri must be festering.'

"'He was, too,' I observed as Mick Beale split like a hare in short range. 'Something you say discombobulate him?'

"Y-z holstered his cig in a mound of rice. 'I'm sorry, but that bitch busts my balls. Masquerades as a hetero here. And off-campus, gluts on his Caligulan jollies with twelve-year-olds. A glass of milk, indeed!'

"One morning shortly after moving to Bangkok, Y. had been awakened by the sobs, not of a twelve-, but a seven-year-old. Jettison of the slums, the child was plaintively crying on Y.'s front steps. Y-z took him in, fed and clothed him, taught him English, brought him up, and sent him to the city's best engineering school. Pom by name, he'd become a successful electrician, with a score of girlfriends. He'd leased his own flat prior to my trip to Thailand: and never visiting Rollo Y. when I happened to, more than two years would pass before I finally met him.

"There's a tradition in Thailand of adopting orphans, not only of persons related to you, but of the indigent in your village, and of the homeless in general. Of course, Rollo Y-z's reason was other than local practice.

"'Pom is my merit with Buddha,' as he once put it. 'Or the storm petrel I have Noahed against my ruin.'"

Cory poured beer. Its head rode over the rim. He swooped to sip it. I said, "Could you crib me on Chain's superstitions? Documents—some anthropology—would be peachy."

He went to his shelves, and found a monograph: *Political Organization and Rituals of the Tai-Lue*. He made that a hard "loo." "Read this tonight. You'll remember that Chain's parents had fled China at the beginning of World War II. Chain belatedly would admit this descent, and leave it there, the implication being, he was Han Chinese. This is the major but somehow also only 'true' Sino group—according to them. Chain's strong negative reaction to my incidental mention of the Montagnard, once, led me to hitchhike up to Nan, a remote northern Thai province that hosts the Tai-Lue. Hill tribes scattered over the Golden Triangle, the Lue place themselves at the top of a highland hierarchy: and put the Montagnard at the bottom. The original (prediaspora) Lue settlements, in the Sip Song Pan Na' region of Yunnan, became vassal states of China in the fourteenth century: and official Chinese territory only a little over a hundred years ago. It's still a wilderness: Marco Million's "India Minor"—his Karajang!

"Chain was conversant with his animist ancestry: the Lue must sacrifice a black buffalo to their thirty-two spirits. Spirits, need I add, who, without this annual appeasement, may take a seductive form and—claiming to have come from some distant continent, no?—be intent on hideous retribution.

"He knew that the Lue's source of protein is the insect larvae discovered in tree-bark and under certain leaves. These can be poisonous insects...

"–A partner from amongst the world's still jungle-dwelling tribes! Yet Chain, haunted by the insupportable notion that he was a sandal above savagery, craved to assimilate in Europe. How misguided—to bury exactly what is delectable about yourself. –An engorgement one's throwback ruminations shrink from yearning for: this Adam! This utopian's daydream! –Jealous, documenter?"

"Not at all. I didn't watch Tarzan or Mohican flix when I was young," I lied.

"*Tant pis pour toi!*" Cory hollered.

"What *factual* evidence do you have of his origins? He *looked* Tai-Lue?"

"Oh, yes, to a T. So did his mother. My hitchhike proved that.'

"A black buffalo!" I realized. "You're saying that the black Minotaur vase..."

"Forced Chain to sit next to it. He hoped the sacrifice it symbolized to him was adequate protection."

"We'll see about *that*, won't we, Cory?"

Cory Simon turned sour. He said, "Am I missing something?"

"I'm not." –He is so primate himself. "Chain's being Lue: further evidence?"

"Came immediately: on our second Sunday. Claiming to have no obligations at home, Chain agreed to an outing at the Dusit Zoo.

"When we reached the Dusit—a long, hot walk—he waxed formal and told me the Thai name for every animal there. While I'd no reason as yet to remember any of them, opening my pad, I jotted each down in hasty transliterations.

"As we worked our way through a wooded area on a path linking the ape cages, two dark boys, I'd say nine or ten, poked their unkempt heads out from behind a gigantic rain tree and began calling to Chain. At first he slighted them. They grew somewhat rhythmic, as if reciting a diatribe, and an apparently memorized one. It wasn't in Thai. Failing to win his attention with this, the boys stepped into the open—ragged-looking ur-chins they were!—and pelted us with stones. Chain about-faced and rushed up to them. All three trembling, a shouting match ensued. Some of their words were as distinct as they were loud—and these I wrote down next to the names of the animals. At last Chain lost his restraint, removed his silver-stretchband watch, and smacked first one, then the other, very hard across their cheeks. Then he knocked their heads together. Both boys, shocked, with dirty hands scrubbing what were sure to become swollen patches, fell back and made off.

"Since one stone had grazed my collar, I was set to get in there myself...when a sensuous zookeeper, flushing a nearby pen, caught my eye. Zookeepers are an atavistic turn-on, don't you think? So close to animals, they are close to animals. When you arrange to date, and they arrive, they're absolutely ursine."

"You've made such arrangements?"

"Often. The sex is fair-to-middling. –Where was I? Oh, yes: Chain returned winded and sodden; and offered: 'My cousin(s) me—bad boy(s).' Then he made tracks, dropping—his color leeching out—'Rollo know them!' When I caught him, he was in front of a cage of orangutan. Beside it were an oyster-omelet cart and white plastic chairs. He said, 'Hungry now.' We sat.

"Chain reviewed the orange-haired, sad-eyed pacifists with irritation, then attended to his chopsticks, which he manipulated aristocratically, keeping his sensitive fingers near the tops of their broader end. After he cleared half his plate, he pushed it away. I asked, 'Why you not finish what we buy?'

"He said: 'Face. Leave food, mean rich. Not need eat (all) what order.'

"I scored, 'You will not do *this* with me.' He didn't budge. He looked at the vendor, then the apes. I pulled at his serving and ate what he'd left.

"To stop the tug, I elucidated, 'Orangutan means "forest man" in Malay.'

"He cried, 'How about—in Malay—*"zoo man"*?' He was boiling.

"I protested, 'Since you naming *only* the animals...' (Again: my Adam.)

"'Always want name,' he sneered. He summoned a tense composure. 'What about tiger, what about elephant—you not like?'

"'Oh, I do! Elephants are my favorite animal.'

"'Sacred animal! Sign for monarchy. Siam look same elephant head. And *name* me—Chain—mean, like elephant.' This was filler. He'd worries beyond errant boys; and Rollo. He gagged: 'And Cory mean: *my* punishment me!'

"He read his watch: 'Go now?' He reflected, and added, 'Have business. You want, I walk apartment you, or you go Rollo, he on way.'

"What he'd been forced to reveal created more ellipses. I told him to pursue his affairs; I'd get to Rollo's at my own pace. He worked his eyes for a whole minute and oscillated on his chair: to him as well, that morning was incomplete. He said he'd see me on Wednesday and promptly departed.

"I sat thoughtfully dabbing my sweat and watching the orangutans, who were watching me, stalling on the hot trek to Rol's. Why did Chain now have pressing business? He'd previously maintained he was free. Ill-behaved relatives, Rollo, and a scrumptious zookeeper hid something else. Nor did I miss his use of 'Siam'—Jim Thompson's preference. My note pad had possible clues.

50

"Rollo Y-z studied my scribbling with deliberation, silently mouthing plausible pronunciations. He was pasted on his favorite armchair, a Qing-style horseshoe. 'It's a hill-tribe dialect,' he mumbled wearily and very warily, 'I couldn't say which.' He returned the pad. I asked him about the boys.

"'How would I know his cousins? I only met him the other night.'

"'Do you know *any* hill-tribe boys?'

"'What for? They wander. I need addresses in case of trouble. Hill tribes are Fourth World. They're not citizens of a recognized, or developing, power. They cross borders like birds. So Chain knocked a smidgen of sense into their noggins? Why allot such dimension to a run-in with beggars?'

"'Allot it *some*thing, or I'll punch the floorboards with all this anarchy.'

"'Punching assembles an order? Sterling! Care for some blo before you start? Here: I can't get up. I'm too mired in anarchy.'

"A mature tokay wiggled along the parquet at the far end of Y-z's lounge. It must have bunked with him, because I saw it there often enough: seemed a foot long, with bluntly human fingers and toes. It sent a tongue to test the smoky air for who was about and barked, 'Toe-kay, toe-kay,' in a slow fade-out, seven times. Nine successive barks assure good luck. That stubborn specimen always quit at six or seven. Like I felt then, at sixes and… –Tokays, of course, are tropical janitors assigned to insect detail, so Westerners encourage them to feel at home. Thais, fuzzy with cause and effect, throw shoes at them.

"I looked around at this now familiar setting. Y-z also housed a squirrel, in a suspended cage by the kitchen. There was a blanket in the cage: his squirrel dusted it off before turning in early every evening. The higher you got, the farther and farther away the walls of his lounge receded. The decorous potted plants wantonly multiplied alongside them. Depressed right then, I was awkwardly sunk in his reshaping butterfly chair, while Rol sat especially stiff on the camphor wood of the horseshoe. Both he and Chain were lying to me.

"And one of them had a memory problem with those hill-tribe boys.

"CHAIN WAS CALMER that Wednesday night, having adjusted to the schism in his tacit third degree. Rol had said: 'By picking at his Mainland influence, you locate the model for Chain's façade. The Chinese are ancestor-worshippers, and endemic to deifying the elders is accepting the advisability of what had been their habits and ideas. Since the elders had it all figured out, a visible restlessness to alter and improve would be sacrilegious. It's saying your forebears—the gods—hadn't got it quite right. Not only is originality, then, and innovation reprehensible: being interesting is suspicious—and undesirable. A Sino male knows his job: to hold down as many as he can, vacation as seldom as possible, earn as much as his skills permit, and leave it all to his children...'

"But Chain, from a tribe minority, had an administrating quarrel in appearing not to rock the boat. Once I'd inadvertently recited it, he requested that I repeat, several times over, 'Mine is a country that strives for freedom and equality for all.' At each recitation, he would rise and shadow-kickbox.

"His political exhibition unsettled me enough to consider leaving town.

"'Where want go?' Chain asked.

"'To a jungle. The thickest is in central Malaysia, just over the border.'

"'Not come back.'

"'Why?'

"'Dangerous. Not come back. Same Jim Thompson (stressed, Tom-*son*).'

"'Oh? What happened to him?'

"'Disappear.'

"'Yes, but how?'

"'TV not say. Lost. Kill maybe.'

"I flashed gabby Randy Wetzel and his tales of Thompson and the Oriental: and Chain's lifelong proximity to that hotel. 'Did you know Jim Thompson?'

"'I not sleep him.'

"I needed to get Chain smashed; to digress, use sidetracks and tangents. *I'd* already had five cheap-gin tonics. He was going slow on his second.

"'Famous expatriate,' I said. 'So many expatriates here.' –An inquest, broadly generalizing, seemed sly enough. Asians holding it bad form to opinionate about another, I'd badger and ensnare him by soliciting his opinion of all the local expats.

"'What about them?' he inquired.

"'Why they live here,' I tried, 'why they live and work here when they could earn four times as much back home?'

"'Live here. Work here,' he said watching my face with strange attention.

"'For example,' I elaborated, 'this week, a Canadian researcher at Mahidol learned he could get $80,000 at a university in Vancouver.' Mick Beale was in my alcoholic thoughts because I knew that bid was giving him insomnia: $80,000—or the teenies at Hua'lompong. *One* in Vancouver could wrap him up.

"No change in Chain's temperature: he recentered himself on the sofa.

"I spiked my sixth tonic with annatto to pierce the cobwebs in this colloquy. That highball led to some spellbound babbling on my part, and airing of Mick's proclivities with more thoroughness than the cautious would. The priority he gave to sex, next to which little else mattered, was obsessing me. I expanded on his talk of *gahlee* and how, according to him, their infiltration of Bangkok's most commonplace haunts had made evading them a continuous chore.

"'I *gahlee*,' Chain responded with a finger crooked at his chest.

"'Well, of course,' I placated, 'we all start to think that way, jumping from bed to bed. And, hell, the provocation! This town is *paved* with good-looks!'

"'You think Thai boy look good?' he asked.

"'Most of them! Rollo thinks so too. Still, I'm not by nature promiscuous. It's the downfall debasing gays: hetero structures make finding a single lover, a monogamous one, so difficult for us.'

"'What you want?' he incised, to push my ramblings to quick solution.

"'You!' I said emphatically.

"'What about me?'

"'You! I want you!'

"'So?—you have.'

"That kind of statement brings up even a drunk.

"'Come on: enough you drink. *Nawn* (sleep)!' he ordered, and without ado began his choreographed disrobing. Before he could complete that enchantment, I tackled him to the floor and used the heels of my hands to part the inconceivable velvet of his inner thighs and bury my nose in them. Their heat and heated scent—floral, umber, torturously sexual. The Himalayan's skin *must* be described as dove-like to the touch; and really, what more could you ask for in the feel of skin: their marshmallow pecs and spongy nips, their flat abdomens, the elongated miracle of their backs?

"EACH PRINTED LESSON was inscribed with the date on which it was to be taught, the approximate number of minutes it should take to teach it, a medical vocabulary to be memorized, and a list of questions to be asked. I might discuss the apposition occasioned by clauses and pronouns, but to stray farther afield risked the chair's carpet. Letting a lesson delay the class convening next was cause for departmental comment; and ending before the bell aroused rumors of pedagogic shortchanging. So from day one, professing Medical English would lack interest, let alone the jumpstart for my sagged authorship, States-side. To boot, Mahidol has massive, omnipresent, raised windows; and beyond these that year continuous construction was in progress: if not with derricks and drills, then other power-tools. Besides not enlarging on the shackling mimeo, I had to read it to the pre-meds at the top of my lungs; and developed a strep throat and finally laryngitis by the middle of the term's second week.

"In between those screaming-sessions one morning, I left the building for a smoke and noticed that the construction workers were all wearing that foreigners' balaclava and outfit, which so successfully conceals (no-work-permit) identities. Returning a glance to my classroom windows, I could see, in a tit-for-tat, that they afforded the laborers on the third-floor scaffold with a clear view of me every day. I experienced the oddest sensation: a vertiginous gliding on a melded swan-Naga. Trance-like, I examined the workers up there: defying coincidence, a faced-away one had the lifted shoulders and hourglass form of the fellow who had given me the bent wire-rim specs and small cigar. When my eyes rested on the reversed triangle of his strong back, he slowly turned and fixed me in his sight.

"In a state that felt as unreal, I reentered my room and seized the cigar from my lectern, where, for unplumbed accountability, I now kept both it and the specs. I walked outside, struck a match, and rather than put it to a Pall Mall, with a deal of difficulty bit its tip and got the cigarillo to take. It did my laryngitis no good, and its smell was offensive: suggesting a charnel ground or more recently dead thing. The dignified worker watched me ignite the stale tobacco, inhale, and sniff its lit end with a scrunched nostril. Then, the movement subtle so that none in his gang would see, he opened his tapered, black right fist just a notch in a gesture of consent, or approval, or confirmation.

"Near the teachers' lockers later that day, I took care to reserve from Rollo Y-z this evident recommitment to the enigmatic alien, who'd blatantly unnerved him on Royal Field: an ebony man, his orbs Sherwood-blue. I complained of my 'somehow' aggravated strep throat. 'Lozenges,' Y-z advised. 'And I'll take you out to Olie on Saturday to invest in the surprise of cosmological relaxers.'

"I asked what that meant. 'I said it's a surprise,' Rollo remonstrated.

"The wat enshrined a 'Footprint of Buddha' with few gold-leaf adhesives—not a favorable prognostication. As a retaliative, it sat in the midst of desiccated cornfields near acres and acres of sugar cane doing less than yeoman's duty. I've the belief that we eventually drove due west, because Khun Mani Vivian—that is, Lady Doctor Vivian—was driving: and she had taken a devious route. Her rationale was a deserted woman's suicide off a bridge accessing the wat more directly. The suicide's ghost would still be on that span, looking to draw Vivian through its railing into the flood below.

"We parked by the monastery section, so the doctor had to wait in the car.

"Rollo and I zigzagged about in a vegetable patch and stooped under a trellis to reach a step-down door, which we opened without knocking (as is permitted). Sitting there ensconced in a rapt audience of teenage novices, his upper half propped on an axe pillow, his saffron robe barely cloaking his bony legs stretched along a mirrored mahogany floor, his head shaved to a bumpy eggshell-tinted pink, was Oliver Augustine Makepeace Littleton himself.

"Himself failed to bat his mole-sided, pickle-colored eyes. Gritting his iodine incisors, he ferociously indicated Rol and flapped: 'You're looking very cuffed with yourself—for a cad who don't return phone calls!'

"'*My* salary covers calls to the border of Burma?' Y-z asked. 'I brought you a waylaid layman. Think a layman might be cured with meditational expertise? When you're not playing lay-man yourself, that is, unto the novitiate?'

"'Frightfully sorry, meditation medicates the strong of mind. Is your mind strong?' Oliver fired at me. '–How many cryptograms can two hill Sambos do in a day on celestial Mount Meru?' He rested his wrists on a warped lute table.

"Was this allusion rhetorical or pointed? I rode it: and dissembled, 'I cannot decrypt a prescription for heat rash, but I *can* decode Ptolemy and Adorno.'

"'*Chappie*: you fall short!' AML whistled. 'The serenity of detumescence is a millionfold more demanding! It requires emptying your mind—a mind encumbered with the abstrusities of pondering and systematic analysis all your wasted life. Suddenly vacating its crannies can cause the chambers of your brain to collapse!'

"'The chambers of Vivian's brain may collapse in the confines of her car outside if you wax too discriminate now,' Rollo forecast, conspicuously ignoring Oliver's interjection of the hill-tribe boys. 'Arrange a vet for when you hit the Big Mango in the next coupla weeks.'

"'Don't see raping and pillaging the Big Backwater in my jammed upcoming weeks, but as you're inviting...'

"'Yeah, we're inviting. Next Sunday, proper channel?'

"'Shall we say high tea, Mr Y.?'

"'I'll fix finger-grub. Thai cukes. And not too many of those. That *is* what the high-toned limey is gorging with tea these days, ain't it?'

"'The *high* ones, yes. Your tea *will* be high? Otherwise, I got obliga—'

"'*If* you insist.'

"This banter went on for a while, their animosity barely disguised as fun and games. The monastery was a furnace, but the substance of our trip—discounting its bonus, that curt slam at mountain boys—and why Rol wouldn't call ahead and provide Olie with the chance to disappear, was to give Doctor Vivian a minute with him. So, after expressing less than unbridled enthusiasm at the prospect of speaking with her, Olie went out to the road, leaving Y-z and me alone with the novices. They sat there unperturbed; and if puzzled by us, internalized it.

"This was when Rol filled me in on Olie's odyssey—and Vivian's: he couldn't in the car, as the doctor spoke English. Rol would postpone program notes; I'd already sampled how thoroughly.

"Oliver was a sixteen-year-old Liverpool guttersnipe when a bored playboy bundled him off to Thailand: for the idle superiority in watching an uneducated orphan flounder in Asia's most alien kingdom. That diversion wearing thin in three weeks, and with nary a word to Olie, never mind a modest handout, the playboy abruptly flew home. So here he was, once again penniless, but now in a strange land, and one lacking the luxury to be amused by his ineptitudes.

"He learned the idiom quickly, as youngsters will when

necessary; and scraped by much as all the homeless do, with temporary and menial jobs, begging, and thievery. In time, he translated Thai when a local merchant trusted that to a kid his age—for satang no adult would have dreamt was a tip. While no beauty-contest winner even as a teenager, Olie had orange hair, a symbol of good fortune in the East. Wealthy Thais felt buggering him would bring them luck—and that, I'm afraid, was how Olie kept the wolf if not wolves from his door. I say afraid, because once you associate sex with money in the mind of the young, you set in motion a corruption that will rage for the rest of their lives. Since the market value of his integrity would never allow him to save enough cash to return to Britain, it lowered him to means, and an idea, of survival that stain the sternest mettle. And Olie was only the most average of persons.

"He learned that monasteries are Sanctuary of indefinite retreat: where the desperate may find food, shelter, and safety… and sex—for he grew, to use an indelicacy here, into a puncher of tickets, a morbid retribution aimed at the whole world. As elsewhere, celibacy is a monk's paramount vow. Yet boys will be boys, and some Thais will be Thais. And monks there are who are grateful for that…

"Khun Mani Vivian was pure exploitation on Oliver's part, in no wise his first, but his longest-lasting and possibly saddest. She was the child of a native and a white foreign father: a frowned-upon union back then and occasion for ostracism. Predictably, her smitten mother, eventually abandoned by her roguish husband, was left to raise Vivian alone amidst the neighbors' scorn and hatred. She was a determined woman and saw to the child's education. Still, from the start, Eurasian and homely, Vivian's marriage prospects were nil. A bit on in life, she encountered young Olie, and though hardly naïve about his lust for men, harbored the ineducable hope that one day he'd need to fructify. Oliver, given how aimless he'd become, saw no point in discouraging her. When short on funds, short of virgins, and too fidgety to reenter a wat, Olie would come a-knocking at Vivian's office and always, alas, be admitted. Once he moved into her three-story house, however, he'd lose most of his freedom: for she kept a jealous eye on him, insisting he be back before dinner, or eleven, and also, quite naturally, constantly badgered him about setting the date. Time and again, then, he would find her wearisome and sneak off in the smog without notice, as they deceiving *him* had neither thought necessary, and be gone for a year or two. Throughout those merciless months, she'd wander the nighttime sois in search of Olie or sit by the phone awaiting the call that stroke after stroke of the clock never came. For if Olie never said yes, he never said no. And Vivian grew old that way, her face lining rapidly after her child-bearing years, happy only when he was near and she at least could fasten her eyes on him with inexplicable adulation.

"Her friends, as custom went, were only a few miscegenationists or half-caste ladies like herself who'd gather to play mahjong and whisper to each other in the warm evenings. That's how I most remember her. When urgently searching for Oliver myself, I lingered in her front garden, smoking quietly and waiting for him. At spaced moments she'd step down through her row of hedges and slip between the Pride of India and scattered Rough Brush trees, her thin shadow behind me eerily leaking under my chair and hesitating beside my sandals. She invited me to sleep in her house; I tried and couldn't for the gunning of motorbikes. But Vivian didn't try to sleep: she paced up and down the adjoining canals, the twisting trawks, dark alleys, and private paths looking for her lover.

"Some years back, when Olie was still in his thirties, he conned Vivian into the airfare and a wad to return to Liverpool, promising he'd land a job there and set up a situation for both of them. He milked the dole as best he could and managed to hang in for fifteen months; he ultimately found, as the majority will who stay abroad, and for fewer crucial combats than he, that home is not where he thought it was. He had listened too long to a different exchange interpreting life and saw now with alien sight, hustled with alien wit. He was part—destiny do its worst— of another people. He reappeared in Bangkok, as purposeless as ever, his tail between his legs, and threw himself alternately on the mercies of the monastic system and the doctor's irresolvable patience.

"Olie left the shale road by the parked car and rejoined Rollo and me. We were coaxing a breeze with bamboo fans the novices had thoughtfully provided. He apologized for his absence: given his recent lapse in the lady's company, he'd been brief just this side of discourtesy.

"'I savvy you twits have perv moves to make, and Vivian has back-to-backs this afternoon,' he said with unconvincing affability. 'Been jolly meeting Cory; and since Mixed-Grille's *chained* up now, I'm keen to give him a nail file.'

"He crouched through a narrow passageway and reemerged after a moment with a shimmering Buddha. Over a foot high, in the lotus position, the figure was slender, confident, and graceful, with a hive of tight curls, long-petal lobes, and a breathlessly extended cone torso. It wore a Siamese spiraling chadok, or crown, of daring length and peered at its lap-held palm with a living gaze and the Orient's ever-haunting semi-smile. Set upon a sturdy, intricately engraved base, this icon was clearly a craftsman's accomplishment, and costly.

"'Welcome to the Land of Semi-Smiles,' Oliver hummed, semi-smiling to me. Half his teeth were missing. 'And for you, Y-z, two wog nippers up the arse!'

"In Rol's flat a few hours on, I grew agitated by the morning's discrepancies.

"'You don't see him often, do you?' I commented.

"'Not often.'

"'And don't return his calls.'

"'Seldom.'

"'Why?'

"He lit a Camel and scrubbed his table with an over-soaked sponge. 'There's a meanness about him. He's petty, and vengeful. Like when we do blo: he struts along the wraparound windows. You understand? So if anyone's nearby, they can see him holding his breath, with the pipe in his outstretched hand. (Y.

used a tiny pipe, preferring not to roll a joint or force the ganja into a partially evacuated cig.) He wants to endanger me, Cory. He feels I deserve it.'

"'You think it's purposeful, not just thoughtlessness?'

"'I'm telling you it is! He'll eat after twelve noon in his monk's robe. That's illegal! It appalls people. He'll touch a woman who's passing with his hem—or an elbow. This is a sin for her. It's *all* purposeful. A white monk is attention-getting enough. He defies the sacrosanct and courts arrest—when he's with me. Even if I didn't have a sensitive job...'

"'You think it's only when he's with you?'

"'I don't care!' Rollo shouted. 'The bastard is blackmailing me!'

"'About what?'

"'Oh, never mind. I didn't say that.'

"But, of course, he did.

"He switched tone. 'Olie's hooked-up, got that? And his back's to a wall.'

"I waited. 'Do you miss his companionship?'

"'No.'

"'Oh?'

"'Not his, not anyone's. If the word "disappointment" means anything, it's most of the people I know.'

"'Tell me,' I asked, handling the marvelous statuette, 'what do you make of his giving me this? It's worth a great deal.'

"'I can't make shit of it. –Another plot.'

"'You think it's worth money, don't you?'

"'Probably.'

"'It's fine workmanship.'

"'That don't mean squat with him. I hoped he'd like you. He doesn't.'

"He opened a tin of tuna and emptied it into a clay bowl emblazoned with burnt-ochre swirls: an authentic example of antediluvian Ban Chiang pottery. He diced an onion and celery stalk and stirred them into the tuna, squeezing a thin half-tube of mayonnaise on top. 'They pack two ounces of sugar into a tube this size,' he seethed. 'You call sugar "white death" now in the States, yes? Be forty years before they hear of that. I'm not exaggerating.'

"'Rol, why did you want me to meet him if he's treacherous? Could he tell us more about the boys at the zoo?'

"'He could tell us how he discovered—or cares—that you encountered them. Could be that ursine agent, a manager of his, who leaked it...'

"'Ursine?'

"'Yeah, Ursa Major! Olie's a gumball—for one of the biggest operators in Thailand. But he'll be punching above his weight—won't he?—if this means he's already agreed to screw you like he does me. –Won't he be, Cory?'

"'Yo! Count on it!' I affirmed—actually confused by Y.'s multiple handouts.

"'Cordie, if you just keep at your rut of cornering me, a jock for deadlocks and irrelevant facts, you will fall sick again... Christ! Why do I even try?'

"Rol had lost time leaving the stall and was whipping his stride to recoup it. Introducing Olie did not have the persuasion he'd bet on—to convince Olie to drop his manager. He cut a sandwich in quarters and angrily pushed it at me.

"I watched Y-z, waited again, and brought to the fore: 'Speaking of ruts, I'm getting real disjointed dealing with the dissatisfied one. I don't satisfy him.'

"'Who?'

"'Chain.'

"'So find someone else,' he grumbled. 'Jerk!'

"Rol's qualification further disjointed me. 'Where?' I fought back.

"He dumped the Bronze Age bowl into the sink and went at cleaning it with the soggy sponge. Finding that impossible, he added his knife and fork, opened the faucet, let it run, and grabbed a towel to dry his hands.

"'*Where?* It's Saturday night, right? Chain said he's working this weekend. You snag a bus to Patpong, you get off, you go to Lome or Bar Harrie's! –Or you sit in Lumpini Park, you take two sticks, you drum them on your belly—and shove them the hell up *your* jammy!!'

"I wanted to say, 'Would you like me to change your diaper?' But didn't.

"AT TRAFFIC-FREE 11 P.M. I'm on a No. 2, thrilled by its careen down Phayathai. It slid left with a bounce onto Rama IV, then right into Silom Road. The first stop there is at the Saladaeng intersection. I buzzed; jumped off; looked both ways for vehicles, saw none, and sped across Silom, hugging the ground for bricks, fissures, sharp-ended gutters, and brass coils that trip pedestrians in their sexual hurry. My anticipation at the edge of a hunting area exonerates me: it gets so out of hand I can hardly breathe. My nipples rise, and my thighs constrict—making the height of an ordinary curb a challenge; and the curb there between the two gay sois was a mini parapet then. Hundreds of flank-to-flank swallows, settled on the inches of telephone line they'd spent the evening arguing over, were peering down like attentive gargoyles. The street was near-deserted: and dark: so that when, hyperventilating, I brought my cramped leg up on the curb and lifted my eyes for the first time since starting across the road, the sight that greeted me came at my chest as a shock, the full, loaded spear of adrenaline, and my heart began pounding in my ears.

"Standing profile, literally in touching distance, with his back against that creaker Randolph Wetzel—Jim Thompson's former partner—with one of Wetzel's fists a bony mound under his singlet, fiercely cupping his breast—and the other in a hauling-grip on his crotch—was Chain.

"Randolph Wetzel!—his frazzled pompadour sweat-pasted to his forehead; his checkered shirt pasted on Chain's shoulders. Gamily shuffling what had been a full nelson, Randy swung Chain from side to side and brought him about in an arc that ended putting Chain's face a foot from mine. Chain squirmed free and froze. The old man, nasty, drunk, and puzzled by this, *baubled* Chain's pecs now: and basket: to rattle a response into what had become immobility.

63

"*Unwanted* frames of déjà vu restricted my glassy vision: I saw a stairwell in my junior high. Howie Paul was the shortest kid in the seventh grade's advanced class: first on assembly lines and first-line-left in class photos. And, somehow, also the heaviest. Burdened with a stack of overdue books, he was taking too long to get to the library. A brazen, braid-muscled tough—much older: almost mature-looking, in fact—a boogey, as we called the hoodlums in the slower homerooms—overtook him, thrust his fist into Howie's shirt, and grabbed his sizable swelling; then bellowed up the staircase to his sycophants: 'Hey, guys, look at this! Real tits!' Howie purpled; his eyes went dead. The boogey's sidekicks arrived. Each, yelling loudly and squawking in agreement, helped himself in turn to cruel and generous, crushing handfuls of Howie's mortified trauma—indelible for life. His and mine.

"Chain dug his nails into Randy's arms. Randy, wondering what had happened, peered over Chain's head, straining to find me. That broken drainpipe looked his full seventy-seven years of age. He gargled, 'You're a—a—pal of Y-z, no? Met you somewhere. Wait—where was it?—don't tell me.'

"Chain offered: 'This friend. Name Randy. –You know Randy Wetzel.'

"Wetzel smirked with approval. 'Chain's an *old* friend of mine. We go back real long. But we still get it on, once a week! Don't we, boy?'

"He squeezed Chain's chest again; and butt. 'Great tits here! *Great* crack!'

"Chain, more steadily, even hard, intoned: 'I *tell* you I know friend(s) you....'

"I whispered—to him or no one, 'Yeah. Rollo and Randy. *Fine* people.'

"The geezer chirped, 'Small world, Bangkok.' He grinned idiotically, drooled, and lapped at his drool. 'Lemme emphasize, got, on balance, a big cock, too!'

"I think I may have said that's nice. Chain tilted the side of his tennis shoe, scraping the pavement. His volume dropped.

'So—have good night.'

"'You also,' I mumbled. 'See that this man doesn't drink any more, O.K.?'

"Randolph Wetzel belched loudly, 'You tops know each other?'

"'Not well,' I concluded. This wasn't meant to cut: it wasn't even a note to myself. There was no direct wire to my brain. I saw only Howie Paul—if possible yet more viscerally than before. We had called him the Blimp.

"I heard Chain say, '*Sawat-dee' cap* (good-bye).'

"'*Sawat-dee' cap*,' I returned.

"The drunk thought to inform me: "'*Cap*" is Mango vernacular for "*crap*".'

"'Yeah... I knew that... I'll be around, Randy.'

"Chain pulled him to and, the old soak stumbling, urged him on. Chain added, for no particular reason, '(We) Go Harrie's.'

"Initially I couldn't see. Then stared in a contrary direction: vaguely, at Soi 4: and sought shadow in the closest building. Securing this cover, I walked like a zombie, stepped into a doorway, and turned. I became aware, by a learnt scent and the glow of its source, that the ursine Englishman who'd menaced Chain on the night I met him—and Chain, tolerantly, had allowed was his boss—was also standing in a doorway, spaced two or three from me.

"He'd witnessed this scene.

"I snubbed him. I watched the barhops. Wetzel was taking giant strides, and Chain, too short-legged for his 'friend,' was making an effort to appear at ease while keeping abreast. Randy was oblivious to Chain's stress in his rapid gait toward further sudsing.

"Before vanishing into Soi 2, Chain paused briefly and searched the street. My reflex was to slip deeper into the dark. My heart continued to hammer. This happenstance wasn't open to question. In that split second when I looked up on Silom and caught their horseplay, I'd understood what I was seeing.

"*Aperture of a thousand pistons!* Randolph Wetzel was a cli-

65

ent. That was that, and nothing in that remotely uncertain. And yet, I rehearsed, on my fourth vodka in Lome—to which I repaired, losing memory of how—Chain *had* told the truth in his way: about working with his family, about being *gahlee*, about knowing Y. and Randolph Wetzel. And, previously, Jim Thompson. Yes, I *had* always thought the neighboring influence of the Oriental was inescapable. Meaning not just the lifestyle it symbolized: its clientele. Little as he said, Chain told the truth—in so clipped a manner as to be dismissed. He worked with his family, but it was only sometimes and not his major source of income; he practiced prostitution, but tourists were not his key customers; he knew Rollo, Olie, and Randy: but how closely, and in what unthinkable capacities? And as with them, Jim Thompson. I *did* believe he'd never slept with him, for such was Chain's gamble with words: but this wasn't all he could tell me about the most celebrated disappearance in the history of modern Asia…

"I ordered a fifth—or eighth tonic. I lip-synced the same thoughts. I saw gossips ragging me. I pumped my arms in defiance. One, returning my defiance with a pronounced mouth tic, was that Eton Atlas, again: Chain and Olie's 'boss.' Wasn't *he* the urgency driving my alien black? He was chinless, smoked a betel-wrapped cigar, and had bulging owl-eyes, enlarged through wire-rim specs.

"I faced the exit. I excluded the world—then smelt that charnel stench engulfing me. Atlas had assumed an attack from directly behind. He dug his nails into my right bicep as Chain had dug his into Randy. And spoke.

"'Whatever in blazes you are, and whichever Hell you call home, quick-to-punch, *keep away from him!* I shall not repeat this.'

"I stood there, a breathing stone. I couldn't turn around. I said:

"'I don't know how to.'

"As much opens the can of worms we will inspect by making your tapes.

"Now: with each dead soldier scolding me here, the table's too crowded for a nightcap. Meaning, I'm as plastered as I got in Lome that evening. We can continue on in, well… two days? By then, I'll have recovered from the hangover, which retaliates for killing them."

THE SECOND DAY

CORY GAVE US A SHOUT at Moon Dormitory two mornings later and claimed something had come up, could we cancel our session. He said he was mindful of my time set aside for Bangkok: I was not to worry, we would complete his interview that week, or when I returned from Beijing. I said, "I know you are conscientious. And I owe you for any unpleasantness your memories cost you."

I rang the next artist on my list, a negative-image photographer, who tried Thailand via the Peace Corps thirty years ago and never left. He was game for that morning. He was no big talker: I was finished by 2:00 p.m.

I went to an internet café. Simon's vignettes—their canny meld of incision and blocks—were ringing a bell. I really had to know more about Cory Simon. I needed a background check, things not in print. I had in mind a PC wiz. William Ned Dilly could break it up for me, no problem.

After I sent the email, I did some exploring to pinpoint the spots Cory had specified. I wanted to concretize them for myself.

Silom is now referred to as the Downtown Business and Financial District. It is also a tourist hub. I snapped a roll of the mishmash. Nothing happened in any shot. No use developing.

Luckily, Cory phoned the next morning. Would I do brunch at the corner of Silom and Saladaeng?

Would I! I fixed a mini-mike into an envelope—not that deceiving figured in my project. With layovers, I like the results of occasionally recording candidly. Cory could always listen to what he said at some point, and censor it or leave it intact according to how it struck him then.

Simon's studio is in a cul-de-sac near the river, between the Royal Orchid Sheraton and Oriental. That nabe is largely Iranian and Pakistani: a cast-iron ghetto, the streets cramped with curry-slops and rooms for subcontinentals in native garb. His court is shabby, and this, or any environment, as field recorders will tell you, colors the tapes they get. So it is pro to tape a person in as many locales as you can, within reason.

I felt with Cory, when he was sober as well as lit.

He got to the northwest end of Saladaeng before me and was talking with two studs, I would say in their midtwenties. These were those bruisers you see there: wearing ribbed-cotton tanks to showcase their awesome lats—also, since the tank-straps were long, rock pectorals with enormous sunny-sides-up. Both were bulging in low-slung Wranglers with wide cowboy belts: not guys I would cross in an alley, but still, poster-types the world over. They were laughing freely, joshing with, and groping Cory. I thought I would like to boff all three. The shorter one wrote on a piece of paper, gave it to Cory, and playfully tapped his ear with a lightning gym-gloved knuckle. The three wai'ed at chin level. Then the Thais took off on the balls of their feet. I waved to him.

He sported a tapered Hawaiian shirt that day, with red, pink, and purple parrots set on a black-and-green jungle. He had on khaki-colored cargo pants with four front pockets, all zippered, and black-and-green camouflage slip-thrus, without socks. Reflector shades bounced from a lanyard on his well-defined chest. He had got a haircut since I saw him and looked younger than before. His tan was deeper in streetlight, his face tougher and a good deal more ominous than with his back to the windows at the World Inn. Noon touched the irises with cerulean in those Asian eyes. At a distant, cursory glance, he argues as Western; but in daytime this seems incorrect: I was now certain he had mixed blood.

In the middle of lunch-rush, he immodestly lifted his shirt, displaying a hard, concave stomach, so as to retie the knot in his waistband.

He said, "Do stewed hocks tempt you? There's a place near-by."

We walked to a shophouse on Soi Saladaeng. As we cleared the open front, Cory dropped our order to a stocky man list-lessly sitting by the stewing vat, then led me into the steamy interior. He beat me to a fold-up facing rear, forcing me to take the wall one. This would let me examine the staff in that basic eatery. A seat away from the street noise also suited my hidden recorder.

There was a well-rounded woman giggling and stirring near the entrance, a preteen girl helping her, and a petite matron-type, perhaps late fifties, who was spooning the hocks onto plates. I counted five tables on either wall; as it was one o'clock the customers were thinning out. The guy who had been idling at the vat brought our order. Setting it down, he abruptly re-turned to his station, opened a tabloid, and read it backwards, starting with the sports pages.

Cory watched him. He said, "I was put in reverse right across the road from where we just met. When I stand there now, it doesn't speak to me. My rupture, wanting for evidence, except that I tell it, could have happened somewhere else. Or, for the purposes of your colleagues, not have happened at all."

"My colleagues?" I asked.

"Sure. Pretending to repossess words, doctoral candidates today compete to alter the past. You draft the irritant 'memory': its Siamese twin is invention, separated at birth: of whose sur-vival it's always unaware."

Memory an irritant? This from a mind with a memory in a million?

Cory thumbed the table: "The man I was, struggling to dis-entangle himself from the intrinsic drift that Chain embodied, no longer exists. So *where* does he dwell now, amongst the reli-quaries required to re-entangle himself for you? Hence neither temporal point—the then and the now—stationary today..."

I jumped: "...the centrifugal force of both renders realign-ment nil."

I plonked kale over my rice. I said, "Hoosegow, Cory! You're as finicky as my advisor. No input is unpolluted. Particularize."

Cory smiled and said, "O.K., I will. I'm going to ask the waiter for our check. When he brings it, get a bead on his face."

He turned and called out: "*Nawng, cap* (Brother, please): *check-bin!*" Then he whispered, "When I knew Chain, his aunt owned this shop: his late mother's kid sister. In those days she ran it by herself. If she is that woman up front, I'm not remembering her. –Don't talk now, he's coming."

The man tallied our check at 50 baht: when he arrived, Cory stared hard at me. I felt that discomfort when you examine someone inappropriately close. He appeared to be in his early thirties, sienna, amply padded, with a wide, cheeky face under a mess of blue-highlighted hair. Set on that lackluster face, frowning at having to serve foreigners, was a diadem of lashes: cupping practically painted, oval, obsidian eyes, crystal in the glint of a ceiling bulb; in their pools as he lowered them, deliberately blank and aimed offside Cory's ear, was a Chinese child-emperor's most prepossessing beauty.

He stood upright and quickly walked away. Seconds later, Cory explained his haste. "That man is Chain's cousin—the younger of the two hill-tribe boys in the Dusit Zoo. With Chain's eyes. –His very eyes! They live, still!"

We sat in Lumpini Park, a short stroll from the foodshop. Cory said it was the Japanese army-camp during the occupation. Afterward, it was reconstructed as a cosmopolitan showpiece. He dangled his arm over our stone seat and sighed, "Yes, many men have made Bangkok their Hades of choice…"

I admired the landscaped arbor with fossil-like leaves in such a variety of greens that I lost count. Yards from us, geese were using the kidney-shaped lake's caterpillar bank for a landing pier. They frightened a toddler tossing candy at them; she dropped her candy bag and scrambled away. Out on the water a pair of swans, one white, one black, sailed serenely toward a disturbance compromising their curiosity near a firehouse-red camelhump bridge.

"Is Lumpini queer?" I asked. "It couldn't be closer to the gay nightspots."

"Is a frog's ass waterproof? There's a Muscle Beach here. The Mr. Thailands, priced sky-high at Club Tawan, bench-press in the afternoon. It's a dirt patch with random free-weights and dilapidated workout machines from the year When. Dig groups? Our chunks in threesomes charge the same as singles this time of day.

"Once, when I was sitting by a gate in broad daylight, a young delinquent paced to and fro in front of me. He wore cutoffs and a billowy T-shirt that fell almost to where he'd cut them off. At length, he looked either way to see if we were reasonably alone. There were two mounted police, but they were cantering in circles by the exit. Then he yanked the T-shirt up to his navel to show me how the cutoffs were belted above his knees, and that his skivvies were still in the wash. He shimmied for me while palming his set like a vendor hawking a wind-up. Then he did wind it up. He had a real thick bush, some Thais do, and a cock so fat he must have felt he need not blush to make it public."

I said, "You have to be crazy to do that!"

"I'm sure *I* blushed. But the juvie never broke his concentration."

"What was he expecting you to do?"

"Hightail it to the men's, and there try on the fit. I suppose his flash suggested whose, or which, opening was to fit. If he cared."

"Don't stop now."

"He made me nervous. Especially since the Mango's finest started clopping in our direction. So I remained a noncommittal audience. As the Mounties came closer, he dropped his shirt and hurried to the toilet, as if to host its door. There the very long mollusk of his tongue, virtually exploring his nostrils, continued to beckon me. I changed my bench as only the cautious, or uppity, would. The horsemen trotted by. The juvie, out of nowhere, reappeared from the opposite direction, stood within two feet of me, and rewound his offer. After all, I hadn't exactly fled, had I?"

"And then?"

"I became indecisive. I glanced beyond him to consider the head. Learning more mores by the minute, I saw another teenager dashing to its door with what I judged a greater emergency than the flasher's: since both the newcomer's hands were in his unzipped fly—what is arguably called a holding action."

"Then?"

"Oh! Thai clinks aren't the Marriott when it comes to accommodations."

"So what finally happened?"

"The showoff must have figured I'd *got* off earlier. Or (to save face) that I was straight. He raced back to the can to administer to the emergency."

"And puppy love triumphed!" I concluded.

"If you like the whole squirm firm. Look around here: you'll spot a manual-labor force, as well as shiftless teens with shanks akimbo—toes tightly curled—or a cleaver beveling their drumsticks."

"Are they all cruising?"

"They're not going over Immanuel Kant's *Critique of Pure Reason*."

"Could some be hustlers?"

"Some. But many do need to hang it out to dry; and will ask for zilch at even a tony hotel—just to submit, as Thais say, to a call of nature."

"Or to practice their English?"

"Their slurping permitting. Well, I am being too clever by half. Lumpini is the town in Nepal where Buddha was born. That statue of Rama VI at the main entrance is considered a deity. People pray on its base. Yet that impressive base nevertheless becomes a stage at dusk: for gold-diggers to strut their stuff."

I said: "O.K.—Chain, his boss, and Randolph Wetzel on Silom Road. What was the aftermath, Cory?" I magnified the sound inside the envelope. But, Jesus! Talk about clumsy! "You're grinning like the dog who leaked a rug," Cory smirked.

"Snaring a fill-in for Chain that night wasn't within reach of the real. So his hairy boss was whistling Dixie: and on indefinite hold. I positioned myself to wait for Randy and Chain to stop into Lome before I left. Then I could *enjoy* their rotten coupling as one does cuts and toothaches. In the flesh they'd bring new pain, as opposed to recycling those Silom moments. We yearn for that diffusion. Or evidence against evidence, we'd only imagined the snag. The dirt didn't come. I ran to Harrie's. Not there! They were gone to lascivious sheets—leaping like satyrs!—and I was obliged to tuk-tuk uptown solo to lick my inoperable waiver on Chain in hideous isolation…or lap at the vodka I stocked, to be precise.

"I hauled my hangover to Rollo Y-z's on Sunday.

"'Devil in the springtime!' Rol began. 'Let us ask where he learned Western conceits like the "devil" and "springtime." His boss and Randy are possibilities. Both belong to a clique of tradesmen, ambassadors-at-large, and informers to the Generals who run this realm.' Y-z went for his pruning shears. 'There is more to Chain than meets the eye, though I agree that with him much meets the eye. The reason you *should* get it so bad doesn't… This news is not welcome—and will become pivotal, if you replace him. Trick Chain into showing his hand. Get him to act like the confidante and right-wing postilion he probably is. Then *he'll* be forced'—here Rol clamped the shears—'to snap Cory Simon out of his life.'

"'Like that?' I wailed.

"'I think not. Don't underestimate him. Come, let's feed this hangover.'

"A decent steamed duck later, I felt more rational, though still a tad hungry. I signaled the waitress, a shy, slender girl who kept her hands calmly clasped. I asked her, '*Mei sapparot*? (Have pineapple?)'

"'*Mei* (Have),' she said.

"I smiled and turned back to Rollo. She remained by the table. I gave Rol the fisheye: 'Why is she standing here? I ordered pineapple for dessert.'

"His response was summary: 'You didn't. You asked her if she has pineapple, and she said she does. You did not say you therefore want some. Thai is literal. *It* has no implications. Your rut does. Wake up!'

"I did wake up. Rol was insisting that I stay with Chain.

"Previous to my collisions with the hegemonic roués raking Chain, he had arranged to fall by at 8:00 p.m that coming Tuesday. I was penning horrific letters to give people my impression of East Asia and address when, to the minute and my disbelief, he tapped softly on my door.

"He wore blue paler than his skin, on his throat a cabalistic amulet with a *yantra* diagram, encased in plastic. Rollo wants me to cultivate him, but he'll want that, I thought. He greeted me in Thai and took his place on the sofa.

"At sea for a sane reaction, I continued to write until I finished the letter. When I closed shop, I flipped my pen into a Toby Jug. Rather than a Toby, it was glazed with a satyr stripping a nymph: thus the image that came to me in Lome. The satyr was lifted in ochre and the nymph in orange and blue. I pushed my bamboo ladder-back away from the desk and urged it around to deal with him.

"Chain had left the sofa with nary a sound and was sitting on his shins under the brace meant for a relic or icon. As directed, I had put Olie's statue up there. Chain was *wai*ing it in humblest obeisance: his hands on top of his head. Then he bent forward, his face a-ground, and flattened his palms on the floor three times. He was shaking, his lips were moving rapidly in silent prayer.

"I spat in the familiar, and with no preface: '*Thoe pen gahlee!* (Thou art a whore!)'

"He stiffened, broke the *wai*, jumped to his feet and rushed at the door, seizing its knob. Once there, uncontested, he reconsidered that reflex and turned toward me, alternating from high dudgeon to intrigue, a shift he over-practiced. Then slowly, his offense began to coalesce: subtly, for his lids widened by the merest fraction, his sinuses clogged, and his nether lip developed signs of pursing, just enough to flash the gleam of his immaculate little teeth.

"He returned to the sofa and, a moment later, offered gently, 'I tell you this.'

"I gasped—with exasperation of course, but the desire to batter him at once took hold, and I had to grab the seat of the ladder-back to stop myself.

"'I think was joke!' I cried.

"'No joke,' he returned, strengthening his tone ever so cautiously.

"'Who believe such talk! A sewer! Every man's sewer! How can this be?!'

"'Must be.'

"'What do you mean *must*? Why are you here? In what do you *lack*? –I think you joking! We say that—it is—just word gay people say!'

"He thought. He looked intimidated, then deprived. It registered in his twitching. He tensed, an apparently genuine, natal want of appropriate response.

"'*Must* be,' he repeated, quite lost. He let his armor go limp.

"I stood up, hunched, and rammed my right into the bamboo seat. It went through with a collective crack, opening my knuckle and wrist in a half-dozen gashes and smearing them with splintered blood. Then, because it was something I wanted to do for weeks, I pulled three left undercuts at the wall on the side of the desk. Its plaster broke into zigzags in a clockwise continuum around my blows; and coming away from the wall, fell out in my face and hair. He witnessed this with a shudder of incredulity and reassembled full alert, rapidly turtling his body inward and appraising mine, so as—assuming a headlong lurch—to tally the frenzy in tandem jabs. His eyes moved quickly along the floor and settled, should it be necessary, on an empty, toppled bottle ready to be enlisted.

"'*How* must—you scum! Itching cunt! You lied!!' I shouted.

"'Not lie,' he rebelled, and pampered a moist mouth with his right backhand, a gesture doing double duty, for it brought it into a defensive position. He'd the discipline to stay with the search in his stare, calculating my bulk in a breakneck throw. I jogged in and revved up for a wild, roundhouse strike—but my fingers were smothered in ooze, and for a critical instant I didn't know why.

"Then he did something unexpected, which was to draw five fast breaths and deeply exhale into a heedful repose that would ventilate his arms for action. His salient aim was to transfer this corporality to me. A minute later he extended both hands: ignoring the splinters sloshing between them when he shut mine together, he cradled that dead clench with warmth. And I let him.

"What did transfer was his burgeoning scorn. That worked a purpose: for after a beat, surmising my adjustment, he dropped my fists, cleaned his with a tissue, sat back, and crossed his legs—the last with the same effect as a pail of cold water, whose dousing was meant to convey his conviction of being quite brainlessly put-upon.

"'*Dek nok!* (Childish outsider!),' he slurred heavily in slang. He waited a while. Then added, 'I think you know. Two times I tell you, so you know.'

"'I not believe!'

"'Have to.'

"'But I not believe you before!'

"'SO: NOW KNOW: –I say, you believe.'

"He paused again for his words' full weight, never letting his umbrage slip from a charged and disapproving study of every inch of me.

"All at once I felt ridiculous. His majestic equanimity was thoroughly faked, for he lived in dimensions we barely acknowledge, where atheistic Theravada, multi-god Hindi, and the multiple systems of multi-god mountain tribes indecisively collide: assimilating him and rendering him indecisive, even about indecisiveness. And here stood I, who couldn't begin to engage all this, guard-up and punching at—what? His philandering? The vigilance of the handlers with whom he'd cast his lot? The infringements I shared with him?

"I'd lost this bout; and aware of that now, was left merely marking time.

"'And so you thought what?' I asked, a tentative peace treaty the meeker.

"'I think you know.'

"'And?'

"'Is O.K.'

"I examined the broken chair. The worst in these clashes is that you didn't measure and can't police your behavior. Claiming to work for his family and a vague Atlas with a retinue of Gypsies was an acronym which, no matter how then expedient, had become a trap for both of us: one for whose suddenly visible magnitude I'd no preparation. My unworldliness, and need, had allowed all his subsequent refinements to glide by undetected. Like his stalling at the zoo, taking forever to dispute that if *I* were opposed to giving him money, he'd keep a date with a sack who wasn't: and adhere to that resolve in future. A major stand, taken right then. I couldn't seize on the dread I inspired, what he was dreaming of or hoped to accomplish, but dropping either him or Rollo was self-destructive given any interpretation. Not, at least, until I was groomed, politically.

"I asked him, 'And Randy?'

"'Know from work. Work in kitchen, *Orien'-tan'*. When I eight, maybe ten. Wash dish. Take order to room. So meet Randy.

"'His friends, too? You meet them?'

"'Some.'

"'You sleep with them?'

"'Some.'

"'All?'

"He laughed. 'How can sleep all? *Some!* This business *me.*'

"Then you become tired, in situations like this: yeah, exhausted. I found the empty bottle near the foot of the sofa and stood it upright on the desk.

"Finally, I said, 'So what we do?'

"'Do nothing.'

"'What you mean?'

"'Not do. Sleep.'

"I went cottonmouthed. 'Take shower,' he added. He intended to, whether I did or no; and otherwise internalizing, he stepped into the bathroom.

"Thais don't indulge a setback: it saps the energy they'll shortly surely need.

"Chain did not speak further that night. When he came out of the shower, he *waied* the icon once more with hands atop his head; then hurried by, shivering in the thermostat's coldest setting, which, against his preference, I insisted on.

"After a futile interval, I switched off the light in the parlor, soaked in the tub, and bandaged my hands. Then I crawled into bed and hugged my half, as close to its edge and far from him as I could: and debated the imperiling, probable roster of his clients. You can sense when a mourner is not sleeping, quiet as he may be. He rested motionless for nearly thirty minutes; then turned softly on his side and, mindful of my dressing, was especially thoughtful in his lovemaking.

"In the dark before dawn he was silent and left with me at 6:00 a.m., since I was due at Mahidol by 7:45. The circles under his eyes were heavy and his face haggard. If his normal twelve retiring hours had struck me as silly before, the reason for it was obvious now. Getting on for a hustler, his time in bed was in direct ratio to how old he'd seem: twenty, to Euros, after his full complement of sleep. That morning, yanked up one-third through his customary marathon, in the wake of a night to disown, he looked his thirty-five years.

"Across the road workers, seeing no humor in it, stood single-file in the parsimonious shade of a telephone pole. I'd be aboard the bus for the usual potholed ride: on its second doorstep. That door never shut for the folk bulging from it, and out the windows: a passenger had to stretch from within and take hold of my collar for the next two hours to make sure I didn't fall off the carrier (falling itself off its wheels) and into the traffic clog. That I was alien to them made no difference in their manhandling of me, a cultural dictate as they saw it.

"'Bus you come,' Chain alerted nodding to his left down

Phayathai. 'I see you tomorrow, eight, nine o'clock.'

"I braved the artery's fender-to-fender; and before infiltrating that curbside dash, reliably breaking from the shade, checked back with my lover on the far walk of the road. His arms at attention, a blur of blue caught in the poisonous fumes, he was keeping a troubled surveillance through still-gummed lids."

The bag that tot had dropped had candy corn kernels. A monitor lizard over four speckled feet long climbed up the bank and shot its tongue at the cellophane. Cory stood, snatched it from the lizard, and made for the edge of the lake. He knelt and held out the offering. The black swan deserted its twin and paddled toward him. Swans are unpredictable. It is geeky to feed them.

He was teasing me with his muscled back. His squatted gluts are so perfect they look computer-generated. I could just about see the beak biting his palm. He bellowed: "Aaaaow!" The bird propelled above the lake and echoed him with a clamor of wings. Cory tumbled. He showed me the wound: a red trough seeping to his right wrist. I ran to him and soaked two paper napkins I had taken in the foodshop, undid my bandanna, and tied them around his hand.

I said, "Should we find an emergency room? Birds can be lethal, skipper!"

"Not yet. Let's see if the bleeding stops. Give it ten minutes. Ferocious beauty, huh? Could have rabies."

"And you'd like to start raving here?"

"Disturb this peaceful setting? Wouldn't dream of it. Nah, I'll cure."

He supported his palm on a mound of dirt. He studied it and the offending beast: it was boiling lather. The swan, not Cory, was astonished: it was sharing the mishap with him. Cory was determined to lie there. So I scooted back to the bench and got the mike.

He followed the swan, and then three drifting rowboats.

"Those gracefully curving rods on temple roofs," he said closing his eyes, "are both the hongsa's neck and the tail of the Naga. Those rods integrate them. The hongsa is a mythical swan:

80

it is Brahma's mount: it connects the oceans with heaven, and guards and directs persons who cross oceans. It is the figure-head and mascot of the royal barge. The Naga is a fanged, seven-headed dragon-snake that protects Buddha. Like the hongsa, which can bite badly, Thais know the Naga has a negative urge as well. Some people say amalgams like this dissolve friction. Yet art is the anfractuous spill of austere friction…

"To those people, these temple rods are shortcuts in consciousness. I keep mine hidden: and gun under the radar. That is why *you* came here. And now that you've secretly recorded my metaphysical ramblings, in addition to openly adding my feck-less face-off with Chain, help me up, huh?"

Chastened, I took hold in his left pit and lifted him to his feet, the first time I had touched him. I was surprised by the width and brick of his underarm.

He said, "I like the effect of your evil bandanna. A rakish knot at the nape. Hair bundling over it in front. I am sorry to swipe your bandanna."

Then Cory abruptly tells me he has a dinner engagement. He will be happy to tape more in his studio after that. I agree. I will check my email.

My hotshot in Oral History is a volunteer general coordina-tor (and gopher) there. He has a major in research skills: e.g., hacking. So William Ned Dilly went apeshit when he saw my message. A real skinny! a blue-uniform! he had clicked. Not dry hits in old rags! What Dilly dug threw off my kilter! His attach-ment, in part, ran a sheet on Cory Simon as long as Simon's (oversized) arm. Whoa! B&Es, drug busts, assault & battery, DWIs, public intoxication—and indecent exposure!

Less of a toughie to factor in is that years ago, Cory had placed well in rodeo competitions: specialized in calf roping. Dill loaded more facts. One was a zinger! Cory suffered a breakdown in his early twenties that lasted fourteen years. Its nature was unclear. Whether he had been institutionalized, and in which institutions and for how long in each, Dill was still investigating.

This dope was too funky. Could it be true? It would mean

that Cory must have met Chain on the heel of his illness. Wrong time!

I was shaky that night: he likes me bushy-tailed (if you will). Imagine, then, my tail*spin* when I found my "evil" bandanna binding more cuts in his palm. He was punishing himself. I kept my yap shut.

OLIVER AUGUSTINE MAKEPEACE LITTLETON tried to get under his skin during the weeks that followed their introduction at the wat. Bopping with that for a while Cory deemed feasible for what he most likely would scrape together.

"I insisted on mid-morning meets with Olie: and that we go to a restaurant then for his secular banquet—before noon. He'd resort to airy abstractions on Mount Meru, central to Buddhist cosmology, with airy gestures that could hardly be holding utensils, making sure he didn't chow down until well past the cutoff point. When I'd frustrate this transparency, he'd flounce into a second eatery at 3:00 p.m., always visible from the street, and, despite *my* abstaining, gorge again. If you ask why the owner served him after noon, I must tell you that sin or no sin, saffron robes or prison stripes, cash is king here. Furthermore, a shop-keep, or waiter, would never dream of taking it upon himself to question the behavior of a monk. There are police for that—if *they* dare.

"We went to wats where whites were domiciled as monks. A handful were serious: most had heroin charges for incentive. Transcendentalism was in fashion. The West never saw Buddhism's rungs as a serf-strategy, abetting the limit on free education, then, to four years. Together, they guaranteed an ongoing cheap labor force to swell the obscene income of a small ruling class.

"Sustained schooling—isn't that requisite to the development of sentiment and sensitivity? Of feeling itself; and of the moral dimension in experience?"

I said, "I don't know. I haven't thought about it. Probably."

"I'd the intuition that Olie only sideswiped reality. Rollo Y-z's 'official' reason for staying in touch with him was that Olie had become his supplier. Rol had a lover, going on a decade, name of Vichai, a field reporter for a Thai newspaper who'd bring him an ounce or two on his weekly or bi-weekly visits. Nine months back, Vichai was assigned to the Red skirmishes in the Golden Triangle. As now, there was also continuous guerrilla warfare with Moslem separatists, *and* Peninsula Reds, all along the elephant's trunk between Phetburi province and Narathiwat. Neither was Vichai a stranger to these. So his show-ups had become infrequent: a weekend in three-four months. This kept the grass widower in a constant state as to Vichai's safety, and in constant contact with Olie. Rol underwrote Olie to bundles-full; Olie's take was his payment for muling; and Y-z recouped his investment-plus by selling to fellow-falang instructors.

"I contributed to the run one day, and Oliver came up with righteous weed. Having no convincing concealing place, I stuck the boo on a shelf under my shirts. Sunday next, I went out to study a building I wanted to write about and, that accomplished, headed home. A quick shower, and my hand fondled the shirts for that sure short trip to a different perspective. It wasn't there—the stash!

"I felt through all the stacked clothing, maybe I'd slipped it into a sock or athletic cup, but, no, it was gone.

"The goodies were gone.

"…The menial had the key to my flat, to dust it every other day—and so did the landlady; but neither would be motivated to search for, care, or even suspect I'd a hoard. The rooms felt polluted. I left and paced the hallway and the garden, trying to retrace my movements during the past few days. I went back in and rang Mr. Y., who advised me to stand outside; he'd be there in a jiff.

"Minutes later, Y-z marched through the compound gate. As he approached me with guarded step, the maid appeared and intercepted him. Rol grilled her; she responded deferentially, and evidently to his qualified satisfaction.

"'The mystery is partly solved!' Rollo shouted, crossing the lawn. 'While you were out a religious paid you a call, and this slavey, with the fawning respect her status owes a monk, admitted him to your quarters with her passkey, there to await you. After a spell, he reemerged: said he had pressing monk-ey business and would call again.'

"'A monk?' I squealed. 'A *white* monk?'

"'Unless you've relations with yellow ones—which, naughty! naughty! Said mole'd devotee grew impatient and stole your stash. Well, what else is a renegade relapse-and-rebound devotee supposed to do?'

"'Wait till I get my foot into that fucker!'

"'But she would not admit the boys.'

"'What boys?'

"'She claims Olie led two dark boys, who were not novices, since they wore no robes, and not Thai. Sound familiar? She made them sit on the stoop. I believe their being black, rather than not Thai, is what decided her.'

"I found Oliver hiding in the attic at Vivian's that evening, cringing on the timberwork like a beaten cur, as if my stick were laced with further burglary from Vivian's medicine cabinet. He yelped: 'Rotted, blasted prat! You with the flick-goofs now? – Marty's losing it, what!'

"'It's the boo, Olie. Go cold turkey.'

"'*You're* cashing him in! Big Marty don't see bloomin' sense!'

"'Olie! Who's Big Marty? Who I think he is?'

"'I'll make it up to you, triple your count the sec I'm flush.'

"That crook flush? I had an iron in the fire besides his penny-ass theft. And I wished he were more coherent. I tried to look less the undercover—or defector—he was seeing. I knelt and took his hand. I smiled, 'Forget Marty. You brought two boys with you. Nine or ten years old?'

"'Uh-huh,' he remembered. 'Figured you'd be daft.'

"'Why? Who are they?'

"'Friends of Rollo's.'

"I said, 'I know that much.' I closed my fingers around his, just this side of crushing them. I breathed: 'Again, who are they?'

"He winced and tried to extricate his hand. 'Runaways.'

"'From Nan?'

"'Not anymore. The Children's Garden.'

84

"'A brothel?'

"'You could say that, yes. Can I have my hand back, please?'

"'Sure,' I told him. 'Forgive my firmness. You can still use your other one to hold the joint.' The reason I'd needlessly hurt him was that I was thinking, 'Must run in the family...' This ventilation isolating Chain, my mind-numbing target, I hadn't the smarts available then to shake Olie—he being so cooperative now—into being cogent about the whole acrostic: my icon, Big Marty, the Gypsies, the 'flick-goofs,' and who or whatever villainy else was sucked in here. Not, I was positive, that he ever was balanced enough to half understand it himself.

"I rose and opened the attic's trapdoor. 'Well, there's much to be said for hill-tribe boys,' I commiserated. 'Perhaps you and Rollo and I will find something appropriate in the near future.'

"He nodded faintly: 'And perhaps you are too good for both of us.'"

Cory stripped off my bandanna. "Speaking of good, it was good of you to lend me this. Want me to put it with my laundry?" He twisted it into a knot.

I said, "Don't bother. I'll rinse it later. So the hairy Eton Atlas got a name."

"Yeah, he got a name," Cory muttered, disgruntled.

"And you leaned on Chain, his star staffer, right after that?"

"With and about what? Chain had a handler in common with Olie, a man named Martin with nipping competitors, over whom he was 'losing it,' and who wished I didn't exist; and preteen relatives that fled a chicken ranch. I lacked a slam dunk. I needed to fight Chain within a formality that would not disappoint—or topple—Rollo. I couldn't locate that arena, given Chain's intractable height—an escalating height: because for the time, Chain, too, was disillusioned with me. I lived with this on the nights he slept at Phayathai.

"That Friday he had an 'engagement' so I took a crack at his after-hours scene in Thaniya Plaza. A wag with pertinent poop might be having *kuaytiaw naam* (veggie soup) there...

"A concession—next to a table that huckstered 'art' photos—was serving the Mutt and Jeff of Patpong: the stand-ups, Philip

Bailey and Soren Cass. Phil Bailey was a retired New Jersey sports-caster. Noticeably tall and bent, his trademarks were an antique fedora raked on his steel-gray hairline and a grimy-white surgical mask. He sometimes went minus the first but never without the surgical mask, which tugged at his long, hooked nose and anchored under his jutting jaw. It was anything but duct tape to him: he was voluble and distinct through its stains. He did have to lower, and then replace it, to slurp. When I asked him about this strong-armed approach to germ warfare, he told me he was considering having his eardrums punctured to lick the city's noise problem.

"Up from trailer-trash, cherubic-faced Soren Cass, a foot shorter and three wider than Philip, was the ex-designer for a millinery shop in Mobile, Alabama. *His* ID was Scarlett O'Hara hats, 'hidin' mah perpetchal bad-hair day,' a new one every sortie. Each, when he swilled, if you moved, would poke you in the eye.

"I'd exchanged notes with this inseparable pair, both in their late been-there-done-that sixties, in various watering holes. That night they were washing down their soup with a bottle of cheap Mekong whiskey. I sauntered up and said, 'You boys killing the taste of the soup or the whiskey?'

"Philip Bailey gagged: 'Cory "the walking wet dream" Simon!' He pushed his ratty fedora back to scratch his very high forehead. 'What are *you* doing *here*?'

"'Well, I… gotta be somewhere,' I cooed.

"'And where better than the foldaway with cock art? –Sure as shit you ain't *chained* down,' Philip Bailey barked. 'Do they have *you* in that collection?'

"I sniffed, 'Not if they're bare-ass. Never pose in my birthday suit.'

"Philip glared. 'Too bad. Randy Wetzel will pay top baht when you do. Says he met you.' I mumbled noncommittally and took the stool next to Philip. 'Know something?' he said, puffing into my face and touching it with his manicured nails, 'if Randy's nostalgic for a beef burger with ketchup and fries, Simon, *your* features are too close to the surface. Don't mean to rile you.'

"I said, 'You don't. Yours, Masked Man, protrude enough for both of us.'

"Soren lisped, 'That is why Phil's the *Lone* Ranger!' Sensing a squall on the horizon, Soren Cass blew at the (pigeon) feathers brimming over his straw hat and screeched into a southernbelle detour: 'Ladies, Ah am keepin' a *ephebe*—keepin' him from his wicked trade! Or mah bank account is, Ah swear. Once y'all cracks the ol' pocketbook, it ha-as no linin'! His kin suffah from a congenital need for houses—in hay-af the counties of Sigh-am. So Ah aim to cut it off!'

"'That's drastic,' Philip Bailey pathetically punned.

"I sentimentalized: 'Find a how-to that won't hurt him, then.'

"Philip snarled, '*None* will! They don't hurt the way we do!'

"'Really? What is *your* sob story?' I asked.

"Philip drained his paper cup and refilled it. 'For three years eleven months I live with a waiter: who hurdled my crapper in All Loads Lead to Lome. I remove him from that iniquity. I relieve him of the bun-pinchers there. Lechers pinch his heinie or not, a waiter drops drinks, he pays for them. I send him to typing school so his heinie can heal. I fly him to my manse in Hoboken; I tour Europe with him; I buy him heaps and wedding bands. But he misses a black and blue behind. It's *less boring* than Hoboken, Prague, autos, school, or me. He *longs* for Rome's fake ollas and plaster torsos. You can take your harlot out of Rome, but you can't etcetera. We have a heart-to-heart. Tears fall like seed in a circle jerk—and I let him go. What was I supposed to do, put cuffs on him? He'd develop anorexia, slip them, and pawn them. Well, the second the fat lady sings, I taxi to Rome: to cry in a wine cooler I learned to stomach tippling with him. I crumble through its colonnades, what do I see at the roselit bar? My own cherished boy! Hitting on a granny is ninety-eight if he's a day. The foolproof hit: one decker stopping Methuselah from caving in, the other picking a pickle, and his tongue lapping the loser's ear like its wax is strap-crud! This! ten minutes after we bawl our lungs out—this! after three years and eleven months. It took me that-and-some before I could see another tramp: it took him diddly to powder his nose and peddle his vault—a vault, to expand, cavernous as the Vatican Dome.'

"Soren hiccupped, 'Girl, that *is* expansive of him.'

"'Why must you always explain?' Philip hollered, ballooning his mask. 'I give granny my road map—to scrounge for traction in that Jersey Tunnel! *This* is how I mean they don't hurt the way we do.'

"'A dated, sweeping generality,' I balked, 'from a bit of a used-car salesman. What did you expect of the type who waits in Rome?'

"'Do tell! So what is your type? –As if I don't know, Cory!'

"'Has to be wearing pants and still breathing,' I quipped.

"'Oh, yeah?' Philip shot back. 'I got some friends ain't so particular.'

"Soren guffawed on a swallow of Mekong, hosing it clear across the Plaza, and fell victim to maniacal shrieks. Spinning on my stool, I swore they outdid normal expat brain decay: I'd met fundies and Republican housewives more liberal. And, my spin confronting me now with the porno table, saw a tall, Isaan Thai gingerly flipping through its Western inventory. He was nicely proportioned, with shoulders returning in a 45-degree angle to his long arms and unbelievably narrow hips. He had bright eyes, light skin, and small hands. His brows were very thick and his hair was kinked, as it is with a scattered number of Thais, and cut close at the sides to form a kind of cylinder rising an inch above his head, there encouraged to curl over a modest thinning area. He had a gentleness in his movements: and a mere glance my way sufficed to show he was aware that the inventory I was taking was of him. I said, 'See anything you like?'

"'Four pictures,' he responded in careful English. 'But they are too dear. I earn 3,600 baht a month. However, my rent is free.'

"'Doing what?'

"'Can't you tell?' he asked, obviously thrown. He straightened up, arched his back, and squared his shoulders.

"'No, sir. How would I?'

"He seemed puzzled. Then considered this, and, somewhat

reluctantly, made an adjustment. He said, 'I am a soldier. An army officer.'

"'Oh.' After a pause, nonplussed since he wasn't in uniform, I corrected myself, I hoped properly. 'Forgive me, I should have known that.'

"'Yes. It is my profession.' He lifted his chin with charming aloofness. He'd assumed I could read his body language: no doubt particular to the forces running the country. He would also reason I'd know his status and rank by the English he used, that it somehow shared the career and class distinctions of Thai.

"'Your name?' I ventured.

"'Jahd. I am twenty-nine.'

"'Cory. I am American.'

"'Yes. I know. Americans have beards.'

"'Jahd, would you like to come to my apartment?'

"'I am afraid,' he answered immediately in an oddly hangdog tone. 'I believe too big for me.' He was looking then at the snap of a nude blond that quite wide venue might give wide berth.

"I challenged him: 'You are army. You mustn't be afraid.'

"'But...'

"'It *won't* be too big.'

"Philip, eavesdropping, poked at my inner elbow and drooled, 'Think what you're doing, Centerfold. Suck any more yellow dick and you'll jaundice.'

"Jahd waited for him to turn his moist mask back to Soren. He shifted his weight with hesitation—and, altogether unself-consciously, his eyes, from the photo to my basket: modified that night by a polystyrene jock cup. 'Still,' he protested, 'I am required to return to the base now. I work in Recruitment tomorrow. But you will not work tomorrow, isn't that so? So you should come with me. I shall wake you up for lunch.'

"'To... Jahd? The army base?'

"'You are *American*. You mustn't be afraid.'

"A sentry with naked bayonet saluted Jahd but stared blind through me. The base was off Phahol'yothin Road, midway between my apartment and the airport. Jahd unlocked a bicycle inside the gate and asked me to saddle its rear rack and hold his narrow hips. Then he pedaled, pretending effortlessly, along a sprawling tree-lined drive and far into the static compound. We skirted a quadrangle of low official buildings and a parked van, through whose open side curtain I glimpsed a skin flick on a small TV. A soldier in fatigues glimpsed us, rolled over, and drew the curtain. We reached the huge housing stations. At that hour there were few lights on: these eerily quiet barracks quickly summoned the appearance of the Dvaravati Foundation at night.

"We rode an elevator to the sixth floor in one of the barracks, then walked a lengthy gallery to the last unit. I removed my shoes and without a sound followed him through an almost empty kitchen and communal area into a spartan bedroom at the back. Calculating that trip as sufficient respectful delay, I shook off my trousers and shorts, then thought to reserve my jock till later: for modesty and his excitement. Yet the hard cup in its pouch would hinder both of us and feel like What-in-hell? if you weren't expecting it. So I dropped my strap to mid-thigh; and, in my haste to extract the imbedded cup, caught my foreskin between its border Styrofoam and solid plastic. 'Ouch!' I shouted. Modest himself, Jahd was undressing with his butt to me: he turned so fast on my cry that I hadn't the time to face away and deal with the disaster under the covers. He looked at my raw, wedged, and fully stretched fold. Raising a brow, he rubbed in, 'Ooh—ugly! Do you want a sterile strip for that?'

"'Sterile? Bite your tongue! How about we pry it loose first?'

"He inched the apparatus apart with a thumb and index and tweezed out my prepuce. He held the consequently sorry-looking member in his palm. 'Now,' he affirmed with annoying relief, 'I shall not have to be afraid.'

"'No, you shall not. I shall.' Lying right-angle to his pelvis, I saved my painful boner from ever brushing against him. So I *couldn't* be too big…

"Jahd's abdomen was surprisingly hirsute: an Occidental bonus. I failed to get lost in that shrubbery, though, for still hearing, and reliving, Philip Bailey's caustic jibes. The officer came into a cloth, then offered it to me and fell asleep.

"I lay awake fixed on his ceiling scattered with little paper stars that held an iridescence they'd borrowed from the bedside lamp when it was briefly lit: instead of creating a magical sky indoors, they encored my sense of being trapped between blankets in the rank chaos of a wet field.

"After an hour or so, the stars began to fade and one by one went out, and I slipped into a troubled sleep. Jahd had informed me that his home province was Ubon Ratchathani, a major site in the Dvaravati era; Philip's hostile comments pulleyed that information down with them, particularly his claim to having friends indifferent as to whether or not their partners were alive. All at once Jahd was deadweight on top of me so that I could hardly breathe, and with sinister strength pinned my arms to the ground while his thighs wedged under mine in an effort to get them to rise. I could feel the dropsical tip of his stiff punching my rump, then boring into its breach and spinning through the helix of a soft faucet. I yanked my hands free, inserted them across his chest, and, to inhale finally, pushed him up into a spread-legged squat. I saw, with sudden horror, his chest-mail of chains (that pun, again) and a spike-studded leather collar with which he'd been trying to slash my face. Then the entire circle of spikes was consecutively blasted by bullets and pieces of his larynx exploded from their holes, returning its light to the corona of stars on the turret of his hair. He was dead, but the bayonet that had emerged from his fold stabbed repeatedly into my intestine, while his fists, now clamped on my shoulders, kept trawling me in to maintain his leverage—though I frantically kicked at his knees, hoping to force-ebb the surge of his pounding seat. He howled with rage, 'Sit up! Quickly, sit up!'

"'What is it?' I gasped, terrified.

"He said, in an undertone, 'You dream bad dream. And you very much perspire. I shall wash your body.'

"He reawakened me for lunch, as he'd programmed. Another career officer, who slept in the unit's second bedroom, joined us. And then three more young men, evidently, and perhaps unlawfully, shacking up there. Each had a hundred questions. Proudly, Jahd maintained: 'We are permitted to register for whatever university courses we wish, without tuition. I selected the English Language, and my grades are the highest at my level. I shall translate for my roommates. Please answer the questions of these Thai people.'

"At dinnertime, yet more personnel, their friends, and enlistees piled in, every one of them gay, all from that landing, the one above, or the barracks in back of and adjacent to Jahd's: forming, I gathered, a lively and substantial community. However, given the battle I'd fought with the cup safekeeping my jewels, I requested Leave: a letdown to those vociferous soldiers. Each fussed over me. So I promised to return the next day. Jahd, enjoying no small amount of reflected glory, accompanied me to the gate, where the sentry again promptly saluted him and then averted his eyes. Riding home, I felt I was still dreaming.

"I got back to the base at Sunday noon, my dickie healed or it had better be. When I stepped into Jahd's quarters, it was crowded with flushed and eager men trying on dresses—for a drag contest to be held in a town east of Bangkok. Some asked, while applying makeup, which wig or gown I thought most glamorous. Still dreaming. Jahd rescued me from the gaggle and took me on a tour of the quad: the ball courts, swimming pool, workout yards, shooting ranges, meeting halls, and offices. He smiled as we approached a drill, its teenage recruits overly bass and baritone in response to the training sergeant. He explained, 'New boys. Every time excited. They bellow.'

"I asked, slowly, 'If the army stages a coup, will you have to fight?'

"He untied and retied his bootlaces, watching the cadets slack to at-ease; and then break into a run. He did not answer, which meant my question had been inappropriate. He said, 'I want you to come and live here with me.'

"Now I stared at the runners. 'Jahd, this is very far from where I teach—'

"'It is equidistant from your present lodgings. If you leave early, the buses going to *Phla Lam Hok* will move fast: faster than the ones starting at Yommarat.'

"'Jahd,' I objected, 'I have too many possessions to fit into your room. And I am used to living alone. My entire life.'

"He looked at me intently. He tightened his belt. 'Then I will stay with you on some days. And some days you shall stay with me.'

"The first night he spent at my flat, Jahd was curious about everything in it. He was more or less comfortable, or went through the motions of appearing so. At sunup, we went to a neighborhood foodshop: there he changed. He was put out the moment the spiffy northwest waiter took the order. His breath caught and he frowned. 'Our waiter speaks improperly. Sit here, and I will fix this.'

"He walked into the kitchen and was gone for three minutes. Then he returned to announce calmly: 'It shall be all right now.'

"But when we strolled the sois off Phayathai—he, of course, was not in uniform—even I noticed that people threw critical looks his way. He lost patience.

"'Everyone we pass believes I am for hire.'

"'Why would they believe that?'

"'Because I am with you. You must *try* to reside on the military grounds.'

"So I tried: and staunchly restrained the following week-ten days, grew less noteworthy than the continuous callers. Jahd and his subsidiaries, taken with some chore, malfeasance, or rousting, tended to ignore me: leave me to the texts I'd bring or his TV's poor reception, all its programs naturally in Thai. I *did* appreciate the invariably stunning bodyguards you see surrounding government officials. Diametric in deportment to zookeepers—in sharp designer suits, alert to minutiae, their heads ever rotating—they are just as arousing. When I thought of zookeepers, I thought of Chain. –Chain and Rollo. Rollo, Olie, and Chain...

"I found a booking agency near the quad and asked about overseas flights. The fares were highway robbery. I said, 'I'm only checking.'

"Jahd cooked with tap water: and the john's compulsory

solitude augmented the not (I thought) that compulsory in his room. He insisted I meet his grandma, with whom he consulted on all priorities, to get her approval of me. Yet I shared few waking hours with Jahd. When not voluntarily ironing uniforms or attending to loan requests, internecine thefts, or the whole company's gripes, his evenings were monopolized by conciliating those disputes for which servicemen everywhere have a peter-measuring penchant. This regimen, his behavior made clear, was expected routine. Several soldiers solicited me for language lessons ('in American'). When I related to Jahd that I'd in no wise moonlight, he, without flinching, and as if translating, told them, 'Mr. Cory will be pleased to teach you American.' And to me in his muffled undertone, 'You must *say* you shall.' So in the end, I read as many of the city-planning files as I could borrow from the municipal libraries (for an article on row houses nagging me); and waited for him, through countless hours, to come to bed.

"He allowed me to enter him infrequently, but his sperm was sweet.

"One night nearly two months later, Jahd was particularly quiet. After I awoke in the dark to beat the predawn rush, and had halfheartedly showered by pouring icy water on myself from a barrel in the bathing closet, he got out of bed and stopped me by the door. 'Listen,' he said in a whisper, 'they are going to transfer me to an encampment in Ubon, next week. I shall earn more money. I shall be close to my family. My parents need me to help with the seeding and harvesting of the rice. I want you to come and live there with me.'

"I shivered; and became damp, feeling as if I were not yet toweled. I placed my fingers on the back of his hand, barring the door, and thought and rethought my now double-laxity for several minutes. It was difficult to see his expression. Finally I responded, 'Jahd, my job is in Bangkok. Are you being reassigned to a war zone? The Khmer Rouge is active again, isn't it?'

"He bided his time.; then, as was his habit, bit his lip, drawing it deeply into his mouth. At length, he reprimanded: 'You will find teaching work in Ubon.'

"'I would be too lonely there. Jahd, I *am* sorry.'

"His great serenity broken, he said with a touch of steel, 'I do not know if you are sorry. What you are is American. That is more important to you than me.'

"'I cannot change what I am. I never asked you to change what you are.'

"'What I am is your lover. Love can have injury. It makes men afraid.'

"He removed my hand from the back of his and stood off, walking into the shadows to hide his face. 'And *I* have accepted that, Cory.'

"He remained silent for a while before squatting uneasily on his ankles and crossing his arms over his knees. He lowered his head.

"'I shall always hate this day for the rest of my life.'"

Cory stops talking here. Both of us stared at his bandages. I lit a cig and said, "You're thinking that Thais—all along—have 'shamed the Greeks'?"

"No," he answered, "I'm thinking that Jahd was my sole alternative to Chain. I'd discover no other in Thailand. I was very, very fond of him."

I objected: "Lovers waste time second-guessing stillborn affairs."

"Spare me the fortune cookie."

"Look, it didn't materialize. You did *not* move to Ubon. Living, openly gay, with their military is fascinating! Except for ancient Athens, I can't imagine this anywhere else. –The *army* kept you with him. You're not being realistic, Cory."

"I'm so glad you know so much about me."

"O.K., I don't. –Please—enlighten me further."

"When I get home that afternoon, depleted, divided, and demoralized, I find a note taped over my lock. It's the reply from an editor at the *Bangkok Post*: for a piece on restoring a district adjacent to Ko Ratanakosin. The editor had reached my landlady and asked her to ask me to come to his suite at the Oriental at 5:00 p.m. I show precisely; he's fairly affable and duly impressed with my résumé; he gives me a deadline, and I'm downstairs by 5:30. Long as I'm there, I decide to examine the original structure. The postwar tower annex that included the editor's kraal was pleasant enough, but the usual.

"Inside the lobby/dining area of the original two-level building, high tea is under way. Immediate I pass the winsome doorman in traditional costume (swept turban, Nehru jacket, tail-tucked pantaloons), I see Chain, in a subdued guayabera, having Cameronian Tea and scones with the stiffly attired Randolph Wetzel. I'd had him spottily after our 'truce': and crassly abstained when Jahd took hold. Chain's back was to me, yet he turned at once, not a whit less stabbing than if I'd tweaked his ear. Nothing for it, then: I'd dig in.

"'Man of the hour!' Randolph shouted. 'Take a load off, will you?'

"Inconsequential chatter ensued to cover this travesty, for Chain and myself, and myself and my new admirer, Randolph Wetzel. To defuse it, I asked Randy if he wouldn't treat me to a look-see of especially the Author's Wing. This request wasn't arbitrary. I hoped that Chain's treading familiar tracks, in my *and* Randy's company, would jar his memories—and, cherry on the pie, their articulation.

"The wing has been renovated a number of times, so it hasn't a nineteenth-century or even pre-'50s patina; but the slender louvers, winding staircase, and fluid inner court, all in wan topaz and awake white, do conjure the extraordinary. We looked at photos of Graham Greene and Alfred Hitchcock and passed suites bearing the nameplates of James Michener, Alec Waugh, and John le Carré. Also silent film star Douglas Fairbanks: a guest with unique promotional value. In one room Somerset Maugham had nearly died of malaria. 'Too bad he didn't,' Wetzel griped.

"In the garden, a caged hill myna, cawing hello in English and Thai, mewled a bottom-note phrase in Thai that repelled Chain: a bonus. His longtime sugar daddy announced his need to visit a 'real' tearoom ('Every fifteen minutes for five- and fifty-five-year-olds, you know'); and soon as Randolph headed for the men's, I sprang on Chain: 'Interesting that you like Cameron Highlands tea (the area from which Thompson had disappeared). Remember before? When you here with Randy—and his friend, Jim Thompson?' His neck muscles tightened.

"'This best tea!' he snit. 'And not like talk about before!'

"'Or Jim Thompson?'

"'For what talk about him?'

"'Then, how about three months ago?'

"'What?' he clicked. The myna cranked up its squawk. Chain trembled.

"'Why your cousins angry?'

"'Cousins?'

"'Hill-tribe boys—at Dusit Zoo.'

"'Because, business same me.'

"'How Rollo know them?'

"'I say, business same me.'

"'Mean what?' I persisted.

"'I say you: young, but business same me.'

"'He go there? Rollo? House they keep boys?'

"'Before, a lot. Now, no. Boy run away.'

"'They throw rock at you—why, Chain?'

"'*I* put boy in house.'

"The myna tinkled the low phrase again. Chain jumped, his eyes fueled: and slipped from direct to outright sassy, his hands on his hips. 'What you think, can have other work, same you? Can do what want?'

"I felt the urgency to force more and different headway under the pressure of Wetzel's imminent return—but was utterly skunked by his loveliness; and a consequent loss of invention. Attendants, plainly disturbed, were watching us. I retreated: 'I not say boys can have other work. I not accuse. I not blame.'

"'*Dee!* (Good!),' he responded to that. 'Maybe blame for no money. I need pay *gahlee* boss, today. For boys! Because run away. –*Me!*'

"Sugar Daddy stumbled along the elegant apses, the grunt still adjusting his fly. He shook, 'Hey, swells, how's about a threesome—'steada cocktails tonight?'

"I said to Chain, 'Tell Randy bye-bye. I want have sec with you.'

"Ample as always, his body was warm, and he was aggressive in reexploring the upper half of mine: weighing it as I sat over him by supporting my elbows on his palms; then taking the measure of my waist in their span. He teased me no end before admitting to my extremity. It was in great shape now.

"I don't recall what we did with the evening, but I roused him at a respectable hour the next morning and, since it was a holiday, claimed I'd like to sightsee. I piloted his drop in diligence to the Jim Thompson House on Klong San Sap: a worn tourist mecca. I've seen the extravagant near-palaces of the parvenu rich in and outside of Chiang Mai, and an education they are, but Thompson's six-building complex is the most *Thai* of Thai homes. Chain's chief interest was a jichimu-wood screen carved with animist insets. These screens stand just within the entry of temples to block Opponents of the Path. Unsheltered in the air, and taunting *me*, was the upright Dvaravati Buddha, a life-size seventh-century limestone: headless, handless, and toeless, the most valuable piece on the site. All the indoor statues have deeply canted orbs, suggesting a Chinese origin, and smiles so circumflex they toy with reviling us, the less enlightened. Chain lingered at them. When he stopped to scrutinize the third or fourth statue, I took his absorption to put to his back: 'What that myna bird say in language Thai?'

"This plunged him into a distinct private quarrel. 'Expression Thai… Cannot tell for English. Umm… French, O.K.? –Mean, like, in language French…' He twisted about, his lips a dagger, and the foot between us pure ice: 'Like, "*Tous beaux:—tous nouveaux.*"'

"When we left, and started into the alley connecting the House with Rama I, we saw, at a distance, four feral men fussing over a stolen supermarket trolley, its contents presumably their entire effects. Three were loading and reloading the groaning carrier; the last peeled down the alley to our approach. He was wearing a tattered violet T, torn boxer undershorts, and a checkered kerchief drawn bandit-style across his face. He held a bo branch and a splint of some sort in his left hand. Striking in height, he was yoke-broad in the shoulders and exceptionally sinewy rather than thin. As we neared him, I'd the cordoned-off sense we were entering an aura, and the alley and its over-sky were falling away. His hair was knotted in thick dread-curls, haphazardly spoking from his scalp and winding in clusters at his throat. What I gleaned of his brow, arms, and bare feet was black, or so black from tar and caked filth as to glow and reflect our subordinate images. And there were those eyes—huge, round, and elegiac, lit in their unforgettable Sherwood-blue. The three of us, this tenacious figure, Chain, and I, were alone in the world. Chain was transfixed; he blocked me from budging; and the man gracefully trespassed into our comfort zone, shuttling his study from Chain to me. He gently touched Chain's fingers and, after, those of mine closest to Chain. Once again, his rasp of recognition. Then, with his narrow, oily frame addressing myself, he pressed a button on his grooved splint, triggering a six-inch blade: and began to whittle the bo branch. He shaped no point to its hacked end; he simply shaved its length with transparent scrapings.

"Chain was a pried-open tomb during all of this: beyond doubt certain we stood in a circle of the palpable spirits he continually saw. I paid him no mind until he pulled at my sleeve. The sanction, or moot, evidently delivered, it was time to go. Chain almost ran to the road with my sleeve in his grip.

"He was groggy when we got there, his red-rimmed lids cradling the bilge forced up by his mix of emotion and flight. He cried—rejectingly—'Street people!'

"'He is not that,' I stamped. 'You *know* him: and he is not street people!'

"For the remainder of the day, Chain was shut; and caught in a quag of suspicion. The man Jim Thompson was the last subject he would entertain. When he fell asleep with his arm fiercely locking my neck that night, I went through the possible constituents of his acquaintance with Thompson; and the general embarrassment this person may, or must, represent for Thais.

I carefully dislodged Chain's hold and got up to urinate. The toilet was a step away, but I chose to use the chamber pot beside the bed. Jim Thompson was a foreigner who had salvaged a distinctly Thai folk art. He was called the Silk Monarch. He had been a world-class textile designer, ingenious colorist, and indefatigable promoter. A super-successful *foreign* businessman. *The* American businessman: without whom, possibly, no one today would recognize, or care about, Thai silk. A Yank who modeled the most perfect and traditional Thai house in the 1950s, when they were considered hopeless curiosities; and a rescuer and collector of Thai art at a time when few natives appeared to have an interest in it. Far more nationals, then, than Chain would find dealing with him acutely uncomfortable… I mulled over the accusation in his French adage—that he was a transitory novelty to me—and how eccentric it was that someone with so pidgin an English should know even one sophisticated French saying. A similarly puzzling phrase he'd spoken floated by that Rollo said was top-dog influenced: but which, it now occurred to me, is a direct translation from the (slowly returning) French. A Pre-Raphaelite genre: *Le diable du printemps.* Why this conspectus on Rollo's part? And why, still dwelling on him, does Rollo deny knowing Chain's cousins; or, for that matter, Chain himself before? Then I realized I was standing buck-naked in the dark with both arms embracing a warm metal chamber pot. I took it to the john.

"I was up ahead of him and wrote a note telling him to wait until I returned. I thought, just beneath it, to rewrite that in French. There is a shop in the Art Nouveau plaza at the edge of the Indian, Pahurat district that sells firearms. I'd seen knives displayed in its windows. I went through dozens of these to find a switchblade that resembled the one the wanderer had. The handle of the weapon I finally selected was carved with Lue-tribe cabala; its button was ivory, the razor a perfect looking glass. It sank neatly into the upper right pocket of my cargo pants. I'd have to wear cargoes, not Levi's.

"When I reached my apartment, Chain was awake, and I believe had already also ventured forth with intent. Because after a quick *Sawat-dee' cap*, he offered those plane tickets to the Ta-rutao archipelago that I told you about in our first interview: the trip in which he not so much initiated as incorporated me into a smattering of his enterprises out-of-town. When I got back from that excursion, every patch of skin I'd exposed peeled off; and I found that I was beginning to drift into a moral crisis of the kind I hadn't experienced since turning twenty.

"I tried to stay on track, to control this rapidly departing, daily sense of self. The best I could think of was to ask Chain to revisit the zoo. He was well onto me there: and sniggered mockingly. Still, in spotting that zookeeper again, and taking him apart—an ursine Uncas, as it were—I did get things right for once. Drafting the Thai economy of consolidation—that man's potentially harmful *and* proper appeal—I'd get pieces of the jig-saw to fall in place.

"I addressed Chain: 'I'd like you to take me to your house.' This raised an eyebrow. I added, 'How long now, you and me? I must face the music.'

"'Face the music?' he repeated.

"'When a fellow dates steady for a certain period, it is cus-tomary to meet his prospective in-laws. Never a breeze, but customary.' These words were purposely too complex for him. I wanted him to deal with his own ideas.

"He puckered his mouth. His eyes rose to an area directly over mine and remained fixed and inexplicit: so as not to design approval or distress. He said, 'Sunday have Sweeping Evil Spirits Out of House day. Good day for you come.'

"I arrived before the other guests in order to give his wom-en the opportunity to adjust to me. I'd be the first Westerner to cross that threshold; he would identify me as a person for whom he worked. Chain had to have some explanation for how he spent his nights and earned his money, let alone the endless calls from parties talking in alien tongue, so he told his folks he 'work for falang.' As the only man in a tribal household, he wasn't closely questioned.

"I'll draw the drape. Come to the casements and look at his

street, lamp-lit. When I got down there, Chain, now Somboon, was in fine fettle, busy in that two-by-four trawk, or sub-soi, you can see from here, stir-frying the more difficult delicacies in the pyramid of food to be served. At the hot, gigantic wok, he wore tight cut-offs and a loose singlet. He joked freely with me. I'd made the decision to join his family, and he was at peace with that. Later, tasting the dishes he cooked, I conceded that Somboon—other than making dubious contacts—had not squandered his youth at the Oriental: he was a chef.

"The first guests pulled up in a '47 Buick and parked across from Chain's trawk, right beside the Hotel Swan. At least I think it was Buick's '47, the most imposing of lowbrow car-models, its high front fenders swooping in a dramatic giraffe-neck decline to kiss the rear ones. The heap had incongruous, too large and showy whitewalls, those starboard jacked over the curb. The three middle-aged Thais who emerged were, to my amazement, evidently impersonating Warner Brothers' cardinal, and iconic, racketeers. Their ringleader, with smug, slick brio and gold molars, his hair slashed center and combed to climb to his temples, recalled the debonair cunning of George Raft. His first gesture was to prink himself, flicking the lint off his padded shoulders, slate blue shirt-jacket slit in rear, matching, cuffed, slate blue trousers, and two-toned spats. The second to jaunt from the auto was clearly fond of James Cagney. He crunched his knuckles, gritted his teeth, and alternated an intense look with an impish grin—meant to simulate suppressing simmering rage. He was Cagney down to his rouged lips, circumflex mustache, eyelash shadow, and well-spaced hairs lined-in to appear to grow in a net above both lids and join his bush brows. The third was a composite of the goons (or if a particular one, I couldn't single out which) that we count on seeing in any movie mob. Monstrous and mechanical, he had a mug that kills unprepared parakeets, marched rather than hoofing it like the other two, and kept a hand breasted to warn he was packing. I glimpsed his holster. Cagney and the Goon, in deference to Raft, used the same tailor and shoe store.

"The trio tripped up to Chain and did not return the *wai* he snapped on his head. After a cursory blink at me, Raft slipped Chain what was obviously a yellow check, folded twice. He sampled what Chain was preparing. Cagney frisked me. Intent on performing even to the use of Warner's English dialogue, he poked Chain, and toothed, 'Who's the commando?'

"Miffed at the insubordination, Raft growled, 'Pipe down!' At that, the Goon, initially oblivious to me, came to alert, swallowed me whole, and gripped his heat. Then the three intruded into the common room on the ground floor.

"Chain's near and distant relatives were few and blessedly less cinematic. His oldest sister, now unmarried, functioned as matriarch. Sister-Number-Two was there, and the aunt with the small daughter. Following the dozen unrelated guests, a school of monks arrived, bearing new brooms and circular bamboo fans. When they lifted them to their faces, the fans symbolized anonymity: and humility. They used the brooms to sweep away the phantoms who'd recently killed Chain's mother with cancer. Raft seized those moments to cough lightly to catch my attention (I was kneeling and praying on Chain's far side) and, soon as he did, pinched hard at Chain's hip. Chain did not react. Then, smacking his lips, Raft forced his polished nails under Chain's cut-offs. Cagney was crumbled over. Defying Thai behavior, he was openly sobbing: in tribute to his idol's most startling display, in the office of a penitentiary warden. The Goon flopped and spraddled, also in defiance of ritual positions. Prompted by Raft, he readjusted to sit ogre-like, rocking on his spats. These, then, were the 'flick-goofs,' about whom Olie had hallucinated; because of whom Martin, 'one of the biggest operators in Thailand,' was 'losing it.' He was certainly losing it if he still entertained notions of exclusivity where Chain was concerned.

"Despite their scene-stealing, the thugs were the elephants in the room: during the candle-and-incense lighting, chanting, and banqueting, no one other than myself dared look at them. *They* virtually photographed me. When I was a kid everyone and his uncle imitated these tough stars: Edward G. Robinson could be added to them. This was those mobsters' pleasure. Only the heedless would trivialize it. When I'd first seen that Buick, I'd dropped my switchblade outside.

"George Raft paid the coven, and the coven and the three hoods left. The grim Goon was chauffeur, and the second they were seated in the heap drove it backwards at a roar out to New Road, the whitewalls in a mean tornado of dust. Don't ask me why: somehow I knew that my dictated switchblade was destined for those whitewalls.

"When the celebrants had gone to well-wishers elsewhere, Somboon led me upstairs to centralize me in his 'private' world: merely a mat in this sleeping space. There, on its edge, was the telephone. –For his panting clients to drool into: from local or oversea receivers: the foretaste of their assignations! Sitting on that mat with him, desperate for anything but, I listened to them. Their drivel bounded about the room and tubed through the cables plugged to my chest.

"Their storm became a Pandemonium in my heart.

"'You see number-one monk?'

"'What?'

"'He do praying, also chanting, head monk?'

"Somboon was referring to an elderly, seemingly strong, well-preserved man. 'Yes. What about him?'

"'He same monk masturbate penis me when I a boy.'

"The polyglot of voices stopped. Somboon moved closer to me. He scoured my face as vain, or ageing, courtesans do a gray glass. He yanked the check from his cut-offs, unfolded it, and handed it over. It was Rollo's monthly salary check, endorsed by Y. and, I presumed, one of the Buick gang. 'A lot men like new boy. Boy nobody touch before. So must have young: for (be) sure. Rollo same this. Randy same, sometime.' He paused. 'This what you want know, yes?'

"I nodded.

"'Before, year before, Randy go Nan with me, for give money to family me in Nan. See young cousin(s) in Nan. Tell me take cousin to Bangkok: for have sec. Then Randy give green jewel box. Very old—box you find…in water in Tarutao. But Randy make drunk and tell Rollo. So Rollo come *baan gahlee* before Randy and do sec first. Randy give money and old-boat box, but

Rollo open cousin first. Both cousin.' He waited again. 'This what you want know?'

"I looked away. 'Yes.'

"'Now, you happy?'

"'I suppose,' I managed feebly. Then: 'No. No, I am not happy.'

"'So for this, before I not tell you.'

"We fought empty air for upwards of an hour. When he heard his sisters climbing the stairs, Chain took me to the trawk's gate. To my inquiry about the under-their-movie-roles-real career criminals, I received the expected two-word answer: 'I employee' …And sexual appetites appeaser. I stared at the squat and wretched Swan Hotel. I had my own deficiencies, accursed urges, and incurable inflexibility. Yet there was no way, now, I would jettison a chance to undo this whole cast's ghoulish antics a-dance in the pit of the soi.

"I muttered, 'And "street people"—the black man?'

"'Hunt,' he said."

"I asked, 'Hunt *you*?'

"I could feel his breath on my arm. 'Yeh. Hunt me, too.'

CORY SIMON WALKED to his curio cabinet, standing right of the casements. He glanced at its contents, and at the mike. Dupes of black-and-gold lacquer art and a mammoth rainbow nautilus he rescued from a beach were framing him. There I saw something he was just then especially projecting: his face itself is representative—a sort of venial scurrility that amounts to an obligation.

Twenty minutes passed. He had all his days about him. When he lit a cig, I thought he would return to the sofa. Instead he used an ashtray on the cabinet. He finished the cig, quickly lit up another, and said:

"There followed a period of madness. Its components were repetitive—called 'compulsive'—thinking, and three distinct obsessions. This climate was the first obsession. I felt like a furnace at full blast, fungously moist all day, and was preoccupied with that. The weather engulfed my brain; invaded the vessels of my body; and defeating attempts to ignore it, produced fantasies of living on Baffin Island, or in Antarctica. I did not feel cold, or even cool, for the next seven years. The second was with food. I avoided dinner as a matter of course. Then I began to cut back my intake at breakfast and lunch. I developed a concern with low-grade, denatured rice and wouldn't eat it. The third obsession was rivalry: keeping a sexual draw. Whenever I detected that Chain had scored, I went sleepless until I had too. But *my* pickup was to wear no price tag. So I set myself a handicap to equal Chain's, whose customers had to come across."

This irritated me. I said, "That never seemed ill-advised to you?"

"Just how well-advised do you behave when you are in love?"

"Forget it. What was the repetitive thinking about? It's what happened with Philip Bailey's bitch, no? 'Compulsive thinking.' Is that a psychiatric term?"

Cory winced. –Ned Dilly, right on! "Yeah. It is. It's rewording the same negative comment someone made, or sequence of comments, hour after hour. Often you respond to them audibly. On truly creative days, you have three or four solid line-ups, numbering perhaps a dozen sentences individually, and you belabor these multiple times but not necessarily in the same order."

"How much time would be devoted to this… wonderful activity?"

"Every spare minute, when I wasn't teaching, reading, or talking. So I cherished falang; and weighed Soren's flit to pool our rents and get a six-room house. Soren Cass was into dragging violent hustlers home and then refusing to pay them: hoping they'd beat him with the straps he provided and carry off everything not nailed down. I figured on heavy bolts for my own doors. When I informed Chain of my plan, he, conversant with Soren's need, said—nonnegotiably—that if I went ahead on this, he'd never visit. I dropped my plea.

"My opportunities to enjoy foreigners, except for Rollo Y-z, were few. To cover their expenses on low hourlies, most expatriates work a long week, and their leisure time by far is spent chasing tail. Chasing tail, male or female, after all, is why they relocate in Thailand. They may find me a surprise as a conversationalist, but our repartees or tête-à-têtes are mere precatting aperitifs."

Cory's new listeners must think he is reciting or quoting from some hidden paper, in original exchanges where he simply cannot be. Do they learn to ignore this? I reminded myself *I* must not: and neglect to investigate its real impact as remembered style. I said, "Can compulsive thinking be controlled?"

"Yes: you slam the heel of your hand onto a table as hard as possible. Then shout, 'Stop!' and count out loud to ten. Then shout: 'STOP!!' again. Now, it won't, at once. So you repeat the procedure. After your palm gets good and red, this bugbear, like a pack of strays you chose to face, will want to back off. So for that day, you're a liberated man... with a bandaged palm."

I asked, "Couldn't Chain have become a sous-chef at the Oriental? I mean, instead of going crooked?"

"No. Early on he rejected an (as yet) unnamed pedophile there: with clout. And that was the end of that. One morning, in the Chinese slum of Yommarat, we came upon a garment factory, its wide doors ajar to create a draft. Rows of shadows sat at sewing machines, closest to the entrance four teenage boys spinning the wheels of their ancient Singers. Sweating profusely, they were stripped to underpants squashed into G-strings. Thin as wren bone, each was as fine of feature as any youngster you'd spot in a bar. Or once had been. The four brightened as we came into view, waved enthusiastically, and grinned in unison, '*Pai nai?* (Where are you going?—the Thai-form of Hello).'

"Chain said, 'Boy here work twelve hour every day. Seven day every week. 18 baht (90 cents) for one day. You want I do like this? I not go school same you. So must work factory. You want I do?'

"I searched the factory wall. Chain persisted: 'You want I not make *gahlee* or gangster? O.K., give 400 baht every day.'

"I kept my eyes averted. Four hundred was most of my salary... –Let me say that in this touchdown-for-touchdown thing, Chain was further handicapped because he never priced himself. Strangers approaching him for sex were expected to know it wasn't free. Should they make inquiries, he said his rate was 'up to you'—*dam jai khun*—literally: 'according to thy heart.' Normally he earned $15 for 'full time.' Some paid five, some fifty. Not bringing up money was another gamble. Had he not gambled our first evening, I'd not have brought him home.

"When I was young, an ageing queen said to me, 'In the end, you always pay for it. And cash is the cheapest way.' But who takes his elders' advice?"

I needed to scratch an itch: "Mind if I ask how Chain was in bed?"

Cory stuttered—sotto voce, "My orgasms with him were nearly nightly. Yet the number unsponsored by mental imagery was so few as to be with me still. Emissions finally required the assistance of a visual narrative involving myself and some lover other than him; at times not even myself; and for the lovers to be active in ways we weren't. Even our infrequent anal sex needed me to be seeing him as somebody else… or that corking him was not what I was doing.

"Chain initiated the lovemaking immediate he flounced into bed—his appeal was to be applauded and continually reassured. He sought a quick climax and was expert at all forms of rapid sex: oral and interlinear, a sack hum-job, and both joints jacked to simultaneous explosion with one man's hand. He kissed well, and at length, exploring the inner lip—which few Thais care to do, saliva being creepy to them. Occasionally he made my nose a fudgsicle. But unless I led with some imaginative splurge, he slacked to his simplest disposition: the dry hump or hand-job. His vigor at night recycled his daytime underwater ballet.

"Videos left him cold, though he'd claim that straight flicks were superior: '…because have different, two same boring.' Skuzzies were scarce, anyhow: Thais fight the *image* of sex (for national face), not its indulgence…"

Cory was trimming his planters here. He crumbled the dead buds in his still good fist and sank them into a wastepaper basket twenty-two feet away. He dusted off his hands, straightened himself, and resumed: "I did not believe it was Randolph Wetzel who gave Chain the gem box: though he might have been its middleman. Chain referred to that antique celadon as if it were a nest egg. Could the hewn, brandy-sedated Randolph Wetzel, in obvious straits, afford it?

"Distracting from this, I'd an advance that called for immediate attention: I needed an authority to nitpick my piece on the row houses and find inaccuracies. Our tropical-disease research man, Mick Beale, admired the area, so hard by his squalid cruising ground. When we went over it at mess one day, I told him how right he'd been about the problems a newcomer would have with *gahlee*. He said: 'Tell ya what, you got to ditch the hooer bars. Pork classy queers. For that you'll want the lingo. Haul ass to Rajdamri and sign up at A.U.A. Put more Thai under your belt—and I don't mean when your fly's unzipped.'

"So on Monday-through-Friday late afternoons, I made it to the American University Alumni Center and Library. Three weeks into Level One, I was doing my homework on its scorched upper-tier: and aware that the droopiest of eyes were aimed at me with adversity. My own adversity aroused, I introduced myself. Confessing to twenty-five, this fellow was peplumed, buccal at both ends, and named, unnervingly, Nok: 'Bird.' His English was fine, so he wasn't there to study it; owning to not use its library, why then was he at the Center? To practice his English with an Anglo? No. He said his mother was an English instructor, which accounted for his fluency, but dodged his work or how he spent his day.

"Nok's rolled-out lazy body struck me as investable.

"He waited for my lesson to finish and led me to an old café on Rajdamri. We talked. Was Nok looking for a lover or a one-night stand? He ping-ponged these questions. Something in his game sounded foul, a mite vicious. So I took a long shot: told him that *I* was in the classifieds for an artless, job-holding companion after some unproductive experience with a chippie.

"'But sir,' Nok finally bit, 'you think a chippie who tempts Red engineers to dynamite on the Mekong is unproductive?'

"I did a theatrical double-take. I said, 'To what is this in reference?'

"'The big dam that the villagers, farmers and fishermen, are protesting.' I fired a quizzical denial. Nok, clearing his throat, pooh-poohed my response with a patronizing 'O' and airy flutter of his hand.

"He copied my address and brought his interference to my flat a few nights later. My article was published by then. I showed it to him: it monopolized the editorial page in an issue of the *Bangkok Post*. He read it slowly and said he was impressed with a foreigner so interested in a block of rundown Siamese streets as to draw up a blueprint to save them. He examined my Buddha, touching its perch, and asked how much I actually knew about this 'stolen' icon.

"Or, for that matter, my lover Chain.

"Nok knows a lot: but what, really, do I? To spell it out? I know he returns a proper reticence to words. I know that he sets the bar almost too high for me: that he reaches for me, and brutalizes desire.

"I said briskly, 'Nok, you were subject to disciplinary action. –Why were you disciplined?'

"'Error! Error!' he cried.

"'So was your coming here,' I registered.

"He shot to his feet and announced that the train to his mother's, where he lived, would soon stop running. Off he went. I fingered him for a toady of Martin and, right then, couldn't appreciably pound the pedal on that: I was consumed with love's sinister sorrow. I should not have been: for though this 'Bird', Mr. Nok, did not return for several weeks, that return was inevitable—and definitive.

"Two days later, the landlady rang my bell. I lifted the peer-drop and saw her standing alongside a brimming youth in some kind of official white uniform, with gold shoulder braids and braids on his cap, carrying what I'd realize was an appointment book. She very stiffly and formally identified the youngster as the private secretary and messenger of Her Serene Highness the Princess D., a person of minor royalty. She *wai*ed the young man, covering her face from hairline to chin, opened her palm in my direction as if giving me over to him, and left us.

"He thanked me for admitting him and said his visit was related to the upkeep of communities currently or formerly on royal property: a matter of pressing concern to the Princess. She therefore owned to a fascination with my article on Praeng Nara: or, as he translated, The Junction. Her Serene Highness desired an audience with me to discuss my thinking on the neighborhood involved. My instant response was that I did not have the clothes appropriate to an audience with royalty. Nor was I conversant with the called-for etiquette.

"He smiled broadly. 'Never mind. I will bring you to a shop where we can outfit you. If you have not the cost of this, I shall arrange to have garments lent to you. When will our excursion be convenient?' He opened the date book and clicked a pen, meaning I'd really no choice in the matter, and waited for me to speak. Simultaneously his eyes roamed my parlor in a casual manner and came to rest on the icon.

"I fumbled, 'I—I guess tomorrow afternoon. Uh, three or four o'clock will be fine.'

"I saw him color: he was agitated. He collected himself and, in a deft transition, made as if my awkwardness was the cause of his discomfort, smiled again, and said, 'Then tomorrow at 3:30 it is!'

"Financially strapped as always and lacking the connivance to inherit a roll in twenty-four hours, I had to fess up to this and work the borrow option. The fit was perfect, the shoulders just right on a lapis lazuli silk single-breasted, with matching tie and shiny brand-name shoes. The messenger instructed me on the protocol and walked me through it twice. He had also informed my dean, not bothering to inform me, that I'd be out all the next day.

"The Princess sat on a slight dais in a northern elm horseshoe chair; beside it was an elm table with a vase holding cheerful yellow orchids. She was young, perhaps not thirty, wore a tailored lavender suit, and was more than gracious. I knelt on one leg at first—afterward assumed a sidewise recline by supporting my weight on my right arm and folded-under right leg;

and took care not to look directly at her. Still, I saw that her lips were animated, her cheeks unnaturally drawn, her dark waves brushed to a full biretta. She was light-skinned to pale, used no cosmetics, and had an amulet suspended from yarn-cord half-hidden in the lapels of her crescent collar, its fastener undone. Her feet shifted ever so uneasily in simple patent leather flats. She expressed a reserved but keen engagement with my ideas, managing the impression, although she probably went through numerous interviews every month, if not week, that I was the very first foreign writer on local buildings with whom she'd the privilege to discourse.

"She explained that the roughly 100 units of which we were speaking once ran through the royal grounds of King Mongkut, and were now under jurisdiction of the Crown Property Bureau. She believed the Talephat Suksa School, a charmingly modest movie-set masonry linking wood buildings, was the district's showpiece. This two-story, constructed during the reign of Chulalongkorn, had been part of his son Prince Narathip's former palace. I agreed, adding that if nothing else its cast-iron spiral staircase and the balcony's filigree-circle woodcarvings made it that. I displayed my blueprints. I said I thought that the original lime wash with emerald borders and shingle roofs should be restored; the nearly identical further units' stucco favored dark to pale canary, with lime and emerald shutters. Nor should the contractors forget the still standing, similar structures out on Tanao Road. Their wash might be in the cream range of cornflower, with the concrete corrugations separating the houses done in a sun-bouncing white. Special attention should be paid to my favorite discovery in the lanes: a Chinese sandstone plaque above the ground-floor corner where the titular trawk joins the klong—a traditional but spectacular relief of the yin-yang globe encased in a rainbow octagon over a hideous good demon with grimacing face and a sword between his teeth: he stares down, and stares off, bad thoughts.

"Whether or not my intended-to-be-lighthearted reminder here of our constant need to control bad thoughts provoked her next response, I do not know. She suddenly wanted to learn

112

what motivated my 'ambitions' for the Pridi Banomyong Building on Soi Thonglor. I stole a glance at her. Her eyes were pink: a puffiness under them revealed that she had not slept well, or had been weeping.

"I said I'd incubating notions about suitably reapportioning the stately edifice in question, which included a small theatre. Yet conversant with no satraps of the former Regent and Prime Minister Pridi, I had no personal investment in a national designation as such. Being a mere guest of Thailand, how could or why would I?

"Satisfied by this comeback or not, Her Serene Highness almost disclosed by directing her further inquiries to my average week in Bangkok: where I worked, how I amused myself, my exact Mahidol duties, if I had 'placed' associates outside its circle; and by firmly establishing the budgetary nature of my lifestyle.

"The audience lasted thirty-five minutes; when her secretary stepped forth and knelt, I had my signal to retreat. He presented me with a silver pin engraved with a spiny-edged, involuted lotus. As I tailed his smart pace through tiled arcades in the meld nineteenth-century Colonial and broad-Thai mansion in which this command appearance was held, I thought to myself: Princess D. knows far more about Praeng Nara and its restoration possibilities than I; and concluded that I'd not been summoned to discuss historic buildings.

"At the street gate (over whose threshold I Olympicked wide berth), the secretary/messenger flexed his shoulders, ignited his winsome smile, and saluted me. I saluted him and about-faced sharply: I'm still unsure if that was correct.

"THE JUNCTION PROJECT ULTIMATELY came to fruition, and the Pridi Banomyong Building is a political landmark today; but I'd no inkling then that this would ever happen. That night my sine qua non was to binge. I hit Harrie's, threw back three tonics at the bar, and ordered a fourth before turning in my size-too-small, big-balled slacks to meet all comers. Harrie's was lit with kliegs and a dozen maddening strobes that flashed the customers on and off and made its great space tentative, if not all wrong. I

113

wasn't certain who or where anyone was, if men were coming or going or even there. The dancers were impossible to watch.

"So I focused on the mezzanine, where less movement would be more intelligible; and lingered there until my eyes adjusted to the purple, vanilla, marine, and orange gels. Its bleachers were divided from the narrow stairs that led to them by a heavy felt curtain, whorehouse-red; this curtain also served to divide the bleachers' planks from the short hall that went to the john. I concentrated on the waist-high rail: and when the vanilla gel lit it enough times, for a full second each time, saw that a man with a peg leg was standing by it, looking down at the bar, and that Chain was sitting nearby, angled toward the higher tiers, with his back gracing me and the dancers below. Two men were seated on the plank above his, both good eaters, but with a considerable difference in bulk and height. On the topmost plank of the bleachers was a slight figure. Could be a pansy.

"As the strobes kept blinking, this is what occurred or appeared to occur: the man with the artificial leg left the rail and climbed the tiers; the gigantic older man held up what must have been a humidor: because he opened it, ostentatiously removed a thin cigar, and gave it to the chunky fellow near him—who, in a quick beige spot, resembled the hostile, spread-hipped, drooplidded Nok. Then the older guy, no doubt the Atlas Martin, in stop-shots, drew what appeared to be a string of stones from his breast pocket and dangled it, in turn, close to the faces of the other four. The stones caught, in succession, a prism's darker colors; when they had reflected these twelve times, Martin, with much (indeterminable) facial adjustment, tied the string around Chain's neck. Martin's specs caught the carousel of colors and dizzy beams of light: there was no shilly-shallying now: he was the same Chain-buff who'd clawed me with his ultimatum: and, too, he of whom the canvassing hermit wished me to be aware. The slight fem seemed to approve, or be delighted by, big Martin's big gesture, but did nothing else I could make out. Nok, or Nok's double, smoked the cigar to peeve the others. They held their noses and dispersed its blue-glow fumes.

114

"I began the stairs two at a time and ran into a block of drunks crawling up and merrymakers clawing down. For a moment it looked like some nocuous pulling and shoving was going to develop. Everyone took a deep breath and stopped: then, one by one, men filed up, and men filed down, flashing on and off.

"In my heart I knew I was already too late: still, I yanked the tassels on the red curtain to coax it aside a foot or so. Only the fruit sat in the bleachers: on close inspection, a nail-chewing, ultra-gaunt gamine—a true fright, whose loud-print single-piece could do for either sex. I asked him where, it being the shank of the evening, his companions had gone, and he said he had none; that he had been in the stands 'alone long evening.' Didn't I think that he, Ekarin, was enough? That saccharine inquiry set up the usual banalities: my age, wages, number of offspring, country of origin. –Ninety-seven, a half-million baht a week, forty-eight children, Fiji. Ekarin reacted to each as if it were Holy Writ; stood with a flourish; minced toward the curtain to indicate he'd be splitting, and noted that if I'd not yet slept in a real *baan Thai*, this would be my opportunity. I said, 'I don't care to travel tonight. How about here, in the toilet?'

"His response was, '*Impetuous!*' ...or it sounded like that. I yanked the tassels again, took his limp wrist, led him down the hall to the men's and into the last, graffiti-enlivened stall. I blew hot air, slipped off my belt, twirled him about, strapped his wrists together, and brought them up between his wings. He groaned with an overdone pretense at pleasure, but when I jerked them higher so that his tapering, painted nails raked his pricy shag, he dropped any play at fun-for-the-weird and waited. I whistled, softly, 'Who are the four men you were with and where did they go?' Elbows up another notch. The big one 'have theatre' and the young ones 'in new show there.' Elbows higher. They went to 'show-practice.' The cripple? 'Not Thai.' What did the gross man give the pretty man? A necklace (of paste) for his costume. What did he give you? Zilch: 'I not in show.'

"I didn't believe a word of this, but as a bit more elbow work was going to fissure them, I cancelled my try. The switchblade would have made this easier: inopportunely, those encumbered cargoes didn't get fast come-ons. I loosened the belt, freed him, and started to slide the catch.

"'What about the fuck?' Ekarin asked.

"I had not ever entertained that; however, he requesting it, I did suddenly wonder what a hole is like padded in paucities equivalent to kitchen mitts. May be tight as a drum. I tore his bloomers apart and gave him a rectal whisk, my middle finger clicking his love button. He shut his doughnut, imprisoning that digit. I counted on this prostate probe to exhaust any necessary consolation: yet Ekarin balked—'Want cock! Give cock!'

"Ekarin was ectomorphic, frangible, and emaciated. His pitching bone-rack and toothy skull furtively mobilized me. My desire beckoned like a stripped-off winding-sheet, as it had sirened the autonomous peter to perk up even in the bleachers. In the toilet he was a blank, an absence. Since he'd next to nothing to engage pound-wise, I stared at whopper-art a foot from my face. After four-five rams, Ekarin screamed: '*Set lao*! (I came!),' tugged my hand, and rubbed it over his gooey dick. It smelled.

"I gasped angrily, '*I* didn't!' and delivered a coupla-three more thrusts. My climax was intense: the most intense I'd had in Thailand. I rinsed myself with the mini-hose attached to crappers here and zipped my slacks. As I pushed the stall-door, he stuffed an unopened *Gauloise* into my back pocket. When I carved a what-the-heck's-this-for? twitch, Ekarin said, 'Pay! *Gahlee dee—khun*!'

"I BEGAN RIDING BUSES that passed A.U.A. in the evening: routed anywhere except to my flat. I needed to think, or agonize, away from Chain.

"There were two empty seats against the rear window in the bus I caught of a misty evening, going out over the bridge to Taksin Circle on the city's west bank. Moments after I took one of them, a milk-skinned man got up from the front of the bus and started haltingly down the aisle on a crutch, his piercing eyes pointedly fixed on mine. He'd a lank build with my height, a mass of glinting curls, and a square, very hard face. He was wearing a lilac jersey and clean white shorts, on his right foot a heavy black-leather sandal. A matching sandal hugged an artificial lower limb, buckled to his left knee with a chrome brace. He twisted into the seat next to me with inordinate difficulty, grasped his crutch with both hands, and aimed it at the aisle. He shuddered for five minutes; then, addressing that emptiness, asked in a steep, quiet voice, *'Vous vous connaissez de moi?'* I nodded. He had tiny ears, a wide, anxious brow, scaled lips, their edges skewed, and cheeks pariah with rheumy hollows. He muted, 'Excuse. My French and English, not good… You—you want to speak with me?'

"I answered: 'Yes, I do.'

"There wasn't a further word between us until we reached his sanctum. He gestured to alight at the Circle, and then toward a nearby train. Sitting or walking with him, I felt that telex the Asian sends with his silent body. What read then was that our meeting on the bus had clinched a stakeout.

"The locomotive was that southwest wobbler whose doors never close. Thais call it the Train to Nowhere: it runs to a stranded fishing village. At the fifth whistle-stop we jumped off, and he bought a package of ice at a grocery there. He lived in a corrugated tin hut alongside the tracks, which held a futon, a floor lamp, a hot plate and tank, an insulated bucket, and a pair of plain armchairs: that confronted each other. He lit the lamp, emptied the ice in the bucket, filled two thick cups with cubes, gave me one, and pointed for me to sit in the chair farther from the futon. He jigged his crutch under the doorknob (a thief breaking in while he slept had to collapse it) and sank into the opposite chair as a man would: its concave seat slouching him slightly, showing no ripple in his waist, and parting his pale thighs. When his shorts tightened his crotch with dampness, he occasionally pulled at their hems, and reset and smoothed his foreshortened limb.

"He sipped from his cup and patently studied me.

"'Look old, but still young,' he began. 'Nickname, Kambuja'—which means descended of Kambu, a Hindu deity: i.e., 'Cambodia.' He explained that he'd fled his homeland after the '79

117

Vietnamese invasion deposed Pol Pot and deported the resident Chinese. He had not lost his leg stepping on a mine, planted by the Red Khmer in their effort to regain power. *'Oui! Ça arrive plus tard.'* Shanghaied in the Gulf, Kambu-ja was forced into slave labor on a Thai fishing boat: paid starvation wages. When his boat was docked one day, its anchor became entangled with the anchor of a neighboring scow: the pilot ordered him to slip over the gunwale and dislodge it. A swell in the breakers caused the two boats to collide, and his left leg was crushed. Kambu-ja worked extra hard when his ship went forth the next morning, but by sundown the captain felt he was hopelessly disabled, not worth his pitiful pay or the yard of deck he slept on, and had the crew toss him into the sea. To drown. He collected jetsam during the night and, drinking rainwater from his palms, floated on it for nine days. 'This rainwater,' he said, indicating our cups.

"On the ninth day, the Thai Coast Guard picked him out of the ocean and brought him to the port of Sattaheap in Trat Province: from there, and in that state, to be sent back to Cambodia. Older Brother *(Phii)* found him in Sattaheap, fed and clothed him, put him in a hospital, and had his lower leg amputated. Older Brother purchased the prosthetic limb and paid good doctors to fit it to his knee. Kambu-ja was now enslaved to Older Brother, obligated at first to do simple things; and when he grew used to the plastic limb, gradually more challenging tasks. He earned wages, and his wages increased.

"Kambu-ja asked, *'Naam yen?* (Water cold?)' I said it was; and wondered aloud if I'd ever seen Older Brother. 'He is big man: upstairs: at Harrie's.' Using a mix of French, Thai, and English, I edgily inquired if he might not elaborate on some of the tasks his current work entailed. I believed he had guided me to his distant home to do just that. The Train to Nowhere clunked by: the tin walls and the floor lamp shook.

"When quiet returned, Kambu-ja asked if I knew that General Pol Pot was in a refugee camp near Sattaheap; that this refugee camp was really a military base; that the 'refugees' were virtual Pol Pot slaves: slaves of the Khmer Rouge, which Pol was reassembling there? I instinctively shivered. I offered him a joint and smoked one myself. While I smoked, he stationed me in the continuous grip of his stabbing eyes. I sensed I should not avert mine—and that he could read my every thought: they might as well be lit with bulbs and crossing my forehead like bulletins. When our jaws clamped, he involuntarily was duplicating mine.

"I relaxed my jaw and stubbed the joint. He deliberately closed his lashless eyes. He made a soft sound; I don't think it was a word. Then he pursed his lips and silently began to make our decision. Should he open his eyes, I shut my own so I couldn't appear to be reading his lips. I said I knew that Pol Pot was in a refugee camp a disc's throw from the Cambodian border; that I didn't know exactly what he and his army were doing there; that I would appreciate it if he, Kambu-ja, would tell me any-thing about these activities that might relate to me: that is, as I put it, 'be my business.'

"It amounted to this: some Pentagon hardheads were still fighting the Vietnam War; and Vietnam was Beijing's historical enemy. Singapore was the city where funds for weaponry, rath-er than the weaponry itself, were being placed by the CIA and Mainland China's confidential agents. From there the money was easily carried by barque and water buffalo to the refugee camp. Mrs. Thatcher was also involved: she found the Khmer Rouge to be 'reasonable people,' and, in fact, was sending mines and instructors for how to plant them (and hand-rockets, field-rockets, and machine guns), either to Singapore or directly to Sattaheap: it being her ministerial belief—in tune with Wash-ington and Beijing—that Pol Pot would rout the Vietnamese cur-rently in, and controlling, Cambodia, and send them packing—'to place they belong.'

"Kambu-ja stopped here, stared at me almost indecently, and reinforced that stare for what seemed a lifetime. I realized I was supposed to ask a question.

"I adjusted myself, the seat *was* uncomfortable now, and fi-nally asked him: 'Who is delegated (*délégué*) to see that Mrs. Thatcher's funds, weapons, and teachers get to Singapore or Sattaheap?'

"Kambu-ja answered, 'Older Brother. He is English.'

119

"I waited, threw him another smoke but was too strung-out to light one myself. I muttered, *'Et qui apporte…* who… and who is the operative who brings the funds from *Beijing* to Sat-taheap?'

"'Chain.'

"I must have paced that shack for twenty minutes, breaking only to refill my water cup. I don't think he watched me, at first. Can all or any of this be true? That Chain is an aide-de-camp—that he mules Chinese money to the Red Khmer—for Pol Pot, inventor of autogenocide, a fiend who murdered over a fifth of his own countrymen? So he'll kill yet more—always the guiltless, the unarmed?

"*A bag man!* I swung at the nearest wall. It rattled and dent-ed deeply. Kambu-ja looked up. Seconds later he split in three—with the three drooling heads of Cerberus. Alternately, he be-came a mutilated brigadier with three scarred faces and three remaining legs. Suddenly I was in a ubiquity of eyes: Kambu-ja's, the grand hermit's, the Royal Messenger's, Rollo's, Nok's, and Ekarin's. It was like the time I was put to bed in a private house in New Orleans, know as *Casa de las Mil Munecas*: and awoke in the middle of the night to see hundreds of empty-eyed litigating dolls denouncing me. I believed them to be the multivision of delirium tremens: but they weren't.

"I measured every inch of the hut before returning to Kam-bu-ja, knocking his restless, truncated knee and listening to my voice in triplicate, 'Hide nothing now!' His anxiety rose; he fought his incomprehension. 'We will unite,' I assured him.

"He stiltedly unbuckled his gleaming metal brace and rested the plastic leg on the floor. It had the effect of undressing. He prevaricated, cupping his stump with his left fingers and, duti-fully said, trembling:

"'Thai people like not—this. Never do, have this… Sometime foreign man *mai son jai* (don't care)… Please. Do not behold me.'

"He turned himself out of his armchair and onto the futon, which had a single pillow and a single white sheet. He drew the sheet across the lower half of his body. He grimaced gauchely. Then he pulled the mulberry jersey over his head, threw it at the door where it dropped on the pad of his crutch, and sat there bare-chested, breathing in tormented gulps and staring at the ceiling. His pallid chest was perfect, almost featureless. Beneath the sheet, he squirmed out of his shorts, wound most of the sheet securely about his amputation, and, with a wretched sigh, continued to sit upright, not making eye contact.

"I stood without volley, took off my clothes, and went and sat at his side. The moment I touched him nakedly, he clamped my shoulders and pushed them back. Reversing the reality, so I'd appear at gunpoint, he entered me with the haste of utter self-abnegation: where nothing more than my endurance could or would be experienced. He seized first one brow and then the other in the vise of his teeth until he had spent in tandem.

"Then he tore up his pillowcase, fell on his side facing away, and began to sob. I lifted myself, flattened him on his stomach, and carefully massaged his spine, the narrows of his waist, and, unbinding the sheet, his non-pliant thighs. I sniffed a lush axilla; I tweezed the vagrant hairs on the scented parchment of his eternal divide, and tasted both. But he was too tight in his gluteal peak and dry, sandpapered sphincter to tongue any farther than that; and from iron triceps to his long-jointed toes. I took his broken branch in my arms like a child; I hugged it, I washed it. He pushed at my forehead; he blocked my mouth with his hands. I dozed, kept from sleep by an ineffectual displacement: that Kambu-ja, not I, had maligned Chain through his injurious solitude...

"I fastened a towel under my hipline and showered in the morning, using an enclosed communal rain-barrel a short walk from his shack. I returned in the towel, dressed, and sentried in his doorway gazing at the garbage field, which a group of hovels called home. It smelled of silage, not sewerage. Kambu-ja, uncharacteristically, ineptly hopped and thumped to his crutch. Clutching it, he entreated, flushed with humility, 'My... my semen... is inside you.' He stepped behind me. 'I... *Je veux vous revoir. Mais je sais je peux pas. C'est la verité.* Because, Chain.'

"'Yes,' I said, half to myself. 'Our Chain is an infection now. He will always be there.'

"Rollo would, too. Rol blocked my dashing to class a month later to refresh his injunction. 'Chain fell by last night. The prideful here don't do that uninvited. Even gave me a gift. Beat around the bush, the usual face-saving ploy, then got to the grit. He suspects you and he are drifting apart.'

"No kidding… I defended myself: 'At this point, Chain is in danger.'

"'Aren't we all!' Rollo fretted, not able, or willing, to grasp my meaning. 'To coin an Americanism, he's looking for a commitment. Drifting is only delay. I told him to weekend with you in Hua Hin. At the Railway Hotel—the Thai answer to romantic dilemmas. So *he'll* be making the effort to aerate the nest.'

"*Chain*—the irrevocable! Fed-up, I asked what deep investment Rol had in that criminal's welfare. He glared, 'In *his*, little. It's yours.'

"The bell rang. His concentrated look enflamed his bromide, 'Wouldn't hurt to help yourself for once, would it?'

"'I'm not?' I asked—weighing Rol's grave and surely ignorant error.

"'Not from where I stand. And, at Hua Hin, check it: the smile was born in Thailand.'

"Prince Purachatra built the Railway Hotel in 1922: a circular, stately edifice hoisted by a conical roof into the skies of the South China Sea. Its girdling twenty-acre garden was rainbowed then with tree-suspended buttercup orchid, violet bougainvillea, and topiary of orange ixora clipped as elephant, peacock, and Singh, the dog-lion. Those equivocations, part human and part bird, showed up everywhere: in paintings; on postcards; as small or man-size statues near temples, and the plazas of the Grand Palace.

"We left our duffels at the hotel and sped to the white beach. He bobbed in the waves—the Chain you adore, a water sprite, a bashful merman, happy as a boy. Afterward, we rented beach chairs and coated each other with coconut oil. His chatter was full of inanities, like the single kitten his family's cat recently had (and a Tom killed—'because, not good for sec'). He laughed as never before.

"At dusk the hotel assumed the lineaments of a strangely disturbing Maxfield Parrish. Its true-to-deco structure allowed for cooling through hidden drafts. The rooms were lit by gaslight, and each had a bombé screen recessed from its French windows. Blocking the sun by day, these summoned devastating constellations to wink through at night. In the teak-paneled room I noticed, and became concerned with, the elm headboard separated by eight inches from the bedding. I'd had an identical one when I was four or five: my head would get caught in that breach, resulting in claustrophobic struggles during my dreams. Back then a child tumbled into a drain on a Midwest lawn. Emergency crews tried to extricate her for three days: *long* days in which the nation held its breath—for few as long as I. Those last hours of her life haunt most of mine: as a tunnel to shadow no recalcitrance deserves or rebellion justifies. To fight that headboard's presence just beyond Chain, I encapsulated his sortilege by undressing him with my mouth. Sensing my panic, his face molten in the brass bowl of the gas fixture, he lowered its wick. That distortion encouraged me, down to his slippers. I ran my incredulous fingers over his heated arms and descended his torso until I took the eiderdown of his backsides: their weight, their shift from languor to imperial fixity, their puckered secret, their concession the arrangement of Angora and eagle. They were— they are now—glabrous and truant, the finest tactility to which I've trembled. I compulsively whispered, as if the phrase would be too lame, trite, or dishonest in English, *'Je t'aime.'*

"And he responded, *'Moi aussi…'*

"I knew, there, this was so for me absolutely; and as absolutely for him: that he shared my intuition of true love's infrequency, its value and its cost. How for its stasis most live; and live to relive; and for whose a-temporality nothing more transporting shall be found as a reason to die.

"Both of us shaking, I let him nudge me around the bombé

screen. We leaned against the vast window and hailed, ourselves adamantine and stellar, a centaur turned toward the nebulae forever arching his bow.

"Lying in the sand the next day, I glanced to my far right, where the shore in an artful swing prized from the sea a small green mountain. On it was a weather-beaten temple; and challenging the eddies at the edge of its precipice, a gigantic, gold-colored image of the Walking Buddha. I knew it addressed sailors. Chain followed my interest: 'Chopsticks Hill. Have little church. Want go see?'

"Our clothes were piled on the blanket, but he chose to make the trip in his maroon bikini: scandalously briefer than a Jarawa's codpiece, it raised two-score eyebrows along the strand. We'd be exploring a temple, so he need not have been so bonkers to accompany. This costume was his ticket to satanic activities: smuggling; the damming of waters certain to flood-out fishers and farmers; the procuring of kids—his kin, no less—sentencing them, as often as not, to deathly disease—his becoming bag man for a mass murderer! I watched him wince and curl his toes on the heated pebbles. I lagged farther and farther behind.

"At the roofless *bot*, or inner chapel, on whose floor glared a disapproving monk, Chain remained unabashed. I tried to skirt him as he gingerly trod the burning stones of the holy altars and pretend for that conflicted life of mine that I didn't know him.

"Of a sudden he was nowhere in sight. I searched within the chapel, then decided he must have left it to examine the Walking Buddha, which rose, simulating a lighthouse, on the hilltop. Sure enough, he was lying on the gulf side of its base, his ear propped on an elbow like the god Narai who sleeps in the ocean. He'd bought a collapsible fan at a souvenir stall and was indolently fanning himself. Spooked by this apathy defiling the sacrosanct and outdoing his exiguous attire, I indicated the fan and sarcastically inquired, 'Hot?'

"'Is not for hot,' he said in his courtly, critical voice.

"'No?'

"'No.' He was staring over the swell to the nimbi gathering on the horizon. 'For keep away evil. In you.'

"Three weeks on, Oliver Makepeace Littleton rang me and asked me to meet him in Thonburi. He would furnish triple the count he owed me. Talk about wanting to see a man concerning an icon—and two sets of fiends.

"He was staying at a Wat Sai located on Klong Dan, and his instructions for getting there were very complex. I was first to cross the river to the west bank by bus, then find the Tachin train; and once aboard, count the number of stops that would bring me to the station a jot north of the compound. He told me to enter by the south gate, walk straight to the principal temple, turn right, and then continue on until I came to the monks' cells. This was easier said than done, because the dominating stupa blocked view of an overall and further hampered the restricted pass-ways between structures.

"When I reached the cells, I could see he was not on any porch. Then, on a stretch of the canal circling the domiciles, I noticed a jetty—with Olie on it: shouting angrily at two young Thais, all three in profile.

"As I started in their direction, something happened that was to puzzle me for two years. I surveyed the path so as to clear the puddles and rubble there; when I looked up, one of the youngsters, in the standard off-blue full sleeves and polyester blue-slacks uniform of an office worker or government employee, moved a step or two toward Olie, then back—and fell into the klong. He grasped the withered timbers to keep from sinking, but the swift, filthy current, splashing over his face, crushed him against them. When I got to the jetty, Olie and the other fellow were struggling to pry him loose from where he'd been rammed and caught in the pilings. When they finally yanked him up, he was gasping for air, his head battered, his cheeks cut, his soaked shirt a gushing and transparent second skin. Despite his hair being partially stuck to his forehead, he'd a visible and amazing widow's peak. He limped to the bank on a costly loafer, its match having been taken by the rapid swirl. He vented his pain and frustration with an exasperated laugh: then thrust his shoed foot forward, flinging that hushpuppy out into the canal. It sailed northward like an unmanned rowboat. This widow-peaked fellow looked my way fast and hard, as if fixing me in his memory; then, joined by his companion, scurried on top the scree toward a spinney; and, somehow, both youngsters instantly disappeared.

"I hopped onto the jetty board and demanded a tell-all. Oliver cut me short: cautioned, 'Don't stand here now. Let's go into that pavilion. Everything ace? Forget those wallydraigles you just saw.'

"He smiled beatifically. It was as if I'd never confronted him about Fourth World boys. Or that men like Martin, the movie-star counterfeits, or even Rollo existed. I'm not convinced that they did for Olie, most of the time.

"The pavilion he pointed to was a half dozen yards from the water, painted black and clearly old. Only its triangular roof, stilt-supported floor, and rear wall were intact. The sides, flush with the klong, except for several warped planks were gone. Olie preceded me to the recess and spread a tabloid on the guano there. He spilt two kilos of bound sticks onto the paper; and, drawing a stiletto from his robe—as a tussle with me came back to him—divided the ganja in thirds. He dumped one third in the fold and shoved it at me. He scowled, 'This should put you in your bloody corner! Kill some now. You'll *know* it's Triangle Red! –Place is putrid. Still, stay down: we can be seen if we stand.'

"He maliciously rolled a memorable-size cigar. Charcoal-chickens, which resemble dwarf tyrannosaurs, high-stepped into the pavilion and pecked his feet. 'Buggers! *They* make it putrid here!'

"Two tokes and I felt like the mummies look in the digs at Ban Chiang. I squatted Thai-style. My hands dropped beyond my knees. He tapped my fingers with the flat of the stiletto and irked, 'A cramp in your grip *this* outing, gorilla?' The stiletto reflected my eyes: aglow with recalling the wanderer's blade and big man's cigar. Olie persisted: 'A short in your overkill? Your knuckle-crunch?'

"I said, 'I'm knuckled under the stick: watch it, Oliver.'

"'It's that touch o' the tar. We *pure*breds don't jump to assumptions.'

"I was facing the rear wall, not in a mind to swat him. I stared at its gold wood-relief: Olie's slur had an unintended target there: speaking of impure, at eye-level, that combination sharp-nosed man and jaunty bird was suggesting a lotus stem to a melon-breasted female of the same species. Their combusting boa-tails, branching gracefully, were repeated as the basic design, which tangled ceiling-wise to engrave the whole paneling, ten-twelve feet high. In those tails, often upside down, doves perched and squirrels climbed.

"I asked, 'What are those combination creatures? I've seen them at Hua Hin. And in Loei, Nan, and Nong Khai.'

"Olie was disappointed that his cheap-shots got no rise. But one man in the drink did for the day. 'The males are kinnara', the females, kinnari'. Above the waist, they're ancient royalty; below, giant birds. They symbolize celestial love and sympathy... –Celestial, since they can fly there, get it? Right to Mount Meru.'

"'And their complicated tails?'

"'Unfurling lotus buds—and dying flames. They picture the cooling effect of Buddha's teachings on human passion. Ruin's named the Golden Pavilion thanks to that relief,' Olie went on, starting to drift. 'Dates to 1703. You see it's not in the style of Wat Sai. A bloke with a hard-to-douse passion had it moved from wherever it was and reassembled here. Strong weed, what?'

"I said, 'Oliver, what's between you and Rollo?'

"'A boy: only Thai I may say I loved. Years ago, Rollo came to a wat in Ko Chang to chisel my grass. He stayed late, and we slept with the boy between us. Got up in the night to go at a flash, and Rol was rooting him. –I'm calling time: a Slimy Pink Monster's due in ten. Sod flaps a lot. Tried fobbing me off, he has.'

"I said, 'Hold it. Afore I blow, can you weigh in on my statue?'

"'*I can!* That saint is a ring of passkeys—and a heartfelt freebee, slope.' Delivered of this sanitization, and both very stoned, he pulled me toward the road to assist me to the train. En route, So I told him that I'd met the cocktease Nok, who knows, or says, that the icon is stolen. And the willowy Ekarin who believes I'd do well, or am doing well, in the life. And the lame Cambodian, a slave for his own handler—

"I stopped because Olie was simply nodding; and, instead of ticking off names, switched to stressing the importance of the position you assume to enable you to grasp the wat's grammar; that big-bellied chedi obstructs relating the yoni and lingam… It made no difference: he wasn't listening.

"I stepped up to the plate: 'What is your read on the 'movie-goofs,' and how are you hooked in to their competition?'

Oliver was standing still: staring at a white sedan parked by the curb, almost hidden by a circle of food carts. A well-favored man in a seersucker suit, wearing reflector glasses, was seated behind the wheel. An unmarked car… Olie's face mottled. He grabbed my forearm: 'It's better if you skedaddle by the klong. Klong Dan will get you to Klong Krung Thep Yai. Know where you'd be?

"'At the double, Cory, the pier!'

"For a minute, the canal was deceptively pellucid. Then the mounting waves signaled the coming of a slim longtail. As I took the rigging to drop into it, I said, 'Sad that you botched the icon for Marty. Shit'll hit the fan for you two now.'

"I had recognized the thief-searcher in the white car.

"He was the royal messenger.

"A week after my junket to Wat Sai, I responded to a bold, rhythmic rapping on my door. It was past midnight. That lackey Nok—who'd cornered me at A.U.A., called Chain a Maoist, and smoked Martin's cigar on Harrie's mezzanine—was stumbling in the hallway, just about to pound again.

"Had I put a match to his breath, my flat would have exploded.

"He groaned peevishly, barged in, and slipped off his shoes, his ample butt lickety-split on my couch. Unemployed Thais make unexpected pit stops with the same frequency they allot to skipping arranged ones, or to ignoring the time they'd set to arrive. Days to the reincarnated haven't the strict agendas single-lifers give them. Nor has time, nor history, the linear scale we bestow on them: and then read into them. As for inappropriate hours, how can any hour be inappropriate when solitude strikes the Asian as pathetic? I ran these abstractions in preference to letting the alarm that entered with Nok at once get the better of me. Hadn't persons who'd recently offended my coma—the Princess and her messenger, Ekarin, Kambu-ja, and even Olie: his sudden over-payback—rapidly intruded with orderly succession in the wake of Nok's initial visit? A soul least sensitive to his surroundings would have butterflies in his stomach.

"Nok began to giggle. To whose detriment, if not mine, did he owe his mirth? I presented a quart of gin. He took ninety minutes to slug a fourth of it, remind me that he was a Muslim from Hat Yai (who shouldn't drink), click the cup with carious teeth, and answer that question. He said: 'Starved. Very starved!'

"I stir-fried glass noodles. He wolfed them down. So he's out of groceries: Martin is seeing to this. –Nok's insolvency: in which my future lurked. It had hatched in his brain—more cemented there than anywhere in Thailand.

"I was his captive now. I'd be for a while. He became invitational: those overlaundered chinos, gloving his slouch in the sofa, outlined nature's generosity. When he stretched himself on the sofa's arm to reach for the gin, at that point on the floor, and presented me with the stimulant of his slabs—his chinos, to the purpose, caught in their crack—I spasmed in the ovate base of operations.

"I rose from my chair, hit the cushions behind him, and undid his snap. Then seizing both waistbands at once, I tugged his chinos and electric skivvies to just below the satin of his dimpled honeydews. Nok appeared to struggle with the protest of a soused tease: half interested and half trying to remember why not to be. I'd no problem with ignoring his only half tumescence.

"Hobbyhorsing back and forth, he finally collapsed on his left side: his pullover sufficiently nudged up by then and his briefs completely nudged down. As a prolonging ploy, he managed a truly annoying, oppositional incantation: which his big brown behind inevitably canceled. I slopped a glob of saliva on the slit of my boner, boosted his right cheek exposing and opening the magenta anus, and slammed my entirety into the draw. Though stuck on the couch and forced, because his legs weren't, into a Greek Cross, I hammered at the lower ridges of that washboard up there like a madman bent on breaking them off.

"*My* guzzling kicked-in the protraction, or I'd have sauced near instantly and let go the abrading for this canary's souvenir. During that thorough ramming, I kept him stationed on his left side with my left hold on his crushed right bicep and my right on his fat and full, still-clothed chop. When he threatened to squirm and upset my tempo, I shifted my right fist and took him by the gonies.

"The fuck is what *I* put into it.

"I extracted my shovel with inconsiderate suddenness the second the orgasm pumped dry so I could watch his expanded, ruby-leaking pit shut in a slow swivel—which, digging-in my digits, I lengthened by pulling both plump buttocks apart: as far as they'd yield. Then I yanked his briefs up to his love knobs and slapped them firmly into his ravine: to stain with the freed sperm, spit, and fecal matter of the plug this esurient minion comfortably foresaw—since my capitulation to Nok had been a certainty—to Nok as well as to my driven self.

"Nok slowly rolled over, sated and dazed. He fumblingly lifted his trousers. He squinted at me, his trump card no longer a dream. Then tried his unsteady feet, drained his last drink and mine, and carved a sloppy path to the door. With a bound, I was there before him. I shouted, 'No!' and blocked his exit. I grabbed and shook him. He radically keeled. 'Not yet!' I warned. He flattened his hair with a wet palm and stared sightlessly.

"'What?'

"'You did this because of Chain. Didn't you?'

"He worked his jaw. 'What I do?'

"'You opened your asshole. *Chain* is the reason!'

"One lid twitched badly. His mouth became agile. 'So?'

"'What is your problem with Chain?'

"'Same yours.'

"I searched his disclosure. What hid there? Nok snarled. –It was Beauty's incision—*both* our destinies: but the weal in his wound. I summed it up: 'Nok—you are being disciplined by the big Englishman for crossing Chain. You impeded—or tried to displace him.'

"He said, quite darkly, 'Sir sees quickly.'

"'Not quickly enough, Nok. And not everything.'

"'That is correct, sir: not everything. I needed to describe sir's prick.'

"…He'd a new carnal notch. How, in accomplishing this, would Nok rescind his trespass? He'd leave my rooms as one does a starting gate.

"Chain, Nok, and I were hanging by our thumbs.

"He puffed his cheeks with contempt and brushed off my grip. Then spun on a heel, and was out. I went to my bathroom window's wire cage.

"For eight or nine minutes, I watched the rotating sprinkler and a line of ants hastening through the grillwork, each lugging its aphid like a tiny surrender flag. The sprinkler must have flooded their nest. I heard doors open and shut.

"It was 2:30 a.m. At last Nok came into view, ambling saddle-sore to the exit in the compound wall. I tried, too soon, to feel he'd called it a night. That downgrade executed a neat turnabout when he reached the wall, then waved broadly in the direction of my lighted cage with his arms high overhead—as if semaphoring a dive-bomber—and bellowed loudly, *very* loudly:

"'THANK YOU FOR FUCKING ME!'

"At 6:45 a.m. I was plowing the cipher of China Box trees when my crimp-faced landlady, bolting from behind a Travelers Palm, snared me. She wore a *chewngsom*, the standing-collar, ankle-length, Hong Kong traffic-stopper. Using a divorced monotone, achieved by barely parting her lips, she frostily announced: 'Khun Cory, my brother—the Police Lieutenant General—wishes to converse with you now in a matter of the gravest importance.'

"She nodded to where said worthy sat, bolt-upright, on a folding chair smack center of the lawn. A second, unoccupied folding chair was squarely facing him: awaiting *my* occupation…

"Well, sport, this has been a lustful double session!"

I chirped, "Chief: it has."

"I'll reserve the calamitous outcome of that hijack by the Police Lieutenant for day after tomorrow."

THE THIRD DAY

MOON DORMITORY IS IN SOI 19, off Sukhumvit Road, Bangkok's major crosstown artery. This used to be the nabe of rich foreigners; today it is hairy. I ate breakfast in the Honey Cone Hotel, a dump near my dormitory. I would have done Sukhumvit, but Tobias York, a Tut mummy look-alike and frequently recorded third-stream pianist, said, chuckling, that he could fit me in that afternoon. So I paid the fee for the Honey Cone's pool: oddly, in its front garden. The stink-o canal across the soi made reading and relaxing there thorny and may have colored the material I was going through.

What I read were two of Cory's essays, both dated 1985: *Greek Influence on the Dvaravati Vishnus in Prachinburi, Thailand* and *Caucasian Buddhists and Other Fakes.* The second is a dud in Cory's output. I trace its polemic to Oliver A. M. Littleton: through it I believe he deflects the animosity he felt toward Chain. I shuddered to think of the bedlam in Cory Simon's heart that Chain had investigated, and what retribution Chain underwent, animating it.

I picked at his current scene. Adding Simon's self-inflicted cuts to his International English, with its tantalizing aura of déjà entendu in even this bilge, I sensed I was getting closer and closer to something I thought I knew much more about than Cory—or I, when selecting him—suspected.

Tobias York laid down the law through the spray of his senile erudition. He wanted to pontificate on everything, joke a lot, and air his pet peeves, rather than elucidate his career. When he stressed an "insight" drawn from his "wisdom," there was no insight. I asked how he spent his time when he was not practicing—on the *piano*—or disking in a sound studio. He could not be doing both every day, all day long. He dripped, *"Pussy cat:* why not let me show you?"

We found a giveaway guide called *Bangkok Gay* in a Silom bar. There is an article there under a pseudonym (*Incidental Nudity*, d. Apr. 2005) that I know only Simon could have written; since Toby and I followed it spot for spot, I prefer to reprint it in place of an inferior personal account:

"Get to Lumpini Park. Sit in the playground by the entrance, the hot seat for hunters just before and after sundown. Park freelancers are straight. But since they tolerated hometown, reciprocal penetration when they were kids, if they see an advantage to it, they still will now. A fast worker can turn a dozen tricks in a night. The unskilled unemployed find their open-apricot a windfall. In the way of getting by, getting corked is a piece of cake. These guys are grungier and more menacing than those you find in bars, so a john should be nifty at handling rough trade. Watch: some johns do the ice-breaking and some take a bench and wait for the hooker to approach them. –The juicy butch prowling around that old China Hand? The Hand will say he can do better if Butch comes to more than a fin: and bundle him off to a hammer-by-the-hour, or his hotel. If it's his hotel, Butch will leave his ID at the desk, a safety net for which your China Hand knows he will be grateful.

"Hanker for something raunchier? Sure you do! Hit the Go-Go palaces. Head for the sub-sois of Silom 6, and look for a neon blaring 'SuperRex.' This sleazereena's big on yardage. Hope yardage doesn't make you feel inadequate.

"They are strangely proportioned at SuperRex: awesome equipment on such diminutive fellows! Here, a real shower set with five bathers scrubbing their friends' backs and backsides is followed by a soapfoam act: a glistening Spiderman slithers along a supine partner and eventually rocks him on a piped-through-the-stage-floor cloud of purple bubblebath. Their pulse-stopper is a rapid fashion trek of twenty or so tense yet well-

greased farm boys dressed in split-second rip-offs—which they rip off in a split second after racing to the apron: disclosing pendulums of whose devastating length few hippopotami boast. Then as many at a throw that space permitting, now in briefs with numbered badges, reassemble in order to be 'offed.' I.e., 'bought off' the premises. This includes a 'house fine' of 350 baht ($8.25) and a separate tip for the youngster currently negotiated at 1,000+ ($25). Go during slow season: prices are better. These curtain calls are the purpose of the preceding entertainment. Caveat emptor: they mayn't stiffen your inadequacy, but affinity: with Harriet Beecher Stowe.

"Man Cock, around the corner, is still in spring training compared with Rex. Its Beer-Dancers, a skinny duo who frig a local brew and squirt the heads in each other's face, might cut their giggling out if they'd coif some first. The unassuming highlight and end to this show is a stoical youth who carries a chair stage center and simply sits down. Then he modestly lowers his jeans to only an inch of thigh, firmly concentrates on his oiled rod, curved to the curve of his belly, and brings a wank to quiet climax. There is more to this than the apparent: every performer I've asked admits the most debasing of his obligations is public masturbating.

"Before you leave Soi 6, peek in at Club Tawan, the uncontested lounge for steroid freaks. Bodies-beautiful sit in a pen apart from the drooling clients; at intervals a L'il Abner gives the crowd a break, peels his posing strap and lazily trips along the catwalk. They are heteros all, haughty to a man, and full of themselves.

"Right now, Bar Space Boys over on Twilight has the naughtiest show in town. It is the most testosterone-rank room I hope ever to inhale. Its house choreographer thinks nothing of lifting from gay Philippine skin flicks—when you enter, a sprig of nude hunks is slouched on a rear bleacher: stroking their consecutive blooms Manila-style. It's something like a circus sideshow; the audience filing in, startled and confronted, tends not to look directly at them. These yankers all have big bushes and bushless perinea—which means, of course, I do. The formal exhibition begins with eight Midnight-Dancers. Midnight Dancing definitely hails from Manila. It's a deliberate and supersinuous roll of the

muscles starting from the abdomen and ramately traveling to the toes and fingertips. The rakishly smiling gyrators have (chemically created?) boners: some interrupt their dance to rub them against the mouths of stageside gawkers. That enticement is followed by a pair of Fire-Eaters in ebony jockstraps who singe their perfectly matching ebony pubes and armpits before making yummy of four alarming torches. Candle-Juggling Ballerinas soon join them and ignite their wicks by plunging the candles in the Fire-Eaters' throats. Then, rather thanklessly, they drip hot wax on the Fire-Eaters and a selected number of hapless gawkers. So the mats and first rows become a bit of a mess: a cleanup squad in jumpsuits rushes on and mops away the stray sparks, solidifying wax, and residue of spittle being dispersed by the hoofers' hoses. When the flames start sputtering for these performers, they're replaced by three ugly drag queens in three different native costumes—native to what disaster areas I couldn't guess. This coy coven's talentless spinning is finally brought to a halt by three gladiators yet more bizarrely attired in assorted and incongruous rhinestoned jackets, embroidered loincloths, leather harnesses, and carved designer boots. Shortly, whether the tall, spread-eagled gladiators remain upright or go horizontal, the smitten femmies lift the gladiators' respective loincloths, slurp up erections, muzzle them with condoms, and deftly insert them into their Vaselined rectums. Then a serious stabbing in triplicate gets underway, in every conceivable posture. Standing on his hands, one Roman pumps upside-down, another doubles his partner over the edge of the platform, and the third cartwheels a queen on his axle and thrusts with his back always to the customers: manfully powerhousing in widening circles and withdrawing with thighs a foot apart so as to give the gapers an unobstructed view of his solid butt and rosy, concentrated grapes. Presently, each gladiator takes hold of a carousel pole and impels his body, unsupported and stiff, with feet in midair, out to a gymnast's full right angle with the pole: and (!) continues his furious pounding. The squad, turned prop-crew, hurries onstage with a pressing bench, pulleys, and swings, squeezing between the screwers so as not to disengage any, or themselves get kicked in the head. They

136

shove the bench under one pair to simply missionary, and hoist the swings for the others to grind on in a gibbon crouch while simultaneously pumping the swings up to a point of return a bare few inches below the rafters. The rubbernecks gasp; and to the accompaniment of accelerating Hot Metal, the squad hauls on more benches—and now chairs, ropes, tackles, and torture racks. The show crescendos with a score of additional ramming couples appearing all over the place, some of them dropping from the ceiling to fill every unoccupied corner of the canvas. The room morphs into a Bosch or Burroughs vision of hell. –Or Politics-and-Purgatory. Or perhaps the actual universe: as we blind suckers previously failed to see it.

"Need a break now? Try the conventional bars, called beer-bars, Soi 4: though, like the 'cool season' here, 'conventional' wants for science. Aside from the wall-to-wall pros and part-timers, brazen as hussies—but then again, they all are—the lechers are half Thai; one-quarter whites; the rest Asian residents, tourists, or salesmen-touching-favorite-base: ageing cruisers hailing anywhere from Borneo to Bangladesh and Yokohama to Mindanao. Most will be glued to the cricket game on two TVs. It's the dangle in the players' sweatpants. The tourists could be anyone. The residents are alcoholic windbags. I call them the Coma People. Know what I mean? There's enough manure in those troughs to fertilize the farms in Mainland China. That's why I feel comfortable there!

"Next go to Adam Garden, an open-till-dawn karaoke. Or the Suriwongse, a decades-old hotel-brothel with twenty-four-hour gay action for the over-seventy set. Camaraderies in its coffee shop enjoy a whiskey-with-prune-juice klatch. Keen-eyed hustlers (and pushers) abound, hoping to give the hots to a soon-to-retire-for-the-night expat or his less blasé visitor. The predators mayn't approach a table of elderlies with whom they are not already acquainted: though some need a light, especially if the greenhorn is alone. The S.O.P. is for the predator to follow the greenhorn into the lobby toilet and call a price—on himself and 90-minute rooms: both high. To save dough, skip the klatch and take a piss ordinaire.

"Lastly, hit Rama IV. At 3:45 a.m. on that main avenue, between Suriwong and Silom, are more streetwalkers than piranha at a feeding frenzy. If you can, find a breach. Tearing from one pedestrian to the next, screaming, 'I go with YOU!', these sharks are easily the most perilous of the sexually employed. They'd as soon slit your pockets and throat as drop their knickers for a last-chance fee."

Simon's article does justice to my adventure. I neglected to say good-bye to Toby York, but fogies his age do not remember things like that.

There was a message from Cory in my box, asking me to come at 10 a.m. I rang his night clerk: said to tell him I had been out drinking and would make it later. Too blitzed to sleep, I googled and Wiki'ed on the PC at Moon for Simon's new hits. I saw, p. 18, a review (d. 2004) of a seller I overlooked: *Clout of Real Iron*. It studies Jesse "The Body" Ventura, the shaved-head former Navy Seal, competitive swimmer, and popular TV wrestler who became the Libertarian Party's governor of Minnesota.

I rethought Cory's build, rodeo days, and buddy-buddy with the gymnasts on Silom and Saladaeng. Were they too, athletes, politically wired?

I got the heebie-jeebies. Tobias York led me through the Triple-X enclave, but that night had Cory Simon written all over its ass.

AT 11 A.M., CORY was not only he-man and wholesome, he was industrious. He took my recorder, mike, and tapes out of my satchel and set them up himself. He said that he amuses older Chinese ladies, like the one near him in a dim sum restaurant, who gargled when he, after stuffing his tummy to the heaving point, dropped an Equal tablet into his coffee. Or the fellow passenger who squealed when he plunged off a bus to retrieve his shades that popped out the window and vaulted back on before the bus pulled away. Yet when it mattered—curse his nemeses—as with his landlady, he chaffed her wrong cheek.

Why was his charm making me uptight? Awful.

"My hemming and hawing to the effect that I already was late for work," he started when he got himself seated, "in my valiant stab at postponing the chat with her brother, proved nil. My hawkish landlady insisted that this wouldn't take that long. In point of irritating fact, it would seem quite the longest time in my life that wouldn't take that long.

"The Police Lieutenant General was a slight man whose single-mindedness bulwarked his frailty. He was maximally insignia'd with braids, rank-medals, and medallions. Any additional dangle, unpropped by his purpose, might well have bent that official into a puzzling position. As he stretched toward me, the better to scrutinize my crusts of aqueous humor, I feared his mouth was intent on reaching my crotch. Even his cap was crunched with status.

"'Mr. Cory! You are *ajaan*, correct?'

"'At *Mahawitialai Mahidon*.'

"'The best medical school in Thailand. Number One!'

"'I'm glad to hear that.'

"'It is a privilege to teach there.'

"'I feel that.'

"'Where do you get these boys?'

"'Uh—what boys?'

"'The boys that come here with you.'

"'They're medical students. I—yes!—give them lessons in Medical English.'

"'After midnight?'

"'Oh. Well, lemme think—they work. Until all hours. It, *jing!* (truly!), is the only time they have.'

"'Khun, where do you get these boys?'

"'Ummm, let's see. Through school. Through contacts… Other pupils recommend English instructors, and then—'

"'Where do you get these boys?'

"'I assume they inquire at the Department of Foreign—'

"'They are not students!!'

"'Uh-huh.'

"'They do not come here for language instruction. Now, Khun, where do you get these boys?'

"I certainly wished he'd change the station. The dew point at sunrise is near peak; I hoped that sopping the downpour from my hairline, which was blinding me, would satisfy his softening-up preamble or gratuitous need to sweat me further. Perhaps it did, for as he went again at the tormenting refrain, 'Khun, where do you get—,' he stopped and tuned to: 'I *know* where you get these boys! In Patpong bars. They are prostitutes.'

"'Really? They don't charge. I—'

"'They are dangerous. You did not know this?'

"'Well, no, I didn't.'

"'They may murder you!'

"'Heavens.'

"'And you are endangering the tenants who live in these houses when you bring such prostitutes home.'

"'I am sorry for that. I really didn't know.'

"'If it was one boy, all right. The same boy. That is all right. But you have many, many.'

"To this tasteless hyperbole, my temperature going over the top and surely rendering my visage rubicund, I had no rejoinder. So he got to the matter: 'Where is that one boy you had? A brown person. The mountain-dweller. Where is he now? Why are there others? Why does he *let* you have others? Listen: a royal secretary came here. Yes, yes, I know he found you. But he returned and did not speak to my sister. He searched your unit. We cannot have that here. Our domestic offered assistance. He wanted to know if the Lue tribe man lived here. She said he did not. His name is Chain. Do you remember him? Why does he not come back and tell those others to keep away? That is why I am worried for you. Without him, you will be murdered here. Do you comprehend me, Ajaan Cory?'

"I did, indeed. This accounted for the doors opening and shutting at 2:30 a.m. the night before. And Nok's coarse fanfare: he was making good on whatever summitry he'd delivered to my landlady prior to that. Was there no limit to the number of persons Nok would address to undo Chain—and me?

"Then, absolutely having to, I said something which I'd never said to anyone before, much less the police, it's expediency notwithstanding: "'Please, sir, please stop, this is very embarrassing for me. I understand what you are saying. I promise you *no* one will come here anymore. I thank you for your warning. I apologize if I have frightened my neighbors. Please accept my apology. And assist, if you would, in begging your sister to forgive me.'

"The policeman's admonishment taken (in spades), and I too down from my loft, he judged I'd copacetically eaten all of the crow for which I'd stomach. You might say I flew as if shot from a rusted cannon—to work.

"My mind sizzled during my four indistinct classes. I couldn't concentrate on—what was it? The sperm duct? the colon? Chain is *wanted* now! What's their problem? He's in a gay bar every night. –Marty must fork up insurance on him… Chain's never worried: about jail. And that cop's z-bend! Is Marty in *this* veneer, holding Chain's love life uppermost? If not a veneer, quite a reversal! Still, Chain *would* be uppermost in solving my setback: the out in my outing.

"—Moral turpitude, man! Can you fathom that? A stratagem stressing moral turpitude! Men come here to stretch a point: so what battening could lie in scuttling that release? Not bring back anyone I cared to?! Ridiculous beyond response. Except it required swift response.

"The lunch-bell bonged and I guzzled the gas to a hall phone. I rang Chain on the assumption he'd be asleep on Soi 36 and was right. I told him to go to Café de Paris and the time I'd need to taxi there. I'd skip A.U.A. I had eluded him for what seemed months. I actually lost count. As His Vigilance despaired, we were unofficially separated. So my call jolted the insulated one, as did the urgency in my voice. That he both picked up that urgency and was disturbed by my choice of locale to discuss it was obvious in his demeanor when he entered the café, where I had arrived ten minutes early and was all nerves.

"What happened next demands detail in order to unravel its consequence. Exact memory is defeated by its convoluted permutations. For starters, Chain wasn't sure he could handle whatever I'd tell him if it had challenges, as he figured it did, surpassing anything in our relationship up till then. In the contest to communicate with him there, I found the first to be his limited English.

"To a calculating degree, he may have simulated incomplete concord—or he may not—but I'm getting ahead of myself.

"He ordered an orange juice and composed his trembling with his elbows on the table and hands locked as the remiss do at emergency business conferences; then took in the blackboard where the plats du jour were chalked in French and, as uneasily, the etchings of the Louvre, Notre Dame, and Sacré Coeur over my head. I retailed my dawn ordeal and the allegation, to all purpose, of adultery. Chain had the reserve not to lay into me here. He did agree about the danger I courted—though I thought he'd little idea of just how and how much. I said my blunder at the Phayathai pad was in leasing it for a single resident. This was why the owners could take legitimate umbrage at an overnight guest. Therefore, my objective was a new flat where frowning at visitors was obviated: by signing up for double occupancy. Did he know of any such? Would he join me now in search of one? And would he help me out by cosigning a lease?

"It is here that Chain may have had genuine trouble in following me. Bear in mind also there's a loss of face in admitting that you don't understand what someone is telling you. To him the proprietors of my current rooms were petit bourgeois reaching for their notion of nouveau prudery. Hence my need for dual residency most anyplace else may have made no sense to him, despite the several ways I phrased that need in the pidgin we had commonly tailored. I'd previously articulated a desire to move to or near Patpong because I wished to live in that gay ghetto and avoid the bottlenecks traveling there. Throw in that I was resigned to deal with its long commute to work as a separate issue. I'll allow that this sentiment may have sounded like I simply preferred Patpong's energy and Silom's atmosphere to the mind-dead ambience of Phayathai-Sri Ayutthaya. As opposed, that is, to anticipating healthy traffic through its unpatrolled turnstiles. I'd been, after all, accused of conjugal laxity. Chain suggested the very area in which we sat, Silom being a district where sleeping-over is essential to commerce. I, hearing this, believed he was conceding as salutary a flat where pickups could be brought with impunity.

"Chain struggled for a while, and smoothed the immaculate tablecloth. Occasionally angst-ridden, he'd look up and around at the small, homey dining room: and, catching himself, return and rebury his focus on my face. He parted his lips when I mentioned the messenger, then winced and slowly closed them—as is obvious, now—wanting to inhibit his distillation.

"At last he inched forward and hushed mellifluously, 'I think is Buddha.'

"'Buddha?' I asked.

"'Buddha you.'

"'The statue?' I saw it as sharply as had it been dropped between us: more remindful of Brancusi's *Bird in Space* than any object of worship: the tangible vacuum alongside, and created by, the gliding from its haunches toward the narrowest waist; and then that continuous emptiness like a boomerang soaring of a sudden broadly out to the armpits, implicitly upward forever. It belonged to no particular period of classical Thai sculpture, with their constricted dictates, nor was it a meld or selection from a number of these. It was a harmony wholly original and unique, a single and individual artist's concept, his very personality and self-styled tools present. It was not without a touch of idolatry.

"'My statue?' I chorused. 'What has *it* to do with what I tell?'

"The idolatrous gleam was in his eye. 'Never mind,' he said quietly.

"Finally Chain raised his chin like resistance-conspirators when they've settled a dreadful option. He stood and pushed in his chair, his burnt persimmon hand lingering on the top cane of its backrest. For an instant more he was stationary. He throated, 'And Ekarin, Kambu-ja, and Nok?' (Bad news travels fast.)

"'Little family thing. Won't necessarily be seeing *those* boys again.'

"He suddenly convulsed, flinging—to my astonishment—at a beach beyond hope his weary and indeterminate obsidians. He as suddenly recovered, and said: "'Come, I show place.'

"We crossed Silom Road to Soi Convent, a long street joining Silom and smazy Sathorn Road. The postnothing architectural monstrosities of North and South Sathorn are divided by a concrete-suffocated, perfectly linear, dengue-fever klong. A flyover took us to the south side and a short walk to a gray, double-for-a-factory, five-story eyesore whose corroded shingle identified it as a lodge: insinuatingly called, The Aphrodite.

"But in '82, the Aphrodite had a poor-man's poetry you could cut with a knife. You passed through the whore-congested coffee shop fronting the street to the ebony, always busy registration desk in an oil-painting and woodcut-hung, heavily shadowed hall that led to an enclosed inner court, monopolized by a deep and sun-splashed swimming pool. The court's walls were painted with maladroit murals depicting Siamese nature scenes, notably its howling gibbons, still-feared tigers, and secretive rhinos pointedly interspersed with cryptozoological Garudas (Vishnu's mount, a birdman, with wings underside his arms, a barbell-lifter's belt, and clawed, otherwise-human legs yawned quite as widely as still believable); and, to be sure, a semblance of the Aphrodite of Milo with her shapely upper limbs and lovely head reimagined. On the court's near walk a ten-foot glass parallelogram riant with live tropical fowl and pigmy trees created a delicate highland see-thru of the blue water and surrounding rooms. We were shown to one two-thirds along the left side of the pool. I peered in, got the impression of a sparse and spacious, high-ceiling teakwood square with an enormous brick-glass oculus facing the court, and told Chain I'd take it.

"We backtracked to the check-in desk to Hancock the registration book; and leave a three-month deposit. I tallied the next day to pack up and provide, even with mishaps, enough time to move—and this is where an unexpected tug-of-war held crucial sway. I again had tremendous difficulty getting Chain to understand, or not resist, what I wanted him to do: namely, cosign the lease. He stalled. With trapped perplexity and renewed misgivings, he weighed my frown: and Sue Ugly's, the omniscient receptionist's (so called for her fright makeup and Gorgon perms).

144

Touching my finger, he prevailed, 'This place have people can come.'

"I pushed the lease at him. 'Sign it! Chain, please!—you not understand?'

"He pouted. Then drew me into the dark and whispered, desperately, 'Here have *gahlee* many, have people-two can!'

"'But want sure,' I insisted, 'not want trouble same-same Phayathai. Sign two. You, me. So can come two, sure.'

"I seized his right hand, walked him back, and skewered the desk pen into it. I pointed to the lines for renters' signatures. He pulled on the pen's bead-link, apparently startled by it, appraised the knowing Gorgon for a last time—she was staring him down, arch, annoyed, and scratchy—and signed.

"He exhaled deeply, sneered with superiority, waited for me to leave the deposit, then marched briskly, his nostrils up and worked, out onto Sathorn. The sun, in sinking, was diamonding the garbage-cluttered klong.

"That night I informed the Lieutenant's sibling of my impending evacuation. Asking to settle my phone, water, and electric bill, I naïvely hoped the harridan wouldn't indicate that I was overreacting. She didn't: imparted no pleasure or displeasure, surprise, relief, or regret. My quick exit was simplifying her life.

"All my belongings fit into my original suitcases. I had asked Chain to show at my new digs at six the next evening. Possessions in hand, I quit Phayathai and was waiting for him in the Aphrodite's corridor at five forty-five: between oils of Buddha taming the elephant, Nalagiri, and Buddha meditating on the Naga. These images are front contenders for duality. No one can know if a particular elephant can be permanently subdued, or a Naga not use its fangs and coils to kill. I contemplated that and wondered why I didn't go on into the room myself, somehow obstructed until Chain arrived.

"There, fractured in the sunset glare—I couldn't see him fully at first—much less comprehend what I saw—was Chain: not come in programmatic expediency, but contorted under crushing impediment as he fought the coffee shop's heavy doors. Positively beaming, he had five or six valises in tow and freshly ironed shirts and trousers on hangers slung over both shoulders, since his arms were busy with laced footwear, a scramble of neckties, and, had they been packed, four drawers of breakable odds and ends.

"This took me a good minute to grasp. I do believe the man to have had his entire effects about him. How to express my defeat? My anger and outrage? Sue Ugly, the manager, and assorted employees were in earshot. So I suppressed my reaction, and a coupla hauls from the desk to the domicile sufficed for our affairs, that political powerhouse's decidedly the more prodigal.

"Pressing it back into service at once, Chain set my statue on top of a small security vault, a strong room in miniature built into the wall between the studio and toilet: it afforded the highest perch. With smug routine, he hung his sartorial wardrobe in the dark armoire; and situated tiny, animistic amulets or reed containers here and there. –Randolph Wetzel's—*supposedly* Randolph's—glazed gem box: that got special attention, centrally honored on one of the two brick tables holding the bed in place. Finished, he nonchalantly announced he had to see some relative (which word was always relative), occupying him for the remainder of the day, but would be back about midnight to christen the mattress with me. Soon as he left, I fell across that new six-foot battlefield, not knowing whether to pound it to pieces or throw in the (Thai) towel.

"–That basilisk! Inverting my very strategy, he'd tried to craft a 180-degree turnabout! Consider it: my relocation included betraying him to the sigmoid, dawn, morn, midday, eve, and into the witching hours—and he, this *manipulator*, had just taken that proctological pipe and snaked it up my own fanny. Why, he could now each and every night, if he wished, bunk right here, a eunuch in a harem of estrus! He'd not so much flipped me the bird as flipped it over on me.

"–Well, for now.

"Because for the *now*, I'd noticed among his effects, a stack of—"

146

I sat closer to Cory, and said, "Wait... for just a second. Before you go on, I want to record anything else you make of Chain's maneuver."

"Oh, boy! ...The Aphrodite was a budget-traveler, typically Thai-tolerant, and streetwalkers' residence. The lease perplexed him. When two guys, especially a mixed couple, cosign a lease, they are declaring they are lovers. A marriage, like hundreds of thousands of straight ones here: without state or holy seal. A gay partnership has similar moral expectations and legal consequences that community pressure and the law may enforce. At first, it *currently* seems, in his push and pull, he believed I'd not known that double signing was extraneous for simple cohabitation: in calling on him, I *was* surrendering to cohabitation. He concluded *he* had not understood—that I, in fact, had all along been demanding that he become my common-law lover. If I put myself in his shoes now, this publishing, in writing, of our moving in together was as open a neighborhood newsletter as a Thai could circulate."

I said, "Cory, I don't buy his resistance. Or concern. What could sleeping around mean to him? He indulged in hooking."

"Utilitarian to his ambition... In being pragmatic, he saw no infidelity. But my job was teaching. Thai males find cheating their prerogative. A Westerner has no such entitlement. Therein his concern."

"You swallowed this?"

"No! It mortifies my sense of justice. Do *you* entertain hemispheric molds?"

"So what, exactly, was Chain up to?"

"Well, not up to, there. Accepting as par for the pact."

"And that's?"

"A given in the giving of face: which of course public bonding *is*. So inherent—once our relationship was shared knowledge with all of Sathorn, Patpong, and Silom—was that afterward, I'd not dare do something to cause him to lose any. This was an understood. To Thais. To Chain. To Sue. Unfortunately, not to me."

"Explain."

"*I* saw his moving in as a punt to create escape-hatch headaches, not a victory that would stop me from behaving as I pleased. Hell, no. –*Au contraire, he* now could be forced to tether and squirm—to smell the rears of men in my pubes, their semen on my fingers, their saliva in my beard."

He played with his ring. I gave him a minute or two here, and said: "Cory, why don't you just tell yourself the truth?"

He was watching a flutter outside the casements. He reached for his teacup. A loose stitch on a shirt button caught his wristwatch and restricted his hand. He recorded: "Thais won't snap an errant thread. They'd be cutting their own or a stranger's lifeline."

He broke the thread and rushed at the window where he hung his broom. A pair of sparrows was plucking its straws. He opened the window, shooed them away, and took the broom inside. "Nest-building season," he frowned. "I forgot that. Those *nok–a-jawk* can carry off a whole broom, piecemeal. Brooms too are bad luck: like feet, they deal with the floor."

Then, tightening its weave, he went to the mike, grabbed it, and proclaimed in a brittle voice: "Chain's care was *thrust* on me!"

"There was a compact," I said.

"It was never mine to make."

"Nor his. –And, so, the truth?"

He sat down. He gulped. "Truth? ...You *will* wrestle with me for possession of this story, won't you? –Hustlers turn men against themselves. Some feel they can't, or needn't, relate decently to hustlers: either considerately or responsibly. Yet certain hustlers may sell application. That commodity is not without value. A friend of mine was a class editor, magazine layout man, and fashion designer: he installed mixed-media shows. Today he's the curator for a Charlottesville museum. He told me he'd once been a part-time callboy. He claimed, 'As I understood it, the money—that I desperately needed then—meant that I go out the same way I came in.' Which he did: discreetly and, as time has proven, with his character and talent intact. There are a few like that...

"Yes, I did want Chain to move in with me. I believe he had

148

to. Of course he had to." Cory peeled a matchstick here. "And I had to live with him. So many knew that, the corrupted and the renunciates: Rollo, Olie, Marty, Kambu-ja, the princess, her investigator, and the hunter: the hermit who hunted. I have a recurrent nightmare of running from crowded room to room and not recognizing anyone in them."

I said, "I predict you won't have that nightmare anymore."

"Good at predicting, huh? *Several* men in my story thought they were…"

"Outstanding! Long as you don't make your mandate come off as chicanery. –You noticed a stack—of what?"

"Embossed business cards." Cory stood the broom like a spear at the edge of the couch. "On my return from a solitary dinner that evening, I had bought a *Bangkok Post*, and I set it on the left bed table while I stripped to my jockeys. In compliance with city law, our thermostat was fixed not to drop the temperature ten degrees lower than whatever it was outdoors. So even near nude I had to stay as still as possible or sweat profusely. I sat on the bed, and when I lifted the paper it pulled the top contact, adhering to it, off a pile of Chain's neatly stacked business cards and slipped it into my lap. I picked it up and read its information in French. It gave two addresses for a Woo Chun-hao: one in Paris and one in Phae Meuang Phil, or Ghost-Land, a remote geological phenomenon in Phrae, the northwest province partly wedged between Phayao and Nan. I heard a key juggling the lock, stuffed the card in my jockeys, and grabbed the *Post*.

"Chain entered with a broad smile and called out, 'What you do?'

"'Read newspaper.'

"His smile soured. He stepped over to me, took the *Post* and, as if it were on sprockets, rotated that semi-rag a full half circle. It's the sort of thing that happens only in Hollywood B's and life: I was holding it upside down. He walked to the wide three-quarter mirror separating the bed and security box and began vigorously brushing his hair. When I glanced at the front-page heads, the first item I saw was *Ghost Busters Catch Entrail-Eating Spooks*—in the vicinity of Phae Meuang Phil! The ghoulies in question, *pii-paub*, feed on raw human inners. Locals were blaming a spate of mysterious disembowelments on the Ghost-Land spirits that had lived in the eroded pillars of rock and soil recently displaced by preliminary diggings for a dam up there. Forty-nine ghosts had been caught, nineteen proving strong-willed *pii-paub*, the rest minor types and strays. All were to be cremated in an elaborate ceremony in four days' time.

"I thought carefully: and then said, 'Important *pii-paub* cremation in province of Phrae. On weekend.'

"'Know this!' Chain stomped with revealing intolerance. He scanned the evocative swirls in our wall paneling. The spirit, Mah Seekai, housing in the tree from which it was made, would travel with it; and, alongside us, be conceivably less pleased than the free-roaming and poisonous jack-o'-lantern indoors.

"Ignoring that, I tentatively tempted, 'Can take pictures... You want go?'

"'This for people stupid, have no school. I not go.'

"'Then let me take picture here,' I adjusted, reaching for our flash camera, and hoping my request sounded offhand. 'For good luck in new home.'

"He ploughed a wayward cowlick, turned smartly about, and offered a choice of poses: straight-on with forearms folded; reflective near-profiles; and the finger-locked ape-crouch down to his popped, contracted thighs. Not exactly a novice at this, I mused, framing and clicking each pose. In fact so far from a novice that he could sufficiently split his concentration and affirm his adversarial potency by noting, 'Have something wait in underwear now beside *cooay*?'

"I headed for Rollo Y-z's the next afternoon, intending, more emphatically, to extend the trip to Phrae to him. He was behind a *Bangkok Post*—the decoy of preference that week—and before I could, threw Section A at me.

"'Savor the center of page 8,' he chuckled.

"A banner there read, *White Monk Cited in Taxi Stickups*.

"The article drooled over a rash of robberies in the past few months. Cabbies reported the criminal fare a fortyish white in holy robes, fluent in Thai, with a half centimeter of orange hair and slit-pupil, green snake eyes. 'He's sunk that low!' Y-z editorialized. 'A common stickup artist. And if the drivers look back when he pulls the pistol, they'll see his stick *is* up!'

"He gargled like a hyena—a Richard Widmark chortle he loved to echo. Y-z bore no small resemblance to Widmark, who rocketed to fame in *Kiss of Death* when he strapped his opponent's elderly mother into her wheelchair, rolled it to a steep staircase, and, quaking with that now-famous sadistic cackle, his eyes an ecstatic white, pushed the invalid, bouncing from step to step, down to her death at the landing. –Y. could do that moment, do it toothsomely.

"While he did, I reworked Olie's 'heartfelt freebee.' Had *its* snatch been as showy a holdup? Every three days Chain encircled that icon with a garland of jasmine buds. The new flat would be off-limits too without unwilted propitiation. I related all this to Rollo. He lit a Krong Thip and wheezed, 'I don't know that you *can* propitiate an iffy legacy, "a ring of passkeys"—from a crud sexually aroused by crime.' A tense theory: offered by a culprit whose crimes, past and present, were themselves sexual. He went on to relish, 'Therefore your new room in the Afro is, doubtless, replete with *pii*. The vicious kind.'

"'I'm sure it is. However, it's not the *pii* in my room I've come to discuss but the forty-nine feasting in Phrae on people's alimentary canals.' At the risk that Rol reprise, self-reflexively, his Widmark hoot, I acquainted him with the slated exorcism and Chain's crepuscular fate-baiting: his smuggling double-cross, dangerous displacement of Nok, PRC fund-running for Pol Pot, Woo's dual address, its link to the PRC's probing—and murders—at the nominated dam site. Reprise it self-reflexively Rol did: laughed so hard he had to dry his tears. He choked out on, 'Lie down with an Asian Mata Hari and I'll be lucky to wake up at all...'

"Then he folded the *Post*, sadly left his Barcelona, and went to stare into the field beyond his kitchen window. He counted its sundrops and marigolds. After a time, he asked, all too painfully, 'What would you like me to do?'

"'Come with me to Phrae. You speak whichever dialects they speak there. I want to know more about Chain.' Rollo brightened. 'These murders will interest your lover, Vichai, as well. He's based nearby. Could be a scoop for him.'

"'Vichai may learn something. I'll call him. But his Thai venues won't cover an insurgent struggle…' He took a dust-cloth, spat on the window, and polished it for eleven minutes with disconcerting elbow grease. He said, 'There, sparkling! Don't feature an obstructed view, myself.

"'When do you want to go?'

"A stout young woman in a multicolored paasin that brushed the jumble of anklets on her bare feet was shoveling the coals in a portable barbecue pit just outside the settlement closest to Phae Meuang Phil. Holding my hand in his, Rollo assessed the woman and her operation with his customary speed. Her flattened, rubbery cuttlefish on bamboo spits resembled twelve-inch manta rays.

"'Good,' he observed as we closed in, 'breakfast isn't quite cooked: she hasn't made her first sale yet. When we reach her, flash your famous pearlies. Flirt a little. Tell her you want *plaa meuk, see aan* (four), give her a ten-baht note, and refuse change. Watch what she does. Approve. Then take a stroll.'

"I obeyed his instructions and was rewarded by her shy, indrawn lips. She handled the tan bill with the respect one accords to a reverential emissary, touched each fish with it, passed it quickly through the uppermost flames, and hooked it to a ribbonned nail crowning a cooling-rack next to the blackened tank.

"I wandered over to what seemed to be more than a thousand people and still coming, gathering around and making way for a ledge-browed, well-fed monk and his entourage. From there I could see Rol chatting it up with the young vendor; and, affecting absentmindedness, periodically gazing toward the crowd. He took the four devilfish and chewed into one while rubbing his stomach, for all the world as if he'd never experienced such ambrosia. He continued to chat and apparently quip while I endured the cynomolgus monk's monotonous rant.

"After a small eternity, Rollo brought me the remnants of our breakfast and said, 'That character is Phra Khru Kittisak something-or-other, a veteran exorcist. This ritual's staked by a village emergency fund. He's the balls to ask for further donations and encouraging the faithful to lap up Khom-inscripted amulets at a while-they-last 15 baht. Royal Grounds Security is creaming for a man of Chain's description. Vichai had that tidbit relayed personally to the cuttlefish girl.'

"'Do we—' I started.

"'No, we don't. Phra Veteran Exorcist is not who I want.'

"We stood by for what felt like an additional hour while the press trampled itself to purchase the talismans. Then a new entourage came into the clearing, one quite differently attired, in wide-hemmed paakamas, with magenta or acid green sashes draped over brocaded waistcoats. Teams of well-barreled buffalo and rib-visible Brahmin cows augmented it, along with lines of black bobtail cats with identical white bibs, white paws, and caracal ears. Swineherds with their charges pranced lightly at the rear. The foremost marchers bore cradles of corpses whose midsections were covered with sheets; centermost, two strong men supported a small person of great age. For the moment, the crowd turned and simply stared at them.

"'Ah-hah!' Rollo cried. 'Our opium doctor! We could be in business. Let me see your photos.'

"He flipped through the portraits I'd taken of Chain at the Aphrodite. 'This one: where he's cogitating—looks right. He may've been doing a lot of that here.'

"The pallbearers laid the bodies in a row, then stood in formation behind the opium doctor. The hunched doctor began to chant and move amongst the dead, stopping by each to pull away its coverlet. The crowd left the Phra in droves and came to mill about the ancient, frightening the animals, which fell into safer bunches and nervously stomped their hooves. Y-z opened his purse and carefully withdrew a necklace of bones and bone chips. 'Here,' he said, 'hook this around my neck. Wait, she is going to speak... –She's telling them that this is what remains of the farmhands and fishermen whose barricade prevented the

diggers from destroying the last soil pillars at the dam site…
The dam will flood the riverside farms and block the fish from
coming to spawn… Our collective future is starvation.'

"Rol's charm-string had a steel crook at one end and receiv-
ing catch at the other. I lifted his straight yellow hair and fastened the accessory on the pale of his neck. The long teeth and
wide dice varied in integrity and boasted few familiar shapes.
All were bleached, and some had dents or deep cracks. 'She's
repeating, ad infinitum, that Ghost-Land's spirits protect the
Chao Phya basin. The farmers were murdered by the military—
and disemboweled, to blame the dwellers in an adjacent world.
But the guilty dwell in this. It's like a refrain.'

"I asked him, 'Can a tribeswoman be an opium doctor?'

"'Tribeswomen, no. Grandmas, yes. Even the army won't
harm an old healer. Especially an activist. Healing cuts both
ways, you know. In a flash, they could look worse than those
farmers.'

"I said, 'I want to see how they look.'

"He held my wrist. He was furious. 'You don't have to see
anything now!'

"'I do.'

"I walked across the stretch of broken earth. When I reached
the mountain people guarding the mutilated, the grievers nearest made way for me. And I entered, at once hypnopompic, not
a display of the eviscerated but a blast of vaulting forms, marble
in their polish, that pulled each other in fractious triplicate and
rivaling inter-struggle toward a surface maniacally deferred.
Ellipsoids, bloated moppets, and boomerang-shapes engulfed
me, their mandibles snapping in frustration. I went with them,
pitched into a swirl wind flapping and smacking my flanks:
the wonderfully animated and ambiguous buoyancy of soaring
pat—both helplessly hoisted and standing in place. The grievers'
chanting was the tendons in my throat, taking the bicker and
quibble of time to a determination.

"I felt a nick, moist with mucous and tickling with bristle,
on either elbow. When I twisted about, two Brahmin, viscously
testing my substance, backed off. Rollo appeared between them

154

and delivered a foul: '*Whatever* wets the pussy?'

"'The wet you see,' I said drying my elbows on my shirttail, 'is their nostrils. Where's your sense of reality?'

"'Or neutrality?' he clicked with mock self-reproof. 'The chant is finished. The protestors are settling down. They won't demonstrate again for a while. We can talk to her now. –Don't look at them anymore!'

"'They are only a thousand dolls,' I said.

"'What?'

"'The éminences grises. Nothing to be scared of, Rol.'

"'Ever hear of a brain transplant?'

"We genuflected, bowing beneath eye-level of the opium doctor, and Rollo leaned forward so that his necklace swung free within reach of her. She reached for it and handled the bones. Swaying a bit, she snorted with satisfaction. Rollo gave her the photograph he'd selected. She squinted at it, her wrinkled lids revealing the rapid movement under them. A moment later, she spoke in a low, measured tone and Y. translated for me in an even softer register:

"'Who is a farang to ask after one of us?'

"'Tell her that the Greeks and Romans have been in the harbors of Siam since the first century,' I instructed Rollo. He did. She topped that with:

"'Why does the farang puff out his chest at me? We have been here for eight millennia!' She cackled—the hollowest of sounds—at her own alacrity; but then went on without reflection and almost in a single breath, 'The man in the image is a go-between for local officials, who illegally transfer land deed titles, and PRC encroachers. Song District will compensate owners of the *rai* (acreage) it confiscates to make room for the dam. But tracts it judges... public, will be under the retainer... of investors. ...The man in the image... is the moon-burst (I think) of... the loveliness he uses to ease (she actually said, lubricate) the negotiations. They call him Chain. He is a malignant force.'

"'I hope I got that right,' Rollo added, 'but I want to ask her something else. I thought the Chinese here were Kuomintang refugees. If she's certain the buyers represent Beijing, that "moon-burst" may be nudging the three of us into the head-lights of history. Nice work if you can get it,' he ended bitterly.

"The opium doctor and he went through a number of quick exchanges. Then he removed his necklace and gave it to her, *wai*ing with his face and hands to the ground. She received the gift with a sustained steepling of her fingers. Rollo got up and said, 'Let's go.'

"As we shot away, I had trouble matching his pace. Once out of hearing, he ruefully muttered, 'If we look alive we'll snag the next bus to Bangkok. It leaves in sixteen minutes. She knows who Vichai is. And me. She's hoping he'll pick up the story. I doubt that myself. I don't doubt that's what motivated her to tell all. She's positive the current land-deed holders are People's Republic of China, not the Kuomintang—however shifty and opportunistic the latter always are. Yet she still may be failing to see the larger picture here.'

"'Of Red land-grabbing in Thailand?' I suggested.

"'God! Why did I have to find this out?'

"Suddenly a skirl went off, as loud as thunder, and the firing of pistols. The gathering, en masse, started running toward us. In mere moments we were in the center of a riot, with those in front streaming past us, people flaying arms or tightening their fists at waist and hipline, bundles being dropped and children dragged or flung upon shoulders. A mournful shrieking came from the field. 'What's hap—' I started to ask.

"'The special operations police and anti-riot squad,' Rollo shouted, peering back at their uniform-armholes looped with double braids. 'They're arresting the grandstanders first. Wouldn't do for *us* to get caught in the roundup. Everyone here is headed for the depot. –Quick!'

"He yanked me to the right down an overgrown path that ended abruptly at a stone ruin, built in the Lan Na period. There was an incomplete gantry and lintel with delicate Hindu figures over an entrance, and a largely crumbling wall surrounding the floor (that we couldn't see) of a medium-size sacrifice room. The roof was gone, of course, but raised altars and a gray limestone lingam remained. 'We might hide here till they stop chasing

156

people,' Rol nervously said. He listened for a second, stepped up quietly on a heap of horizontal scaffolding, and held one eye to a break in the wall. 'Oops, I don't think so,' he whispered.

"'Why? What's the matter?'

"'Get a gander in there.'

"I climbed onto the wood and put my eye where his had been. Nearest in sight was a handful of MPs patrolling scores of handcuffed young men: who carpeted the sacrifice area, all face down in its trampled grass. They were shoeless and shirtless, with the handcuffs set in their coccyges, not an inch to spare between their parallel bodies. Except for being belly down and having no disclosed internal organs, they excitedly recalled the assembled cadavers. At the far periphery, the police were stripping and searching newly arrived young men: to discover, variously, saws, hatchets, slingshots, ping-pong bombs, pine bats, and blunt knives. These they identified with tags and were throwing in a heap; escorting their owners to a point in the carpet: shoving those there aside, and laying batons on the newcomers' bare backs, doubling them over until they prized a spot amongst the luckless demonstrators who preceded them.

"Y-z tweaked my sleeve: deciding (for me), 'That picnic's full. Let's skiddoo. I spotted a road where we can grab us a *sawng thaew* (two-bench truck) to the train. A motorcade will commandeer the buses for Black Marias. ...Have you seen enough? Or do you fancy billet in this bachelor's party?'

"'Lotta skin,' I said.

"'*Tell* me.'

"When I turned to follow Y., we had to push through the fleeing who were now headed to the ruin, as yet unaware of its trap. That's when I sorted him out: Chain—in a conical rice-paddy hat pulled improbably low over his brow and an indigo-dyed farmer's shirt with bowstrings rather than buttons and buttonholes. Loose blue pajama-pants reaching to his calves and an unconvincing mustache completed his disguise. His wild stare locked on mine with *un*disguised anguish for the briefest of polemics; then he darted sidewise, his floating plaits a close match in color to the shirt and pants, enabling him to meld with the rest of the

157

longhaired runners and be thoroughly hidden.

"I saw no reason then to tell Rol that Chain had tailed me. True, he may've had squalor to dispatch in this Ghost-Land event; but given his renown with the mountain folk, he could not have relied on exhibiting his (superficially concealed) museum-quality assets that day to do much to keep them intact.

"Perhaps he'd tailed *us*. For what would I have learned alone? Was Rollo's becoming advised of his hijinks there what worried him? Rollo and Vichai?

"We crouched, climbed through a hill of thickets, snapping thorns and breaking rotted branches along the way, and came out onto a part dirt, part paved road. In time, a few buffalo carts clopped by. Near you, these are splendid beasts, glassy of hide, their horns like Viking helmets; and unbelievably enormous. Rollo breathed, 'Now we stew. Quiet, isn't it? Who'd guess we're in trekking range of a mass arrest. Wonder how many were seriously hurt. Or shot.'

"'Shot?'

"'They'll probably disembowel them, too.'

"Rollo could not have known that I knew what he was sitting on. Hadn't I watched his boss, Martin, ostentatiously bestow that necklace of chips on Chain—on Harrie's mezzanine? Rol had *said* that Chain brought him a gift when he visited unannounced, determined to urge Rol to reconcile himself and me… This necklace was a prod as maverick as my Buddha.

"I asked, 'Why do the palace police have trouble nabbing Chain? He *lives* in Harrie's and Lome. Must be big baht there, and here, shielding him.'

"'How astute!' Rollo withered. 'A laced cigarette?' He tossed one to me and lit his own, forgetting mine. I watched him puff.

"I complained: 'And why do *you* think *I* am the Devil in the—'

"'Springtime? You ever wanna say you're not, wait till I get earplugs.'

"Irked, I pushed it, 'What adorns the necklace you gave the old shaman?'

"'Dinosaur bones.'

"I gasped. '*Dinosaur* bones?'

158

"'Animists and Buddhists don't believe in dinosaurs. The reconstructions in Jurassic halls are a Western hoax. But she knows what they are—and how much they're worth. I hope she uses their cash-in to further her cause.' He quashed his half-smoked joint in the gravel. 'Hope for your sake. *And* Chain's.'

"I stammered, 'But the value… they must be worth—I can't imagine what they're worth! A small fortune. Why did you give them to her?'

"Rollo's skin literally prickled. 'Cordie, this is important for you.'

"Forty minutes into the ride south in the belching truck, on jammed and splintered sidelong benches screwed into its hold, I remained dumbfounded. Were those bones unearthed in the diggings at Phae Meuang Phil? Had Rollo's battle to keep caring really turned up a purpose—in me? Squashed next to me, his breathing had become regular; his lids almost shut, he allowed himself to bump easily with the road.

"I abruptly shook him. 'But—' I began.

"'I was only giving them back,' he said.

"In the city, I lost a fast clash with Chain—over what I, or we both, now knew: he wasn't there for thirteen days. I lived with the chance that his tradecraft had so badly slipped, he'd been netted in Phrae by the royal or military police; and became insomniac. I went sleepless, except for an hour on the third day, before wandering dazed into his research lab to seek Mick Beale's counsel. Fractionally hypochondriac, Mick Beale furnished the names of a European general practitioner and an Asian chiropractor. 'Don't be cheap,' that cheapskate urged, 'try both.'

"A flaccid-waist and bag-bellied nurse with stains on her uniform opened the door to the practitioner's double-duty office and operating theatre—in effect, an alkie's trough. He was sixty and had the alcoholic's proverbial spidered nose.

"'I wish you bring me different disorder,' he sighed. His accent made guessing his nationality impossible. It had no regional origin. It was an earache unconsciously concocted from years of speaking a deliberately broken and highly enounced, imbecilic English so as to be understood by sickies whose native tongue is never English. An expatriate is a person who speaks two languages poorly; expatriates who develop this no-man's mangle save their own are linguistically ludicrous altogether. It is useless to call: they've no conception of—and can't hear— what you're referring to. He closed: 'No ill harder to treat. Pills not do. You are insomnic because you are unhappy. And I cannot make you happy.'

"So on to spinal manipulation. A sign near Samsen Junction, back then a forlorn suburb, read: *Chiropractic: Japanese Massage*. Japanese? Would he come from behind and slam me upside the cranium with a Taiko cane?

"Actually, Manipulator Hitoshi Kimura's therapy was crass. It wasn't a torso adjustment in that melting uncooled house, it was a nerve-massage, tracing an invariable route from temple to toe and taking exactly thirty-seven minutes at every appointment. Hitoshi would place a white handkerchief on the area he intended to pressure; and, very delicately, apply his fingertips. Soft-chinned and shadowy, he'd ask me to strip before mounting his padded table. Thereinafter, if I'd be so kind as to dispatch my huggies as well, and just pull on the freshly bleached Jacuzzisock he provided. 'Good,' he'd encourage as I'd lower my heat-plummeted and oscillating eggs into that loose fit, where one or the other dropped out when he'd tell me to switch to a different side or roll and bend my knee. I'd flinch at the lapses in which his knuckles lightly smudged either testis or a ridge of alerted follicles—but supposed this scarf-like getup had ritualistic significance or was operatively essential to his procedure.

"A stuck-at-half-open louver between his waiting lounge and treatment parlor allowed me to watch Hitoshi work on clients ahead of me. I saw that no matter the problem, the cure was that nerve-massage. And that Hitoshi Kimura's other patients, all of them Asian, never removed their clothes. He'd administer through whatever they happened to be wearing, as U.S. chiropractors do.

"During this wakeful period, I spent my drowsy evenings smoking stick with Khun Apirak. Khun Apirak, who read and wrote in several languages, was Chain's father-substitute. He afforded his hovel in a Chinatown alley by translating, and answering with multiple pleas for money, johns' letters to anxious prostitutes. Apirak was wispy-haired, dry-humored, very wide of mouth, and genuinely good-natured. He accepted me on face value for the simple reason that I oversaw Chain when he couldn't. I liked him a lot: and exceptionally high one night, thought it wasn't impolitic to ask him what he made of Hitoshi's request that I, alone, undress. Rocking on his mat, tickled pink, an expressive glow in the clear skin of his bobbing throat, the scribe courteously simulated reflecting.

"I asked, 'Khun, do you laugh at my expense?'

"'No,' Apirak smiled. 'Asia man want see falang. At your expense.'

"Undeterred, I went to Hitoshi's table every day. Just resting on a slab for thirty-seven minutes with a stranger prodding my privates seemed to make the trip worthwhile. My appointment time always the same, I almost always was home by 3:05 in the afternoon. At the ninth massage, an excursion of giggling Japanese ladies was there: tuning for that probe I gathered they felt was naughty de rigueur on a Bangkok break. So I huffed and wilted while those housewives took their turns and didn't get to the Aphrodite until a quarter to six.

"When I opened the door, Chain was in the room. His trousers were soaked and bunched at his thighs—he'd been caught midtown, where steep ground-levels latrine the floods—and was taxing (and wetting) the floor tile with furious pacing, literal pacing, his features demonically contorted, his eyes shooting fire, his lips bitten to the point of blood. Sweaty and stinky myself, I put down my books and asked him what was amiss.

"He bleated: '*You see Thai-boy!*'

"It took me a bit to digest the wild sight of him; and shunt *his* bedfellows: which I'd been counting on locking horns over first thing I saw him. A calamitous bit, for I must have appeared to be fishing. I stuttered, 'Wha– what you mean?'

"'*You see Thai-boy! You see Thai-boy!*' he fumed again—with magnificent contempt. 'Think I not know?'

161

"'But why?'

"'Every day come 3:05. Today not come. Come 5:45. You see Thai-boy!'

"'But *why*?'

"'Afternoon sec!!'

"I sat on a pillow, whichever was closest: probably his, seeing as this caused him to raise his brows and heighten his outrage. So he'd been spying on me daily. Well, given his provincial enterprise, that was reassuring. It suggests he believed I'd a residual of self-respect. I might be hosting an ecologist in there, or specialist on border-crossing backslapping. I looked away from him while I reconsidered: between the damming and deforestation, not only Phrae but all of Yunnan was destined for a disastrous, or even no, future. Or did this very idea make Chain gloat: i.e., *was* this his idea? And a subsidiary puzzle: if Chain is so highly connected in his political dealings, why does he live in such straits? Is it because their footmen generally see little of the cavaliers' cavalier profits? If not, where is, and what becomes of, his money?

"His cursing and growling brought me back to the matter at hand. Hitoshi was not Thai, not a boy, and his manipulations not precisely what Chain would mean by 'sec'—though I confess to a grin as I retrieved the subversive kneading in what he could denounce as an airtight alibi. Chain registered my grin ferociously, his muscles rippling like a rabid pinscher. The preposterousness of his imputation—he gets laid six ways from Sunday—combined with the tactile afterimage and pun of the balls of the massager's fingertips made me—lamentably—start to laugh.

"'This funny? I funny?' Chain exploded, frothing between clenched teeth and twisting that into a snarl.

"I swallowed—with the certainty of hell rising to greet me otherwise—'Why you not ask Khun Apirak what I do after doctor? After hard work and after doctor? Last two weeks you see him, huh?'

"'Not have picture-falang, now!' he cried: referring to the scribe's fondness for male action-shots with the larger, or all, participants white; and his own habit of visiting Apirak with

162

porn depicting such orgies. Apirak, filmy-eyed and computably internal, would devour it. I embarked on the reason for my being tardy, patting the bed covers to indicate that he should join me. He wouldn't: though he did stop cursing as he listened, and bend toward me, as if to block my worming through or around a condemning disclosure.

"I went on to ask why, since he was the city's handsomest man, I'd want or need to fornicate with someone else, fully aware that this wasn't the most convincing argument to offer a Thai: comeliness aside, many live for variety. I tried speaking about my unattractively drawn face, my sleep-deprived depletion, my time-demanding job. These defenses were ineffective: boys are lustful rather than picky; studs staring at tight buns are no longer tired; and pokes can be wedged into the briefest of bank trips or window browsing.

"Then I surrendered to crude representations: old egrets, which, perched on a swamp-tree branch, suddenly die, and hang there in death upside down, secure until parasites from within or without decompose their rigor-mortised claws; and Chain removing his slippers of the Gods. Chain's feet were caked, bistre and dun under the toenails, his crumpled pants live with the vermin of urban flood, his voice no longer nuanced but a toneless bark, his striding gruff, not imperially graceful—how mutable, and burdensome, his seraphic looks...

"His trial exhausting me, resenting and then thoroughly resenting the unjust charge, I grew ill-tempered myself and yanked him to the bedside, at an angle that forced him to fall next to me. His resistance was a fraction weak of what he'd have wanted to fend off capitulating. That close to him now, I declared, 'Chain, I not have sec with Thai-boy because *I am saying* I not. You not trust me?'

"'No!' he announced. Dreadfully.

"'How—*how* you can live with man you not trust? How sleep, more than one year, with man, and you not trust?'

"I realized this shock, this protest was specious as well. Sex requires no mutual trust. Our shacking up could be mere convenience: financial for him, and valuable for me since I gained those hours wasted cruising. A mute tension followed. I mulled over the possibility that behind his automatic outburst might lie the pain of recited experience. His hustling would sour most Westerners contemplating fidelity. Yet *I* lived with his inability to perceive, and dismissing out of hand, the foreigner's scorn for that trade—not to mention his other ingenuities. I turned to my original intent. I said: 'And District of Song? In Phrae?'

"He shouted: 'This business m— business YOU and me!' His gaze went to the oculus, through whose glass blocks the light was compromising, then to the puddles on the floor. He mumbled, miserably, 'You not find boy in Phrae?'

"'No, I did not.'

"'In Phrae, *fan* Rollo, newspaper man, want know too much. You too.'

"I said: 'Business. Business you and me. What about Woo Chun-hao?'

"'Contact me, in Phrae.'

"'And his other address—Paris, the rue Victor Hugo?'

"'He agent. Woo also agent there. For me. In Paris.'

"Regretful, he sniffled: 'Ah, *and Randy...*' –Yes: Randy, Raft, and Martin.

"Slowly, very slowly now, he appeared to want to be convinced of my innocence on that day—as if the opposite, his soul spilled and spent, and shared with mine intractably, would be unendurable. His body went slack. He appealed to the recriminatory grain in the walls. By the evident perplexity in his look I assumed that the spirit, Mah Seekai, had found a mascot in me.

"When I felt his terror ease, I whispered, felicitous and pledging, and directly into his eyes: 'You believe me, Chain?'

"He rose and wearily gathered the photos I'd taken of him and some gifts he had bought for his family. Then he examined every pore in my face, successfully penetrating me from a source I'd been culpably late to fathom.

"And at last, answered me, very quietly.

"'I not know.'

"WHY HAD HIS GODS selected me? Why had they promoted, arranged for, and elected me as his narcotic? I junked my calendar for the next few months. I skipped Philip Bailey's grievance-airing cocktail hour; plus student evaluations, college boards, and the diction-lab, Chain's incremental demands thoroughly monitoring my latitude. I tore at chocolate bunnies, though, their sienna chips and ebony drool redesigning my day's attire. They were prey-like providers of energy; they restored eight of the pounds I'd shed.

"I tried to integrate Chain—that is, to ground our bond's imprecision—by giving him swimming and English lessons. Thais are a riverine people, yet not many swim. He learned to do laps as fast as I, but found clearing between my legs underwater more fun: that way, he could tickle my thighs and whatnot else. He also insisted on lying in bed while tolerating his English lessons, so my coaching lasted no longer than it took him to become aroused: about ten minutes. He'd shudder, turn on his stomach, and burn, 'Very open now. O.K. for me...'

"When this proximal student-teacher relationship caused more ambivalent reactions, he'd suddenly solder his lips to mine, his teeth a small corrugation of relentless reinforcement, and hold the back of my head to prevent me from jerking away. Then he'd drop his own head and drive his chin into my collarbone with painful rupture, his nails cutting my triceps.

"I'd go to these persuasive invites to reassure him because they revealed a cardinal aspect of his deferments through lovemaking: the subverting of facts that made him uncomfortable. Apirak sporadically taught English, French, German, and Teochew; and Chain approached him for the necessary readers and grammars. These were hand-me-downs for first-graders, replete with childish illustrations. Deny that as I would, Chain knew this, and they humiliated him. After a certain age, Thais deem returning to rhetoric inappropriate. Therefore, as a feckless student, he'd frustrate my setting up many sessions. When I rebuked him for squandering my benefit and scored his abysmal pidgin, he rationalized, 'English not language people Thai. You understand, no? How I speak, enough for me.'

"My comparative isolation was broken when Philip Bailey

called to say he was organizing a raft trip down the River Kwai. Would I care to come along and bring a boy—whoever, at the moment, might be my number-one? I told Philip to count me in; however, I'd bring no companion.

He said, 'You'll be the only fruit who ain't.'

"I asked who else was sailing. 'Besides Soren Cass, Randolph Wetzel, and Martin Pitt—Volker Altmuller and George Bryning. So you'll meet two new falang. Then, behind their backs, you can try and date their lovers. You know what kept-boys are made of.'

"'A little brown spot.' Philip Bailey enjoyed that.

"Rollo said, 'Now, when you go on this adventure, I don't want you to drink.'

"'Why not?' I inquired.

"'Because when you drink you can't stop telling the truth.'

"'Recently that happens when I'm sober. But, still… I'll toke instead.'

"'Good, here's an ounce. Three hundred baht, please.'

"Randy Wetzel, Philip Bailey, Soren Cass, Volker Altmuller, George Bryning, and Martin, surnamed Pitt: men whose bridges had burned them…—the last of whom ached to burn all mine! Soren Cass, wearing a noblewoman's brimming hat onto which cloves of real mangosteen were clamped, was drunk when he approached the hired minibus transporting us to a bank on the Lesser River Kwai. I assumed the need for his anesthetic before leaving his flat was apparent in the partner he brought: a not quite young and avidly threatening hustler named Euryporn. Euryporn grunted rather than spoke, and seldom at that. He'd a fierce, unbelievably angular face with vehement eyes, ever alert, and a brush of hair that sprouted on his projected chin and ran under his jaw to the gullet, a kind of Mohawk taxonomically supporting, in default of cresting, his skull. He kept a proscribed distance from Soren Cass, if not all of us—more dumped than showed Soren into the van. This thrilled Bonita (if you will), a six-foot-two, big-breasted lady-boy in a 1940s print escorting the surgical-masked Philip Bailey: Bailey, whose pep on that venture would be (surreptitiously) near zero.

"George Bryning was a massive former soccer player, now in flabby shape, with a sandy, flourishing ponytail, I'd say in his early thirties, a raw-silk wholesaler who shuttled between Darwin and Indochina several times a year. George was flounder-faced with street-dumb and popping dead pupils, short-tempered, outclassed, and knee-jerk in judgment, what we'd call today a fringe member of the Australian bourgeois left. He'd an arguable eye for young rice-paddy workers: one was his current companion. Bryning preoccupied himself with deciphering the group's alphabet; but held to making a categorical imperative of his own Down-Under benighted and parochial life.

"Volker Altmuller lived—and longed not to—in Cologne; so he inveigled to reside here, nine months out of twelve. He bragged of panting from orgy to orgy, and at the drop of a Soren Cass hat enumerated his daily conquests: on the order of three in the morning, four more by dinnertime, he lost count of how many during the evening and night. Dubious of his arithmetic, I believed his dedication. About forty, forty-five, his scaly features were secretionary, summoning those of the Aphrodite's poolside Garudas as they brandished a snake, their sole diet. Volker's only aim other than anus was to be a celebrated painter: from the portfolio he constantly carried, where all entries were crayon-scribbling—an idiot's take on abstract expressionism—I gathered a poststructural one. To survive with his befuddlement, Volker concocted a universe allowing him to define his output as 'romantic'—in rebuke to what galleries hung, which he labeled 'cynical.' This filtered fantasy world, with its thousands of blind spots supposedly making sense and success of his failure, rendering it as valid as any man's product, was utterly impregnable, though the boob was a near teetotaler, a train-conductor no less who kept regular hours. Wrecks who construe weltanschauungs to avoid confronting what is so can be, apart from dogmatic and infuriating, a peril to others, since they are normally impervious to activities not perceived as direct assaults on their protective fabrication. His 'lover' was nondescript, as must, by necessity, have been his orgiastic tastes, and I don't remember him well.

"Martin Pitt, Chain's illegible Brit 'boss,' puffy-faced, fold-necked, paunchy, hairy, and immense, was passing as an executive of sorts in Esso's offshore oil fields, southeast on the peninsula. He clearly did study the Asian stock markets and had an encyclopedic knowledge of Thai politics—as he spun it, a priority for the foreign investor or property holder. Martin must have been in his mid-forties. He was generally pasty—and chinless: his identifying feature. He summarized people from under half-closed lids; was cerebral, fatalistic, and deliberate in step. His cold-sore lips were bit brown, and he'd that disturbing mouth tic. His eyes within the bent wire-specs were ice-pink. Pitt gave the impression of guarding his back; in the van, he was unable to avoid checking the rear window.

"I adopted his sham of nonrecognition, and asked: 'Expecting someone?'

"He said, 'Three cinema luminaries.'

"–Etonian Martin Pitt, the theatre-owner who handled Chain, Olie, Ekarin, and Nok—and was *Phii*, Older Brother, Kambu-ja's master. The man whose ultimatum to me would be henceforth no longer on hold.

"Randolph Wetzel you know, so I'll say only that he looked immeasurably thinner than when I'd last seen him. What I *will* italicize are the small fellows Pitt and Wetzel brought with them… Boys really, not fellows: the hill-tribe boys, Chain's cousins! At this point, one ten, perhaps, the other eleven years old. Both boasted that family crop of unruly blue hair, now relatively subdued. Their clothes, with rummage-sale price tags still attached, were somewhat better fitting than when I'd encountered them in the Dusit Zoo. *His* eyes, Chain's eyes—but their other features far less refined, their teeth chipped, their cheeks sodden. They, or someone, had thought it cute if both, at least for this outing, had female names: the younger boy Pavena, and the older Kineetha. I'll leave you to hear the thunder I did when I saw them. Neither retained myself: the altercation in the zoo had given them no reason to page-trace me.

"Do I sound superior here? Globals tend to, describing each other."

When Cory asked me this, I needed to switch tapes and got

busy with that. When I finished, he had opened his shirt and crisscrossed his arms. With opposite fingers, he was twisting his nipples. "What *are* you up to?" I squealed. "Nice chest expansion.... but aren't there guys who'll do that for you?"

"Do what?"

"Pinch your paps."

He snapped his neck. He looked found-out. He said, "Wow... dig it: when I was pubescent I experienced constant pounding in this area, the area around the nipples. Our doctor claimed it was the equivalent of what a girl my age would sense: her incubatory breasts. Not to worry, that it actually was... growing pains. Happened now because, can you imagine, I felt that pressure and tried to relieve it when I saw those kids get into the van that day. Philip derided my indecency with a hackneyed, 'Self-gratification: in the end, the wisest kind.'

"Soren criticized that: 'Depends which end.'" Cory buttoned his shirt.

"Bonita had to help Soren Cass onto the raft, because Euryporn, abusively, wasn't about to. Then, speaking Thai, Bonita introduced him to the cook, captain, and navigator, who came along with this flat vessel of startling size. When Soren stood there nonplused, the captain managed, 'Pleasure all mine.'

"Soren snapped, 'Ah hope it won't always be!'

"Bonita reprimanded, 'In Thailand twelveteen years and you not talk Thai?'

"'What!' Soren cried. 'An' have folk accuse me of goin' native?! Next y'all be askin' why Ah don't don a sarong and walk around barefoot altogether!'

"The gender reassignment saw to the sports activity. The second we entered calm green river, she cast tire tubes overboard and screamed for the fit to dive, come up inside them, and let the circling tubes carry them downstream. As we'd near hidden, dangerous rocks in too-swift white-water rapids, she'd screech in mock hysteria, 'Womens aboard!' And when I'd dally, wanting to try my skill at negotiating some of those passes, she'd shout, 'Include you, Esther William!'

"At one point, servant to my tension, I swam underwater

169

pressing the fronts of my hands against slab after slippery slab until I cleared a lengthy stretch of rapids. I rested on a temporary sandbar: and watched the sudden, to-be-idiomatic action on the raft. Martin Pitt threw Pavena and Kineetha into the river; when they surfaced and attempted to climb back, he placed his left foot on the head of Kineetha, and then Pavena, and repeatedly submerged them. Within minutes, they were gulping, gasping, and desperately clawing the sideboards. Mucous poured from their noses. The Thais were appalled by this putting of a foot on top of the children's heads, the falang seemed confused by Martin's brutality, and all were stunned, motionless.

"I bettered the rapids and struck out for the craft, seeing through the rinse that widow-peaked boy who, after speaking to Olie, fell or was pushed into the Wat Sai klong. I paddled along the vessel's windward, went under, and rose between the brothers in a gushing fount. I grabbed Pitt's ankle, as he was about to stomp on Pavena again, and toppled him. He flattened with a hiss. I encircled Pavena's waist and hoisted the child just high enough to climb for himself; Kineetha took that opportunity to also scramble onboard. I kept sight level with the splints and made no contact with the scattered groupings, let alone Martin Pitt. Then I caught a swivel at a rigging bolt, let the drift pull me to even my breath, and looked up. Martin had Pavena in a clinch, and Randolph Wetzel had hold of Kineetha. They tore the boys' bathing suits off and slapped them until they knelt. Then crushed their purpled faces to the planks, spread their legs, and buggered them in full view of everyone present.

"The navigator moored the raft at dusk; and the cook set to poaching trout and seafood, bedded by longan, melon, and manzanilla. Volker, growing anxious, noted, 'Dese veekend-squeezes, very young and lovely, *nicht war?*'

"Pitt growled, 'Pro tem! *We* have what it takes to pare the Mango. Which is money! Besides, *my* toit for the weekend has been too pared.'

"Volker showed stress. 'Zey are quiet as vell. Still vater runs deep.'

"'Here?' Martin objected, chewing his stinky cigarillo. 'Non-transparency says skive off! Eleven centuries and these slants still don't know that!'

"Soren awoke: '*Deep!* Scratch a Brit deep anuff and y'all find a colonialist.'

"'Or, superficially,' Philip Bailey grumbled, X-raying Martin.

"Martin snorted, 'Did I just *hear* a DOA (Drunk On Arrival) retrofag from the land of no law and disorder?'

"'Not this one,' Soren choked. 'Musta been Centerfold over there.'

"'Soren Cass!' Martin Pitt sneered, focusing on the belle. Then came the inevitable: 'What is Cass called when he's at home?'

"Middle name always Cass. Mah complete name is Soren Cass Blackblatt.'

"'I thought so!' Martin groaned. 'You people who believe it's your birthright to teach shouldn't try to live in the East. *You* invented the West, and it's all you understand. You're unicultural. You can't click biculturally! Stay home!'

"'But Ah converted—to atheism!' Soren riposted. Then George Bryning perked up and hollered about words like 'retrofag': Out-of-the-Closet is a weapon, mate! –He objected to *commodifying* gayness. Randolph Wetzel said expansionist hell! When you creeps scrap meters n' centigrade, n' sample feet n' Fahrenheit, you'll be over the outfield with the Stars n' Stripes. Soren Blackblatt took one for the road, which road on that levee led to where masked Philip was nodding, and Bonita donning her nightgown. Bonita counseled Soren to 'not hear' *pla whan cow*—'white whale,' mind you—and maternally crumpling his sachet of Black Label, she bunkered between Soren and Phil.

"I sat by the campfire, hoping to learn something, anything. The Thais were telling folk tales. When it was my turn, I recycled my tour through a subterranean Ripley's Museum in Chung-li, a grim, unknown slum of millions kept out of sight on the dark side of an airport it shares with Taipei. In its depths is a 'mermaid' stuck together with a stepped-on porpoise skeleton and a small monkey's skull with the foraging jaw of a barracuda. The money-boys were all-ears as I reached a green Spaceman, accurate to the Humpty-Dumpty head and tiny body, found in a nearby field. When I got to the Lycanthropic Mummy and was describing its unkempt, patchy beard and, albeit fig-leaf-sufficient, hirsute lower region—like, oh yes! my recurring satyr—forcing the Thais to huddle protectively en masse, I gagged on how puerile and malignant this display of my impotence was.

"That's when I felt my Y-z purchase an extraneous bulge in my pocket. None of this demimonde being users, I'd escape their deadweight in private. And why give them a drop on me? I rallied, and sure enough stumbled, because despite my promise to Rol, I *had* tested the quality of locally brewed Black Label. I ducked into the thickets some sixty yards from the campfire and squatted in the mud. As I pressed, all thumbs, the tobacco out of two Krong Thips and began stuffing the chopped boo through them, a mango shower broke. I drew my windbreaker over my hands to prevent the ganja's getting wet; and in that awkward crouch spilled enough for a high. I had smoked about an inch of the second cig when I heard the dripping twigs cracking. I couldn't be mistaken: cracking, at a distance, both to the left and right of me. With stoned paranoia, I buried the joint in the marl and wrestled to look ruminative, as if discharging rice-constipation—or its swamp gas, seeing as how I'd neglected to lower my pants.

"Volker Altmuller whispered huskily, 'Vhat you do, Cory?'

"The men's in Thai cities are crowded cruising clubs, but a can on the Kwai? Volker's puss was keyed, disjointed, and repellent. He was crawling on all fours, clumsily displacing the compost in his way, and swatting mosquitoes.

"'Fishing for monkey-headed mermen. I'm not up to anus this evening,' I answered.

"Volker rattled, 'Monkey-headed? I just saw one!'

"'Where?'

"'Here! I see a wild man. Black. Very tall and skinny. With fuzzy hair.'

"'Really? You're drinking too much. –What is he wearing?' I asked.

"'Just shorts. He has a club, a big stick. Maybe zey live around here.'

"'They do not.' –The scaffold worker, the street person, the hunter… How did he learn I was making this trip? He had to be tracking someone else. The brothers? Randolph? Martin Pitt? *Martin*: his small cigars, his wire-rim, pebble specs: duplicates of the objects the hunter gave me in *Sanam Luang*.

"Volker said, 'I have to converse with you.'

"'Can't imagine about what.'

"'Do you know of Martin Pitt vell?'

"'I met him three weeks after I arrived. Three weeks after that, he tried to narrow my fucking field. He may've been correct to do so. He may not.'

"'He is never correct!' His gutturals darkened, their fumes just the feather that could deck me then.

"'Oh?'

"'I remember him. First I do not. But now I do.' Intolerable as he was, I had to tolerate him: this German was truly suffering. Gulping, he continued: 'I am visiting Siam since I am nineteen. Have you hear told the Children's Garden?'

"'An acquaintance mentioned it.'

"'It is on the highest roof in Soi Twilight. Martin owns it. He owns all the bars in zat building.'

"'And?'

"'I was up to zere ten years ago. Zat is when I meet him the third time. Randy can say it operates still. Bar on middle-floor, too. Martin owns zem.'

"Whiskey condenses time and ganja stretches it: so Volker's sentences, so meaningfully imparted, seemed to shut-fast and yet never close in competing with the chorus of vicious bugs. I hadn't registered a painless purchase on the bank: and with my arches locked and butt-tips anchored in the mire, could not, for the post of Lome-plaster I'd become, maneuver to find one.

"'Middle-floor is a Go-Go auction. Boys eighteen to twenty-two.'

"'I hate Go-Go palaces.' My ankles, too, were killing me.

173

"'Always it is full. You cannot get near the bar. Also the Children's Garden. Packed all the nights.'

"His drift wouldn't drift downstream. With every pronouncement tandem to nothing I could referee preceding it, I was nevertheless glad that the downpour hid Volker from the frenzy that must have been mastering my dilated pupils. I directed them elsewhere, as if summoned by the gold-epauletted mermen vouched for in Siamese paintings, since I could hear their siren in the scree: it had the sound of a gamelan. His human voice melted into the lick and hush of the ripples that those creatures and the raindrops were inscribing on the water.

"'The Children's Garden is a fenced arbor, a bar at one end and cubicles at the other. All the boys are six or seven. *Six* or *seven* years old! Do you hear? Vhat are you listening to? Zey dance in the arbor with you. Zeir faces come up to your belt. Zey lean zeir heads against your stomach, Cory, and rub your thing until you get hard. Zey say, "Mister, you not want fucking bum me? Please, Mister, fuck small bum me tonight." I drink a liter of rum and run down the stairs. But I see zeir faces everywhere. I cannot screw for a month.'

"I braced myself on a fallen tree and sprang to my feet. Volker rose after I did and stood almost touching me, scratching his bites. I stopped him and held his hand. I couldn't tell whether or not I was hearing right, hearing the song, or hearing, really, anything at all. We stared at the river.

"'Martin Pitt?' I asked. 'Are you sure?'

"'Ya. When he lighted his cigarillo… He has gotten old. He has changed his look. But zis cigarillo, you cannot forget its smell. He smoked zem in the Go-Go. On the rooftop, too. Zat dead deer smell is together in my thinking forever with the smell of the snot—and the nur in the bellybuttons—of zose six-year-olds. Grown men took zem to the cubicles and… Cory! Cory!'

"'But *you* didn't?'

"'Oh, no! No! I am not a monster! When I smell zat smoke again today, I tell Martin I know who he is.'

"'Did he deny it?'

"'Deny it?? He ask me, very calmly, "Don't you like children?"

I said: "What I like or do not like do not matter. I would like cutting the throats of two or three people in Thailand, but I do not. Zere are things you do not do in zis world. And zere are reasons you *must* not!'"

"'What did he say, then?'

"'He said, "Oh: so you're one of those. Listen, Volker, that's how these tykes make their living. Otherwise, they would be sleeping under a highway with rodents, not men, and starving to death. I am giving them a chance to keep on living. Do you want to support every slum yourself? If not, shut up!'"

"Then shut up is precisely what Volker Altmuller did: a magnified retreat, because, as though struck dumb by his report, the rain as well withdrew. For him, reality's own lost child, this was perhaps a pioneering resolve—and its instinct was to seek the aid of Martin Pitt's accomplice. I went through Volker's unguarded confidence in my sympathies: of Chain's connection to all this, his betrayal of his cousins—and Oliver Littleton and Rollo Y-z's obvious investment in it.

"Finally, Volker said, 'So now he is being very acid with me. He is constantly making slashing comments. I had to get away from him.'

"I asked: 'When and how did you meet Martin the *first* time?'

"He sneered, 'Oh! Zat had to do with the Thompson heads.'

"'Thompson? Jim Thompson?'

"'Him. In 1960 my money was stole in Phetchabun province, so I helped to pack three old heads and drive zem to Bangkok. Zey were in full relief: white limestone—a Buddha, a Bodhisattva, and one I do not know; the backs all rough: zey were sawed off something. Zey were very heavy. I was assisting Martin Pitt. He said he cut zem from a cave wall in Khao Sam Rot Mountain, near Sri Thep ruin. He was not ashamed to tell me, he was proud. He sold zem to Jim Thompson for a very high price. A year later he found me again. He had two more heads. Thompson bought also those. He was a big collector, you know.'

"I said, 'Didn't anyone object? That's national treasure.'

"'Fine Arts Department! Zey took the five heads without paying for zem. Prime Minister Sarit Thanarat's wife was making up herself a silk business. She copied Thompson's designs. So people talk, she is behind zat grab.'

"'What did Thompson do?'

"'Jim? In the end, nothing. You cannot fight City Hall. He wanted to leave his complete collection to Thailand anyhow. Quite soon his bitterness becomes a legend: for zis country's ingratitude—or maybe just the government's...'

"'And six years after that he disappeared,' I thought out loud. 'Leaving an open pack of cigarettes on his table in the Cameron resort.'

"Volker stood ground, auditioning me. 'Later I learn *Martin* stole my money, to make me come in wiz him. And now he has zat on me. A noose. Cory, I want you to know all zis thing about Martin Pitt. Is zat O.K.?'

"'Yes.'

"'And?'

"'I'm twisted, Volker.'

"'Police kick Martin out of Thailand. Zey take him in handcuffs to a plane. But now he comes back, free as a bird. To carry right on. Zat's Thailand. Do you believe me? Martin is not hard to recognize. He is lacking a chin.'

"'Um. And big on a mouth tic.'

"'Vhat are you going to do?'

"'Here? Keep the meter running. Mr. Pitt has no affiliates here.'

"'But—'

"'Volker, *thank* you. Very much. Mind returning to the windbags?'

"Right then I'd only two goals: straightening up and not staying any longer alone with Volker. This was to make small difference: because when we reached the camp, several complications, to put it mildly, occurred in rapid succession. Following the rain, the captain was rekindling the fire. Martin and Randolph were sitting closest to it; and Volker and I, other side the fire, stationed opposite them. I'd the feeling that, shoulder to shoulder with me, the German wanted to prove he was *my* henchman now. However, when the flames shot skyward, he stared at my illuminated face and, whatever contortions it wore, stepped militantly away. That sharp movement caused Randy to study me as if searching for the cause—but also as if he had not seen me there before. Could be he hadn't: there'd been a sense of wandering about him all day. He squinted and said: 'Ah, Simon!—welcome, welcome! Marty, this is Cory Simon, a modern-history writer. He does the trenches, too—in sexual custody—of Chain.'

"Immense Martin corrected his specs, resting them higher. Their thick lenses upped his orbs to twice their size. He asked, 'Chain?'

"'Yeah, Chain. –Remember? …Wait, uh, Somboon: he was called Somboon then… at the Oriental?'

"Martin blinked. 'As I were next in queue. Who could forget? The brat in room service—a chef-in-training, no? –Pretty little blackarse?'

"'That there's the whipper,' Randy Wetzel enthused. 'Tell Cory about it.'

"Pitt took in his tongue: he'd obviously linked these double entendres before. 'I go *ball*istic—ten years old, wasn't he? But what bad buy! Somboon rejects me! Well, this pig-headed poof tries to. He kick-boxes. I belt off to the kitchen and tell them he's surly: to cancel his cooking instructions *and* room-service gig or I'll kiss the management—with whom I am nightly tight— and assure the cooks' dismissals. Tipping like a prince, I inform them that they are to send him straightway to my room with Chateau Lafite one last time. I shave my pubes in front of him. I want him to see my *hole* revolver—what a whack's for certs with a stiff-upper. Boys: he would *not* handle *ma pièce d'occasion!* So I hit him hard with the bottle, curl him over my knees—and use the bubbly's neck to make a snicket out of his ginnel. Then get at his poop, proper. There was blood all over the suite, red as… well, the cherry that chap just lost!'

"Pitt and Wetzel burst into lubricous laughter. Volker lunged between the fire and myself and threw his back up against me. Randolph tossed his head from side to side with deafening whoops; then seized his cane and struggled to his feet, confronting me with the oval of his yawn, slimed and black as a ditch. His lips quivered fearsomely, attempting, I guess, to shape some gibe, or to scoff, or bellow in derision. Instead, they froze and locked into that globe as if about to blow me a smoke ring. Only a terrible howl emerged, like a mule's imaginary labor cry, that brought the company to alert. He looked wildly everywhere, as one does who needs to be someplace urgent, and hobbled like a driven gnome toward the snoring, hat-crested hill that was Soren. Yet when he reached him, and was evidently horrified, he spindled under torsion on his cane and tripped backward, landing chest-up on Soren as on a torture wheel, except that his head touched the grass at the far side of Soren; and lay there soundlessly. I shifted Volker Altmuller aside and sprinted the distance to Randy. Leaning across the heap's determined immobility, I lifted Randy's head as gently as I could—had him sitting up, using Soren as a sofa, and steadied him at eye-level with me. He searched my face… appeared bewildered. His first phrase was fast: 'You must visit the Allied War Cemetery!' Then he tumbled: '…I fought there… I fought with…'

"I said, 'With Jim?'

"'No… no, Jim was in the OSS. I fought with *Seri Thai.* Is he here?'

"I stalled. 'Um, he'll be along shortly… Don't worry: he won't leave you, Randy. –Do you know who I am?'

"'Sure. You're with the kid.'

"'The kid?'

"'The room service. The kid who brings PM Sarit's codes under a napkin.' For a long moment, the old man juggled; and gawked; then he carefully pinched the dissepiment of my nostrils: 'Veers counterclockwise… lotta gloves connected there, lotta gloves. Now *you're* worried. Kid's sharp. –Don't worry—he won't leave you. *Too sharp!*' He laughed—freely; and soon bitterly.

"I watched his color drain, starting at the moist glabella and leaving his jowls and throat. Bonita had awakened and was kneeling on her shins beside us. She asked, her brows tightly knit, 'What is it?'

"I spoke softly, 'He is having a stroke.'

"'But... I don't see—'

"'You will. We'll need a stretcher.' I glanced back at the campfire, where Soren Cass had gone to whine that Randy'd crushed his Easter bonnet—and the other whites stood censuring us—and called for help. Only Euryporn came. He took Randy's pulse. Bonita spoke a few words in Thai. I hastened into the woods, cut two more or less suitable branches, and stripped them with my switchblade until they could serve as poles. Bonita found gowns in her trousseau and set to binding the branches. Euryporn and I lifted Randolph onto the makeshift litter, and with his feet at my end so they'd not face the Thai, carried him to the captain. Explaining that Randy had to be taken to a Bangkok hospital as quickly as possible, I asked the captain where the nearest railway station was. He said at Kanchanaburi, eight hours upriver, a train stopping there at 5:15. I insisted: 'Then we'll have to start as soon as you pack things up.'

"'Current very strong—nighttime now, rock make wreck,' he objected.

"'Have River Kwai in your heart,' I said. 'You'll do it.'

"I pulled away from him so he couldn't argue further; and away from the weekenders—who, aside from Bonita and Euryporn, were grumbling loudly (so I'd overhear) that Wetzel was peeing on their parade; since Simon's no quack, how does he know, maybe the geezer's not all that ill; but, such notwithstanding, who put the half-caste in charge around here? By then Randy's arms were flailing every which way and his speech had become incoherent. I went to the bank, sluiced water under my eyes, and watched the lightning wink half-second puzzles too brief to read. The humidity close to the river felt like an overcoat. I seethed in solitude, actually looking for the hunter; then heard the anxious exploring in a languid 'observation,' intentionally made behind me:

"'This Herr Volker Altmuller is a chip off the old block, he is.'

"That prickly broad 'a' and those clipped-up-into-the-gum consonants. I stared before me, sweating in spats, and tore a nail. After a pause Martin Pitt went on: 'I discovered these hayseeds on the city's dumps: Pavena and Kineetha. They were digging for soda-pop bags, preferably with straws, picking them out of knee-deep rubbish. For recycling. Their pay was a baht for three hundred bags.' I remained very still. In that held-breath, awaiting Pitt's convoluted summation, a paralysis rose from the pain in my shins that I feared, reaching my ribs, would stop my heart. He said: 'As for Chain, I'm sorry. But I interdicted you, no? Chain set the hayseeds onto the dumps after they fled the cathouse... Hence, you've yourself to condemn. –And he'd a gravitous radiance in his little tunic. We are both men: so you know how it is... Emission accomplished.'

"My father used to beat me regularly when I was a boy and sometimes, frustrated that he couldn't inflict sufficient harm, insert his finger into me.

"All at once, the two of us crouched in reflex to a boom— an explosion so shattering that I can liken it only to a foghorn blasting off a yard away from you. When we unbent, realizing we'd shown our cards, Martin was standing beside me with his thumbs in his pockets; and, shuffling to cut his loss and run, deprecated, 'That sound is just frogs. People think it's their mating call. It is not. They aren't always horny. They croak like that after it rains because they are cold.'

"I finally spoke. *'Cold?* Well! I cannot tell them where else to go to get warm.' A rictus erased Pitt's grin. His apprehension escalated: I was mad. I said, 'I know your fuckup whitearse Olie. Not your two boys. Volker had zero to add. And, emphatically, Randy is wrong: I'm merely Chain's client. He has many.'

"The Lesser Kwai joins the Greater at the town of Kanchanaburi. Trucks parked at its dock shuttle rafters to the railroad. A driver claimed the train was due late: by four hours. I told him, 'Take me to the Allied Cemetery.'

"En route we passed the famous bridge, its bombed center ever wanting repair, most of the original intact: a disappointing truss, ordinary, unobtrusive, functional. The driver, as I knew, would not enter the cemetery. I walked into the British section, grateful—thus far—to be alone. Would sparring with Martin undo his ligatures on *two* hirelings? I'd no comfort to offer Wetzel beyond what Bonita was dispensing. I had to examine my involuntary response, my effort to rescue Randy: did it hold not Randy but myself foremost? Did I do it to extend my leverage with Chain? Was it to abort his unpredictable reaction, a shift in his uniformity, if Randy were suddenly lost?

"I absorbed the flat graveyard, automatically hearing a cinematic voiceover clicking off the cliché, 'Scanning this pleasant landscape, who could imagine the atrocities that once took place right here?' I'd no trouble at all. The Japanese Death March was in flickering silhouette, starving and dropping these buried young lives in its stagger to construct and cross that Bridge. Resting on a number of the tombstones are letters, hand-written by the bereaved and left there for their dead sons to read. I read some of them. The dark hermit stood at the far end of the field. I did nothing to indicate that I saw him. I didn't think I had to. I wrote my own note, placed it on a tombstone, and cried. And I have cried ever since… whenever that cloudy dawn finds its shameless reason to return.

"We got Randy to the St. Louis Hospital, near the Chao Phya on Sathorn. Then the three of us, Euryporn and Bonita on either side of me, sat and waited in the emergency room. The brush under Euryporn's throat sufficed to scatter the nurses. Bonita, checking herself in her compact-mirror, freshened her lipstick. She said to me, 'Why you no have boy same everybody else? You have nice form. Can take Kineetha. He free now.'

"Sometimes, in Thailand, you cannot believe your ears.

"At last the examining doctor showed, looked about, and spotted us. He confirmed my diagnosis: it was a major stroke. Randolph Wetzel could be expected to sink gradually, perhaps into a coma. For the moment he'd stabilized and was relatively insensitive to pain. It was a time to see and still speak with him.

"We found Randy supported by huge pillows, all sorts of tubes attached to his wrists and nose. His eyes were filmy. As we approached, they seemed to clear enough for him to locate us. He was embarrassed when he tried to talk: he could hear his slurring. The right side of his face was paralyzed. He took me in from head to toe and smiled with the good corner of his mouth when he came to rest his vision between my legs.

"He spouted, writhed, and worked hard to pronounce, softly and approvingly, 'Not exactly corn kernels, are they?' "

I said to Cory, "Can I ask you about your father?"

"No! you cannot. You think I'm made of rhino hide. That is a legacy which discomforts me. He would pound his fist on my behind and push his index up; and when it reached as far as it would, crook it brutally. I couldn't understand what he was doing, or why. He stopped when I was nine, and I thereinafter never thought about it until that night with Martin Pitt. And at no time since—until right now. That is what I will say.

"I telephoned Chain from the St. Louis lobby; first trying Soi 36; and reached him at the Afro. I sketched the mishap, listed the hospital's all-welcome hours, and told him to go there at once, that I'd see him late that evening. On the phone, as proscribed, he let slip no emotion.

"When I hung up, Euryporn, sensing my continuing anxiety, threw his arm around my shoulder, manfully grasped it, and flashed that profound Thai smile that says, 'Never mind: everything is, or will be, O.K.' Then I thanked him and Bonita, quickly *wai*ed them, and headed directly for Rollo Y-z's.

"He opened to my knocking with a cheerful, 'Home is the *hunter*, home from the hill, and the sailor home from sea! Tell me all a—' His voice broke off. He gazed, aghast, into my face. He said, 'It was Chain who gave me the necklace of dinosaur bones. I, in turn, gave it to the opium doctor.'

"'I know that,' I stated impatiently.

"'It was a bribe. It was meant to get me to soften you up to him. How *he* came by it, I've not an inkling…'"

Rollo slumped to his Barcelona; and moments later delivered what sounded like a prepared confession he'd prefer to make now and be done with. 'So the hunt has yield— Do you remember that first job I accepted as counselor at a summer camp? One day I took the kids on a picnic. A little girl, maybe five or six, said she had to pee. I told her to go in the bushes.

She emerged after a while and said she couldn't. I said go there, by the water, it's easier. She returned again, claiming to have no success. So I accompanied her to the river, out of sight of the others, and ordered her to pull down her bloomers and squat. She did: with no result. I knelt beside her, told her to listen to the stream gushing over the stepping-stones, and placed my palm under her and rubbed her gently. I smoothed her feather. Something about rivers, what you hear in the hush of rivers: as you do. She puddled in my palm: it felt warm, invitingly warm, and viscous. Another time, in the camp's pool, I played a game of tossing her over my back and managed again to slip my fingers along her crevice. She wanted to play in that pool with me every day. Children are seductive… They're flirtatious… A boy there would come to my room before dinner in only his bathing suit— I was still in mine—and insist I show him some wrestling holds. …It doesn't happen often. It *hasn't* happened often… This is the blackmail: Olie's blackmail—the ruin he always threatens. He's gathered ragamuffins *he* brought me: who, for a few baht, will make accusations. No, I haven't done it often. Cory, I've tried not to hurt anyone. And you're an old friend. Was this visit necessary?'

"I had remained motionless while Rollo spoke, leaning against his cabinet of paperboard cartons, no more looking at him than he at me. 'I suppose not,' I slowly exhaled. I let myself out onto his gallery.

"He called: 'Haven't you one more question to ask me?'

"I stopped, holding my back to him. 'Yes. Why, from the day I "introduced" him, have you wanted me to stay with Chain?'

"'So: isn't that for your good, Cordie? And how about thanking me?'

"'For…?'

"'Chain.'

"I walked half the distance of his gallery before pausing. 'Thank you.'

"I wandered uptown for hours, any place I could think of where a fidgety Altmuller, and the necropolis of Pitt, had no possible business. I'd remembered seeing something when I was a boy. We lived near a beach then. On occasion I went there alone long after sundown. Above the beach was an old boardwalk. Poor or homeless people often slept under it—in cold, damp, black sand strewn with food scraps and broken green bottles. When I was tiptoeing over this offal one night, I saw that two policemen had trapped between them an adolescent girl. Having opened her blouse, the one in front of her was gripping her pendulous breasts; while the one in back, who'd hitched up her skirt, was massaging her buttocks, his fingers slipping along and well into the pubescent length of her lips. A few weeks later a local newspaper featured the story of two cops who were busted for repeatedly raping a fifteen-year-old runaway—in return for not arresting her, allowing her instead to live in that wet, filthy sand. The split-second sight of this assault—for I knew exactly what I had come upon and, as a witness, ran off—accompanied, importantly, by its verbal account—plundered me as well: lit hot sparklers in my chest and sculptured and scummed my knickers. It does to this day. Which is why, after I know all, the battle of pardon and the unpardonable palsies. As it did on *this* evening, when rather than meet that battle, I chose to plan what to ask Chain, how Randy seemed, how he, Chain, was taking it, and so forth. This deficiency partly reports on why, when I got to the Afro, I couldn't adequately put two and two together. The other part is that the backlash I encountered when I entered the hotel was set to spin very shortly before. *Necessarily*, on that very same day.

"I walked the gauntlet of frescoes—those tigers, gibbons, and Garudas—and when I reached my door found it was double locked. I kicked and pounded until Chain undid the bolts. I stepped in; and, stung, saw seven menacing Thais seated on the floor engaged in a card game, their legs akimbo, hastily covering fifty-baht bills spread on the tiles. This, then, is how Chain's illegal earnings vanish: they are lost in his equally illegal pursuit of gambling! –He is using me for this highly policed addiction, and minutes after leaving the hospital, was the inscription registering first. His crimes, and yet one more, I'd come to anticipate, no, to count on, but that he'd bring them home—in a whores' den and losers' flophouse not mattering: even the fresco beasts don't shit in their lair. Taking for granted now that given his nature, he'd deal with his distress re Randy by quickly seeking to distract himself, I still said, without preliminaries, 'I want them to leave.'

"No one moved. Conceivably none of them spoke English, yet my meaning was clear: *in*conceivable (to them) was to be unceremoniously asked to get up and get out by someone who'd just barged in. Glued to their stations around the game, they stared daggers at me. The poolside floods, filtering the oculus, lent their umbrage a perilous gleam. They were all tattooed and wore Northeast or mountain-tribe head kerchiefs; except for the youngest, who was dressed, incongruously, as an office worker in a blue shirt and black tie with polyester pants.

"I seized the triangular, heavy axe pillows heaped on the bed, and booming, 'Get the hell out!' threw these at them in a rage.

"They still hesitated, uncertain of the protocol in such a situation, and looked to Chain for a hint. He hid his eyes and indicated the open exit. Then the tattooed thugs reluctantly collected their cash and cards, stood severally, and filed past in front of me. Chain held the door for them, excusing my behavior in an undertone. The last to rise was the well-clad youngster. He sidled up and smugly confronted me with a *wai:* perched and ridiculed on his razor-backed widow's peak; and drooled in impeccable U.S. English: 'We regret antagonizing you, sir. My name is Daeng. I carry a gift for you. Kindly accept it.' He unbuckled his satchel and produced a half-gallon of alcohol. He cradled that weight under both hands and extended it toward me, smiling with ambiguity. I mindlessly took it: because in exchanging suppositional reproaches with him, and inspecting his surly carriage, my prudence was elsewhere—I thought for a moment I knew him.

"Then he immediately left. I slammed the door, threw the latch, and hurled at Chain, '*Did* you visit Randolph?'

"'Visit! So?'

"Undercut by the flatness of that, I tried degrading him—revving up to the audacity of this violation. Reeling, near berserk, I

185

stressed how alarmed I was, lacking the criminal funds protecting *him*, at learning now of his compulsion to daily re-endanger our predicament.

"'Feel here not place me' was his incredulous defense.

"'It's not!' I shouted. '*I* pay the rent. *I* buy the food! *I* sign the electric and water bill! *You* are my guest. This is *not* a casino!'

"'Lose face, you, me,' he responded dolefully. 'Boy bring vodka—and yell. Yell always, not care what.'

"I examined the oversized bottle: a Russian import, quite the most expensive in Thailand. I said, 'That one, office worker. How buy this?'

"'Not buy: take. Take out back: American Embassy. Daeng work Embassy. Have big parties, that place. Friend he, bring truck. Falang drunk: men Thai take vodka, one hundred and sixty case. Do a lot. –Now no more. Get caught.'

"I covered the bottle with a towel and vacantly watched him shift about, antsy and trapped. Having lost face, he couldn't, in a huff, tail the gamblers to escape my further vitriol. Chain needed, for the present, to avoid his fellow Thais.

"I went to the phone and rang Rollo. Amazingly, he sounded relaxed, preoccupied, his usual self, his greeting not the least contrite.

"'Have you *seen* Olie recently?' I asked.

"'Yeah. In stir.'

"'Oh? For what?'

"'Wouldn't say. I gave him thirty cryptograms. Thrice what he deserves.'

"'When?'

"'Saturday before last.'

"'Do you know a young and attractive employee at the American Embassy, a sort of smart aleck? Has a widow's peak that rivals Aquanetta's? Name's Daeng?'

"'Daeng? Maybe. I believe Oliver brought a trick around here once, said he worked at the embassy. Something I should know?'

"'Not yet.'

"I put down the phone. Where I'd seen him before had come back to me. Daeng was the lad who'd fallen or been pushed into

Klong Dan when he'd stood on the jetty there talking with Olie. The day I'd made it to Thonburi to get my ganja—with interest: feloniously prodigal. I inquired if Chain knew Daeng well.

"'For play card. Only few year. He live America (when) he young.'

"End of that lead, since Chain wouldn't deal with Olie: or so he maintained. But Olie could be sprung by now. Free: today! I gave my dumbbells a break and worked out while I thought this through. There was the unmarked car to factor in: with Princess D.'s messenger, who'd scratched for Chain and tracked Olie, sitting in it. Chain; Olie; Olie's ganja; and the stolen icon: that messenger's concern, not with retrieving it when he re-searched my flat—just its whereabouts. *Au moins,* he'd made a mental note of me at the wat. And surely gleaned that I was not newly acquainted with Olie. Wat Sai isn't easy to find, and how did I know he was holed up there? I rang Rollo Y-z again:

"'Now what?'

"'Did Olie ask you to buy some liquor lately? At, say, a discount?'

"'Vodka.'

"'Gotcha.' I hung up.

"Well, be wise to make certain there's no blo in our room, but that's really it. –Except for the icon—which murkily *did* broker a world outside: and precisely because nobody wanted it! Also, good guess, not fiddle about with polishing off this Stoli. In fact, best to get cracking on that right away...

"Chain was in no disposition to help me and questioned the advisability of attempting to dent half a gallon. *I*, after a tonicked seventh shot, no longer fret with advisability. What, in living with him, was ever advisable? I fixed on the Buddha, fancying now, if I tried hard enough, I'd stare it down. Chain followed my struggle. I said to him:

"'You see this Buddha me before?'

"'Before what?'

"'Before I have?'

"'Yeh.'

"'Where?'

187

"'For what you ask? Not business you!'

"'Temper, temper…' I smiled. He flopped into bed—and claimed he'd seen a monkey with its paw in a hole: an astrological bad luck sign. He was guilty as sin. I tickled his tummy. Annoyed, or pretending to be, he slapped my hand.

"'You know about Jim and five Buddha heads? Jim Thompson?' I pursued.

"'That one buy. –Museum take.'

"'Buy from who?'

"'Not know!'

"'Think know! …I think you *know*.'

"He pulled on the bedsheet and twisted it around his head, like the hermit's balaclava minus vents; and risking suffocation, lay like that for five minutes. Then he loosened it enough to expose his mouth, and got out: '–Big man English, boss me. Not good. Khun Jim buy—from my boss me, *not good!*'

"I smoked our remaining ganja sticks and slugged back, sans enumerating, additional highballs while wondering why Daeng, since he'd been caught, was still employed. Wouldn't the embassy have fired him—if not worse: brought charges, had *him* arrested? Or was this how he came to be shoved into the klong? Embezzling one hundred and sixty cases of Yank Stoli at a throw is a lucrative operation—uncovering it could avoid the potential exposé of a stunning U.S. taxpayers' rip-off. So they'd have relished learning who else was in on it. Who else better as middleman—and possible instigator in the first place—than someone white? A monk, to boot? Get a higher price from white consumers. So, threatened with prison, I speculated, but told if he sang he could go free and keep his job, Daeng sang. Did all this end there, or were Pitt's trumped-ups tossed in?—like implicating *me* in the vodka, Chain's gambling, and Olie's dope? Daeng: the stoolie on the Stoli, I mused amused as I sank, miserably, into the swirling klong of sleep…

"When I stepped dripping out of the shower at 6:00 a.m., Chain was sitting on the edge of the mattress, rubbing his eyes.

"'Where you try go last night?' he yawned.

"'What you mean?'

"'Last night, middle of night, I wake up—because you boxing door. –Look for lock, want open, want go out.'

"'You joke now?'

"'No joke! Ask *pai nai?* Have no clothes. Naked! *And:* you not know me!'

"'Why you joke?'

"'Cory, I say, no joke… –I take you bed. After, quiet.'

"I toweled myself and dressed. He had curled up and put the pillows over his face. I picked them off; kissed him quickly; and, in the way of placating him, admitted, 'I very drunk. –*Mao-mao*. Don't worry.'

"'How not worry? Live with crazy man.'

"I in no wise dismissed this sleepwalking. While waiting for the bus, I shook with the remembrance that my dad had been what they've since identified as a 'reactive' somnambulist, especially during puberty. He was twelve when his family lived on the top floor of a nine-story tenement. He would climb the stairs to the roof in his sleep and balance along its foot-wide parapet. Discovering his trysting place, his terrified parents had to grab his nightshirt—in a nerve-wracking hush that wouldn't startle him, or he'd have pulled free of it and plunged to the street. In time they shackled him to his steel bed frame. My dad was legendarily powerful, even at twelve, and would snap the shackles, break his chains, and get on with his weekly—or nightly—balancing act."

I drew a blank on this illness. I said, "He did grow out of it, no?"

"Not before his parents were forced to rent a ground-floor apartment… and fix bolts on its doorway and hide the keys. But I can't say he ever grew out of it. In current parley, that 'motility' merely shed its literalness. Because I vividly recall as a child—believing I was dreaming—watching him leave his room in his sleep and tilt on invisible wires.

"We alternated the days we went to see Randolph, Chain and I: since Chain (glowering) derided my hunch that he'd benefit if we went together. I assumed Chain skipped his turn more than once. Randy chatted briefly, often stared into space, and generally weakened. It bid fair that Chain had something to do with the thefts of the five Buddha heads, as well as *my* Buddha, like at least pinpointing their original locations. I'd spot Herr Altmuller in the mobbed soi along Bangkok Bank, artlessly elbowing through the squeeze. Feeling I shouldn't, or needn't, I'd refrain from attracting his notice. I was positive that the world was about to attract mine. And so, in its ecliptic redeployment, it was.

"Rollo Y-z had lent me a typewriter that must have been vintage in the '40s. When I was down to my knuckles with jabbing one night, tracking the Olympic abs—read, Hellenistic—on ancient Hindu statues suspiciously stored in warehouses east of the city, Chain decided to irk me: skated morose figure-eights behind my back. This meant he wanted to talk: or was almost but not quite certain he did. To grant him time to work up courage, I let him stew until I'd hoisted a white flag on an over-tense cohesion. Then I whinnied, 'Yes, what is it?'

"He sat on the tiles and lifted huge, bovine eyes. He moistened his parched lips. 'Have dream,' he said.

"The dream was set in our room at the Aphrodite, but it invoked a wood staircase, flush with the wall facing our bed, that led to a platform: there was no opening in the ceiling to a second floor. A salt-and-pepper-bearded, heavy-set, older than middle-aged man sat on the landing and peered down at Chain, who lay nude and supine at the foot of the stairs.

"Chain had this dream five nights in succession. He assured me this forecast that he'd shortly hear from its co-star: –Albert, the proprietor of Café de la Vertu, a bistro in Paris.

"Albert sent Chain Christmas cards: none having arrived in '83 accounted for Chain's deepening morbidity since Christmas—'No Randy; I not care Randy.' Chain insisted he was psychic: he invariably dreamt of something important before it actually occurred. He devoted an hour to tangible proofs. Mah Seekai, attentive in the wall, was too graphic for me now to dismiss the preternatural out of hand. I interpreted the five nights as the five-fold path of Buddha; and his realized predictions as déjà vu. Animists easily believe that many people have prophecy; yet somehow it seldom wins them the city lottery.

"Albert's Xmas card arrived, pursing the dreams, three months late: addressed to Soi Rongphasi Cow, and Chain had picked it up that morning. What all this rigmarole was really about was that he needed me to read it for him—and was loath to show it to me. He preferred Khun Apirak not learn what it said and hadn't the fee extorted elsewhere for a French translation. Moreover, he was adamant in his reluctance to let a disinterested stranger, but in days conceivable tattler, see its contents. Trying to coax it from him would not have been quality time. I'd let him attempt to decipher it himself for a while; eventually he'd have to fail and usher me in. I'd act indifferent; and conceal my fear of what its message held for me.

"He safe-kept the seasonal greeting in a breast pocket; and by the (again magical) fifth afternoon devised a compromise too naïve to jeer at. He'd present the card in one hand and with his other cover most of the writing with a napkin, slowly lowering it as I translated each sentence. That way, if we reached a no-no section, he could yank away those secrets. A fragile procedure, this. I had to sit with my own hands behind me; any attempt to adjust a cramp—which brought them suddenly forward—precipitated an instant withholding of the revelations. So it all required patience—and no fast moves…

"It was a large card; while I don't retain the crèche or crosses on the Euro-trash flap, the remaining folds had an anal-retentive, minuscule, and closely lined script. It took two full afternoons of bickering to get to read this affidavit, but here's the gist of it:

"It opened conventionally with Year-End salutations and inquiries after the health of Chain and his family. Then an acknowledgment of Albert's dearth of missives—that this after all is due to Chain's continuing stubbornness, and that he must shoulder the blame for it himself, since Chain has not responded to four very specific letters mailed on such and such previous dates. Albert *knows* that Chain is waiting for airfare back to Paris: he can't possibly send that until Chain follows through on his request, a request Albert reminds him he made in Paris, and thenceforth repeated in every letter.

"To wit: Chain must go north and scout out parents looking to sell a sixteen-year-old son for circa 800 USD: but 300 would be better. Chain is to aim for that: three hundred. Then cash for the boy's trip will be money-ordered to Chain: who will find it futile to use to return himself—for in that case, Albert shall not underwrite his French visa. After the boy deplanes in Paris, Albert guarantees he'll DHL a fare for Chain.

"Chain ripped the card in two! He shrieked that he was no fool: once he boarded a boy on to Paris he could never expect Albert to forward a ticket for *him* to return! There I agreed. Thrown by the pleasure I was clutching, courtesy of Chain's torment, I forewent a response to Albert's treachery. Besides, the above fitfully translated, I needed some background to it in order to understand what I was reading; after an hour tedious with equivocation, Chain provided this:

"The reason he'd come back—the last time, days in advance of meeting me—was to renew his French six-month visa. *–I* realized it was then that he also did his Pol Pot runs. Chain reserved the exact number of round-trip flights he'd previously made; I estimate they were thinned out over a decade. Immediately prior to his final flight, Albert had imposed his need for a toy-boy from, vaguely, Phrae or Utaradit, where such sales are common. Chain refused to specify which town or village: and studied me distrustfully on my third urging. Before his initial journey, he had taken a crash course in French at the Alliance Française—a reinforced memory for him: since the Alliance stands alongside the Aphrodite. But hadn't Chain selected the Afro himself?

"In Paris, he became cashier at Café de la Vertu; and nursed Albert's invalid mother, who fawned on him. She loved when he fixed Thai food. He devoted his time off to attending her bed and sometimes slept in her room. I assume her death shortly before that last visa/Pol Pot run had much to do with his sudden dispensability. This brings us to *why* Albert is in the market for a boy when Chain clicked so well—a topic saved for the closing paragraphs.

"They declare this shall be the last plea for a second boy, that Albert is worn down with reiterating its necessity. By the summer of 1981, he'd found Chain's conduct insufferable. Albert feels house-confined, like a detainee—or a music-grinder's *monkey (!)* on a leash. He can go nowhere without Chain's duplicating his steps, a shadow with a spyglass on his every move; he has no free will, with Chain a private eye preventing his even talking to another young man. He cannot breathe for Chain's tailing him; he is suffocated by Chain's megalithic possessiveness: an unreasonably assumed proprietary when it is he, Albert, who employs Chain, supports Chain, loves Chain. Yet this very true love cannot withstand such limitations, so crazed an imprisonment. If he pays for two Thais, then he, paying the piper, calls the tune. This is not to proclaim he necessarily wishes to be unfaithful, but he certainly has that prerogative. What grievance needs Chain have remedied—who owes him everything: a life in Europe, generous vacations, an easy job, trips home, a warm new family, the fulfillment of his Occidental dream? Whence, then, this assault?

"He asserts he can handle—or juggle—two lovers and still wants Chain as both lover and friend, as well as trusted employee. It ends on that note, with grave protestations of enduring affection, etc., etc. And the card is signed, 'Forever, Albert de Crescent.'

"As I say, Chain, at will, tore the billet-doux out of sight; I endured this, largely by registering his macho reaction to someone else in a triad's driving seat. He listened, mortified, to its climactic accusation, denouncing it as 'sanitary napkin' from a sexual butterfly and enemy, the lies of sewerage incapable of feelings, a superannuated child-molester, a traitor to Thailand and its democratic hopes! So virtuoso a rage! Then he thoroughly demolished the card and fled.

"The watchdog gone, I collected the greeting's fragments and placed them on the bed. I had to see that signature again. 'Albert de Crescent.' Where had I heard that name before? And how many persons could have so odd a name?

"I headed for Suan Plu, found a 7-eleven, bought a pint of decent brandy, and lit out for the hospital: if I stepped on it I'd make its evening open hours. Randolph didn't recognize me at first; the pint was more familiar: he let me slip it under his pillow 'for later, when they turn down the lights.'

"I said: 'Randy, did Héloïse de Crescent have a brother—perhaps years younger than she?'

"He gasped, 'Just a nip now, no one's looking.' Before I could stop him, he had out the flask, its cap twisted off, and two fingers gulped away.

"'Remember?' I persisted, slipping the pint back under cover.

"'Sure,' he smiled, wiping his mouth with the sleeve of his pajamas. 'What you wanna know? Name is Albert. He's born 1926. Héloïse is born in 1911. I remember these things like they was yesterday. But I can't remember yesterday.'

"'Did you meet him here in Bangkok?'

"'Uh-huh. Albert comes to visit his sister every so often. Back around, let's see… '57, first time.'

"'Is that when he met Chain?'

"'Humm—come to think of it, yeah, musta been, at the Oriental. But he looks him up on subsequent trips. Takes to the kid. Who doesn't?'

"'And takes him to Paris—finally?'

"'Yeah… Why not? Chain is legal age by then, eighteen or so, maybe more. I see him in Paris myself. He's doin' just fine.'

"'So you went there a lot?'

"'To rendezvous with Jim. Import/export deals, I think …Often… plans for a renova—… And sometimes we visit Héloïse. By then, Jim buries the hatchet with her. Or hopes he does. I get a different take on that. –Little hustler, Chain, ain't he? In the best sense of the word. Does O.K. for himself.'

"Randy began to gag and trailed off. When he composed himself, his eyes went blank. An attendant poked his head in and signaled closing time; I told him I'd be only a minute. I leaned in to Randy's ear and whispered, 'I assume Sarit Thanarat was field marshal then. You say Chain carried his codes under a napkin.

To whom?' His gaze remained vacant. I whispered again, 'Randy, for whom?'

"He focused slightly. 'For the former regent, Prime Minister Pridi.'

"'Pridi Banomyong?'

"'Him. Chain delivers them to Jim, of course. But Jim was to pass them on. Jim and Pridi, both those guys are ultraliberals— didn't I tell you this?'

"'Does he, then?'

"'I don't know, Cory. I'm not involved in big political maneuvers anymore. It's strictly silk for me. Pridi was deposed in 1947, you must know that. And the name "Siam" gets changed back to "Thailand" two years later... Pridi goes to China, what he does after that, I don't keep up... Can I have another sip?'

"'Soon as I leave.' The attendant stomped, now, with an intolerant frown. Randy noticed him, became confused, and began to babble. I rose, smoothed his limp hands, and started for the door. He watched me walking away from the bed: and, with a telling effort, called out, 'Pridi died last year in Paris! ...Jim always sees him *there*. Pridi lives mostly in Canton for twenty years, but Jim goes to see him in Paris. I think Chain also meets Pridi there. Something to do with getting Pridi back into Thailand... and bringing him back as *prime minister!* Ya see, Mr. Simon, Chain has expressions... that are all his own. And no one can... duplicate... his solid footfall. When you're with him, you think... you can touch *every*thing... that is not in the room.'

"The attendant came close to manhandling me. During that night Randy finished what remained in the bottle and in the morning suffered a second stroke. There was no foretelling this, but those words of Randolph Wetzel, architect and gentleman— his tribute to Chain—were to be the last I would hear him say.

"I went to the Alliance before retiring. Lacking a new third degree for Chain, preferably a French-related discomfiture, the Alliance would be the place to find one. An ad on their corkboard argued for attention: a lecture-demo of Sri Lankan fire-eating *commencer demain soir* at the Thai Language school on Yenakat Road, a nearly deserted forest lane south of and parallel to Sathorn. I chose that. The event and its precise location might rattle him. –I underestimated them.

"I geared up for introducing the 'diversion' to him, then lost objectivity when, hour after hour, he failed to appear. I thought about that irritating woman Héloïse de Crescent, and how her sympathies following surrender had militantly disfavored independence for French Indochina. She'd have rubbed raw against Pridi and Thompson, let alone Randolph… Finally, I fell asleep in my chair.

"I bounced when Chain came in, the clock reading 4:25 a.m., and automatically shouted: 'I not want—'

"'*This* how you like!' he shouted back and got into bed with all his clothes on. He never went to sleep and left at dawn when I did, claiming he'd go to the hospital that morning. When I returned from work, I found him in the room, leaning over the bed table gently caressing his celadon jewel box. I'd checked at the Arts Department and learned this item was trawled to the surface in 1974: from the first fifteenth-century shipwreck discovered in the Gulf of Siam. He'd quietly open and close that empty minaudière during the next half hour.

"After I put down my briefcase, undressed, showered, and had a cigarette, he said, rather softly, 'You give him drink?'

"I made no response. Carefully and detachedly, he described Randolph's condition: Randolph was in coma. He ended with, 'Now just you, me.'

"'But Randy's still a—'

"He cut in quickly: '–Will die.'

"The route I chose to get to the language school that night took us along the moat at the Civil Aviation Centre to a walled switchback. Its street sign read, in Thai and English, 'Soi Pridi.' I stopped there and looked up at it, as though to discern if we were walking in the correct direction, because I wanted to make sure he saw it. He did, but had no reaction then.

"When we turned into Yenakat, that lane was pitch black: we virtually fell over a massive tree trunk. Chain told me to strike my lighter so we could see what was there. When I did, I instantly froze; but *he* stood back, set to flee. The center of the trunk, blasted by age, was a natural simulacrum of a temple scroll's entrance to hell. Within that crater was a clumsily painted Phra Malai, in the guise of a monk, floating over a cauldron scrum with the bug-eyed condemned. The duck- and crocodile-headed demons that stoke the fire were lifting their flaming fingers to *wai* the flying Phra. This vaginal crevice and the larger branches of the now-obvious pipal tree wore red and yellow sashes. Cycloramic offerings—tiny shrines, cooked rice, fruit and fruit drinks, incense and joss sticks, and figurines of Lao and Taoist deities— were stacked as merlons to block egress from the bark. Ominous objects representing unidentifiable fauna, votive tablets, and ideogramic tentacles swayed above us at the edge of the area I could illuminate. I sensed that *area* beyond it had vanished, as in the Thompson House soi. The dark hermit and hunter wasn't visible: yet we knew he was there. In his stead, in the viper-nest roots, were miniature spirit-servants, or mediums. Each had a spear piercing his jowls, and some, the flagellants, beat bloodied hatchets on their bodies. Chain's knees buckled under him, and his utter loss of strength riled me enough to nelson him and prevent his bolting. 'Stand here!' I instructed. 'For shame!' Minutes passed and nothing moved. I pushed him on.

"Chain's terror at the tree, however, withered before his fury the second he saw the fire-eaters in their loose loin-swaddles. He took the island ritual to be an ignorant display of unshod savagery—one I'd already seen and maliciously planned to expose him to. He insisted that we leave mid-performance and run, not walk, diametric to the haunted monarch—a route so circumferential that by the time we reached the mouth of Soi Pridi, he was exhausted. He leaned against the street pole there. As my eyes traveled up the pole to its sign, he trepidantly followed them and read aloud: 'Pridi.' It dawning on him then that his connection to this name was instrumental to his present ordeal, he finally felt it would help him to comment. He prinked a volitional fan of blue waves over his short right sideburn and said: 'Hero man. Albert not like him.'

"I stirred. 'He try get you hurt him?'

"'He try, he try: I not listen. What I care Albert?'

"'How did—'

"'Enough, Cory. I not want talk this. You think Thailand America? Maybe—(pausing here, to find a phrase he'd heard)— maybe you "tired of living"?'

"Then he clammed up. For what remained of our journey I considered the ways in which Albert de Crescent may have wanted him to, or thought Chain could, betray Pridi: and until last year may yet have wanted him to. Strung out myself by the bo's doormat to Downstairs, when I entered our room and spied his celadon again, I was driven to share the book I was reading. He would take his lumps for making me turn my human control over to spirits at Hell's grating. I *had* scouted the locations: at high noon—and at high noon experienced little. That night I'd seen Héloïse, Abelard, and Albert amongst the penitents. To play his ill-advised ethnic sensitivity, I pointed to a passage in the medieval chronicle of a Portuguese soldier of fortune who describes active cannibals in the hinterland north of Chiang Mai. Chain wouldn't speak to me for days.

"DURING HIS REFRESHED WITHDRAWAL, which brings us to circa March '84, Philip Bailey, the Vs of his ears anchoring a joint and a pencil in addition to the straps of his surgical mask, elected to counsel me:

"'New York and London are museums—tomorrow *is* in Asia,' he chewed. 'But I'm worried about the company you keep.' I thought, and the company *that* company keeps: like Albert de Crescent, Martin Pitt, and General Pol Pot. Bailey went on to say who I banged, babe, was my affair, yet I still ought to upgrade my bumps. He suggested a snooker club overlooking the municipal racetrack where choicer Thais, not altogether distant from matters of interest to me, and better for my health, were generally 'on tap.' I skipped investigating his toss-up concern with my health and went.

"When I did, two upper-crust Thais were standing center-room: a psychiatry professor and a sociologist, both in their thirties, both keen, lean, intelligent, and stylish, their wide cliff-like cheekbones dropping to cruel ravines and long, tight lips. The professor had known Jim Thompson and been invited to a number of the dinners Jim was famous for. I pretended to only polite curiosity: and learned that Jim favored casseroles heaped with bread crumbs, served champagne in old jam jars, and (bringing him closer than I might have wanted) had contrived those jungle gardens in the city's five-star hotels and designed the silk costumes for the original *King and I*. Then the gossip turned to the abuses and subversive in miscegenation. The sociologist noted, 'On occasion, my peer and I work as a special-tastes team for farang ourselves.'

"As a result of their similar appearance, the overpowering effect of their partnership, the erotic topic under discussion, and the highballs I was consuming, these two accomplices schooled abroad made an indelible impression on me: they were to populate my dreams for the balance of my time in Bangkok; and spice my sleep for years. In the maiden dream, I was standing on the moonlit, shipwrecked Gulf of Thailand gazing out over the ocean, where a Yaksha, an imaginary, squat dwarf, and a Makara, a truncated dragon with a cat's spine and haunches, were sitting in the waves. Then a graceful Harihara, or four-armed combination of Siva and Vishnu, came gliding across the water and up onto the beach. Once there, it fissioned, not into Siva and Vishnu, but the professor and his comrade: discalced but in their flapping, memorized silk shirts and trim trousers. Nonchalantly, they approached me, the professor taking a position to my left and the sociologist one that blocked retreat. The professor engaged me in diversionary small talk concerning the *Ramakian* creatures and play of light upon the inlet; and stretching my waistband, fingered my member, bending slightly to massage it. He did this principally to distract me from the sociologist: who, reaching around and unknotting my drawstring, thumbed down my sweatpants to discover no jockeys; and, with bile, seize that advantage to grip my buttocks individually in order to keep them prized apart and deftly enter me. The dream broke my sleep. Not deflated by anus interruptus, I had to revive this vignette consciously and masturbate to it to overcome my wakefulness.

"When the dream recurred, the mythic figures got short shrift and segued to the tight-tummied seducers. Or they'd start with stretching my waistband to 'slap the monkey.' In time, as soon as I saw the fabulous pewter-skinned images, I'd sit up and turn on the bed lamp.

"This scenario reads like the teenage runaway and the boardwalk cops. However, the enshrining of the encounters at the snooker-hall that evening as archetypal punitive surrender—justifiably eroticized—is conclusively owed to the plump and late-intruding Nok. Nok: the scheming putty, whom Martin Pitt in his power games played against Chain. When I saw Nok, Chain's competitor-errant for Martin's blessing, appear, I felt the thumb I'd been hanging by slip from its ledge and lower me into a region for which every inch had to be contended.

"At first he assumed the role of junior member in this opprobrious elite and took liberties with them as the hungriest and, tolerated by age, more habitually unpredictable of the moonlighters guzzling there. Guzzling he *was*: lit on arrival. Then, without warning, Nok put his chips on an irreversible audacity: he suddenly unbuttoned my shirt in front of the others, and firmly cupping my left pec, sucked on its nipple. He sucked like a starved stepchild for a full minute, making a high-pitched gurgling and nestling clatter. And I *had* to greenlight him. Having already circulated the tilt and measure of my prong where that would do slapdash damage, posting his intimacy with me for the whole city to condemn seemed exactly the eviction whose finality I required. A previously uninvolved gang at the pool table approached us the better to watch him feed—and hear that amplified sound track. One amongst them was absolutely glued to his activity; though out of uniform and in neat, played-down bar-hopping garb, I knew him at once: it was the royal messenger. Had he been staking me out, Nok, both, or just by happenstance relaxing there? Whatever his mission, his eyes remained peeled with blatant disapproval on Nok until the latter, purring at my belly and tickling a stair to my neck, re-buttoned my shirt, finished his jug, and scrambled for the exit. The messenger walked to the bar and stared at his own reflection in its silver mirror... and at the door, clearly undecided whether to stay still or leave. He at no point examined me, either directly or through the mirror. There were several extended moments in which nothing was heard except the low love-plea on the jukebox.

"Then, deadpan, the psychiatrist warranted: 'That Hat Yai Muslim Nok is a commercializer—when he's otherwise unemployed! His clients are quite perverse. Men who have lost, and lived on to become their own mothers.'

"I nodded perfunctorily, stepped away from the unsettling pair, and covered the stretch to the messenger, carefully plonking myself between him and the door. I belted, 'Sawat-dee cap! How's Princess D. these days?' He was stunned: he had not placed me before; and floundered for a buoy. So he'd not been tracking *me*. In fact, he was finding it hard to link me up as louche and compliant wet nurse to Nok's public nourishment. His face cramped.

"'Sawat-dee cap,' he sulked. 'I—I know your friend. The monk.'

"I said, 'Oh, do you? Oliver? From where?'

"He fumbled, evidently not accustomed to flexed, or any, cross-examination, and dealt me a trump: 'The summer palace—in Phrae. He was a guest of Her Serene Highness.'

"'Ah, what woman can resist the mole on that toothless charmer? Can I buy you a drink, Khun? A statuette went missing shortly after he was there?'

"The secretary was dumbfounded. 'How does Mr. Cory know that?'

"'Khun—' I began.

"'My name is Kob.'

"'Kob, I didn't take it. –Why didn't you?'

"Without his regimental cap, Kob's delicate features were improbably boyish: a skittery gosling on a hawk's quest. He sulked again, 'Neither did Nok.'

"'But I ask, when you searched my room when I was out, why didn't *you?*'

"He wisely judged that a try at getting past me to the exit would be useless—as well as confessional—and claimed he wouldn't mind a martini. I ordered one; and when it stood before him, challenged his dodge: 'Nok *is* a treasure-smuggler, isn't he, son?' Kob seized the stemware, brushed the pick stabbing its onion, which dropped on the counter, and gulped down the cocktail—a drinking-novice, too. I continued, 'What you mean is, it doesn't matter whether Nok, Oliver, or I stole the statuette. You want the man who organized such a complicated theft: number-one in a royal and other brazen crimes. Have you come across a film enthusiast who might swipe movie memorabilia—even before a go at gold, devotional artifacts? Or an oil plumber twice your size, armored with fur like an animal, who wears corrective lenses joined by a damaged bridge?'

"Kob looked confused: no quisling ever appeared so guilty. He gasped, haplessly, 'I am afraid that I have not. Cory has? There is a reward for the proper and respectful recovery of that Buddha…'

"'A reward,' I whistled. 'Good …Very good.' I worked on my own tumbler, hugging his side and attempting through body language to express support. For whatever untapped resource, I did not feel as undone as that poor fellow looked. I'd no need to ask if Nok had reached him and told him the icon was in my flat. That inevitable had gone its way: insisting *I* must plant the tree worth shaking. Nor could my co-sleuth know what world else was arbitrated here. Pensively drafting Kob as a fourth party with whom to seal a contract, I assured him, 'Listen to me, brother, we will set this to rights. Please: give me your card.'

"IN APRIL, I'D LEARN—from Chain—of Nok's slur earlier that evening, which sheds more light on his calculation. Nok had run into Chain, thought of me, and taunted him for his rebarbative failure of patriotism in Nan, Loei, and Phrae, sanctimoniously claiming it was necessitated by Chain's blasphemous love for an undead outsider. So when later making the pool hall a pit stop and noticing three hookers there who were Chain's soul-mates, he knew lapping at me would not take an angel's hiccup to come to Chain's attention. His insult was multimotivated: to disgrace his downgrader in re-proving me a bagatelle; to court max antagonism (a local compulsion); and the suicidal triumph in slapping a perceived social inferior (Chain) with a revenge-requiring loss of face.

"After Kob thanked me, and excused himself, I cycled my scrofulous hooching. Can't say to where—I'm assuming the usual ossuaries. Of course, the fool and the drunkard find their way home. I did that. And passed out.

"When Chain came in, his shuffling woke me. I glanced at the clock on the bed table, though the table stood a half foot lower than the mattress and you had to rise slightly to see anything on it. Chain, who slept on the opposite side, often asked me to tell him the time. Once I quarreled, 'Why you not lift your head and read clock yourself?' He'd elucidated, 'For what? Know *you* do for me!' There was a giant, opaque jar of vitamins on the congested table obscuring the face of the clock; I needed to nudge it aside. It was past 5:00 a.m.

"I rubbed my eyes: I was still flying. I watched Chain disrobe, a labored pavane of exaggerated insouciance, then strut pointlessly here and there, fake yawns, and slip into bed. He appropriated the entire top sheet.

"'What you do with him?' I yawned myself.

"'What people gay do,' he rejoined deliciously.

"–Screwing: which wasn't always required …contrary to opinion, and especially with him, not a requirement at all in many paid trysts.

"'Did it hurt?' I asked.

"'No!' he stomped. Then with supreme flippancy, scorned: 'I enjoy!'

"I lay very still. So he goaded further:

"'He suck toes me too. And asshole. I *enjoy!!*'

"I dove for the vitamin jar, swept it up, and swung it toward him. He caught my wrist in midair—he was more than nimble when acting as instigator—twisted the jar free and smashed it into my forehead. The blood spouted across the pillows in a fraction of a second. Chain hauled off and threw the bottle at the wall of spirits. It shattered, scattering hundreds of vitamin tabs in every direction. Then we went for broke with a torrent of knuckles; he, being sober, pummeled to effect while I didn't— pinned me to the mattress by chairing on my chest and gripping my right hand in his left: then galvanized his own freed right to whack my brow a dozen times with all his strength.

"He stopped, leapt from the bed, lit the fluorescent, and cried: *'Bah khun!* (You're crazy!) Put clothes now! –Hospital!'

"He was tessellated with blood—it cost precious minutes to realize it was mine, and to parse his meaning: wounds fester fast in the tropics—we had to get those he'd inflicted treated quickly. I felt for where the blood was oozing, centimeters be- hind the hairline over my left eyebrow, and from my nose and lower lip. I vomited. Chain lugged me, still vomiting, past the nightwatch, offering him no explanation but demanding he or- der a taxi: *'Rao, rao!* (Real fast!)'

"I first started to feel the pain in the emergency room of Bangkok Nursing. Promoted to a nauseous victim of dry heaves, I was clear enough to sign myself in. The closest-concerned at- tend operations here in order to coax the patient's soul to re- main housed in his body. While my hairline was being shaved, my cuts cleansed, and stitches put through by a calm woman surgeon, that closest-concerned leaned across the operating bench and pressed hard on my inner elbow. His admonition to my soul was anything but orthodox and registered as a promise more likely to persuade it to flee than stay in its temple. He said: 'Nok!—that one, I know. I know how he make! I get that one for this. And *you* too! *Both!'*

"I looked a mess. A cotton swab, a half inch wide and three in length, was sewed into the suture on my head like a silly white bow tilted too far forward: it bobbed when I walked. Another small swab rode shotgun with my swollen nose. What a buffoon, in front of a class! Late as it was when we reached the Afro, I rang Rollo Y-z to tell our chair I'd be absent.

"'Tell her yourself!' he retorted curtly and hung up.

"The vanishing taillight on his resuscitated conscience? 7:55 a.m. Monday, I'd trouble thinking. The painkillers were augmenting the alcohol. Revolted at last by dependency's roadblocks, I switched gear and called Soren Cass Blackblatt, firm now in my resolve to pin down Pitt's most frequented hideout.

"Soren was jubilant: and stepping on my purpose, he offered a gift—plus, inadvertently, a warning. 'Basic-call-ee, Ah don't like people, but Ah like y'all: n' oughta present a sailor-boy's cap! It's *so* you! Ah gotchall a hip-kerchief instead: the very rage, stateside. Come in various shades, indicatin' your sexshul nature: bellicose, submissive, cooin', or dirty. –Bought apricot: *that* don't imply nothin'. So it's a icebreaker. Ah'll drop it by.'

"'And have *Ah* fresh dish for you, muscles! Philipa Bailey copped the kick-boxin'-sportscaster gig on English radio—answers her daydream: it'll keep her off the streets.'

"'Now, guess who we had to pick off the street, followin' Philipa's interview? Herr Volker Altmuller! Remember her? Me and Phil found her barefoot on Yenakat—her feet were cruddy! But that ain't all: so was her clothes, what she still had on, stinky n' stiff like they never seen soap, they could get up and swish on their own. She was laughin', laughin', dear heart, like the mechanical lady shills a freak show. And tellin' us, "Zhere are Englishmen in *meine* room!" Her face was swiped with chocolate. She loves Mars Bars. They're to consume! Not use for a base! We subdued Volker and took her to Bangkok Christian. They'd have no truck with her: thought the chocolate was shit and suggested the nut shed in Thonburi. Did she do a Baby Jane there, screamin' *that* bin was fulla Brits! They put her on downers. Had to. She's still there, Cora. Orderlies say hasta be. We hit on the Kraut NGOs—they wouldn't fool with her, neither. Same her relations, who *Ah* coughed-up to call in Cologne! Ah read her beads: a broken-ass sexpat loser: *Ah read her beads before*, don't say Ah didn't. Forget visitin': she don't know no one. Won't for a era. Maybe never.'

"Dammit, pushed over-the-edge, I bedeviled myself... I lisped sorrow; and cut to my inquiry re Pitt. Soren asked (Lord-a-day!) why'd a body scratch for that cracker?; then spilt, 'The Mah Seekai, a tradin' post in the Soi of Lost Souls.'

"'The Mah Seekai?' I echoed. 'Now didn't I know that?'

"'Wha'd you say, heart?'

"'Nothing. Listen, thanks for the gift and info. Talk to you soon.'

"I'd begun to theorize on Volker's disaster when the phone rang. I feared it was Soren, eager to add worse news. It was Rollo, his voice steadier than when I'd called. 'Look, Cory, I'll tell Madame you'll be late. Grab a tuk-tuk. Invent an excuse—a car accident. Madame's not pleased with you as is. Staying out could give her notions. Ignore the cotton and your kids will too. I know you can do it.'

"I went with Rol's perfect advice. Even the security guard, whom I passed twice daily outside the Alliance, did not acknowledge a change in my appearance. This Isaan fellow had the most uplifting of all Thai smiles: and worked it for me that morning as he always did, though I always returned a default smile. Nubile security guards were paid a buck a day: which I figured sponsored his great smile: I'd not shop on our front step.

"Venturing into the Mah Seekai was another matter: the swabs did inhibit that—as did Chain, now bent on vengeance. He harped on Nok's nourishing stint and announced he'd remain till my scalp healed, then leave me.

"'Not need to wait,' I told him. 'You can leave now.'

"'Can not,' he responded.

"'Why?'

"'I do like this, Buddha not like me.'

"'Why?'

"'You alone, Thailand. Not have family. No friends.'

"'I have Rollo.'

"'This not friend. He come, he not come: same-same him.'

"I asked, incapable of an act in kind, 'If you love me, how you free to leave?'

"'I not love you,' he stated flatly.

"'You don't?'

"'No. Pity you.' He'd flipped through a Thai-English diction-ary while sorting the laundry and had found the word 'pity.' He dangled his soiled annatto briefs, his eyes witching to their whites; and mocking the Peking emperors who gave their robes to a favorite, dropped them on my feet. 'Buddha give me merit I have pity you. But you finish cut on head, I finish you.'

"That evening I went to update myself on Randolph Wetzel's condition and officially learned he'd suffered a third stroke: re-covery was not diagnosed. Closure endorsed I sit sentry outside his room. A few of his cronies came by, and one of them, Crisp-in Dearborn, wearing a derby and scratching his insect welts, stopped to speak with me. Shaping his reminiscing proved no problem: I was able to confirm that after *Seri Thai* dissolved, Randolph had gradually leaned left, along with Jim Thompson's inclination, following Jim's emergence from the OSS. With Jim's disappearance, on Easter Day 1967, Randy had seemed to lose interest in life. He'd 'graduated to an unabashed lecher' and 'a rather committed drinker.' Dearborn did not know a boy called Somboon, or anyone presently who answered to Chain; nor had he ever met Sarit or Pridi. But he chuckled in noting that the Thai government had banned *The King and I*—in which Jim so featured. Seeing it as 'slighting the monarchy,' they'd consid-ered it a boost to Red subversion. Then he told me not to worry about the 'arrangements': Randy's cremation would take place in a spire that he himself had architected. A lump formed in my throat.

"My stitches were removed later that week. Chain faltered on his threat to leave just then, and I let sleeping dogs lie. He leisurely dropped: 'Can go out now, no hat. Not St. Louis. Randy dead.'

"'Maybe I should rethink Chain,' Rollo mused, psyching my

state that night. When I slumped in, he'd been listening to Philip on his old shortwave. 'A job's a job, but sexing with strangers when your closest companion for years is dying? Thais don't dismiss their loyalties. –Some Americans might…'

"'Might what?' I asked from my half stupor.

"'Might what! Might what! –Pretend to no allegiance! Achille and me.'

"'Rollo…' I started to prevaricate.

"'You don't discuss it: or we don't. We must, now. If you hang in here, we must. I cheated with Achille to survive… *You* tempted me, you challenged me. And "Johnny" Achille Vitte was cow-flop, no, a turd? He cooperated.'

"'Wasn't I too being disloyal?' I confessed. 'I put my medication on the stand beside my pillow so that Johnny would have to sleep between us that night. Friends' motives can be murky. Maybe to show off; or to test you and him.'

"'And neither passed that test. Persons close to me expect so much. I can't handle that. I've held up for others in my own fashion, but not when it's ironclad—not holding up, helping out, or any coming-across whatsoever. I'm not obligated in Thailand, that's why I live here. I don't have to prove anything to anyone. No, when you come down to it, not anything at all.'

"'Rollo,' I submitted, forced now to deal with Oliver Littleton and Randolph Wetzel's identical experience, 'it isn't right to test people, either. What test do I invigilate now with Chain? Well, Johnny did learn our vernacular. No longer Achille, he's as Apple as émigrés get. I'm uncomfortable. Let's stop this. What's on the static there, other than Philip Bailey?'

"He snapped back. 'Real weird news. There seems to be a form of cancer infecting only gay men. They're calling it "gay cancer."'

"'Where is that?'

"'San Francisco. New York, too. Probably just a fluke. A momentary scare.'

"'Always something…' I murmured.

"'You look ashen. Randy Wetzel is beyond betrayals. And you will succeed with Chain: he has feelings to spare. Buy tranqs and chill out.' He walked me to his bamboo plant; stared into it as if it were vitreous; and chafed a hand in the hollow of my back. I don't recall his ever doing that before. He concluded:

"'We got you this hustler, politically caught-up, because that exact binding is what you require right now. –Cordie—*so what?* How can flailing yourself, or despising the three of us, alter your nature? Your *temporary* nature?'

"He broke a smile too ingratiating for even his canine to compromise. Yet it wasn't until I reached the Alliance, received its security guard's impartial smile, and returned a truly outstanding one that I knew I was going to mend.

"SUFFICIENTLY EASTERN in binocular by then to accept that gifts—painstakingly chosen—are road signs, I had to try Blackblatt's kerchief to see where it took me. It was the size of a small flag; tied to a hip-loop, you left it to flap alongside your calf. Chain hated the kerchief: he pointed to a screaming, teenage *peuan gong* (group of knit friends) who alone in Harrie's were as saucily accessorized as I. That 'second-family' shrieked nightly on an overhang, oblivious to the annoyance of those nearby, or specifically to disturb and annoy. 'They not care now—the young ones,' Chain deplored. 'Before, not scream same.'

"I scrutinized the campers and isolated one ephebe as pornstar hot—also patrician in feature. On Friday, when I started to leave Harrie's, this splendid hottie kneed the doorjamb, blocked the exit, and felt my kerchief. Fad-apprised, he bleated, 'Apricot mean "up-to-you": so where you *go?*'

"'Not like money-boy.'

"'No money-boy! O no money-boy!' he haughtily protested.

"I snatched at the 'gift' his tantrum promised. And O snatched every check—*his* face dictating numerous checks; and mine, that each would involve a varied and hectic sex glut spermed to the last drop over a killing fifty-seven hours.

"O ordered supper at a gay bistro with a secret second floor on Silom Road: called for a liter of Absolut and that famed and expensive specialty, seafood steamed in a hen-shaped tinsel. Then he located his car. Yes, this teenager had the keys to, or outright ownership of, a spanking new, low-slung convertible—firehouse red, should plebeian pedestrians be myopic. From there, to make sense, or use, of having wheels, he drove us to a drawn-curtain motel. You steer directly through a brown canvas in these: and into a one-car garage while the canvas falls behind your auto, effectively concealing it from public view. In seconds a shutter, level with the driver's window, rises ten inches and out comes an open palm. The driver greases this palm with an optimistic time-tab. The palm withdraws, the shutter descends. Then you hop-to and climb to a sweatshop above the garage appointed with mirrored walls and ceiling, an orgy-size bed, a bidet, a commode, three towels, and a shower-faucet. It is the epitome of tell-no-tales: excluded eyes never see who you and your sweetie or sweeties are.

"O dropped back on the bed immediately; I held his legs up and parted like a pair of scissors to clear off his slacks and Jezebel designer-shorts. Then, as his legs were conveniently reaching for the roof and I standing at the foot of the bed, I grabbed the napes of his heels, sank my tube in his tiny buttocks, and let it alarm his lower intestine, bladder, quivering liver, and the tinseled seafood like the rented escort I assumed I now was. He whistled. Then cried, 'I love—I love this. I love this! I LOVE THIS!!!' He struck the verbiage soon as he shot but kept vigorously grinding his nates to insure that mine not lose their momentum. This was to stimulate an ecstasy uniquely Southeast Asian: sucking on the tip of one index finger while your other middle and index massage the mucus on top of and under your partner's tongue. Then he switched hands, and, after three or four hand-exchanges, shot again. Here I joined him, those emissions heightened and, for customer-turnover purposes, hastened by the extracurricular views of which we'd avail ourselves: I of my labor in the mirror at the head of the bed, he of my scrunched heinie in the mirrored wall opposite.

"Parched following my own double orgasm, and certain I'd dislocated my sacroiliac, I tripped down the stair, making the soda machine in the motel's yard. There I ran into a stud returning from the dispenser in nothing but a pointless towel: he was mopping his brow with its lifted hem. He grinned sympathetically, summoned his breath, and managed to wheeze, 'Very much work, *chai mai?*'

"We left at 6:00 a.m. and drove to O's house. I hesitated: that faux-Greek citadel was his family's home. But O guaranteed an all-clear for the weekend. This unfortunate building had no width: it misered a single living space on each floor. A tin spiral screwed to the fifth and final one, O's bedroom. Its wallpaper was posters of muscle-bound straw-heads, all Caucasian. He unearthed a vial of liquid popper and his Euro-porn treasury and watched with glee as I read the rags and inhaled the amyl nitrate; watched, that is, as best he could whilst bobbing to gargle like my joint was the last stick of sugarcane.

"He danced a centuries-old Lan Na lakhon, framed in the stained-glass insets of his Palladian window, itself inset under the gaudy eaves of that parvenu structure. He said this backdrop wasn't arbitrary, that its colors were those of the kerchiefs Yankees wear; and he'd adore my teaching him what each shade sexually represents via consecutive sampling, experienced clockwise from inset to inset. As he was so young, O's ostiole was now too tight for my irritated tool; and though he'd a variety of local lubes in his john, O insisted any intercourse be au naturel. So I asked him to salivate as I did: and with our combined effort moistening my journeyman, doggied him to widen his *prima via*. Then, he well burrowed, I was able to do my colorful duty upwards of several hours. That haunting slant of his inner eye, his elastic ribcage, and aromatic flanks assisted my topspin until I had worn my knees to the bone. Wiping the blood-beads on them, I felt I'd adequately sung for my supper. But I was yet to learn about this teen…

"O treated me to a sumptuous brunch and three cartons of Pall Mall. Then back to his home: in that inning, for straight, home-plate prostration. The shag dispatched, he invited me to a wedding that afternoon. I thought I read O's lascivious mind, needed time-out, and asked him to swing by the Afro where

211

I could throw together a suitable outfit. Thai tricks have no sense of privacy: when they visit your residence, it evidently is a point of politeness with them to inspect every scattered page, unsealed letter, and stray envelope; to slide back the panels on closets; open your drawers; and uncork, to the last, the containers in your fridge. O, in a circular tour of the room, did just this with uncommon thoroughness, climaxing at my Buddha, whose chadok he sacrilegiously touched.

"Suddenly he asked if I smoked ganja. I lied. Why share that liability? I'd already shared my icon with a hyper-experienced squeeze.

"He clucked, 'You take heroin?'

"'No!' I slammed. –The first flat tire on my holiday. 'Do you?'

"'Sometimes.'

"Someone who 'sometimes' takes heroin? On surface, mistaken generosity, he slid off his belt, unzipped its billfold, and produced a thin packet fastened with two green, crisscrossing rubber bands. 'Here, if you need it.'

"I said, 'I don't, O, save it. Let me wash before I dress. I'll be done quick.' When I was, he was in our bed: separate sheets pulled across his back and legs, his small, bare, and relentless butt the sole proposal visible…

"I sensed a setup: that wedding was held in an auditorium on my army base! It *is* a rent-out for gatherings often unrelated to the military. The ghost of my recruiting officer would be there. –Jahd was always present—to insure I take my bitter medicine. The table assigned us further roiled me. At it was O's entire *peuan gong*, including a snare I'd not connected with his group, yet certainly knew: skeletal Ekarin, the gamine I'd toilet-poked: a ranker in Martin Pitt's cabal. Ekarin shoved a trivet between O and me. The queens were already cutting-up: this conservative atmosphere being an opportunity ferociously superior to Patpong. Hot to the ears, I tried to be inconspicuous; Ekarin, spoiling to expose me, indicated a gaunt and ugly old man at a joining table and shrieked: 'He my exact type! I must to crave him. Must!' I smiled. So Ekarin blared: '*Gahlee*, I not need give you cigarette here! Have many now, no?'

"There were hundreds of guests: in more, the more face: who, soon as they swallowed dessert, barreled for the door. O said: 'Courtesy. Not leave mean still hungry. Mean host not good host.' Shall *I* follow suit? What would I accomplish? I went home with the hottie. And—exploiting images of Jahd—had my last spritz with O. This never pacifies Jahd. When O's erection later tapped me, I awoke in mid-bout to sweat its ongoing rounds. I'd seen him slipping to the canvas, shot, Jahd's head between his or my bloody knees, bathed in its dreadful gloaming.

"Hauling a rucksack of unsolicited gifts, I reached the Afro at 7:00 a.m. on the fourth day, looped, stuffed, and jism-dry. Chain was at the desk. Dressed up to step out the previous night, he obviously had not. He'd been sketching. He usually traced Japanese cartoons. His portrait that morning lifted a demon from the poolside murals, a grotty, bearded male with human flesh punctured on its tusks and horns. Print above the keratin read: 'THIS IS CORY.'

"Utterly defrocked, he rose and put down his pencil. I pleaded, 'Tomorrow, you, me, go Harrie's—O.K.?' He left without a word.

"At the onset of the weekend, O had been forthright: his Belgian partner was shortly expected. Then the two would be flying to Europe, where his lover had registered O in a prestigious school. So I was not surprised when Chain and I got to Harrie's to see O prominently there in the company of this Belgian. Men used to mount a kind of bandstand that protruded onto the dance floor for no particular reason other than to be seen and receive the approval and/or jeers of the crowd. Four men on that bandstand now won my application. The first was O's prize: he could not have been more than twenty, twenty-one, a flawless cinnamon-blond magnificently pumped through his tricolor T-shirt, a Primo Carnera with breeding, as tall, gunned, and covetable as the bodybuilders who functioned as wallpaper in O's boudoir. Respecting transpacific protocol, I made no sign of recognition—pulled on an O Pall Mall and absorbed O's foreign boyfriend: and benefactor. Most gays would give five years for a tumble with him. Yet Primo Carnera had bought O: and O had bought *me* for a last fling. I'd apparently re-earned my spurs: once again a meaningful contender. –Or the East's easiest victim! For I'd noticed two other persons, initially upstaged by the dynamic duo: the plotting Nok and Ekarin. They had taken a step forward so as to be abreast of the duo and were leering directly down at Chain and me. If I could see around corners, as by then was urgent, I'd have been able, after Ekarin, to spot treasure-smuggler Nok wedged up the pipeline. I thought, All right, I will have to clip their wings.

"Chain felt my concentration and wanted to learn what called it. I isolated O and the Belgian for him: but Chain, who'd no interest in whites just turned twenty, and blotted them out, saw only O, poised and pointedly turned away—and weighty Nok and weightless Ekarin, pointedly staring us down.

"'O?' he questioned. 'He good friend Daeng.'

"'Daeng! –Daeng he work American Embassy? Live in America before?'

"'Him.'

"'My knuckles found my chin, that conventional reflex. I said, '…And *fan* O—man Belgian—maybe he live Paris, not Belgium? Put O in Paris school?'

"'Think. Think true.'

"'You *see* man Belgian in Paris? See with Albert? He friend of Albert?'

"'No! Maybe… I not sec young, nice-looking. Never like man, he blond.'

"I felt that ice-hole in the center of my back which the paranoid feel passing a cop. It spreads to their gut. My face must have iced as well: Chain, rather than return his coworkers' stare, examined it, arching a brow.

"'For what you look me?'

"'Why you not tell me before O pal of Daeng? And *fan* O friend Albert?'

"'For what tell?' he cawed, starting to move on. 'You not care this!'

"The next afternoon I made the insane asylum in Thonburi. Volker Altmuller deserved monitoring, and I could use whatever he'd divulge. He was strapped to an iron chair; I watched him through a barred window. 'With these sex addicts, their disease, and the diseases they pick up...,' his presiding caretaker radiated—and promptly stopped when he recognized me. The man was none other than the psychiatry professor at the snooker bar. More unctuous and insinuative at work, he then, in terse précis, announced they'd found traces of pig-scabies tablets in Altmuller's blood, which they believed had triggered his seizure; and thought when his body eliminated that poison he would return to normal. He'd not—had in fact remained violent—and when not violent, given to complaining that there were Englishmen in his cell.

"'There's only *one* Englishman,' I said. The psychiatrist's eyes narrowed. I added, 'I am not English.'

"'Who'd guess you were? Still, criminals often return to the scene of their defacement. To relive the exhilaration—and make sure they left no clues.'

"'Glad you told me,' I chirped, 'I need to brush up on my criminology. But *I'm* not a jailer—in whose varsity transits the brownnoser Nok.'

"He said, 'And *I* am not a slugger—for Her Serene Highness, Princess D.'

"His Pitt-leanings aligned, I was rapt by his perjury. Coincidence couldn't account for the conformity in the many men hounding me. Seeking to relieve some tension, I asked Chain for his worn clothes: I'd clean them. He laughed, stripped, and uncharacteristically buck-naked, taunted me as I scrubbed away in our tub. Involved with trying to connect the incremental hints at *my* guilt, and thrown by their deflectable ease, I was slow to see Chain edging along the rim of the tub with extended arms, as if that rim, in a terrible déjà vu, were my father's tightrope. When he'd earned my devastated jolt, his penis rose. 'Why you hard?' I asked, my heart in my mouth.

"'Because, watch me!' he said with that supercilious tone

used to answer a stupid question. He skittered on until he reached me, his boner brushing my lips. Perhaps to defuse the dread of my dad's balancing-act—with an ungovernably attendant priapism—I licked the moist slit of his urethra; but, the taboo against incest restraining me, went no further.

"That night I bent over Lome's balcony rail to watch Chain dancing below. He was wearing nacreous-floral Indian cottons: a bone-button blouse and cord-waist terrycloth slacks: the '60s-style payment of a recent client and a novelty only to Bangkok by then. His parochialism in showing off this outmoded dress upped my critical scrutiny. There were deep crescents under his eyes and flab at his triceps when he'd lift them, his loose, accordioned sleeves advertising this new imperfection. He looked older to me, far older than usual: my father's age when he most threatened and aroused me.

"His first gray hairs had appeared. Reflecting and reflected in our big mirror, he'd pluck them out. They were zigzagged like lightning, dead as nails: Chain said he was plucking them for that reason, not because they were gray.

"'First few same this: after come many,' he waived, digging in his heels.

"At midnight, in a carbon of Albert, came autumn's more crushing evidence. Chain had annual returnees. As prearranged, an Austrian rendezvoused with him. When he saw Chain, he felt less hot to trot, and politely expressed that, for they'd partied over many years. This would be the last: if not that season then the next, or the one catching up with that. 'Never mind,' he braced the Austrian. 'You want, I introduce friend more young. You point who, I know, I introduce.'

"I advised him that his beehive permitted all the more gray to twinkle. He met me on Silom Road the next afternoon: with a poodle-cut. He had cut off the legs of his Levi's as well: at their jagged hem you could see the bottoms of his brunette cheeks. That display pegged Chain as a prossie. So I shuttled us toward Saladaeng. We'd closet in the ham-hock shop where you and I ate. When he sensed my destiny, he abruptly told me to lunch alone. I asked why.

"'Aunt me, owner. You want I go there for she see what I am?'

"This disparaging nod to his core-tool broke a sound barrier: before I could capitalize on that, he whispered, 'Across street— Thai-boy Daeng!'

"'Where?'

"He glanced discreetly at a satay trolley opposite his aunt's place and added, taking off, 'One talk with Olie.'

"Two yardbirds: embezzler Daeng and, sharing his kabob, the thief Olie, in flashy civvies. Neither had noticed me; I swerved into the ham-hock shop and hurried to a dark table. From there I could study them indiscernibly. I gave Chain's aunt an order and settled myself. Whatever their previous, literal falling-out on the jetty, they were locked in an earnest, amicable tête-à-tête now, and smiled frequently. –Daeng—were his arrogant eyes laurel or walnut? I'd remember only that widow's peak. He was no standard-issue embassy jerk, to whom my stay meant nothing. And Oliver? Well, small the mischief outside that man's ken.

"Confirming this, within the hour, my suppositions were rewarded—if rewarded is the accurate adjective here. Antiquated specs, paunch, pasty face, his scourge of height, chinless, jowly, mouth tic and all, Martin Pitt appeared, coming up from Sathorn; both rose to greet him, Daeng executing a tentative, nostril-level *wai* and Oliver heartily shaking his hand. The three of them proceeded to stand there conversing for what I clocked as thirty-six minutes, with Oliver sometimes translating for Daeng and Pitt making emphatic count-offs on his stubby fingers. Suddenly Pitt hauled back and smacked Olie across the temple. He immediately after jiggled his nose with that paternal-Mafia, cliché gesture; but soon as Olie recouped his stance and breathed more easily, smacked his shaved crown so hard I could see the red welt planted on its pimply pink. Daeng cowered during this but kept in position; the Thai passersby ducked and circled them, not daring to look directly. For a time, Martin engaged in a lengthy explanation, in the course of which with hands and feet he indicated the ground, if not the exact patch supporting them. Finally, Martin removed a wad of bills from his drip-dry shirt and, in a practiced sleight of hand, slipped it to Olie. They continued to speak for four minutes, then parted, Martin turning into a tight subsoi that would let out on Sathorn, the embezzlers crossing Saladaeng—as luck would have it—to take a table in the shophouse.

"I had no choice. I needed to pass them. Oliver saw me, used his cuff to wipe his snot, and said: 'Don't sit down! We're too doss to swing a cat.'

"'Wasn't my intention,' I responded. '–On a roll, sport.'

"I ran to North Sathorn, hooked a right, and stepped under the trees by the Anglican Church. Pitt crossed the canal and, surprisingly, started to walk what would become the hour-long distance to the river. He had not brought—or wished to drive—his car. I could shadow him. It's difficult for people with good vision to spot someone other-side the canal, and Martin's vision was not good.

"He entered a tiny Indian travel agency near the dock; and I swatted flies in the hedged porch of an ice cream parlor three shops away. When he left the agency, Pitt moved toward the pier. At midday, he'd conceivably spend forty minutes waiting for a longtail. I stumbled into the Indian service and gave its motherly administrator an award-winning performance. I was a flustered, ignorant tourist who'd little idea of where to go and only three days to go there: perhaps that gent preceding me was headed some place interesting? He was. Just where? Ubon Ratchathani. And what would one visit there, a gent like that? Well, he'd made arrangements for a bike going out to the cliff paintings, not necessarily the most popular, accessible, or safest destination in the area. My, oh, my! sounds scrumptious! Two flights a day, sir: 'gent' was taking tomorrow's later one. Well! *I've* no such time. So *I'll* grab the early one. And could you book me that bike?

"Luckily, I'd cashed a recent royalty check: and paid in a jiff. When I hit the rocking platform, Martin Pitt was nowhere in sight. Guess that would have been too much to expect. Then again, it would make no more sense boarding the same boat than would the same plane.

"I called gal Friday at Foreign Languages and told her I had food-poisoning, to get me a sub, I'd return soon as I rallied. Wanting to think through just how scatterbrained I was acting, or correctly within a hair of Chain's head, I took the water-taxi to the last stops on the Chao Phya, and back, eight times: not minding the polluted spindrift sporadically flung at me: in fact, hardly conscious of it.

"My plan was to reach the cliffs well in advance of Martin Pitt, build a hutch from which to observe him, and when he arrived, do whatever our tournament suggested was best. The flight was an hour and five minutes, and an airport bus connected me with one passing Khong Jiam, a peninsula created by the meeting of the Moon and Mekong rivers: Pha Taem, the cliff in question, was twelve and a half miles from there. Ubon itself is a sprawling, sleepy town whose thick dust had been temporarily dispersed by our strategists when they'd illegally used its airport to bomb Lao. Jahd was quartered in that forsaken city.

When I alighted at Khong Jiam, I found the hired motorbike, but the cyclist flatly refused to ride near the Mekong. When I asked why, he said: 'Pathet Lao.' The Joint Thai-U.S. Military would have prevented the Pathet Lao from crossing the Mekong by then; yet there was no arguing with this stubborn, suspicious guy. He pointed to the distant rise of Pha Taem: a marker affirming that I'd nothing for it to beat Pitt than to smear my exposed skin with liquid-powder and start at once. I'd brought my mystic switchblade and a canteen of water.

"That canteen grew heavier as I tramped across the most forlorn terrain I've seen to date, a hazy and barren remoteness its few inhabitants historically thought was the end of the world. I lightened that canteen faster than prudent, since the temperature, as I'd later check, was pushing 120. But other than pause to tissue-cleanse my blur, to keep the rise in sight, I marched on.

"I'd lost all sense of time and, unfortunately, reality when a far-off paddling fisherman's unreal lullaby reached me and I finally saw the Mekong. Parked beside the sheer drop on its incongruous, tilted whitewalls was a vehicle I recognized—and, in hindsight, would revision permanently. It was the battered

'47 Buick, its front fenders gracefully swooping to the rear ones. The three big-leaguers' Buick—those spoofs of film noir stars: who'd sampled Chain at his Spirit-Banishing ritual. It was empty. I framed it in mind and began scuttling a trail descending from the bluff; then snapped-to when I heard gunshots. Their echo rebounded softly: as if from across the river. Too heat-dazed to care, I clambered on. It had to be bored teenage soldiers with nothing more exciting to do when they spied me than shoot off their obsolete rifles, which could scarcely reach across that span.

The first cliff painting is a compressed impression of life in 1,000 B.C.: splayed human hands remindful of Arabian halt-signs to Djinns, fishermen and fish traps, and a beetle as large as an apparently under-attack and skidding elephant. As I stopped to examine the partially peeled elephant, a deafening shot rang out: a bullet hit the beast's hindquarter, bounced off, ricocheted from hissing rock to rock, and wheezed over the side of the cliff. I dropped to the trail and stayed down a minute or two. Nothing further. Then I cautiously rose slightly, only enough to ascertain the angle of the bullet, an indent left in the red-clay rubbing. It was slanted sharply upward, meaning the shot had to have been aimed from an advantage beneath me—consistent with the ledge on which I was perched. I'd a mere instant to certify this, for a foot of the drawing surrounding the hit crumbled away and splattered on the path. So much for the universal halt-hands and the checkered prehistory they teach. I parted the thick center in a cluster of cacti along the ledge and, adequately camouflaged, peered over the cliff. What I saw then meant the end of some world.

"About thirty feet below, in his cuffed slate-blue trousers and shirt-jacket, teetering by a fire on a flatiron, which topped lesser rocks extending the shoreline, was the ogre-like and mechanical Goon, the Buick's chauffeur, the grimmest of the trio of hoods: whose brains I'd the opinion could fit in a thimble and still have room for his dick. The Cambodian boatman, Kambu-ja, draped in a red tunic, was balanced behind him on his prosthetic leg, braced by his crutch locked in his left armpit. The Goon's rifle had dropped useless on his two-toned spats, and Kambu-ja, with what had to be a fired fishing-rod reel, was burning that wire into his neck—in effect, garroting him. The ghoul's blanched tongue was bloated, his neck visibly sizzling; Kambu-ja was amazingly still, his strength all in the grip that twisted the wire. The chauffeur's face went blank with nary an utter, and the Cambodian effortlessly swung him about and onto a lower rock, where he shifted in the wash. Kambu-ja prodded him with the ferrule of his crutch: no response. My rejected lover was gripping the Goon's holster pistol in his left hand. Long minutes passed. He methodically lifted his head. I was standing now. We watched each other for a while; a faint curl gathered on his upper lip; and then with a flick of the pistol, he indicated that I should retreat.

"I crawled along the trail, hugging the taller cacti to block further view of me, and made the summit of the bluff. I scalloped with the switchblade; then twisted, as Kambu-ja had, and punctured the four whitewalls. They fizzled one by one; the Buick flattened onto the earth. Totally exposed on that desolate wasteland, I started the long retreat. I'd never known why that trio unjustly saw me as a stag, so perilously contentious for Chain. Now they surely would. If the remaining two had come for the ride, hidden where they were, they'd not ride back.

"I had lots to worry through during the dehydration of my return trek. How did the racketeers learn that I'd go out to Pha Taem? Was that travel agent, the motherly Indian, not so much Mama as a crack thespian—in cahoots with those thugs? And I thought *I* was nominee for best supporting actor (supporting guess who?)! The trio's presence at and footing of his family's ritual says they need, let alone savor, guess-who. Why? Other than serve as their fourth (penetrated) poker-hand, what is Chain's function for them? How do *I* interfere with that?

"Or had Martin Pitt, reducing my confidence now, been aware of me in the ham-hock shop; led me (he'd no car) to Sarah Bernhardt; and launched my trip?

"For the corkage intended for him?

221

"As cash is king here, did Sarah Bernhardt, not reading me as anyone's confederate, just shuffle me on? If I weren't cricket, the trio could always...

"That left Kambu-ja. My lame Cambodian may, or mayn't, have already been by the Mekong awaiting a boat—and not one arriving with lateen sails and a merrily painted bow. I postponed dealing with that...

"It wasn't something I wanted to think about. ...Even though, he'd have let the Goon do Pitt.

"I spent the night at a former G.I. brothel in Ubon—where, maddeningly, my thoughts dwelt more with Jahd than Martin Pitt and the crooks—and hopped the first flight to Bangkok in the morning. Twenty-five miles and a murder in the oven of Isaan not enough, I traipsed Patpong when I got there, alternately reviewing having been so close to and yet definitively divided from Jahd; and that motorbike driver at Khong Jiam. He'd been gruff, rough, and evasive with me. He'd dangled a black steel, silver-winged helmet, glassy eyes set on a purple-to-violet, stubbled pigeon face, short, burly arms, strong and nervously shifting bowlegs. The Daredevil is in the details. Had the Goon greased that biker not to take me to Pha Taem so he'd have time to set up? —I recalled a Swiss girl who fucked every bike boy she managed to flag until the police, citing this incitement, deported her. Too true: my quick stiff when sighting Thai toughs with white women...

"I sensed two men were deliberately walking behind me: Asian-style, holding hands. I turned, adrenaline-geared for anything now—but not, cruelly, additional envy: it was Chain, woeful, and the slick ringleader of the erstwhile trio. Chain bragged, 'This Khun Maitri. Employer. Meet before, house me.'

"Maitri, saber-rattling, corrected him: 'It's George Raft to you, marine.'

"'Couldn't be more so! My consolations for your chauffeur,' I temporized.

"'Yeah, ain't that a kick? Got caught on the business end of a fishing rod. Mighta blown a tire the way he drove. Or the four of 'em. Marine.'

"I said, 'A marine when you were expecting Pitt—weren't you? *I* was.'

"I bit my gum and waited. Maitri prinked his imaginary lint and let me drop. What *was* Chain doing? Oh yes: I'd not slept one night at the Aphrodite. Fed up, I split: and charged from toilet to toilet in each department store on Silom; stood next to each lug relieving himself and gawked at his leaker; then switched from bench to bench in the park, wherever something a fraction tolerable was sunning itself. Assured he'd check me responding to all sprays, I hoped against hope he'd acknowledge *my* hopes. Chain was a snake eating its tail.

"In Lome that evening, still with Maitri, Chain sulked three yards away and cast conceits of mourning at me. Maitri was provoking him. Facing the cut-crystal mirror, Maitri, rubbed with skin-whitener, wallowed in his self-aggrandizing image and made his deriding of a foreign lowlife obvious to the lowlifes guzzling there.

"Before Chain could work up the nerve to ask me where I'd spent the night, I accosted him with where had *Phii* spent last night? 'Rob tomb,' he answered directly; and to curfew my cruising, volunteered to expand on that. Martin Pitt, Nok, and Ekarin had flown to the northern Thai-Burmese border to loot the ceramics in its newly discovered burial grounds. They'd reappeared with a haul, including bird-design bowls and plain or appliqué plates, elephant, buffalo, dog, and wet nurse figurines, an anointing kendi with a gourd-shaped spout, and celadon vessels. The mountain people of four to seven centuries ago didn't cremate their dead: they buried them in fetal positions; and considered celadons kilned in China to be the most desirable objects with which to line their graves. The green of celadon represents growth; its hardness eternity; and its capturing light reflects Heaven. They were looting the cemeteries of Chain's ancestors; therefore he did not accompany them. He'd passed the night at the Afro instead, wondering where I was.

"Finding him so erudite, I thought to grill him about Maitri, whom he labeled a card-shark, when I centered the admiration of a not-too-smart-looking chub, who was was impervious to

Chain-as-warden because he was new to Bangkok, spoke no English, and didn't operate with a full six-pack. He'd just come out as well: and concerning what he'd care to accomplish in bed was a tabula rasa. His mongolism, and the tweak he'd grow more selective, magnetized me. When Chain disappeared for last call, I urged the dimwit toward the exit. Slipping through a gap I'd failed to see, Chain stepped between us.

"'Where take simple man?' he cried.

"'Home!' I stated, losing a beat before I realized the gravity of this: that I'd not, to *his* knowledge, previously brought home a trick. We would pass the desk, coffee shop, and corridors. Nor did the hour strike me as hors de ligne: I'd never stopped *Chain's* 2:00 a.m. socializing at Thaniya Plaza.

"He followed us into Soi 4. Followed isn't exact. Chain moved in concert with me, slamming his shoulder against my sleeve—to stagger my advance and discourage the automaton. Succeeding in neither, he swung to the front of us and pressed his weight on my chest to stymie me altogether. He was livid, his eyes protuberant with supplication.

"I sideswiped him and resumed pace with the departing customers. Chain kept jumping at me: he nailed my forearms. The halfwit watched the struggle with confusion. He'd stall when we stalled, then continue on when I did.

"Chain rebuilt his barrier, and yet more desperately—despite its attracting shame-shooting notice—his strength savage and his lips quivering with curses he could barely formulate. He began to push me backwards. Stonily determined, I hesitated merely to circle around him.

"When the three of us reached the road and he saw that I'd head toward Convent and plough by foot to our room, Chain broke from us and hurried away in a panic, instantly lost in the throng of gays now negotiating en masse with the tuk-tuks and cabs that braked to snatch them at the mouth of the soi.

"On Convent, I explained to my (I think) pencil-pusher, whose name (I think) was Goi, that Chain was nuts and to just ignore him. Otherwise we shared little, Goi not having been able to learn hello in English. I got through that stroll by tuning for how his thick thighs and highly appointed stuck-together glutes would pry once I'd drop his drawers for him. I hoped they wouldn't have heat mold: a distinct possibility, since he kept pulling on his shorts and shifting his hang, first from along the left-leg seam to the right, then visa versa: had he a fungus, either side would not ease the itch but reversing it might.

"–Our door was unlocked! When I opened it, Chain was there, hysterically stuffing clothes into his suitcases. He looked out of his mind. How did he beat us back? Then I knew: my latest Harpy: motorcyclists. He must have sped like the Flash and paid double: those cowboys had the homeward-bound competing at 1:00 a.m. He demanded the key to the security vault; had he not been waiting for that, he'd have been gone before we arrived. Too uncoordinated to insert the key, I did it for him. He swept out his *yantra* amulet and the celadon box while strangling on the words: 'You mine, *mine!*—but now not want! Not want more! This bed *us!* You shit on bed! Shit on sheets!'

"Then he spat at Goi, seized his suitcases, and battled with the door.

"'I finish you! I not come back forever!!'

"He shattered the door shut so that it shook for creeping seconds afterwards. I said, dismissively, to Goi, '*Kohn nan pen gangster*. And Equality-campaigner.'

"'*Aaah, Equality,*' he culled, as though that meant something to him.

"I ripped the Velcro of his shorts. –And first saw a thin packet next to him—which took but a snap to recognize. It was fastened with two green, crisscrossing rubber bands: the heroin O had proffered: and must have stuffed in the armoire while I showered. Chain, tossing his garments over the bedspread in advance of packing them just now, had dislodged it. Not noticing the object, or caring, he'd let it lie where it fell. When I passed on that powder, O didn't think I nonetheless mainlined; or could sell it; didn't secure it between the clothes as a surprise.

"It was another blatant plant. Courtesy of Pitt.

"This new 'gift' sent me into orbit. Goi's bowling pins suddenly appalled me. Groping them would replicate the illicit in

225

fondling a statue of Thanatos. I politely asked him to leave. As uncomprehending as ever, he complied.

"No sooner was he gone than the phone rang. –Chain, calling from Soi 36. In his frenzy, he'd flown by Devil-bike to his house as well. 'What you do now?!' he extorted, pitched at the stridence of fifteen minutes before.

"'Nothing,' I answered. 'He go.'

"Chain crashed the phone. He dialed a half-hour later, armed with abuse re my perfidy, worthlessness, infidelity, and continual calumny of two years' standing. Then peace for the next twenty-three hours. When he rang again from Soi 36, I gathered he'd stayed put between calls. To his asking how I was occupied, I said by crapping our bed with a trick less simple than Goi. 'Not believe! Not possible!!' he gasped—hanging up with that eardrum ache.

"The following night, he expanded on this note of disbelief: since I couldn't humanly have the abscission to be drilling new items…

"On the third night I expected his call: the only fresh emphasis consisted of retaking that vow (four or five times) not to return to or live in the Aphrodite.

"I had no one there. My nights were spoken for by trying to fit Daeng, Olie, O, Kambu-ja—and the hunter—into Martin Pitt's Machiavellianism—and Chain's lethal and irreconcilable obligations that so entrenched me.

"As for the wrenching I shared in his wounds, rallied to his bay, exposed to predation, and made accomplice to a killing, I still felt all this was a well-prepped opponent I could take. Because I really expected Chain, as I knew him, to move back—in, given, say, a week or two.

"But he never did."

THE FOURTH DAY

WHEN THE PILOT ANNOUNCED we were over Nan Province and then Yunnan in South China, I dreamt about Chain's forbears: sitting up, disarranged, in their pillaged graves down there…

A Minneapolis composer had lived in Xian for thirteen years. A Texas painter and missionary had thrived in Beijing for eighty. I could not put off the dates I had set for them. So I would spend my last days with Cory Simon in one week's time. Besides these two artists and the Great Wall, Sundial Temple, and Forbidden City, I wanted to get to the capital's central library. What I would be looking up was the Chinese take on Thailand during the Second World War.

I hired a translator for its Mandarin documents. She was a history major, an intelligent young woman. She was ingenious in accessing the sparse official line on the person of most concern to me: Pridi Banomyong. According to her, this rebellious law professor, regent to the boy-king, was the only Thai in power who believed at the onset of hostilities that the Japs would not prevail. The summary fall of strategic Pacific islands, the Philippines, and Singapore had been impressive: Japan was conquering the Far East, the Subcontinent, Australasia, and Austronesia. When she occupied the Gulf of Thailand, fearing a similar fate, Thailand declared war on the U.S. and Britain, on January 5, 1942.

Significant authorities in Bangkok and Washington agreed with Pridi that Japan's defeat at Midway, in June of that year, was the beginning of her eventual collapse. So Pridi was working on how, as Japan's ally, Thailand could keep its sovereignty in the peace treaties. He created *Seri Thai*, a minuscule but expedient resistance movement; and in late 1942 marched ranks northward, ostensibly to engage borderline China: but, in league with us, actually to swell the Allied troops already fighting in Yunnan. This succeeded because he knew the Japanese would welcome not having to control the entire Thai army, then stationed in Bangkok. Pridi won the day again with a full exchange of Brit and Yank prisoners in Thailand for all Thai prisoners held by England and the States. The Japs began their retreat in '43. In September 1944 the nation's Police Force finally gave its unqualified support to Pridi's *Seri Thai.*

Then the regent tangled with Admiral Mountbatten's clamor for Thailand's surrender: since that would legitimize her postwar turnover to Britain as the spoils of war; or her division amongst the Euro colonials. Pridi applied at once for a seat in the U.N. Roosevelt, who had had the foresight to reject the Thai declaration of war, now had the teeth to oppose Mountbatten's plan for the peninsula. He stated that Thailand, which hosted a resistance and was never legally at war, could not surrender. Claiming that the "selfishness" of Great Britain and France had cost countless American lives, he set about dismantling their empires: and bringing as much of Asia as possible under the U.S. canopy, since the U.S. would obviously get majority credit for victory in the East.

A general election in 1946 empowered a civilian, democratic government under Pridi. A year later his former partner, Field Marshall Phibun, slandered him with pinko designs for renamed Siam *and* precipitating the mysterious death of his charge, the present king's nineteen-year-old brother, and forced Pridi into exile. So harking back to his role in ending Siam's absolute monarchy in 1932, and even short-lived abolishing of it, despite his military acumen, lasting progressive legislature, and preservation of the realm's political boundary, Pridi Banomyong was, until 2000, virtually written out of history.

I now understood Cory's anxieties over Chain's work for the anathematized former leader. Then I ran into stumbling blocks. A library official became suspicious of me, precisely because my reading involved Siam, Pridi, and China, and held me for questioning about papers of permit for this file or that. State-permit for public documents? That dude wasted several days grunting through my tapes. He turned totally sour because he found them bonzo. My translator was arrested; I did not see her again. I thought a Mother of the Revolution they brought in would do what I really was afraid of: confiscate my unduped cassettes. Flashing my pearlies à la Simon, I got her to settle for a stern socialistic lecture on my "wholesale disregard for the citizens' welfare," and to restore my belongings. More flirting and some yuan got me a visa extension so I could re-date my R.T.

A self-imposed delay, and a pain in the ass making clear to her, was chat emailing in China with my PC-detective at Columbia. Otherwise I would have no time to integrate William Ned Dilly's fresh ammo. Dill was blocked in advanced research: it kept cross-referencing someone else he could not bring up.

I clicked in: "Find anything about Direct Illumination?"

Dill typed back: "Direct Illumination?? Of what? Are u losing it out there? No such animal! Our man has *health* problems. One is related to myoclonus. That's a heart-stopping nosedive, seconds after he falls asleep—gives sufferers the impression they're dying. Another is Cheyne-Stokes syndrome: his breath cuts off the moment he's asleep, or an hour or two later, and induces his gasping for air and horrendous sweat-panics. Cory Simon's father, or this other person's father, had the same seizures—and died during one of them."

I checked back into the Moon and rang Cory to arrange a new meeting five days late. He said he was busy for the next forty-eight hours. An 8:30 a.m. start two days from then would be fine. I had two days to kill.

Cory had penciled a map to locate Saran Rom, a park near Chinatown, when I asked him where to catch exclusively Thai and Sino-Thai cruising. "Mind the *hongsa* there: that park's informative." It would be—in spades.

Saran Rom is Sino-Modern in design, catty-corner with Wat Po, the home of the huge Reclining Buddha. Teochew use it at dawn for t'ai chi, and it is crammed with joggers till closing. Where you enter, eleven putti are straddling the *hongsa* in a multitiered fountain, the uppermost and the five on the second tier blowing conch shells. I followed a path that wound through a figure-eight lake to the Garden of the Gauntlets of Sharp-edged Stones. People walk these cryptographic mosaics bare-foot to strengthen the sole and heel, and, I suppose, the soul. What a tenderfoot I was on its hardly blunted pebbles! After ten minutes, I flopped in a Kang, or Thinking Pavilion. Thai hustlers lie on the grass all around it; or squat inside, dangling a smoke.

As I sat in the pavilion with senior Chinese, who were read-ing the menu, two cross-dressed hustlers rose from its center and stepped off the rim to horseplay. They dodged and danced, then bulled in with spin kicks slashing at stomachs and punches out to make mincemeat. It was a bout of Muay Thai, the nation-al, deadly art of kick-boxing. How wacko this was: merely fool-ing—spindly flits in such a skilled and violent display. But—and here's the "but"—and what is so hard to get my head around—that these nance gold-diggers should provide *my* Illumination stabs at gender-bender apotheosis! Like a slam upside *my* head, I all at once remembered Parinya Kiatbusada.

In 1997 a sixteen-year-old transvestite of that name (known affectionately as Nong Tum) became the kingdom's most famous athlete—if I have it correctly, an undefeated, lipstick-wearing kick-boxer, who hunched his opponents' shoulders with rapid, walking-and-blocking elbow cuts; and with a spin-to-right-leg kick that hooked his neck, decked the challenger. Then he undid the braids ribbonned in his crown, planted a kiss on the loser's cheek, pirouetted on point, and swished about to the whistling from his bet-collecting admirers. He honored and elevated the lady-boy with a brief career, then forsook the ring, and applied to be transsexed and live out his days as a woman. The munici-pal judicial system intervened to forestall an international scan-dal: said he was too young to make a decision like that. The con-troversy raged for three years. In mid-2000, Parinya Kiatbusada squared away with the scalpel.

–Parinya Kiatbusada's first pro-boxing name had been In-seedam: *Black Eagle*.

So—watching those drag queens whack, knee, jump, and stomp—I finally snapped my fingers. Well, well, well!! Clue after clue rubbed in my face, from the Jolly Boy sumo wrestler, Cory's athletic Thai friends, his skipping-rope, Jesse Ventura, Randolph Wetzel's delirious ramblings—and a man's body not keeping secrets for him—to Dill's caveat that deep research on Cory Simon constantly references someone else, and *I* had made no connection!

It is called *Pugilist*, an autobiography by Joshua Seabrooke. It was published in the '60s for the sizable U.S. market then in confessions of sensitive, secretly tormented jocks. Seabrooke was an undefeated twenty-one-year-old contender with all doors open to him. Yet he abruptly threw in the towel. I read it as an adolescent, at a time when I would lap up anything gay. I had found a charred copy on the ash heaps of a gutted tenement in Hell's Kitchen. That is why the story had eluded me and most of its details were still fuzzy. But there, in that cautionary tale, is the signature style: Cory Simon's ornate, photograph-finish, triplethink subordinates, his same protases and collocations—that had itched me from the instant he let go his lip and each night after when I underlined baroque or troublesome phrases in his many articles.

Pugilist recounts the early life of a good-looking boxer, depicted as the susceptible son of a "mid-Victorian" father who forced him into prizefighting. This, of course, so as to double for the elder and realize his own dream of excelling in the "manly art of self-defense." It scores the criminal tie-ins endemic to the "sweet suicide," which were seriously undermining Joshua's stability, and the Erinys involved in a man's dedication to twisted patronal approval. Three chapters are devoted to a celebrated knockout match that left his "foe" paralyzed. This is followed by Seabrooke's battle with proxy paralysis approaching the title fight and his curt withdrawal from competition.

That withdrawal, it emerges, is because the author was homosexual: and to his dad's and the fans' dismay, wanted to live as one—an impossibility, even if the contender had tried his best to closet himself, in those days as it would be now. The bio sold well for a year; then it and Seabrooke vanished without a trace.

So there you have it: Simon's fixation on AWOL athletes, Thai huskies, and underground freaks. And why he met Rollo Y-z in a clinic. When I left the park I tipped my reversed baseball-cap to the Gabriel-like clarion putti and stone *hongsa*: a swan: to which Cory had fed, punitively, candied corn.

I emailed William Ned Dilly and told him to scare up Joshua Seabrooke. I said I would check tomorrow to see what he found and went to bed pleased.

Dill's reply registered early in the evening: he could tie in, balance out, and identify Cory Simon as the boxer Joshua Seabrooke. He tracked nothing more on gangland investments in him, or torpedo harassing, than is already included in the Seabrooke bio. I felt guilty, a little disorganized, and had trouble getting dressed in the morning. I misplaced my wallet: I would not be able to take the skytrain or subway. With the coins on me for only two buses, I grabbed a 136 and did not recognize my stop on Rama IV. The next one brought me into the smell of a shabby nabe, the Klong Toey pig and fish market. I tore up a pedestrian bridge to run down a 115 that would eventually bear left and drop me in walking distance of Cory. I reached its farther stair before grasping a zinger I passed: and whipped out my automatic developer. Supine, fast asleep there, was a scavenger no more than nine. An erection tented his threadbare Bermudas by what had to have been an awesome eleven inches! "Thailand in a nutshell!" I would surprise Cory.

That never happened: at exactly 8:30 a.m., he was crocked. He let me seat myself; and apart from the koel's joining him, soliloquized.

"That same junior high school, the one with the active stairwell, had a sprawling playground that could be just as active at lunchtime. When the hour for lunch ended, a gong went off and the whole student population had to freeze for a full minute. Then an identical gong would split your ears, and it was the signal for utter chaos: everybody broke the freeze and trampled on each other to get to the doors. The second this mayhem began, one day—that first second, being when you were most unguarded and looking for the best route through that scramble—an expert fist gripped my cock and balls, completely cupped whatever I had, firmly squeezed the thing entire, then withdrew so instantly that I had no idea whose hand it was. I saw only the competing mob. I did as instantly understand, however, that this was, to be so adroit, a many times practiced and calculated pretense at so-called stealing your manhood. It took some training, thinking out, and selection of scorn-worthy victims well in advance. I was certain a homophobe, a self-deceived slumgullion had done it, a boogie of the sort that assaulted Howie Paul, but I'd no way of knowing if he understood how much he enjoyed making his supposed revelation—or how much I did. And still do. He had demonstrated how much we both would. If he did not know that then, whatever he currently does to get off, I hope he knows it now. How does a Singha sound to you?

"I was not yet twenty when I ran into Audie Ellenport, a demure, long-lashed, towering lad of eighteen shielding himself against an insignificant drizzle with a parasol. The night was dark, but a Village streetlamp hit the carnations and rose of Sharon on his parasol—moments before he hit on me. Audie was a fast worker, and though I disliked young guys back then, he knew what *he* liked and disdained to mince words. 'Mince' is appropriate: he crowed it was societal mincing that got him thrown off his mom's estate in a small and exclusive Connecticut burg. Audie saw himself as a true queen, though his seven-feet, one-and-a-half-inches made agreeing with him difficult for others. He was driven to publicize what he was certain he was, a teenage bottom in search of his muscular knight. The platinum tints of his flaxen hair glowed in the mist, and torture them as he would into Dietrich locks or a Garbo pageboy, they'd revert to the swept layers of a naturally groomed linebacker. Ditto for his skyscraper frame and the manly grace with which its immensity moved—an ad-man's ideal for every male product, airbrushing extraneous.

"*Unnervingly*, Ellenport explained that he used his floral umbrella now as a tightrope parasol to tip the scale on the world others insisted was his and the one he wanted entry to. 'She caught me stepping out with this when I thought she was visiting kin and that was the end of my days in the nest' must be, all told, a confessional first in come-on history. Don't ask me why, but I *tout de suite* discovered myself in his five-story walk-up, a fruitily furnished attic, sipping cheap wine and audience to the epic of his split identity."

"I don't have to ask you why," I slipped in. Cory didn't hear that.

"He alluded to the effeminacy of even his name, pinching his nose as he said it to exaggerate a nasal. Still, his range was the bass you'd expect from his size, not the mezzo he was striving to achieve. Then the conversation died. Audie correctly surmised that left to my inclination I'd make no move—except to move politely on. So he tossed me over his shoulder with ease as one does an injured or fainted man in films and bore me to his bed, custom-tailored for giants. Feeling as ridiculous as disinclined, I attempted to sit up on his spread of Queen Anne's lace, and so imply quitting it. Foolish me: I was about to learn how, when necessary, that Conan bulk could be utilized. A flat palm planted in the center of my sternum, he imprinted me on the lace with all the persuasion of an elephant's forefoot and stripped me clean in six seconds. Even my socks were nowhere in sight. Then he cut the only wattage in the room, a gooseneck clamped on the headboard, and, still crushing me in place, undid his fly and climbed in next to me. You know, it's wiser to cower as prides of lion do than get your rump taken down by a pachyderm. Or shredded to pulp as the case might be, in which case you'd not have the correct curves for another that night anyway. I unbuttoned his pink blouse and located Audie's nearest nipple: a nipple not merely prodigiously enlarged, but perched upon a mound of breast! In pointed fact—excuse that qualifier—it was

234

quite the longest, quite the largest and very most solid, pointing nipple atilt the highest pointed peak that ever I had the fortune to maul.

"I went wild. I hooked his armpit as I do to steady a ticklish partner and set to work on those record-breaking attractions. Nibbling would be wrong to say: inhaling the whole milker is more like it, with a hand shoring up the udder so as to center his teat in the suction. Now, I have no need to hide my orality; but during this unrestrained consumption, Audie's breath slowed. He was stiff: unresponsive. And he wasn't bashful. So I shot up out of my gorging fit and hovered close to his face in the dark to ask without words, 'Hey there! Audie! Ain'tcha interested?'

"That's when he turbidly sighed: with defection; or despair.

"'I'm still in the leagues… –basketball,' he muttered sadly, snapping on the gooseneck. I blinked. Audie stretched out in the glare of the bulb, sighing again.

"I said, 'What's the matter?'

"'Look!' he answered flatly. I hesitated, and did, and saw from that vantage—my face touching his—the pale pyramids lifting his nipples, tall as cannikins. Yet these inverted funnels, however startling for a man, were really very lovely, somewhat nubile, like those of a precocious schoolgirl.

"'They're beautiful,' I admired. 'Soft as soufflé—and should be tasty as all get-out! Too bad you can't taste them, too.'

"He failed to crack a smile. He stared emptily at me. I said, 'May I continue? Please?'

"Again, no reaction. I weighed both breasts and dented them as gently as possible. I watched myself molding each and then raised my lids to his gaze, a lover's plea for license to resume. He pouted, and the pout began to quiver.

"He managed to say: 'I have eight paps.'

"You'll identify with my concealing any show of confusion. I pivoted into a Narcissus-leaning-over-the-brook, that brook being his torso: this only natural and surely compulsory then. He adjusted the gooseneck to throw even more harsh light along his body.

"Directly beneath the developed breasts were two smaller

hillocks, proportioned with smaller areolas. Below these were two areolas approximately normal in size for a boy his age and no appreciable glandular swelling. A fourth set—of quite tiny paps, their nimbi in mauve—rested a half-inch above his waist. He respired heavily, and the tremors reached into his pelvis.

"'Teams of anatomists… studied me—when I was fourteen. Three times. Today I won't let them near me. They don't know where I am. …Three times is enough.'

"'What did they decide?' I asked, keeping his level tone.

"'Nothing revolutionary. The opposite: that I am some kind of throwback. To when we were all animals.'

"I let myself look at the phenomenon for another minute while rubbing his nearest arm. Truth is, I was as moved by the expansiveness of his thorax, abdomen, and stomach, all handsomely fleshed, with creamy skin, rose highlights here and there, as by the eight male mammae. When I thought my confirmation of his reverential zoological epoch was respectfully completed, I said: 'I hope you realize it's going to take me a long time to cover all these titties every night. So maybe we ought to get started right away.'

"At long last, he smiled.

"'And do you mind if we keep that bulb burning? I need to see your nips as well. I can't come just eating them.'"

Cory glanced toward the refrigerator, considering a trip for more booze. He stood—and then forgot his goal. His eyes had that drunk's off-focus. Like the small difference between his formal speech and his writing, I find little variation in Cory's speech whether he is sober, tipsy, or in blackout.

I said, "So what happened to you and Audie Ellenport?"

He became testy. He cleared his throat. "There was no sensation in the lower nips, certainly not the nethermost twin: those were a waste of time. As for the other six, I can't, in all truth, say he enjoyed the attention I paid them. I never really knew. Yet should I have simply ignored them?"

"I don't know. What else?"

"Had the yardstick of a walrus, a goat's burlap sack, and a

very wide anus, but maybe that's normal for men his height."

"I mean to your relationship?"

"Oh. I told you his success with his alter ego was severely limited. His straining to behave like my dutiful wife irritated me: no end. I'd have much rather been with the athlete the rest of the world believed Audie to be... And his recapitulation of his... evolutionary, anatomical baggage led to rages that constantly led to his getting fired and therefore back on his rent. I've neglected those rages—and how they recalled mine. Also, it felt inappropriate buggering someone so large, like inching up an elm until you reached the navel knot. He was a tree whose top branches no lover could find. As inclination to bop him dwindled, his rages grew in intensity. One night, during a lip lashing for delaying, so to speak, outside my purview, his landlord chose to visit and demand five months' rent. –Audie tears open the door and clearly takes this guy for some alter ego of *mine*. He grabs him, pitches him a foot above his head, and fastballs him bellowing over the entire bank of stairs. I fly down those stairs myself, twisting and leaping—down a dark siphon—step over the stain the landlord has become, and disappear in that murk for good."

The koel scolded. Cory made the fridge. He seized a beer, popped the cap with his teeth, and sucked its neck. I said, "Were there any partners with whom you did not hug the ropes (here Cory twinged)... that we could categorize with...?"

"'Vestigial structure' is the phrase you want. Yes. He had a tail. Or two inches of one at the base of his spine. But Jack wasn't important. Either that tail bothered him too much or it was I he couldn't be bothered with, but we were a short-lived twosome. There was Dorothea, called Dorothea because her female protuberances protruded farther than her male—as with representations of Buddha, which are always hermaphroditic. The cross-gendered here, of course, with their 'honey pussies'; and a cherub-faced composer with six fingers on both hands. The oddest of all was an Antichrist with small horns in upstate New York, or he believed he was, and so did the Pope, who secretly traveled to Courtland to check him out."

Cory stumbled along the casements. "I haven't thought about Audie since I was twenty. Last night I did. So I liquored up. I failed the event that is Audie Ellenport. I didn't experience him. Is that what they mean by 'exotic' flight?"

"I'm not sure," I pretended. He began to scrutinize me like a doctor trying to determine how much difficulty you will have with his bad news. He moved closer, bent over me, and slurred:

"Do you know why I selected *you* to complete my flight?"

"Yes," I answered, biting my tongue.

Cory leaned into my face. "We need to develop the strength to avoid doing a thing we shouldn't. Like, resort to whatever it is in our *voice* that summons the otherwise inenarrable vision—in front of a myna bird all too capable of… and craving to appropriate… our sound and none of its substance."

He went to the door. "Let's meet again. I'll leave a message on the Moon." He futilely pulled on the slip bolt, not remembering that he never threw it after I entered. This spoiled a dramatic period to his insufferable utterance.

"Allow me," I offered, turning the knob. He grinned, ambivalently. "And I lost my wallet. Would you have change for a bus?"

THE FIFTH DAY

TALK ABOUT AN UNFOUNDED ACCUSATION! I was totally bitter, turned off by just having to see him. Would Cory pull that shit again?

Needing another break from him, I followed his leads to overlooked subjects in town. A few were successful. I also fell by his current cafés and bars, not without profit: they yielded witnesses to the freak-outs he refers to. Fools cross him while he is swilling—fools, I could tell when I met them, who goad or victimize a drunk. Some of those skirmishes had got Cory up for deportation.

At our next meet I was in free-fall. He refused to broker my knowing hints. I took in this boxer, this miraculously still-not-wasted guy. And then, once again, that face. What I confronted him with was:

"Are you part Asian?"

He laughed. "I am asked that here once a week. Thais realize I'm not Thai, although many think I'm one-half Han. Or pure-bred Korean; or Japanese. You must have noticed Hokkaido men with long and pinched or aquiline noses; and whiskers that suggest Walt Whitman cropped his too closely."

"Now I'm asking."

"I believe my dad was part Siberian. His paternal uncle was the Kajak of the Mongolian Cavalry: literally, 'Father of the Birds.' They fly fierce Mongolian eagles: so he was Eaglemaster, or the Commanding Falconer, a revered position. A hunter. The Preeminent Messenger. And killer."

"I see!"

"I hope minimal relevance. This Eaglemaster bore no chicks:. Therefore, when he learned my dad had an infant son, he wired the States demanding I be sent to Ulan Bator. He bound himself to school me as his heir in the equestrian force and offered a minor treasure in return, noting that my fertile father could and would sire more sons. My dad, having been brought to the Promised Land (via Kushito and the Bering Sea) when he was twelve, felt no allegiance whatsoever to war-torn tundra and dynastic obligations. He'd speak only English in front of me and concealed his uncle's command, not wishing a child of even slightly mixed blood to live under more prejudice than necessary in racist America. The result was that instead of being groomed to privilege with mystic importance, I came of age in penurious obscurity."

"Could you be a full one-fourth Mongol, then?"

"I don't know... Or care. A *pied noir?* My dad skirted that touchy point. The information I have is from my mother—a subject of the Crown, who was taken from London to Amherst as a toddler and never bothered to naturalize. My father remained East-World superstitious. Wary of attempts to kidnap me: attempts with real muscle, he stopped corresponding with his relatives on the steppes, changed his name, and moved his little family from city to town to outlying burg with the frequency of a fugitive. And was mum in ever making *me* privy to his yellow forebears. Or trepidations."

"Do you really believe that your life, writing, thinking, and all, would have been rosier over here?"

"It would certainly have appeared more glamorous, for a while. Indeed, more me. The straps of those killers on my very wrist! But with the disintegration of communism and the hungry democracy that replaced it in 1990—no: at that juncture, if not years before... Look, people persist in the person they've actually been—I've been American—and just consolidate to clarify that."

To contradict, I asked if his visits might be to take on his denied Asian identity—with Chain's denied Lue-descent dovetailing neatly. Consider his handle: aren't eagle-straps a steel chain? "Hokey!" Cory bridled at what he called my "convolutions." "–Time for Psychology 101? I feel comfortable with who I am. Chain did not." So Cory's single concession, here, is that his prizefighting name, Josh Seabrooke, was an alias—as his pen name, "Cory Simon," is.

He said, "Oughtn't we pick up where I left off, before your trip to China? My strategy thereabouts was to nail those planters of 'circumstantial' evidence: O, Olie, and Daeng. O was in Paris: to link his heroin-plant to Pitt depended on the others. Olie—Pitt had slipped him a wad. Olie: who used me as cache for his Triangle weed and stolen icon. He failing, the vodka-bearing Daeng could update his stool-pigeon act on Olie—or on his 'good friend' O.

"The moment I left work on the day previous to intersession—the fourth day after Chain's farewell—I directed a tuk-tuk to Dr. Vivian's. I didn't phone: if Olie was there, warned in advance, he'd scat. Vivian was confused when I barged into her office. She had not laid eyes on Olie for months. Nevertheless, she became excited, seizing at the straw that I must have arranged to meet him at her place. She prevailed on me to wait. I told her I had much to do if he was not 'home.' Still, she dispatched her patients and set to high tea, and eventually a feast. I found excuses as she worked to explore the attic, upstairs bedrooms, and toolshed; but knew lingering now was to commiserate with the suffering woman, not a casting of the spell she believed it might be that would draw Olie to her house. I held on until 1:00 a.m. while Vivian paced behind my wickerwork chair in the garden, was taunted by the jagged leaves of her fishtail trees, scoured neighboring soi after soi, and finally broke down in tears.

"The next morning I stood sentry in the proximity of the American Embassy on Wireless Road, hoping Daeng would eat lunch off the premises. It'd be iffy to snag him on job. He could argue he was buried in accounting, (rigged) invoices, and inventories. More tuned: issue a complaint of lecherous attention. Plus I had to isolate him, as I'd have Olie. I sweated abjectly under the study of our guards till 2:00 p.m., then gave up on his exiting for lunch, not on my determnation, sweltered in Lumpini

Park for three hours, and was back by those fortress-gates at five. At six-fifteen Daeng at last emerged, carrying a portfolio and shouldering a satchel. He took the red light and sat in the outbound kiosk, opposite the embassy. His salient raiment was a pink blazer: the perfect punk. Instants later, I asked him, 'Are *these* togs waterproof? Oh, I forgot, you're not in the money now.'

"He reeked with imperturbability: and rested his portfolio on the tarsus of his shoes. His languid, bottle-green eyes (so that's what they were!) examined me. 'What is it that you want?' he snuffed.

"'As pleasant a conversation as possible. Over dinner?'

"'I am due at my family's for dinner.'

"'Cocktails, then,' I smiled. 'Tab's on me.'

"'I do not drink,' he replied, steadily.

"'We'll have them fix you a scarlet fruit juice with sponging orchid-sprigs. I'm sure you have time for one tumbler, since I am an American citizen who knows that you, if not drinking liquor, use it for more than embezzling.'

"A lonely waitress was sweeping the floor in a practically empty jazz-joint on nearby Sarasin. I ordered Daeng their kitschiest Shirley Temple: a parasol leaned over its rim—and, yes, it *was* embossed with a rose of Sharon—and watched as he tried to summon his customary incivility and partially fail. Then told him, in respect of his limited happy hour, I'd get right to the meat of the matter—namely: I was certain he'd handsomely paid, and provided the convertible and extravagant funds, for his good friend O to cruise me, entertain me royally, and plant heroin in my room; that he was on dealing if lax terms with the thief Oliver Littleton; and had improper understandings— like where to dump vodka and play cards—with the English off-shore-oil man and smuggler of natural treasure Martin Pitt.

"'Swell!' he responded, loosening his tie, the arrogance re-entering his body language and gaining momentum there. This relief demonstrated the speed of his suspicion that I'd really no serviceable, incriminating information. So—in a roll peppered with Americanisms—he brazenly bragged: 'Olivier and I used to trick. He liked porking me. Now we're partners, moonlighting partners. I produce the goods and transfer the bribes and he provides the customers. We do not see business practices here as narrowly as Euros do. If Oliver is the thief you want, he is in Lan Na now, plundering its forests for logs *and* its monasteries' precious manuscripts. Oliver does not mind sleeping in a *baan ling* (monkey house). It depends on how porky his cellmates are. As for Martin Pitt, he is an animal apart. He and Oliver are presently feuding over how to exploit a certain icon of Buddha. And you, Cory, work with Marin Pitt as well. You exhibit this very icon—in order to betray them: for profit. A princess is its keeper. I had to smile when Olie got you to think it was yours. Buddha is in everybody. He cannot belong to one man. Where do you breeds get such ideas? Is it because *you* belong nowhere?'

"I said, '*Or* everywhere! Hold it. That statue…'

"'Do you think O is blind?'

"'But—how could I work with… Pitt runs an outfit that smuggles children!'

"'So?' he flared. 'Aren't you part of that enterprise?'

"I had to keep looking as insulted as he. 'Who accuses me of this?'

"'Martin Pitt. He has boarding-pass stubs.'

"'To Ubon?'

"'That is for Nok and Chain to tell you. And the loan shark, Maitri.'

"'Chain to tell—?'

"'Yes, Chain. You do remember *him?* The man who accompanied Martin to collect Jim Thompson in a Malay jungle.'

"I concentrated; and saw it: 'And to which assembly Martin could always own up: saying Chain's acquaintance with Pridi pacified Thompson's misgivings?'

"'This is not *my* fix. It is yours. Chain would be safe without you.'

"I had ordered gin and blue curaçao for myself. It was time to take a stiff sip. I did. I let it heat my throat; agonized; then asked, my voice as even as I could manage: 'These children, are they being smuggled in from Burma and Laos? Or Vietnam…? They arrive by the cliffs of Pha Taem, don't they?'

"He used the parasol to stir his drink. 'That, too, is none of my business.'

"They're brought to brothels in Thailand—or maybe Cambodia?'

"'Not at all!' he returned—stupefied, if I read him correctly. 'Only a suitable handful will become indentured servants.' Then he swallowed his juice, knit his brow, and lurched forward. 'But surely you know this!'

"'Do I?'

"He was so close now I thought his widow's peak would knife me. 'A few will be crippled and put out as beggars here. The rest will be harvested.'

"'"Harvested"?'

"'Their organs: eyes, lungs, kidneys, livers. For experiment and transplants. Very costly transplants.'

"'And how would I know that?' I throated, feeling my jaw lock and my hands go cold.

"'Because, Khun, you are one of the men who traffics in such children! Did you think I was not aware of this? If you did, you have another blank spot.'

"Here was the point to finish my gin. And a pledge of innocence worthless, to appear unruffled. 'Trustworthy proof of anything else?'

"'That you certainly trade in heroin. O never lied to me. But that is a minor investment with persons like you, isn't it?' He disdainfully reshouldered his satchel, a rudeness meant to indicate *he* was ending our colloquy.

"As Daeng jammed his chair into the table, I asked, hoping I was audible, 'These children, the donors, do they survive those operations?'

"'Some,' he said reproachfully. 'Not when they take their heart, of course.'

"That night I tracked a clean-cut white-collar type: who was enticing me. He led me to the Depot Tavern, which serves travelers arriving at the Northern Bus Terminal and passengers waiting to board and go out to the airport, or destinies beyond. In light of Chain's presence at Jim Thompson's disappearance, and Pitt's consequent hold on him, Daeng's slander, and the number of lawbreakers prepared to yea-say him, I couldn't be blamed for wondering if I shouldn't scare up the scratch and head for the airport myself. After I'd slugged three highballs, I heard the name Pridi several times and naturally thought I was hearing things. I had been staring at the bar's grimy sawdust, and turned to the short arm of the L-shaped counter where the name was being dropped. The enticer and two others were poring over a fan of snapshots. The farthest was angled to engage his companions: that angle also afforded a view of me. This fellow distinctly said 'Pridi' once more, shuffled the photos, made eye contact, and gestured for me to join the group. The white-collar, barely glancing my way, evinced no surprise when he, Boonlert, a compact, high-strung featherweight, told them he'd like to make love now with the foreigner. Boonlert offered to cover the taxi and a hot-sheets motel—providing that *I* not ask him to pay in addition for the sex. Considering my physiognomy after Daeng, easily available in the gin mill's mirror, my playing-for-pay gave unwarranted confidence new dimension.

"We taxied down to Rama IV, hooked a left into a still dirt lane, and jolted from one mouth of that bleak, winding soi to the other ten fruitless times. Boonlert couldn't locate the motel he had in mind: huskily said he was puzzled, ordered the driver to back up twenty paces, and settled the fare. We got out on a slippery trough under a hole he'd spotted in a corrugated bulwark. Soon as the taxi pulled off, he signaled that we were to climb through the hole: into what I saw was a deserted estate, or one in whose dilapidated mansion every occupant was asleep. When I asked why, he said, 'Because I cannot wait.'

"Once inside the garden, if watching, the mansion's yet-quick inhabitants were content to be silent. The caterwauling witnesses in its forbidding field were another matter. For that was dense with the most bizarre and moonlit statuary. Grotesque Gothic creatures, tusked demons, and caped witches stood in circles; long-clawed gargoyles and grinning Minotaurs flanked them;

and the Thai Underworld's Damonen and Fire-slaves, Baal, Ra, Haros, six sad saints, and Satan loomed on guard of these: all weather-beaten, viridescent, all on pedestals, all well over eight feet tall. There too was Thanatos, the Greek and Sanskrit god of death, his crocodile snoot fit with razor incisors. Boonlert took my hand and wove through this infernal outdoor museum, this weed-choked collected menace—until we reached a mound of overturned soil he thought would do and pulled us onto it. A frantic bottom, he X-ed his lifted feet and created a barrier to intimacy by crunching his denims and briefs no higher than his knees. When I entered him, he grittily and desperately jacked off.

"The moment he came, his heat dissolved. His frenetic submission had been retaliatory… He sat aside and began the story of his last seventeen years. He had flown in from Paris that very noon and was resisting the trip to Pattaya, his hometown. He said he was obliged to pal in Bangkok with his *peuan gong* prior to seeing his family. He fuzzed and jumbled this, as persons will an explanation not half intended to convince. He'd gone to Paris when he was twenty-one at the invitation of his uncle, a waiter, who'd promised him a job as his busboy. But that included his *uncle's* mining a vein in Boonlert's rectum—nightly. This man being his mother's brother, Boonlert was trapped, conflicted, and depressed throughout the stay he'd been gullible enough to believe would teach him a trade, let him build a bank account, and return to his village a near-dignitary. You know when someone disclosing terrible secrets can seem preoccupied with something else? Scattered in the misery of incest was a current weight and deeper affliction. I looked at the image of Thanatos. The slits of its tunic revealed distended, striding, very muscular human thighs. 'Where are we?' I asked.

"'Thais call this the Soi of Lost Souls.'

"'Because of these statues?'

"'More. The men who finish on it. In the fleabags. You see them drunk, or using needles, in the dirty bars and shophouses.'

"'Gentlemen without prospect,' I said. 'If this is the Soi of Lost Souls, then the Mah Seekai is here.'

"'*That* is still open?' he asked with amazement.

"'I don't know. I never went. You could say I'm not ready to.'

"'Do not!' He paused. 'But, maybe you must… Listen, I shall rent a room so we can shower. And, listen again, tomorrow you will come with me to Pattaya.'

"His home was a *baan Thai* in back of the roads that parallel the beach. As we neared its verandah, his mother, mashing green curry on her knees, did not stop working to greet him, let alone me. Thais aren't big on familial emoting, but this control seemed borderline outrageous. Boonlert showed us to his sleeping space, a screen partitioning in a corner of the square one-floor. He looked at a picture of the king on the wall, eyed me thoughtfully, put his forefinger in my mouth, then went to speak with his mother. He found me again in the gloom of his foldaway corner and said we were to tour the village on his motorbike.

"He steered through the bush jungle, instead, in starts and halts. I thought he was lost, the forest having assumed an unfamiliar look to him. As I pitched forward riding pillion, though, I could tell he was multiply changing his mind. During his zigzags, he studied the surrounding undergrowth in a 360-degree search.

"Then I heard an accelerator gunned to explosive volume, and with a crash of branches saw a cyclist in a silver-winged black helmet mow the coppice twenty yards to our right and cannon directly toward us. He was bent to the bars; the helmet had a gray visor that hid his whole face. Boonlert gripped the gas gear, turned into a low thicket, and took off at top speed. The determined and burly armed rider, his bowlegs more than apparent now, roared closely after us until we reached the open avenue. There, where tourists and pedestrians were bustling about, he squeezed his brake, reversed direction, and disappeared into the jungle.

"My fingers clutched in his ribs by now, I felt Boonlert's heart pounding wildly. He drove straight on to the beach. We dismounted. 'Swim!' he said. 'In your underpants—swim!'

"I kept my shorts on (the switchblade was in them) and dashed into the ocean. Boonlert sank to his haunches in the shadow of his bike. For over an hour he signaled to me to remain in the water while he kept sentinel, his revolving vision a nonstop lighthouse on every water-skier, sunbather, and stroller along the boardwalk. The shore is legendary there; as I rode the lengthy waves or paddled in the gentle breakers, bathtub-warm, I rehashed that headlong chase. Behind our attacker's blind-visor were eyes pinched at a pigeon nose and a jaw darkened with violet stubble. Pattaya was a fraction of its present area, and nowhere as meretricious then or uniformly Hun and Russian. Still, the scent of organized crime pervaded that port even in those days: I wondered if that was the source of Boonlert's peril—and, were this so, the reluctant, inherited, or initiative nature of my host's involvement. On the motorbike I had felt how taut and wired his spare body was. To this day I cannot remember his features for their permanent notches of anxiety.

"Counter-treading the ebb and petting my blade, I thought how the gamblers were taking no chance with one of their inner circle, again.

"We ate on the floor with the extended family. A low-keyed conversation accompanied the meal. One by one, each contributed an opinion, allowing his tone to reveal nothing beyond solemnity. My presence almost unacknowledged, I assumed I was extraneous… When his mother suddenly became agitated, her words pell-mell and shrill, the others hushed her and continued eating.

"At sundown, Boonlert announced it was time to retire. He unrolled a mat in his dark corner; while I sprawled on it and squirmed out of my clothes, he steepled above me with parted legs: sharing, guarding, owning.

"'I shall be married now,' he whispered. 'But my fiancée has not come to the house. Don't make any noise.'

"He stripped, folded his jeans and polo shirt, and lowered his dead weight on me. From that position, he massaged my insteps, anklebones, shins, caps, and hamstrings; then retraced them in quick, hard holds. He kissed me with the tightlipped pressure Asians apply when they aren't used to kissing. I'd have questioned the prudence of making love within feet of his family had not the circumstance, muted as it was and repeating the Lost Souls' muted awareness, dictated hardly breathing. He struggled to trigger by friction, gasped his summit, and, after a strange denial, grabbed my neck, buckled dry for several seconds, and at last pounded through in short, separate spurts.

"Feeling by morning like a jackal's well-marked territory and ill-considered, temporary buffer, I thought it only decent to ask him to take me to the bus so I could finally be out of his way. With the fewest words, he indicated he'd prefer to drive me to the sights visitors enjoy on the Gulf. So we spent the day doing that. Was I a distraction? I imagined, given village protocol, the immediate threat was his nuptial dilemma. Itched by the possibility that I was impeded through not knowing how he shared with me the racketeers' desire to take him out, as he stared at the horizon, I asked him directly if the motorcycle attack was related to whatever problem concerned his fiancée. He turned in a frenzy and cried, 'Cory, it is *you* this motorbike man tries to kill!'

"I scanned the Gulf. I said, 'How do you know me?'

"'The snapshots.'

"'That you and your friends were examining in the tavern?'

"'Yes. Kob took them.'

"'Kob?'

"'He is a royal secretary.'

"'Ah! –I am standing near Wat Sai in those shots? With a white monk?'

"'Maybe Wat Sai. My *peuan gong* showed them to me because I had just arrived. And then there—there you were. That is the way of the Buddha.'

"'Yes, it is. Did, by chance, your friend *lure* me to the Depot Tavern? To help out the Buddha?' He smiled bashfully. 'Why? Lert, tell me why.' No answer. For some reason, he was holding his crotch. 'In the Depot Tavern, you mentioned the name Pridi Banomyong. More than once. –Boonlert: why?'

"'It is not good to say here.' He nudged a stone with the tip of his sandal. I gently moved his hand away from his crotch. He muttered, '…I assisted him. My uncle hated me for this. When Pridi died, I decided to leave Paris.'

"I said, 'There cannot be many Thais living in Paris now. They probably form a sort of community: everyone knows each other. The Thais who work for Pridi must certainly know each other. Did you know a man named Chain? –A man named Chain *and* Somboon?'

"Boonlert's eyes widen with pleasure. 'Yes! There *was* a man there once they sometimes called Chain and sometimes Somboon. How do you know that?'

"'The Buddha told me. What did this Somboon do for Pridi?'

"'We never spoke. I suppose he relayed, or ran, money. And arranged for people to meet. He scouted-out spots. He reached people: he knew a lot of languages. –Yes: Somboon picked safe places where men could meet.'

"'And did Buddha, or agents in Pridi's group, also tell you about Martin Pitt? And the cyclist with silver wings on his black helmet?'

"'They did,' he admitted. Then he seized my arm, as if, for two days, he'd been bursting to ask: 'Why does Khun Martin want to kill *you?*'

"'I am not certain that it is he.'

"His face darkened. 'Martin Pitt has power… He has jurisdiction.'

"'*More* than I once thought. And you are consigned to protect me. You are a good man, Boonlert. But *I* must protect myself, now.'

"That night his lovemaking was immeasurably closer. He inhaled my brows, nose, and ears; he attempted to chip my teeth with his. He caught my throat in his mouth and seemed to breathe forever into it. He sustained an immaculate bonding. He became a grenadier of unsuspected skill and unerring informality; and finally a Hindu dancer, his carnal ventures a cosmogram encasing Time itself. Hours after intercourse, he contemplated, 'You purr like a cat. Now, Khun Cory, you purr like a cat.'

"At dawn, he biked me to the bus stop and waited for the express to Bangkok. Then he instructed, 'If you can, *please*, go to the Mawchit Station on Viphavadi Rangsit at 11:00 a.m. one week from today. I will meet you there.'

"WHEN I PUSHED THROUGH the Troy City door of the Aphrodite, I was face-to-face with a seated Chain: defensive, prissy, and fulminating. I ambled toward him and dropped, matter-of-factly: 'Why you not ask for key at desk?'

"'I not live here.'

"Heeling him to the room, I stared at a plain white string on his wrist and a stylized blue tattoo right-side the hairline of his neck. I assumed this must be some very special or favored beast (which one, to irritate him, I'd not query); and that both embellishments had been acquired to ward off the malignant spirits—in guess who? –No, I concluded: but you plan, if not to *live*, to hang out here a lot, or why show up so well armored?

"I knew by his rotten mood that this morning was not his first attempt to visit me: it would take him thirty seconds to ask where I'd been all weekend. In ten, I marshaled an outline of Pattaya that deleted its sex and stressed the harrowing escape. Identifying Lert as Prime Minister Pridi's assistant in Paris, I asked why Lert had been assigned to protect me and implored me to meet him at Mawchit.

"Chain listened intently, this turbulence affirming the jinx, however different from the one he'd anticipated and steeled himself against at our reunion.

"He walked to the open door and stood there watching repairmen wearing greasy drawers and nothing else, their diagonal obliques ridging and relaxing as they doubled over or knelt and pulled, snaking a faulty drain-off at the pool. He dithered too long. And when I joined him, his eyeballs embargoed: to restrict my reading the obstacles he was trying to put in batting order.

"'Bike man and Lert? Lert love you, yes? Not nice-looking,

yet love you. Mean we have problem more now (with) Pridi. This why I say tired of living.'

"'You or me?' I asked him. 'Did you think Jim Thompson was, too?'

"'What?'

"'Tired of living?' He simply stared; then gulped.

"Chain would never bring back his clothes, the celadon case, or other effects. He'd never formally return. But the golden whore still felt obliged to hedge.

"Rollo Y-z had been in Cambodia for a spell. He'd volunteered for emergency aid work there and was scheduled to come home that day. I found him fumbling on his gallery: trying to lock up. He exclaimed, 'Ah-hah, there you are! You've been hunting for Olie, haven't you? Got me a gabfest for an hour or so. Don't leave.' He let me in. 'Pick the brains in this. And wait.' He tossed me a sheaf secured to a clipboard and stepped outside again.

"'My son!' he announced, alarming me, and left.

"The pages were proofs for his new *Bangkok Post* column: an entry disputing an article of mine on interpreting bas-relief lintels that lack linguistic inscription. He thought you couldn't. Rollo's adding a chatty and personal touch in this weekly column, over a preference for the academic and arcane, was making him a buzz in Bangkok's anemic reading circles. I became so absorbed—or disgruntled—that I hardly noticed how very late he was in reappearing.

"He was grim. He telegraphed his anxiety by changing his outfit several pointless times and then falling into a rattan chair that faced away from me. I took a seat opposite him. 'Well,' he began: 'my son, Pom, gambles. His losses are staggering. *That* is why I can't repatriate. The taxes and loans I currently owe exceed 48,000 USD. The baht I hoard get nibbled to nothing by Pom's debts.'

"'Must Pom's debts be paid? I mean, must *you?*'

"He chuckled, ridiculing me. 'A favor, a minor favor, a mere good word will buy a torpedo—you've learned that. So if *I* don't come across, and quick…'

"I'd never heard him so acerbic. 'Sixteen years raising Pom—so he could keep me in perpetual bankruptcy! I need to tell you something else. The loan sharks at this meet brought up Mr. Littleton… I disown him. It's eons since I've felt sympathy for that shakedown artist. Olie's had a hundred chances and I've forgiven him a hundred times. But this concerns the statue.'

"'My Buddha icon?'

"'Yeah. It's gold. At least the outer coating is: so of course they'd say so is the whole thing. Cory— they know you have it.'

"'And?'

"'Guess where Olie copped it?'

"I said, 'Olie or Nok copped it from the collection of a princess.'

"Rollo paled. '*Did* they? Well, haven't *you* been busy! But, O.K., they sold it to these movie-spoof mobsters. And then *re*-stole it from *them!* That is just so Olie! *And* Nok! –*So much* those ineffable dickheads!'

"I said, 'Does one movie-spoof, named Maitri, think he's George Raft?'

"'Yeah. The other, James Cagney. Like I say, haven't *you* been busy!'

"Rol stalked to the rack where he sets his dishes to dry and was, as I could predict, agitated by their appearance. He rearranged the plates, ascending in size. 'Those sharks want partial payment…of the value they're grossly exaggerating.'

"I asked, 'Why not the statue itself?'

"'They can't peddle that piece right now. Right now parliament's down on the sale of national treasure, especially Buddha images: *and seriously*, I imagine, if it was swiped from a princess. Inspectors are all over the place. What these guys require is hard cash; and revenge on Nok and Olie.'

"'How do you know that "bird," Mr. Nok?'

"'*How? How?* Do we have to go through that again? He brings me boys! The right boys.'

"'Why did these loan sharks tell you about this double-dipping?'

"'Obviously they hope I will—and can—bail out Olie and Nok.

As I always bail out Pom. But I neither can nor will.'

"'What's next?'

"'Next, Cory? Don't you understand? When they learn Olie and Nok can't raise the money, what they'll take for face is the both of them.'

"'Take their—?'

"'Yes, exactly: their lives. They're not fooling around!'

"I said, 'I left a note in the Allied Cemetery on the Kwai promising the entombed I'd devote my days to the diminution of the father.'

"'Great!' Rollo responded. 'Just what we need: non-sequiturs!'

"I crossed my hands. Rollo grit: 'Are you *following* me? You have a vault. It's brick and built into a brick wall: it's actually a protrusion from that wall?'

"'Uh-huh.'

"'Buy the best bolt in some lock-shop, and put the Buddha in the Aphrodite's vault. ...Buddha and Aphrodite: "Big joke!" George Raft would say!'

"I reasoned then: So that's it! The kingpins are indeed tangling, though not specifically for the icon...

"I squirmed, 'Is crippling persons to make them beggars legal here?'

"'You mean, are the laws against that enforced? –No.'

"'But kidnapping foreigners to extract their organs must be.'

"'Oh, sure. There's still a U.N.! Why are you asking me this?'

"'Because Daeng insists I belong to a ring that smuggles children into Thailand for the most heinous experiments. Nightmares alone could imagine them. I'm sure Mr. Nok convinced Daeng of that. Ditto Maitri and Cagney. I suspect those sharks invest in a less efficient ring. By offering me—as part of a Pol Pot internationally connected and competing operation—Nok won favor with them. He gained this leverage, and then got more favor and face reporting that I am doubly guilty: having, to boot, finagled their icon. They believe I am laughing and gnawing at them, truly gnawing.'

"'Wow...' Rollo whistled softly. He went to the cage where

his squirrel was manically circling. He stiffened, his nails gripping its bars. The squirrel bit him.

"I said, 'Wait a minute here, you wait a minute, Rol. I know what I do and what I have not done!'

"'*Do* you, Cory? I'm relieved to hear that. I assume you also know *who* does and has not done whatever this is! We've got to stop patrols from finding that statue! Thais say Buddha enlightens: eventually. Look toward an abbreviated "eventually." At the moment, I'm wishing you'd never come to Thailand. But I'll get over that. For today, stash the damn thing like I told you.'

"He painfully twisted and took me in aslant, his angle sufficing to expose the glower of conflicted condemnation. Then he bore his eyes into mine, cognizant of my resentment, and my struggling with something somewhere else.

"He said, 'It's Chain, isn't it?'

"Shortly after I reached the Afro, bolt in tow, the phone rang. Chain—image-saving: he'd be along in a few hours rather than immediately. When he joined me, I stretched my arm across his waist and held his hip, resumed thinking, and let the intended provocation of his lateness go at that.

"He was still in the Land of his insulated Nod when I ferried to Thonburi with two objectives in mind. First, I wanted to see the chart on Volker Altmuller's progress; and second, talk with that attending psychiatrist: about squelching Nok. I coaxed a nurse into translating Volker's chart: it confirmed the swine poisoning previously noted, and now traces of other poisons.

"I waited until his caretaker came on duty. 'That iron chair is for the violent and violently hallucinating,' he haughtily lectured with his trademark confidence.

"'Handy things,' I said. 'Have you spoken to Nok recently?'

"'Not last night. Are you suggesting that your sometime lover—'

"'Mendacity isn't hallucinating, Doctor. Nok has not been shooting pool?'

"'I say, not last night. You cannot count on men whose mothers raised them to suckle on bar patrons as if they were sows.

–Without social skills: so that they remain mother-dependent all their lives,' he started dogmatically and went like a speeding train. The upshot was, he chorused not to have seen Nok for days and—in a mordant tone—would find it passing strange if he should, now.

"When I walked through the Aphrodite's dark hallway and into the court's blinding sunlight, I heard a commotion on an upper corridor. Chain, at last awake, was sitting in our room, buffing his nails. 'Falang dead,' he announced.

"'Falang dead!' I shouted. 'Who? How?'

"'Sssssh!' he cautioned with a finger to his lips. He identified the man by pantomiming a long ponytail, an all-round flabbiness, with a dopey expression and massive shoulders. Then mimicked circling his throat with a rope or cloth and a suspension from the ceiling. It was George Bryning, that Australian silk-salesman on the River Kwai raft, who had moved into the Afro some weeks back; from whom I'd kept my distance as the forgettable limb of a trip I'd like, but could not afford, to forget. I raced up the stairwell to a congregation of tenants, popinjay cops, and plainclothesmen blocking the door to a narrow unit. The tenants were muttering to one another and the police shut-mouthed, filling in forms or stepping away for the precinct photographer. George was lying in the short foyer, his bare soles disrespectfully aimed at the crowd outside. He was shirtless, his weedy fields of axial hair perfectly still. The famously ample flaxen fall cushioned his scarred head; his open right-clutch, as tremendous and disproportionate as the encapsulating hand of the *David*, yet wanting in any pellet, summarized and recentered the *David's* eternal doubt. A kneeling and weeping, frail boy kissed his brow; and, to reinstate his impatient spirit, was kneading his throat with what I guessed was Bryning's shirt and the instrument of his dispatch. An old neighbor reprised the rumor that George had been a heroin addict: his buddy could be seen at the corridor's end, crying. Though he stood in shadow and with his back deferentially to the rest of the people there, I was certain this buddy was Martin… Martin Pitt.

"I measured my time descending the stairs. If Martin is at the

Afro now, then he knows I am: and have been for quite a while. Since my returns from Pha Taem and Pattaya, there's *not* been a third try at picking me off. Only reason for that, feint, dodge, and delay it as I would, is that Chain is here… I leaned against a court demon and recalled what I could about George Bryning. Might not Martin, in this disaster as in Volker's, be more than the simply bereaved? Beyond recording his soapy pallor, I'd been remiss with George. Philip Bailey had told me he'd found that wispy boy in Chiang Rai: ever since, common to Thailand, he was led around with a ringbolt through his nose; and, familiar enough in Chiang Rai, had developed a taste for junk. So he'd rapidly slid down flights on which *I* had shaky sea legs. The cops were pressing no one. Junkies are dispensable…and replaceable. For who do you think sells them the junk?"

I sighed: "Sure, sure!" His "sea-legs" phrase made me see Cory just then more as a buccaneer than a boxer. And suggested my asking: "*Popinjay* cops?"

"Oh, yes! In this ghastly climate, their brown uniforms are formfitting. The lenticular calves and thighs are pleatless, so personal is their tailoring—so individual. The seat hugs all buttocks, whether salad-bowls or saucers. Casing the torso and deltoids, it's especially skintight: a zipper under the false shirt-buttons ensures they don't pull—a sensually rigged and dizzying subversion feeding the belief that this is the most eroticized of cultures. In that close hallway, the juxtaposition of sex, a killer, and the police overwhelmed the static impact of suicide. Uncalled turgor would cement that threesome; and they'd join my cabinet of captured pictures in their power to deter me for years.

"I wandered into the coffee shop, ordered an arabica, and went through the divisive aspects of the above like a man given fight only when opponents eat his entrails. Soren Cass Blackblatt and Philip Bailey seemed too tanked a version of Mutt and Jeff by now to consult in all this. I walked back and looked at our room through the great terrarium of pigmy trees and parakeets. The door was ajar. Was Chain encouraging mosquitoes to drift in and bite us; or was a 'grieving' Englishman visiting him? Before I'd a grip on *how* to step by and see, four husky deliverymen

257

rolled two packages and a used fridge over the threshold. By the time I entered the room, the fridge was plugged in and Chain was opening the cartons: which contained an electric burner and a full set of cutlery, including a large steel fork and a gleaming butcher's knife. 'Today, eat well!' the headman exalted. He smiled, *wai*ed us, and departed with his helpers. I figured Chain would boast that *he* had come up with the fold for these household goods; then go deaf on my grill re the event upstairs, suicide being another embarrassment (or ill-portent) the Thai cannot identify. In my brief absence, he'd appointed the place with twenty votive sticks, since Bryning's ghost was sure to harry the Afro till the end of the era. George's floor-mates were already finding vacancies elsewhere. But the otherworldly form which Bryning assumed was only part motivation for the deodar swirl surrounding Chain, now insouciantly clipping his toenails. He hummed:

"'Nok dead too.'

"'Nok!!' I gasped.

"'One suck nipples you in snooker club.'

"'I *know* who Nok is! What you mean he's dead?'

"'Motorbike: he fall off backseat. Neck—broke. Dead right away. Happen this morning. So I not see.'

"'Cost 2,300 baht have motorbike-boy kill someone.'

"'Where I get 2,300 baht?'

"'And upstairs? George Bryning—Martin Pitt—*this* you also not see?'

"'Not!' he gurgled ardently, saliva vigorously moistening the damson hollow at the left corner of his lips. 'Not see anything! For what you ask?'

"'For what?? For *what*, Chain?!'

"'I say you before: Martin Pitt, him I not like. –George upstairs: not know.'

"I flushed the juice in a plastic quart down the toilet, filled it with ice cubes, grabbed my vodka, and poured to the top. Gulp after gulp, I swallowed as much as I dared, quaking enough to cave in. Chain followed me from a profile, delicious cunning curled on his tongue: which shot out, shuttling like a lizard's exploring the vibrations of heat. He pocketed his clip and emery board.

"He lied: 'Think Muslim problem. In south. Nok Muslim.' Then he swung, with perfect detachment, 'Want talk dream now.'

"'*Really?*' I couldn't avoid the sarcasm. It misfires with Asians: accepting no Innocence before a Fall from Grace, they slip its target. –There *was* Maitri and Cagney to consider: promptly collecting their debt, rather than no doubt enlarge it by trusting a vengeful turncoat, flighty at best. Even in name.

"Chain's dream of course was precognitive. It featured a lanky, charitable Swede. 'Tom client. Come every year. Make tour: Rayong, Ko Sumet. I also tour guide.' His cadence reeked with celebratory apprehension. He defiantly crossed his legs. And continued humming.

"'You get letter from Tom?' I asked.

"'True.'

"'Before or after you have this dream?'

"'Uh—after.'

"'I'll bet.'

"'What?'

"'*Mai b'lai.* How long this tour?'

"'Twenty-one day. Four week, maybe. –Why you look me?'

"I began dusting the refrigerator and trying to sort the cutlery. I gave up on the latter and heaped it all on the now free top of the vault. His news, hitting me hard, was partly preempted by visions of Bryning's lemon skin, Martin's tears, the gutsy Maitri—and Nok, beside a motorcycle. Chain had scored the night before, and on other nights in the last few months, but had not screwed any man twice. Those contacts were carefully 'short-time.' A holiday sprint seemed intolerable when the qualitatively equal, two-hour tricking had not. My head was pounding. 'This is cruel,' I heard myself entreat.

"'This not cruel,' he objected, unaware of the degree to which the alcohol then was holding back the tedious paralysis. 'Cruel when I go, not say. This cruel. You not know I am where. So I tell you him. Because not come for seven, eight day. Why you drink? Is afternoon.'

"I spilt half the container while awkwardly trying to flatten socks. He sank into the bed on a pillow-pile and faked relaxation. He was pliant; and preparing. I fought my increasing rigidity. He said, 'I not want like this.'

"'What *do* you want?'

"'Live with you. In U.S.! Forever: with you.'

"To that inconceivable punch, my muscles loosened, enabling me to shuffle toward him and then slide, gathering the sheets to support a recline. Sitting up I'd be quivering. He tensed slightly and clenched both fists.

"'And we would be together forever? You, me?'

"'Sure. I want.'

"'Every night?'

"'No! Not *every* night! Sometime have sec somebody different. One time a month. Maybe one time two month. Not interesting, always same person.'

"'Oh…' I unlocked his fists, feeling this fresh razor, and had to be honest: 'If you sleep other man in U.S. *just one time*, I rid of you. I throw you out.'

"He bit hard. 'So, what *you* really want, Cory?' What I really wanted was to be able to wear a fedora the way Dana Andrews could. I was ashamed, in fact frightened, that his possibly arranging for Nok's bike 'accident' had not, by half, automatically dismissed his ambition. To measure my derangement then, it was heightening his appeal. Filtering his proviso, I was questioning the merit in a necessity to have intercourse with him alone for the rest of my life.

"I thickly, hopelessly reminded him: 'But you say you not love me.'

"'Why I here!' he snapped. 'You look I do, not I say!'

"Assuming that he had preplanned the option he was giving me; and that disclosing Nok's death, Bryning's 'suicide,' and Tom's imminent arrival were threats intended to stack it, his next strategy appeared to be simply rounding those off with what he'd have taken for granted would be a dependable coup de grace. I saw his arms in score, like those on dancers in friezes of Javanese pageants, begin to come at me. Each was sleeved in brown, the semiotic dark brown and glove-tight sleeves of the lewd police, ignoring us.

"I submitted to the multiple grapple the better to strike him at closer range: strike at the pampered felon that Rollo Y-z, a black hermit, and Kambu-ja imposed on me. I gave him the time to lambently open my fly, then confessed that I'd never emitted spontaneously during our entire two and a half years of love-making. It wasn't difficult to clarify. I said that to finish with him, I needed to think of someone else. I was confident he'd fully understand me: hustlers know what shutting their eyes and seeing Mark Spitz and Tony Leung—or, today, nature-boy Jeff Corwin and basketball-wiz Yao Ming—is all about. Unthwarted, and to sight dispassionately, he resorted at once to professional amends. He concentrated on rolling three joints of ganja, and after I had smoked two and he one, doused his hands in capfuls of lubricant. Fixing my face with a decisive stare, he used both to coat my flaccidity and bring it to point. Lying back comfortably, his thighs chamois and palmate, and continuing all ten fingers' gentle, circular touch, he slowly, ever so slowly, teased me into his cavity and motored by pulsing his gluts: so that his colon flexed me in rather than suffer an invasion.

"'Now not think,' he said. 'Not think nothing.'

"The adagio was mellow and our balance effortless: a victory of individual testosterone elected in unison. My respiring inaudibly cohered, suspended, and accelerated with his. His whole coordinated body quietly drained the last drop of semen from mine. Yes! An unsponsored orgasm. Nonnarrated: my first with him. Then I turned him on all fours, soothing and stationing him...

"We may have smoked more ganja after that, or I may have had more vodka. I don't remember, because I must have gone into blackout; and neither remember falling asleep. What I remember is that I dreamt about my maternal grandmother. When she was too old to live by herself, my parents welcomed her, and

261

she shared my bedroom. Frequently she rose screaming in the middle of the night. In my dream, I was lying in that bedroom and listening to someone mount the stairs. I cringed, expecting my father: but could tell by her fretted footfall that it was she. She reached the landing, came into view, and stood out there, her hands folded, composedly watching me. Then she closed the door. I don't recall anything else; and if there was more to that dream, wish very much now that I could.

"Ferrotypes of her husband, my grandfather, can be mistaken for me: in Belle Époque suits—especially after a shower, when my hair is slicked back. Once, holding a ferrotype and comparing it to me, she gasped, 'Josh!' This man deserted her and their seven small children to run off with another woman. She herself was celebrated for her knee-length hair, always more marine than black. Though she wore it fairly short by the time she was living with us, I complimented her one evening on its beautiful blue color.

"'It is not blue now,' she said, 'it is gray.'

"Then her eyes narrowed with opprobrium, making me quite uncomfortable. I knew she believed I'd inherit his defection of inborn duty; and asked, guiltily, 'Grandma, how did you raise a brood of seven all by yourself?'

"'I took the pins out of my hair and let it drop to my knees. And put on a grass skirt and went around the corner.'

"Years after he had absconded, my granddad tried to come back. He wrote from an African city and pleaded with her. She told him to stay where he was.

"When I opened my lids, the dream having been so vital, I naturally thought I was in my upper-floor room and searched the space before me for confirmation. My arms and legs were racked with pain. I attempted to move them and found I couldn't. I felt like Volker Altmuller. The night lamp, its shade shredded but bulb intact, threw shadows on the table crushed against the wall; both upturned folding chairs; and, scattered everywhere, the laundered articles we'd hung to dry in the loo. Chain, his gallantry gone, was hunched sadly at the far end of the bed, lock-jawed and looking away from me. It took me a while to recognize him.

"'What time is it?' I mumbled.

"'Midnight and a half.'

"We had bought a short clothesline for still-damp garments, and it was then that I first saw it: severally wound and tightly knotting my wrists and ankles. Amazed, though not yet alarmed, I sputtered: 'What is this?'

"He held up the cleaver, which I'd placed with the cutlery on top of the vault, and replied:

"'What is *this?!*'

"'Butcher knife. So? Untie rope.'

"He moved his right shoulder closer to me and indicated three deep-garnet maul marks on it; and two fresh gashes on his nearest neck muscle.

"'Did I—?'

"'Yes,' he intoned. 'Want get out door again. And cannot. Then you find knife. You stab—five time. I punching you, take away knife. But take ten minute for do it. I put rope like this. You not remember?'

"'No, nothing. –I not think true!'

"'Must.'

"And so, as lost a battle as I could imagine and still remain wanting, trying, or hoping: to be myself and live with him. Chain undid the knots, wrapped the definitive blade in a towel—a towel soaked with blood—and stuffed it into his duffel. He stumbled to the oculus and stood in its prism, his right side facing me: with those wounds, which had destroyed his blue tattoo.

"Then said, 'I go house me now.'

I exclaimed, "But you draw a blank on all—"

"No, not quite," Cory interrupted. "When he told me, I did get flashes, blurs of struggling with him, but they were split-second jump cuts; and possibly a response to suggestion. I mean, had he not offered his account, the flickered and puzzling dream-frames that I did retain would surely have left me in a day or two. Yet let me move on: how I tackled this danger within, and found myself forced to, will become clear today.

"Chain's annual, Tom, was due on Sunday morning. Chain spent that Saturday night at home with his family: and dropped by before busing up to the airport. His pretext was that he needed a burgundy money-belt of mine, since none of his would match the slacks he'd chosen. I was certain he really saw mine as an Ariadne's thread…or *symbolic* chastity belt: as if any such thing could exist.

He as naïvely hoped his stopping-off would be a *passe-partout* for his impending junket. My mood showed it wasn't. So he returned the next afternoon, claiming that Tom had decided to sightsee in Bangkok, prior to renting an auto on Thursday and driving them elsewhere. He stripped at once and jumped into bed. 'Quickly,' he urged, 'not have time too many. Must go hotel Tom fifteen o'clock.'

"Tailing Chain was child's play, because it would never have dawned on my determined politico that, in capitulating to his charms that afternoon, I'd finally surrendered all self-respect. He hopped a pedicab idling outside the Afro, and I grabbed the one replacing it. 'Go same him: but he not know,' I instructed. Complicitly winking, the driver kept a strict four vehicles behind Chain's cab. It pulled over at the Narai, a vertical Deco-update in Patpong. My man slowed and parked at a discreet distance. I tipped him extravagantly.

"Then, cloak-and-dagger style, shielded in the lobby by an urn glazed with dragons, I thought I was in for the longest and sickest stretch of this brain-dead compulsion: they could be balling now or sipping cocktails on a penthouse terrace for hours. One with a river view! To my happy surprise they weren't: they were down in exactly nine minutes. Patpong was the usual furnace that day, yet Tom, endearingly, was wearing a knitted watch cap. Less endearingly, his Swedish ringlets descended from it in annoying reminder of the Pallas Athena at Lome. Unbeknownst to me then, that watch cap was hiding a sizable tonsure. Hands in the leather pockets of his denim bell-bottoms, slightly round-shouldered, and straining to appear at ease and dignified, I doubt he was forty—a fit, pleasant six-footer who found it normal to buy sex. Of course, Chain was his 'guide and escort'; and Tom's brief holiday inhibited nailing a not-for-profit companion. Had I an appropriate lover anywhere? Not even the habit of looking for one.

"Two were looking for me, just left-side the Narai: a sweaty Frenchman, midfifties, and a thirtyish, broad-faced Thai. The Frenchie fumbled, half loony, in a garbled Franglais: *'On a besoin de toi tout suite chez l'Hotel Swan'*—the Swan, opposite Chain's house in Soi 36. An infelicity committed within spitting distance of where he was born, brought up, and still lived was a gross violation, inconsiderate and unnecessary. –Put bluntly: Chain deserved nothing less.

"The Swan Hotel was sleazeville run wild. The Thai leaped its worn steps to the third floor and dashed into their room. When the Frenchman and I got there a minute later, he was stark na-ked and supine on the concave bed—not an eager beaver: he was drunk or drugged. He squinted at me and drew his knees up to his nips. The Frenchman, nude lickety-split, got on his hairy back alongside the Thai and also tossed up his legs: so I'd a quartet of jackknifed limbs and a beet-red duet of puckering gourami. 'Fuck, fuck us!' the Frenchman demanded.

"I studied the psychedelic diptych, chose the stoned Thai, and entered him. He began to scream. 'He doesn't like it,' I said.

"'He like! He like!' the Frenchman agitated. 'Look: legs stay-ing up!' They were, though reluctantly: he held them in place with a grip on his caps. He'd no option until ordered otherwise. The Latin beamed, 'I train him! I train him!'

"The Thai started to drip. I pulled out. His Frenchie scowled, and hissed, *'Alors: moi! Vite! Baises!!'*

"I shifted obediently on the inclined mattress and forced my sprinkled blister to part the moist mat that veiled his sagging cheeks. He revolved unrhythmically on the axis and moments later I was soft. He was furious. *'Lui, encore!'*

"Robot-like, I switched sewers. On this try, blood as well as feces pooled through the sheets. I withdrew, lifted the passive fellow in my arms, and carried him into the toilet. I lowered him onto the commode and kept him there with a thumb on his shoulder. I'll give you dollars to doughnuts he didn't know what was happening. Behind me, the Frenchman, blue-balled and oblivious, was playing octopus to my every crack and crevice. 'Can't you see he's in pain?' I admonished, watching the Thai bend his head to the bowl and heave.

"'*Pas de tout!* He trained! He go in Paree: assistant-wholesale—buy wholesale! Fuck *me* now, fuck again!' As neutral—and opportunistic—as I was determined to act, I could not. The small, cheap room stank of discharge, ganja, stale vomit, and defecation…and, shortly, urine: the Frenchman, whether from urogenital reflex or to coarsen his excitement, began pissing on the floor. Then he forsook his agenda: hoisting his partner off the toilet, he dumped him on the bed: and produced darning-stick dildos. He told me, '*Nous faites comme ça!*'

"I shoved these bowling pins into their familiar sockets and coordinated my fist-twisting until I felt that pair's excruciation in my own wrists and forearms. Fortunately, during this corkscrew, the wholesaler and the apple of his widened eye beat off. Then I commanded the slaves to shrimp me (eat out my toes); and afterward pull on my socks and shoes.

"Avoiding the tears on the Thai's face, I bolted the broken stairs. I hesitated by the Swan's entrance to see if Chain was in the soi—a preposterous guilt, since he at the time was painting the town with Tom. I raced along Rongphasi; started New Road; and slackened to prowl around a teenager staring at a soup-vendor. I asked him his name. Brightening, he said, 'Jiap.' He was homely, gangly, and scrawny. A bag o' bones would be so right, now! I bought him soup, watched him slurp, and learned his goal was to become a *mia chow*—'rent wife'—for which he'd journeyed to *Krung Thep*. Having no schooling or skills, he was under the fabled impression that a pale walking-wallet rendered such liabilities negligible, should he raise the railroad fare and baht for a week's unfurnished.

"'*Phra* (Buddha) not give Jiap good life. Karma me: I bad boy in life before. Find one Yerman. He want take me Yermany. I not want go. I afraid he sell me.'

"'Sell you?'

"'True! My friend me in Phetchabun: Yerman sell him in Yermany. Tell him come Berlin vacation, but sell him.'

"'To whom?'

"'Friends him. Sell for sec. Get many money. Keep him in house, not let out, keep one year. After send home.'

"Jiap waxed morose…visibly plummeted to solder my education…then gauged the moment favorable. Hence:

"'Have dream before in Phetchabun, see you in dream.'

"'Me?'

"'You sure, Khun Cory. Have beard, nose broke, black hair—half-half same you—falang *and* Chine—same very big, same-same strong. Have shirt you, wristwatch you. Too many time I have dream, after dream every time true.'

"'So you are psychic, eh?'

"'Khun make Jiap *mia chow, Phra* make place high for Khun, next life.'

"'Let me tell you something, Jiap. Yankee not have next life!'

"He was shocked; and choked on the creakiest guttural I've heard: *'Why??'*

"Why indeed! Because we are infinitely more blessed than Buddhists. In his coop in a stilt-house built over the remnant of a sluggish klong, Jiap dropped his trousers—but did not remove them—with none of the preamble he'd devised for his pitch. He assumed that completely cooperative invitation: one's chin is planted on the floorboards and folded-arms and armpits flattened on them as well; while the nether region, supported on steadied shins and knees, yawns up at you. His buttless, brandy-colored hole disclosed as many of its recessed incorporates as he could get to surface and palpitate. All that pulsed was that orange suction. I retreated at this insulting directive from another faux-passive partner, even if *he* self-deceptively construed presenting a depository as his duty—in its entirety. Then my thoughts turned ugly: that rear is too meager, its trough too wide, worn, and unappealing—who'd believe he could sell *him?* And petty: I couldn't pick a more suited coterie for tricking into bondsmen than these slatterns. Yet in the end his semi-nakedness and perfected exemption did affect the irrefutable arousal in the submissive, freshly dead, victims of accident, a killed soldier…

"I bought us dinner in a klong café and listened to Jiap arrange his life until nearly eleven o'clock. Then flagged a bus.

"–I actually fled him, overtaken by images of the suddenly, violently dead. Young Vietnamese in hitched-up diapers, their ankles roped to tanks tractoring them to graves—a haul, tearing the filthy fabric of makeshift swaddling, their flat, convex privates and softly mounded backsides often exposed, I'd pinned these sepias to walls in bedrooms long forgotten and wanked. I had buggered Jiap, multiply buggered him, for three exhausting hours.

"I went to Lome. I'd find a stranger who'd understand. Or be simpatico.

"On its sardined balcony, I was pushed toward the W.C. To avoid getting battered by its swing-doors, I stood adjacent to them. My awkward parachuting there stirred the interest of a young Caucasian emerging from the men's; wasting no time, he made that interest obvious.

"Andrew. A brown-weave cardigan was pulled over a white pullover with a '50s-style upturned collar trimmed in tan. If Andrew wasn't ill or anemic, he was enviously impervious to hellish clime. His eyes were violet, his strawberry mane hilled in a pompadour, grooved with a spaced-tooth comb. And the gracious smile of this unique distraction!

"He was from Vermont. 'I'm twenty-six. When I was fifteen, I felt like the shell for an Asian who wanted out: felt I oughta live in the Orient. I flew to Thailand. Each year I moved to a different Oriental country. So in eleven years, I got to stay in all of them. Thailand being the first, I had to come back and say good-bye to it: because I'm flying home tomorrow. I finally know where it is. Wanna go to my hotel with me?'

"*Chain* invaded. He'd have been chomping at the bit when I entered the bar; then told Tom he'd an ache to whiz. I asked for permission to bang with the white boy. When he drew breath for a reflex thumbs-down, I held my ground: 'Chain, is only falang! I not have falang for two-three year!'

268

"'Will rain,' he said curtly. Meaning somehow that should cramp me.

"'Have umbrella.'

"He defiantly paused; frowned; considered (that Caucasians were irrelevant, I suppose); and consented.

"Andrew's luggage was stacked in the center of his room, and a new outfit hung in the closet. We sat on the bed. I confessed I'd be intrigued to learn what led him to the discovery that his white skin wasn't concealing an Asian.

"'Oh, that's easy,' he said. 'I was starting to feel like Ganymede.'

"'As in, "—and the eagle?"' I asked, surprised.

"'Yes. As in: "—the eagle-as-Asia!"'

"'Doesn't the eagle bear Ganymede off to Olympus?' I carped. 'Where he can listen to the whisperings of the gods?'

"'It's still an abduction. That's not at all ideal if you want to eavesdrop. Also, I've got some form of cancer. The doctors here can't identify it. Maybe in America they can. They should be able to treat it. See: my fingers are swollen.'

"He splayed both hands under a lamp, and I saw that the final joint in each digit, ruby when compared to the off-ivory of his knuckles, was enlarged by more than a third. A bolt of lightning lit the room, immediately followed by the cascade of a loud monsoon. Andrew went to the shut window, opened it, cupped his ears at the quarreling sound, and said, 'O.K., now there's your gods. Can you make *anything* of that? And they're not whispering! So come on: stop it, don't bug God's line. –Gimme an appetite for Vermont.'

"We sixty-nined, my lips homesick in his soft, roux-scented thighs, his salty, pliable seat, the snood of his spiced and maple groin. He cradled me in the reposed embrace of his arms and legs all night, rocking to the patter of that downpour: oddly paternal for someone his age. An Occidental boy's unfamiliar body and thoughts! He catered, and so deferred to me, that I could not warn him that home is a direction, not a place. Andrew gave me his card in the morning, engraved with a Seoul and a Montpellier address.

"'Call me when you get to the States,' he smiled. It was such a gentle, generous smile."

I took a ciggy and said, "The protective tattoo that you 'destroyed'—Chain's tattoo, on the side of his neck, was of an eagle, wasn't it?"

"Yes, it was," Cory admitted. "I treasured Andrew's card for many years... The images mauling me the day before returned; they called for my circulating in the sphere I should: and there, doing what I must. By nightfall I was smashed and in Harrie's. To be safe from the trample of dancers, I went to a wallflower niche on the main floor and plonked on a pullout chair. Bar Harrie's radiated away from the chair for acres, and the phantoms in a lower hall of hell gyrated on them. My shelter was bursting with agitation: it was imperative to know, as well as who we apparently are, who might we be. Then, from my perch, in a split in the revelers, I saw Chain. He turned into the arena with Tom. Tom was guileless. No way I'd dislike Tom. Chain, to the contrary, laughing bewitchingly, seized their spin to taunt his rivals, and me, with his comely catch. By parading Tom, he made maximum—and final—capital. My dad and I had duked it out when I told him I was gay. He literally said, 'Put 'em up!' and started to cry. He—wrong about everything—to *that* undying dad was I trying to prove my fiber? This Thai endurance test: for which of my oversights was it atoning? The rounds I can go or rippings take—who profits from a penitence so abysmally imprecise?

"At that pivotal moment, the Cambodian Kambu-ja appeared. Somewhere to my left, the onlookers parted for him, and not knowing why at first, I thought it was Jahd, inevitably amputated. Kambu-ja braced on his crutch and one firm leg and did not come closer. His quiet terror played an Inquisition on my adequacy. Re-seeing them in banned print-offs and smuggled footage, his face duplicated the implacable masks of the Khmer Rouge from whom he'd escaped: invoked the shrapnel puncturing on the spines and stomachs of their victims, the limp bow of a slain man's gland, the pry of his bare buttocks; the dented skulls of Pom and Olie as Maitri crushes them; Nok's snapped

270

neck; Jahd's certain fate; the bizarre and intolerable infatuation in struggling to butcher Chain.

"I sprang to my feet, causing the pullout chair to shut and collapse, echoing behind me, and bullied through the cruisers to the ticket gate, oblivious to whose elbows I was knocking aside or how many highballs I was splattering on this tourist and that hooker. I hardly heard their cries of disgust.

"I ran the gauntlet of Soi 4, tropic shirts, feinted blocks, and toothy jeers a smear of rainbow, and tore into the speeding traffic on Silom. A cabbie screeched his brake, but as I'd come from nowhere to him it was too late and he hit me. I turned at the blast of his horn and his headlights in the chevron of my eye, so that I fell confronting him, sternum and arms stretched over the bonnet, one tire riding an inch or two onto the toe of my right foot. The driver, like a cinemascope head-shot thrown up before me, was rigid with horror; I think my own face must have registered the shock of surprise more than hurt, and that only when I saw the blood from my fingers spot his windshield. There was a sharp bolt through my hipline and a simultaneous blank sensation in my foot. He had brought the taxi to a total stop in the instant that I doubled over its engine; I jounced on it for several seconds, pitched off the hood, swerved sidewise a step nix of oncoming vehicles, and took off across the road without looking back.

"I must have instinctually caught a tuk-tuk; and returned to partial consciousness in our bathroom, running water on the lesions and trying to assess the damage; then, with pillowslips wrapped around wherever, most likely crawled into bed—and was out. When I awoke, I was a speed bag of black and blue and aches the hangover would not let me locate. 'Hangover' is rankly precipitous: I was still drunk. I cut some cotton gauze, and using a full parcel of Band-Aids—and Scotch tape, no less—managed to dress two fingers on my right hand, four on my left, and my right long and big toes.

"The phone rang; I nudged it off the hook. It was the sportscaster Philip Bailey: he of the *surgical* mask. 'I can meet you to-

night at the Mah Seekai. It's a ten-minute walk from the stadium.'

"'Tonight?'

"'Cory—you don't sound too good.'

"'That's not true: I'm better than usual. Quite a bit better…'

"'I'll believe that when I see it. You did wanna jaw with Martin Pitt as soon as possible, didn't you? He said he'll show tonight.'

"'Fab! How's seven, seven-thirty?'

"I needed Philip: there was no telling what would happen
if Martin had me alone, or I him. My limp was not too bad, and
Philip thought tourniquets were my second skin.

"Hidden as it is, the Soi of Lost Souls isn't far from the Afro;
or that bo tree of dark fame. The Mah Seekai was a shophouse
there, ochre-washed inside and out. It had an outdoor table and
maybe a dozen within its step-down interior. There was an expected shingle depicting the spirit above the door, unexpected
thick lace curtains on the front windows, and a collection of
Mah Seekai statues standing about, varying in size from two to
six feet. She wears a red sarong or an ochre breast wrap and
waist-to-ankle gown; has long oatmeal or henna hair, loose or
taken in a tail over her bare left shoulder. Her cupped hands offer pink petals. On one top-knotted version, her left hand held
her right wrist. She always looks pleased. You instantly knew
this was a breathing space, plus trading post, for addicts and
dealers, beachcombers, fugitives, Goa garbage, dole-scam scum,
last-stop whores, and perennial fakes and failures in a city where,
to a certain extent, they can fake it: male, female, and undecided.
A Muslim prostitute in a green half-burka and miniskirt slipped
from huddled group to group.

"Phil recognized a weed-peddler at a back table; bought him
a bottle of Chivas Regal; small-talked him for a while; got to business; and then translated for me. 'It's no-go, now. No-chin was
here yesterday with his retainer, but they've sailed to Hollow
Mountain in the Similan Islands on something big. This joker
doesn't know what. Or when they'll be back. A' course, these
here cats got lip-ice on their assholes.'

"I said, 'The joker has sleepless eyes. Ask him to describe the retainer.'

"He did; and they went at that for longer than I anticipated. Evidently the retainer fascinated our peddler. He claimed he wore a cap pulled to his kohled lashes and a black silk scarf that covered the rest of his features. The Thai weed-peddler could still tell this fellow was unusually fine looking; and as he wanted to take a complete gander, found an excuse to rise suddenly, 'accidently' hook the scarf, and pull it away. He rhapsodized on the 'retainer's' beguiling attributes; but what surprised him were the deep cuts on the 'retainer's' neck, a number of them and just beginning to heal.

"Once outside, I remarked: 'Martin Pitt may have gone to the Similans. His retainer didn't.'

"'Yeah,' Philip snorted. '–Arrogant and shitty of me. *He* could be anywhere.'

"I said, 'Phil, I can't.'

"He dealt with this for a moment, adjusting his crumpled fedora. He touched my Band-Aids. 'Feel nude without these? Excuse my verdict, Cory: you're not in shape to be at Hollow Mountain tomorrow morning. Come to my condo, will ya? I'll fix supper.'

"Philip Bailey's condo was the standard claustrophobic four-room with low ceilings in a new Cleopatra's Needle jarring the skyline. It had clapboard walls and no character. Nothing about it said Bangkok: it could have been in Cincinnati. He cooked a simple stir-fry and served it in his dining alcove before finding words. 'Cory, I know a poke overgrazing his land.'

"'Why? Do I give the impression of pushing it?'

"'No. Being pushed *to* it.'

"I said, 'That so? I may've roped cows. I don't herd them.'

"'Check, babe. You do something that falls in closer with me. I'm a boxing broadcaster—was for years in the States. I don't know much about what goes on in places where I'm not: but if I'm in a stadium, or on a street, I see every detail and I see it fast.'

"'Do I look as if I belong in a stadium?'

"'Not now. Still, you've been in them, plenty of them. My job

273

is to watch men. Each line of work has its carriage: and men have the carriage of their line of work. I wasn't in your stadia. I *was* on a raft with you, and I *was* on the riverbank where we camped. I've been in dozens of gin mills here, sometimes saucing with you: and sometimes doing an autopsy on you, alone and accompanied, when you were too plastered to see I was there. I've also been out a lot with Marty Pitt. Especially at the Mah Seekai: kick-boxers and their managers make deals there, arrange dives, and can be interviewed. So don't kid yourself: I'm familiar with this so-called retainer and what he is, and means, to Marty. And you.'

"I thumbed the table: 'In place of wine, you serve vinegar at home?'

"'We've got water tonight, period. Cory, you're carrying a live bomb under your arm. Do you think it's a good idea to live with a person like him?'

"'I've never had a choice.'

"'I've never understood what suckers mean when they say something like that.' Philip lifted his surgical mask to eat. His chin had a cleft as deep and shadowed as Richard Conte's. He said, 'Not to crowd your daydream: but did you know that Chain was involved with Jim Thompson's disappearance?'

"And Marty was with him when it happened. Don't swap with me, Phil.'

"Bailey, taken off guard, dropped his fork. He was a southpaw. 'And you still want—Cory, this has to do with the CIA…'

"'How about you cut the evangelical act and just tell me what you know.'

"'I know it was Chain who set up a meeting for Thompson in the Cameron Highlands on the afternoon he disap—'

"'With whom?'

"'That I don't know. No one knows.'

"I said, 'Then why don't you juggle with the CIA's great interest in this—in Jim Thompson's disappearance—or should I say, great lack of interest in it?'

"'*Cory*, there's also his older sister's death by bludgeoning to tally here—in Pennsylvania four months later—*and* her son's "suicide" shortly after that!'

"'Yes, indeed: and the CIA's equally nodding interest in the violent deaths of Mrs. Katherine Thompson Wood and her son.'

"'Does this mean that you have some idea of who Thompson was supposed to meet? Or did?'

"'Some idea.'

"'What does "some" mean?'

"'It means that Chain or Martin Pitt will have to tell us, doesn't it? Your scanty inside dope must've led you there. Your taking that info's road-signs, Phil, no further since Easter Sunday 1967 gives your caution, moral balance, and quick eyes a pair of clay feet. Or so it seems to me.'

"Philip scratched his nose and clutched a napkin, his vulgar wit muffled in half-chewed suet. 'But, Cory, we—you and I—must think about number one first: our precarious futures here, *our self-preservation...*'

"'Exactly, Philip. Exactly that.'

"IT COST ME A WEEK to strengthen enough to go out to the islands, and I'd no assurance that Martin Pitt would still be 'on something big.' I checked daily at the Mah Seekai, and no one had seen him in town or heard of his return.

"The Similan Islands are Thai; they sit in the Andaman Sea, midway between Peninsula Myanmar and Malaysia. Tatters in the mist reveal the limestone crags and bristlecone pines of their picture-book inverted mountains, which surface from the waves like a brigade of vaulting leviathans. These are the isle peaks in epic, the furniture of dreams. Ocean billows swell sufficiently only twice a day for canoes to ride them into the creek within a particular hollow mountain there. On the rotunda ceiling of its hollow the celebrated blind swiftlets build their nests. Sea Gypsies from nearby outcrops, risking their very lives, scale hemp rope suspended from hundreds of feet to harvest their saliva-flavored nests: destined for that famous soup in China's most exclusive restaurants. These birds are thus robbed of their eggs and chicks. A face-accumulating ingestion, the wealthy Han prize straws stained with the chicks' blood. I watched those grappling, iron-fisted harvesters vanish into the coal-black heights… Asians have looked at the world in so many unimportant ways; yet the unicolor swiftlet is blind, since *any* vision whatsoever serves no purpose in the damp reaches of that unlit realm.

"Illuminated by torches planted for the climbers, one lithe Gypsy in rolled denims and a checkered wool cap with a short bill was being over-watchful—of me. When I turned toward him, he softened a gasp and stepped back mumbling into a group of his fellows. He gutted the torches, and all of them melted away. I'd experienced this rapid melting away previously: they could only have recognized me from the calm pool and haunting cascade where Chain had bathed on that island west of Tarutao.

"The boatman who'd taken me to the site was waiting for me by the edge of the creek. I let him wait, choosing to follow the fleeing Gypsies, and stumbled in the direction I thought they had gone. For a while there was nothing at all to see; then, at a measurable distance, a single torch was re-ignited. When its flames caught, they reflected the group of Gypsies. In its midst was a huge white man wearing a pith helmet who was skewering a hole with and for the incendiary; and instructing a climber anchoring a dangling twine of hemp. Using heavy rocks, the latter secured the hemp-end to the ground beside the torch. The Euro peered into my proximity, pointed to the rocks, and though he couldn't be sure of exactly where I was, miraculously tipped his helmet directly at me. I wasn't a hundred percent on this, because I sensed by its draft a correlative shuffling behind me. Immediately after, each man assumed his place in a set of bobbing canoes and waited briefly for the back flush; then took it to paddle quickly out and along toward the cathedral-shaped entrance to the creek.

"I approached the 'message' they'd prepared by the light of the torch they had left for me. They'd guaranteed I'd lift the rocks and dislodge the hemp rope. I did, and it sprang up in a sizzle, while its weighted, opposite end plunged to the earth. It was ghastly weighted—with a hanged man. The corpse wore a slate blue shirt-jacket, cuffed trousers, and two-toned spats. It was Pitt's competitor who impersonated James Cagney. His neck was dwindled to that of a chicken, but his mouth stubbornly retained its grit-tooth grin. A cobweb of hair rose above blank, disbelieving eyes. A scrawled note was pinned to his jacket. I knelt and read it. It said: 'I ain't so tough, ma.'

"I angrily cut twenty feet off the twine with my switchblade, coiled it, and dropped it in my knapsack. –Gallows humor—an appropriate put-down in Pitt's abattoir: and just the jab to prep me. I seized the torch and swirled it to signal my boatman farther up the spumed creek's bank.

"I hit town after nightfall and shot a taxi to the Soi of Lost Souls. He'd be there now. And so he was, sitting cross-legged at the Mah Seekai's outside table: sipping tea, chomping his cigarillo, and encircling notices in the *Financial Times*. Distractingly, the wire of his specs was so twisted at the bridge that the left lens was not on par with the right one. Even seated, Pitt's head nearly touched the spirit's shingle. Waving a cramped claw to fake surprise, he called out:

"'The mixed-blood—with eyes of aquamarine! Join me?'

"'I'd be thrilled,' I said, 'to sully the table of a *full* blood.'

"A tight smile. 'I no sooner see you than I recall our chinwag on the River Kwai. The tell-tales'\ trip with Pavena and Kineetha, remember?'

"I nodded, 'And the presently bananas Volker Altmuller... and dead George Bryning. So, what has happened to those hilltribe boys?'

"'Oh, they're still around. I bull them both now,' he answered steadily. Then, as steadily, 'Find caves in mountains irresistible, what?'

"'Painted palisades, too.' I thought I could hear my knees knocking.

"'Ah! –The angry, castellated cliff of Pha Taem—and the busy knucklebone boulders beneath it. Are you wondering why the film fanatics tried to pop you?'

"'No. They were disappointed, but since they believe I'm your consigliere, figured why not? And those versatile sharks would have succeeded—if you and your boys weren't so deft at thinning out gents who step on your toes.'

"'Kambu-ja is a rider to that. ...Funny to think of you as my consigliere.'

"'I wish I could laugh.'

"'You still might,' he responded, holding me hard. Then he gazed off: to win him the time to dwell on a very misjudged tactic. How truly ursine he was up close, appareled in all that hair. He squirmed, and said: '*Caves* have a certain "revisit-the-womb" appeal. They're a descent into the nether lands: with the goal— once you're comfortable there—of ascending from them forever after. Tickle you? Confronting caves isn't always easy. And they are *not* ultimatums.'

"'Fascinating,' I yawned, trying to hide a tardy, airtight intent.

"'Good. I know of a lulu in Sara'buri. A must for incorrigibles. I'm driving over tomorrow. Care to come? Or is my Havana's eidetic stench a deterrent?'

"'No. But what's *your* reason for going?'

"'Batshit.' I recoiled. Would he call Chain 'batshit'? I locked my hands and locked with his seagull pupils. He blew a smoke ring of 'eidetic stench': it wobbled toward me and settled around my clasped hands. 'A doozy!' he self-congratulated.

"'Enough!' Pitt finalized. 'As I said before, we *are* both men. Disunited by a blackarse. And this round will be mano a mano. Be here at 8:00 a.m.: with your knapsack, head-torch, lunch in a plastic bag, goggles, and Wellingtons.'

"On the road up in his Benz I ciphered my intent: asking, 'Think Mah Seekai will flex her muscle, mob-house-confined in the Soi of Lost Souls?'

"'I don't fritter work days with Thai mythology—or Thai itself.'

"'Haven't cared to acquire the language?'

"'What for? Reckon they've got something interesting to say?'

"I decided to be direct: 'What could the late George Bryning have done—or even known, other than what Volker told him?'

"'That was enough, Cory.'

"'I won't feel guilty about this. Volker chose to confide in me.'

"'Then,' Martin rapped with acceptable bonhomie, '*he* is guilty.'

"I chipped at his claim: 'So you're here for business? Batshit, was it?'

"'That's *one* revenue. Bat guano is used for fertilizer. Its margin's ripping!'

"The province of Sara'buri is a few hours drive northeast of Bangkok. It is largely level green plains; humid rice fields; and the last range in the Himalayas. Pitt took a steep incline slowly, cut the ignition, and pulled his emergency brake at a small mountain monastery. He said, 'There are three tham, or caves, here. That big goofy Buddha guards the entrance to this one, the best known: because its first hall has an ancient relief. The monastery you see houses the relief's worshippers. Keen for a squiz?'

"The carving isn't sedate; nor grounded, as Buddhist sculpture invariably is. Pitt said: 'Gaffers here insist it depicts the Gautama preaching to Siva and Vishnu. Bunkum! That flying figure is too melodramatic to be Buddha. It's Brahma: which dates this art to the Hindu period, third or fourth century.'

"'Have an eye for art history?'

"'R*ather!* Nets me a mint… –Your ordeal is in the third cave, the deepest and longest. To that we must hike through: and back. Sorry, there's no alternative. No way off the mountain, other end.'

"We drove a stretch downhill, parked the Mercedes, adjusted our forehead flashlights, and slipped into the low-roof escarpment that constitutes the mouth of Tham Damonen. We had to crouch and at points crawl to clear that space. When the slope enabled us to stand, Martin put on a rain-poncho, draping him from head to knee. This poncho seemed too warm, even for the relative cool I could feel at the site of the initial stalactites: it was to disguise him. Pitt encouraged, 'The rest's upright: so we can make some headway here.' Then he moved at a speed, given his gut-overhang, that proved how at home he was in the twisting passages. For me, footing on slippery stones in the narrows between alluvia and over slabs and cavities while wading in waist-high stagnant ponds wasn't lenient—nor was sidestepping colossal spiders, ten-inch silverfish, and, of course, bats and bat excretion. Pitt had the height on me; I, though not in top shape, had a few years. Would this call for work below the belt, Pitt's groin? –My nostrils miasmal with his necrosis, I'd told the would-be rent wife, scrawny Jiap, to 'Stretch that gash, stretch it wider, bitch! Use your hands. Don't make me hit you!'

"In no time at all Pitt disappeared, and I was abandoned to the company of the earliest of our species, in whose dwelling or tomb we were intruding—*and* my concern that a sudden and unseasonable storm could cause a flash flood. The result? Ignominiously drowning in this unlikely—or *quite likely*—place.

"The strap securing my bulb was too tight. When I removed it to shift the clip, I became aware of a dim halo barely discernable under a shelf at some point behind me. An instant later, it was out. I continued on, pretending not to have noticed anything, until I touched a suitable protrusion and squeezed into its cleft. I doused my beam of light, waited several seconds, and then searched back along the trail. A held-breath on, I'd a quick glimpse of a lean, barefoot monk palming a candle, treading carefully with the use of a staff, and eagerly peering ahead. Then, apparently puzzled, or cognizant of the turnabout, he himself ducked behind a buttress and the candlelight was gone.

"A monk. Not Olie. This fellow's too tall, broad, and dark.

"After what I clocked at an hour and seventeen minutes, I caught up with Martin, edgily reclining on an unexpected, and relatively substantial, sandy beach. I flopped down next to him and tried, 'Someone is following us.'

"'A Stone Age man with a truncheon?' he asked, not in the least flippant.

"'A monk with a candle. What do you mean, Stone Age?'

"Martin sniggered. He fingered the bridge of his specs, inwardly dueling. He said, 'My slave Kambu-ja is the wild card here. Without him, things might have gone uneasily on indefinitely. Know him intimately, don't you?'

"I asked, 'Is this monk also a wild card?'

"'No, he comes along with the package.' Then, pretending to insouciantly speculate: 'That monk probably saw us enter and has nothing better to do than tag along and satisfy his curiosity. Pay it no mind. See these ashes? The guano shovelers camp here.' He began to scrawl stick-symbols in the clammy flat sand with a sharp, medium-size pick. He yanked his water canteen from his backpack, winked, 'Bottoms-up!', dallied over three thoughtful swallows, and offered it to me. 'Cory: even when he lived with bloody Albert, he hooked in the Parisian saunas.'

"'Whom are we discussing now?' I felt myself getting warm.

"Martin filled his chest and blew out impatiently. I wondered if his stick-art was directions for accomplices, but making a visual sweep of the wide beach and similar figures etched about this inner sanctum, decided that was beneath him. It was nerves. Still, I seized his pick and scrambled the scratches; then blurted, 'It's Maoist money that's behind the dams in the north, isn't it?'

"He gushed, 'Of course it is! Somboon was born in 1946, during Bangkok's Chinese-Siamese riots. He was *born* into them. There was street fighting in large communities that had no light. Black markets and smuggling. Cholera and plague were rampant. Under Phibun, Thailand had never declared war on China. Rubbing the local Chinese the wrong way, Phibun recognized the puppet government set up by the Japs. And Jap Beijing took over the hill-tribe states. His home: Somboon's real home. I put it to you that his hatred for Thailand is ancestral. It's implacable. You'll never change that.'

"'You mean military-controlled Thailand. Pridi changed that—or tried to.'

"'Briefly. After a year as prime minister, a coup led by Phibun deposed him.'

"I said, staring Martin down, 'But Pridi never gave up, did he?'

"Martin examined me closely. 'Not been kipping, I daresay.'

281

"Jumping the gun, I asked, 'Where does Jim Thompson fit into this?'

"He pulled a large white handkerchief from his poncho pocket and wiped his wiry chest. He poked a half-yard millipede curled by his muddy Wellington. '...We needn't be afraid of these. It's their smaller cousins, the centipedes, that have the poisonous fore-fangs. –*As I know* Volker Altmuller told you, I met Thompson when I sold him the five Buddha heads, sawed-off from statues in two caves not far from here. Jim, of course, didn't realize they were pilfered. That sale became what he called a trauma for him, second only to Phibun's slaughter of his then closest friends—a trauma that turned his more-than-liberal views into radical ambitions. I didn't think he'd inform on me, he wasn't the sort who did things like that; but I needed to be sure.'

"'And believed if you said you'd help Jim help Pridi stage another coup—as late as 1967—he'd stay shut-mouthed. A coup that could be made possible only with the backing of Beijing.'

"'Smart, as well as in good nick,' Martin noted, with professional admiration. 'Anything else you've sifted by your lonesome?'

"'Yes: Beijing's terms for assisting Pridi Banomyong caused complications. I've no way of guessing what those were.'

"'Oh, that Mandarin become Thailand's official second language. And Chinese seats in the new Thai legislative. Lots of them.'

"'Enough to eventually vote in China's take-over?'

"'In time, I suppose... Well, its colonization... They're already in Burma and the rest of Southeast Asia. Japan may have failed: China won't. Businessmen like me—'

"'...Cannot fight the inevitable,' I concluded for him. 'And Chain's involvement in all of this? Besides, like you, running a bursary and artillery parts to Pol Pot?'

"'I have to smile at how often I heard the nig say, "I middle-class," or "I falang." It makes even me feel sorry. Pridi was in exile in Beijing then. Chain, or Somboon as I call him, was used to contact Pridi Banomyong.'

"I said, 'And arrange his meeting with Jim Thompson in

Cameron Highlands. Jim, believing Pridi could be instrumental in ending the Vietnam War, planned to contribute impressive funding—and, more importantly, his incredibly numerous influential connections. But the CIA, with funds to spare of their own, got wind of this. On Easter Sunday, when Chain informed Jim that Pridi's aides were waiting to pick him up, it wasn't those aides, but agents of the C—'

"'And you, Guv, want to know who was funded to inform *them*.'

"'No problem guessing that, Martin. Pol Pot has the full backing of the CIA. I'd like to know more of the Cagney noose you have around Chain.'

"'Well, couldn't I always go to the CIA and claim Chain is at the stress point of fessing up publicly to Thompson's fatal turnover to them?'

"'Would you do that to Chain?' I asked.

"'Would you force me to?'

"I thought he'd extraneously add that the ball was in my court. He'd no need to harp on that. 'Wasting you wouldn't win Chain,' he said sadly: 'best way to lose him permanently. So if Guv's got his breath, let's not loiter.'

"We resumed our trek. I kept Pitt in constant view. It was his great passion for Chain that had asked me along. He wanted, or hoped—like Philip Bailey—that he could put me straight. But he'd meant 'wasting' me in a way that Chain knew it was he who'd done the wasting. I safeguarded his pick in my fatigues.

"Not fearful like Martin, I too was preoccupied with the 'monk' in our wake. I straggled at all obtrusions, assuming my hermit would identify himself... Yet my familiar dignitary remained familiarly diligent: shaded the candle to obscure his face and took care to mostly hide his dark form.

"There were innumerable openings in surrounding formations through which one could squirm into lesser passageways. These we never ventured into; and two hours on, Martin finally announced we'd reached our objective. It was the end of the major trail, and what a strange near-hallucination the climax of this trail. All at once the constricting walls relented: and giving way to a breach of forty feet, disclosed up there a startling sunbath, furnished and fractured by a jagged, oval exit. Nearly as high, a narrow and lengthy wood-slat ramp had been constructed. It gradationally sloped to a rickety stair. We, below, were ensconced by burlap sacks of guano, heaped on top of each other in piles of thirty-to-fifty. A handful of men were visible in the sky-burst; farther down along the ramp a crowd of perhaps small animals appeared to be huddled under an enormous tarpaulin or blanket: I could see it shuddering slightly but could not discern more than that. Martin advised, 'There's another, lower exit—behind, you see, those brown stalagmites. Use it, and wait for me on the mountainside. Eat the lunch you brought. Here, take mine too, and make certain both plastic bags keep secure— you'll have to do some swimming near the egress. I'm about to gyp the salesman. If he sees you, you'll scare him off.'

"'Scare him off?' I asked. 'Is this negotiation illegal?'

"'Illegal?' Pitt snickered. 'Harvesting batshit erodes the sedimentary strata here. Our planet's unrecoverable record. Wise up, Cory.'

"I started the path he indicated: then shut my light, retraced my steps, and lay flat on my stomach—in a perfect if reeking position to watch Pitt climb the ladder and wobble across the rocking ramp. He conferred with the four or five men near the exit. Each stripped to the waist, I fancied that they were displaying for him the dependable abs of seasoned truck-loaders. More seriously, I gleaned he speaks pidgin Thai to be speaking at all, and that Tham Damonen must have a rear road: both of which Martin had denied. Presently the group walked back to where the blanket was and partially lifted it. They inspected whatever was under that covering for a while; then turned and teetered toward the sunlight, where they became single-stroke silhouettes and continued to talk for about ten minutes. I was afraid to lie in the crud for longer than that, given as Martin, still concealed in the poncho, might suddenly head for the stair, and I first had to make my way out through the underground lake.

"The water was too visceral and complicated to be repulsive. It was thick and lukewarm, as our incubatory soup is said to have been; penetrating my clothes, it softly enwrapped and explored my testicles with the fingers-aswirl of the primordial dead. I swam behind the stentorian waterfall, quite close to the egress, and eventually lifted myself up into blinding daylight. I took two steps out onto the tufted patch right there—and the earth under me fell away! I plunged some fifteen feet before hitting the ground in a tight shaft. Luckily, I'd been cushioned by the grass and dirt that had fallen with me. Momentarily blank, or dazed, but my adrenaline near peak, I set about assessing the damages. Bleeding, to be sure, from countless cuts, with aches at elbows, my left scapula and knee—and this was the last time I could wear what remained of my fatigues—yet nothing actually broken, other than my ego. Of all things: a pitfall, a literal pitfall!

"–Just how pat, how green could I be? How unprepared for what that brute would think to do? Wasn't this cave a final round: not an exhibition match? Well, Martin *did* forecast a descent: before an uphill gradient. I would make that true. I would never give him Chain.

"I examined the shaft. Several men could fit in it: no doubt the size and shape of forest rangers, the province police, or whoever arrests guano-traders. The slate sky, fringed by weeds, was six-foot across. There were scattered divots affording no leverage and a half-dozen limestone ledges left projecting as high as my hip: any above them had been removed.

"Then he appeared, a vague outline, a shadowy specter in the circle of the sky: the monk. A full minute passed, neither of us budging. Finally he pointed a finger down at me, I thought to the top of my head: so I dutifully touched it. He nodded negatively and continued to gesture. He was indicating my knapsack. I removed the soaked bag and opened it. –The hemp rope—of course!—still there. I tapped it and looked up. He smiled broadly. I'd no need to wonder how he knew I had it. I remembered that the hermit had dogged Martin in Hollow Mountain as well and saw me take it. I noosed it: but the shaft was too narrow to permit using that rope as a lariat from the floor. So I climbed to the highest ledge and drove Martin's pick into the limestone at a level with my belt, and, second, the switchblade a half-yard above it. I clawed the divots to raise my right foot onto the pick's handle and my left very lightly onto the switchblade's. Holding fast to a chip in the rock with my racked left arm, I danced the rope beneath me long as I could and then swung the noose up at the mouth of the pit. Three tries failed, their arc wasn't sufficient. I closed my eyes, waited to inhale deeply, and, waltzing it till I felt I'd bleed my nails in the crevice, let fling again. This time he caught it. I heard him whoop: an atonal symphony, quite the most unlikely human sound. I expected him to drop the noose on some sturdy scar or tree up there, but he didn't, he held onto it and shook his hands to indicate that I start my climb. Not the easiest way for him to be doing this, I thought, while I wound my end about my waist. Just in time: the handles of the pick and the blade both broke off and disappeared, propelling me into a dizzying spin. When the spin came to rest, I discovered the blistering grasp-over-painful-grasp, despite years of training exactly so to strengthen my wrists, no easy matter. It took, with constant slipping, a good five minutes for me to mount the shaft; when he got under my arms to hoist me up the last few feet, he still would not let go the rope.

"That is how I had my long-awaited, inclusive look at him: while he kept tight the rope between us. –Tamarind-tall, with a head of profuse hair, graying in wiry knots. Every rib stood forth; his joints were sharp, their skin cracked. His lips were also cracked, his nose flat, his ears delicate sprouts. His eyes, real Sherwood-blue, were large as stones. His overall coloring was a weave of many shades, from high yellow to polished purple; in his drawn, animated visage were the features, shapes, and structure of every race on earth.

"He pointed to his heart and said, simply, 'Jarawa.'

"So there you have it, my hermit, the evidently immune Stone Age man, who'd sailed from South or Middle Andaman and wandered throughout Thailand. His tribe consists of three hundred and fifty people, practitioners of spiritual science and paranormal technologies. They heard their islands wobbling four days previous to last year's tsunami, the tsunami of 'Biblical proportions'; saw their beasts leave the coastlines and move up-ground; and went to safety with them. Customarily, they are hostile to outsiders: I was not to learn whether he'd actually ordained in Thai Theravada—since, if converted, he'd be Andaman Hindu—or ever know if his entrusting of and remitting to me involved a harm that Martin Pitt had personally done him or only detectably spearheaded. Yet the intention in his manhunt would, now that I'd infected and isolated Pitt, become transparent.

"The Jarawa coiled the hemp rope and returned it, in polite exchange for my knapsack. Then, using his stave to poke under the foliage, he strode some thirty paces along the mountain. There he beckoned to me, and when I reached him, pointed to a huge centipede he had nudged from its nest. He dipped into my sack, removed the look-alike lunches, and, seeming to be certain which one was mine, gave it to me. I arranged Martin Pitt's bag on the grass, opened it, borrowed the Jarawa's staff, lifted the centipede on it, and dropped it inside. I urged Martin's sandwich over the centipede with the tip of the stave, returned it to the Jarawa, and presently stood away while he stared at me. He held that transfixing stare until it burrowed into my head; then shifted his eyes to Martin Pitt's bag. When I nodded, he pulled my right earlobe, which I took to mean an oath, half bowed, and quickly walked off. My hunter, street person, construction worker, and monk—*the* conduit accommodating my divisions—slipped between stands of bamboo, not budging a leaf, and vanished.

"Moments later, Martin emerged from the lower exit and eagerly approached the exposed trap. He peered into it—and stiffened, as if from sunstroke. Then, amazingly, recovered; and scanning the brush, located me. I was eating my tuna fish sandwich when he drew near. I asked him if his was 'meat.' He laughed elegiacally; sighed, suggesting a private affirmation; doffed his poncho; and sat on a moss-rock. He gazed over the valley, lush with farms, washing lines, and forest: his rustic and completed, final height in the Far East. Except for his mouth tic, he was outwardly motionless for the longest while. His inflamed tongue circled and dripped like a fatted escargot. Seated, he boasted an area mass a third greater than mine; yet I, as a 'definitive' gift, had a pin to deflate it.

"We heard motors rev, a vehicle skid and experience difficulty driving away. He turned at the sound, curbed his tic, and liberally studied me. I was voluble with blood—and visibly aroused. He took this in, shivering at its deviance.

"He testified: 'The Maitri gang couldn't expect me to have the strength to be cramping the gimp, as well—or Olie: barking mad, that clown is. And with Nok snuffed now… What *is* strength? Thick skin? Living alone? Isn't in my ambit. Not many things can undo a flourishing empire. But love is one of them.'

"'That's real white,' I noted placidly. 'I grove on your approbation.'

"'Buggerall! I meant Chain's, not yours,' he corrected, frostily.

"'No sweat: let me thank you for *him*.' I saw the shattered remnants of his dentures fencing his escargot: and they reminded me to pick a dilled pickle out of my lunch bag and loudly munch on it. 'Aren't you hungry?' I asked.

"'So I am, so I am!' he recuperated, throwing back his arm whilst keeping me under scrutiny. He rustled and fiddled in his waiting bag. I thought of Chain's insect-eating forebears. I whispered, 'Strip entirely, not just your poncho… Use your hands to stretch open *that* pit—your hands, I say! Don't make me hit you!' His specs popped off, his pink eyes enlarged, and he screamed in pain. The spasm that followed was violent. Then, re-commanding his Goliath-like bulk, he directed his spry other arm to extract the stricken one.

"'Here, here, cherry-buster,' I reprimanded, 'we can't have you losing your renowned peepers in a godforsaken wilderness. Or soiling your lovely fur. Please, let me, until you coordinate.' I retrieved his glasses, put them in my breast pocket, and slowly buttoned it.

"'Cory!' he cried, 'I'm—'

"'It's the sun: and our caving, man: your weight. Let's get you to a hospital, Mr. *Phii*, I'm quite familiar with three of the best.'

"'Stop, stop, you don't understa—'

"'I *do*. You're afraid I'll forget your lunch. Small chance—*that lunch!* Grab... grip my butt—my "small bum me"—with your good arm. O.K., that's it. Now, ready? Bit of a climb, returning to the egress: do brace yourself.'

"'Stop, Cory, listen, there's a closer way down. Men up there—trucks! If it's the snot-noses—'

"'What snot-noses? You're delirious, Martin. You told me yourself there's no rear road to carry them off. We mustn't dally. Could be a stroke, come on like Randy's. Or something you ate: from the dish you fed to Volker Altmuller.'

"He struggled like the pro he was, but his critical-fight was gone. I lugged, squired, and dragged him. When we reached the cave, I wormed-out the rope and said, 'Recognize this bit of twine? I'm recycling it. Have an issue with that?'

"I held him still, stepped behind him, and knotted the hemp's end between his shoulder blades. I casually draped the noose on his now very bad shoulder. A large bat darted over the subterranean lake in varied, swift coronets. Watching it, Martin turned sardonic: 'A homonym for bat is "good luck." In Mandarin. Chinese: like Chain, you bastard. My Sea Gypsies eat them.'

"I circled Martin, redressed him with stage-sympathy, pampered the noose, slipped it onto my right welly, and jumped the steep bank. 'Not exactly refreshing, this muck, so keep your mouth shut, now,' I cautioned—adding: 'Just a moment, I have to put on my goggles. *You* won't need any.' He looked terrified. I jingled the rope a little: and, in the water, felt my drip of pre-cum. Then I yanked it hard and he fell forward and sank beneath the surface. He rose all but immediately, gulping for air, and splashed about in a fury. That sting of the arthropod notwithstanding, there was plenty of life left in him. I let him flounder and cry as long as he would, since I knew that if any of the slavers were still on the ramp, the waterfall would more than cover his squeals for help; and I wanted him relatively relaxed for the haul across the lake. When he had exhausted himself and his useless grimacing at me, I leisurely started my swim to the far shore. The tightening knot and noose, as I'd worked them out on either end of the rope, insured that he would be towed behind me with his face down. I did wish he weren't so over-weight. The lone bat swooped inquisitively back and forth above us. In mid-lake, I could see the ramp; but by then Martin was making only a lullabied ripple. The bend on the shore that I had in mind was not within sight of the ramp. When I attained that bend and its coarse pebble-beach, which was scarcely lit by the higher exit, I rested for a few minutes and admired the body's impotent float. Then I trawled him in, undid the knot set in his spine, put that (U-turned) blood-caked hemp into my pack, and set Martin prone on the pebbles, in a submissive position that would look as if he'd fallen right there: succumbing to the in-sect poison, should anyone take the trouble of a postmortem. Knowing foolproof evidence of his demise would, justifiably, be warranted, I wanted him easily located and not at the bottom of the lake.

"His trousers had immodestly slipped to reveal that his stin-gy cheeks, like so many fat men, near flattened on his sacrum. Had Pitt sometimes worn trouserless chaps to display this gro-tesque fiasco to Chain and torment him with it? Still, I excruci-ated over my embolus finally to enter him, or to just ejaculate on his cleavage: as, reassuringly, barbarous warriors would have. It was probably the centipede bite on his wedding-ring finger that inhibited me. Resembling the blue-red fossils of antediluvian in-sects, it cloistered his finger—and rectum. That bite was Martin Pitt's apposite wedding band.

"I retraced our unlit path until I'd gone a safe distance, and there clicked on my headlight and switched gears for the two-some-hours' trip back.

"When I bellied through the low-roofed escarpment and stood once more in glaring sunlight, beside me, as I expected, was the Jarawa on his crook, tall and chivalrous. His people are normally small; it occurred to me that his stature may have been what singled him out for the surveillance that ended here. I lowered my head to my secret guide, and the Jarawa turned his downhill of us. A *songthaew* full of monks but for one seat-space was waiting on the road by the monastery. I calmly took my vin-dicated place, glanced discreetly at the Stone Age dignitary, and from then on stared in a full trance at my lap.

"The van headed, I realized intentionally, in a direction away from Bangkok; when we parked at the fourth sizable settlement on its route, I alighted and caught a bus back to Bangkok. I reached the Afro by late evening, went through my papers, and, finding his card, called Kob, the royal secretary; and asked him to meet me at the snooker bar shortly after opening day next, about 8:00 p.m. Then sat on the bed—and before I could stretch myself out was asleep.

"Kob was leaning on a cue stick, lost in a theoretical configuration of billiard balls, when I found him alone in the club at the appointed hour. He was so engrossed that he neither saw nor heard me enter. I tiptoed up to him, burdened with a shopping bag, and skipped Pitt's spectacles across the pool table. Automatically, without looking at me, his hand reached for and felt their bent rim. I'd lost no time wondering why Martin had not had it straightened. I would ask, but was fairly certain it was Chain, Kambu-ja, or the Jarawa man who'd at one point struck him and caused that damage. And that Martin had preserved this distinctive corkscrew twist as a salute to fate: a concession to, or reminder of, his someday having to answer to his triple liability.

"The fortune that Martin Pitt must have spent on bribes had previously ransomed him from persons like Kob. When Kob finished fondling Pitt's legacy, and I reclaimed it for further use, he slowly raised his eyes. They met mine squarely, and I said, being very careful with my tones, 'Tham Damonen.'

"Sensitive, but conservative as ever, he insularly smiled. Then his wonderful face betrayed both relief and satisfaction. I asked him if he'd care for an orange soda. We went to the bar, and I took a large cardboard box from the shopping bag and placed it on the counter. When the bartender left us to search for a soda out back, I told Kob to unwrap and open the colorfully packaged box. He did and extracted, with a war-cry, the notorious icon of his years-long search.

"He waited a bare second before *wai*ing the Buddha with

hands atop his head, and then me, the pyramid of his palms still there. Then he gracefully brought them to his waist in a reverential fold and remained staring at the Buddha. I'd never seen such gratitude. The burnished gold of the icon's sweep was darkly reddened in the bar bulbs. The Phra's lids seemed to flutter, to become aware of, and acknowledge, the trembling messenger and me. When he saw the bartender returning, Kob piously lifted the statue and returned it to the box.

"He said: '…Two days, perhaps… so we shall have time to… uh, pay homage in the cave. Then will you come to the palace to collect the reward?'

"Want to go to the movies?"

I was startled. "What did you say?" I asked Cory.

"I'd like to know if you'd care to go to the movies now."

"Hey! I'm still in the story. –What are you talking about?"

"You'll have stories aplenty in the theatre we're headed for. It's right down the street. Five minutes. Quick, get your things together. Better yet, leave them and fetch them later. You don't want to be guarding anything other than the family's future in *this* amusement spot."

We scrammed and shot along New Road; crossed the intersection at Silom and legged it past the first soi. Before I could get with the chaos on that side, Cory squirted, "*Voilà:* see the cashier sleeping there?"

We were facing a cul-de-sac. The cinema was blocked by an outdoor eatery with Formica tables. At the dead-end, a skip and a jump behind them, was a lean-to: the theatre's retired booth, "50 Baht" scrawled on its blackwashed window. Cory fixed 100 baht under the belt of a crone snoring on a stool in the alley, then lifted a curtain that figured as the joint's outside wall. He said, "Stand here till you get used to the dark." I was glad to do just that. Cory himself made it along the rake within and posed against the first pillar he found.

A fluorescent in the stinky toilet was the dump's only light. Vintage soft-core marred the screen. When my eyes adjusted I saw that no one was watching anyhow. The house was about twenty percent filled, and every other seat was slashed, I supposed to remove its wires and stuffing. That did not bother the customers either: you could say they were busy providing their own entertainment.

A short geek wearing a newsboy's cap approached Cory and gawked at him. After what I took to be Cory's approximation of the standoff period—about sixty seconds—he moved to the center of a back row and picked the last of three adjacent seats that still had stuffing. His admirer seemed to think five seconds did for the succeeding delay, then squeezed through and sat a seat away from him. Half a minute on, he was sitting alongside Cory: massaging both their bulges.

I waddled ten rows down the rake and arbitrarily chose a seat. Not feeling fuzzy, I watched the flick. A mixed couple in the altogether was embracing behind a fish bowl: so you saw some tropical fish. The audience was sprinkled with couples—these not mixed, and into mutual hand-jobs. They were also playing musical chairs. A lot. A head might dive and bob a bit. Otherwise it was quiet, the spark of a cig or joint here and there.

Of all unflattering possibilities, a woman, I'd guess to be in her midthirties, came and plonked next to me. She was a finicky shopper: she opened my fly and fingered for size. I stopped breathing. I stared at the movie. I couldn't tell if I was getting hard or not. She knocked her breasts against my thigh. I think my heart also stopped. Then I heard a raspberry. –Cory's.

The woman went down and proved a maven. She had a well-developed neck and was determined and talented. Me, a total wreck. I needed fifteen minutes to discharge. She swallowed her drillings, wiped her lips with a lace handkerchief, thoughtfully buttoned my fly, circumspectly rose, and left the theatre.

Cory had waited in the cul-de-sac. "A Queer Theorist, eh?" he snorted. "So who are *you*, really?"

THE SIXTH DAY

CORY WAS FASHIONABLY OUTFITTED in a military-style, black Thai shirt and trim gray slacks when he greeted me for our last recording at nine the following night. I mentioned at once that I would not publish our work in standard interview form. I would like to narrate it, keeping some of my impressions and comments.

He said, "I don't like that idea. Since I did the lion's share of speaking, as I stated at the beginning I wanted to, that will reduce you to a frame."

"What's wrong with that?" I asked.

"If you become a parochial frame—which ferments inconclusiveness—*is* the printing's periphery, how it becomes a 'complete and whole thing,' beyond whom there is no appeal—you will jeopardize the reader."

I said, "I heard that cliché before: nobody's as parochial as a New Yorker."

Cory laughed. "Hopeless! We'll talk about this later, O.K.?"

"O.K. And so now, the coda."

He started with: "The reward—it amounted to something like six thousand dollars. Soon as I claimed it, I phoned Philip Bailey and asked him if he'd be in for the next hour or two. Sounding depressed, he said he would.

"He was out of sorts because his cirrhosis was acting up and the AM station was canceling his kick-box blow-for-blow in English. The sponsors had complained of limited listenership. He also groused, 'I had to birch Blackblatt and do his taste-for-waste again yesterday. Getting to hate that. Money's good, though.'

"I shared his negativity over a beer, and then introduced: 'You have a bookcase of beaverzines, don't you? Could you let me abscond with three or four quality ones in return for a night on the town and the Twilight's most expensive Go-Go boy? Phil, look alive!' Not surprisingly, he did.

"'Now, how's that for a deal!' he enthused.

"I selected the raunchiest—full-page activity shots of Euro models blistering in pink—and headed for an antique shop I'd cased on Sukhumvit. In its window was a porcelain Manikhet, the magical Siamese flying stallion, two feet high. It was not rearing, though every meticulously suggested muscle in its legs indicated that it would. This gold-harnessed horse, like the Kinnara, embarks for heaven. The difference is, it transports kings and celebrated soldiers. I was en route to Chain's sharp-visioned mentor, Khun Apirak; and if he were to shoot-in short and tough, felt him worthy of tying that mount up in a clinch.

"Khun Apirak was delighted, if bewildered, by the zeens and the horse, and hesitated to accept them until I told him they were only fair in exchange for what I'd appreciate his doing. Namely: not simply to write to me in future at Chain's behest, but to add facts and a few observations of his own. The old man didn't know what I meant right then, but I'd the faith that he eventually would.

"Seconds before it closed, I got to a nearby travel agency on Brothel Row in Chinatown. Philip Bailey had scrambled to recommend it for the soonest possible discount flights. As a French or Japanese holiday season was on the horizon, all airlines were booked for months: there was only one seat they expected to come free on Cathay Pacific in eighteen days, if I paid in cash and that very minute.

"'Can do!' I informed the agent.

"Dissolving my university contract was not as expeditiously accomplished, and made more tricky by my need to get on with it stealthily. The reason is that Tom, Chain's client, pruned his stay, and Chain took to bedeviling the Afro. He'd lounge about in the afternoons, gamble in the evening, and retire there every night. When I questioned what lurked behind his exuberant mood, he grabbed a seat, knit his knees, and buoyantly exclaimed, 'Because now I *not gahlee!* Have you! –Have someone: a boy *not* same-same *gahlee!*'

"'That is wonderful,' I responded, feeling anything but, myself.

"The impasse at Mahidol was the chair: she couldn't believe that a lecturer would break a contract good for life. She sent me to the dean; when I served notice on him, pleading ill health, he, knuckling under to school-face, shouted, 'You are not sick! You are *home*sick. Is different!' I had to say, precious face aside, it's a matter of my less-precious life. For this, a native physician (scratch that quack Caucasian) was required: without a native confirming that I was knocking at death's door, I'd not get my work-stamp cancelled: hence no exit-permit. Here's where Rollo hit on an intern to write a moribund-certificate. As visual aids to his affidavit, he accepted earlier candids of me in a slingshot at the pool that make the POWs in *A Town Like Alice* appear robust. Our intern's superiors had to cosign his affidavit: and these were off five-days. I invited Rollo to spend that time north, in Sukhothai, Siam's first capital: a tourist destiny for its neatly cleared and restored ruins. I'd much to relate; and to give him a check.

"It rained every day there, and when we got to a strikingly narrow pyramid—a progressively more slender set of stairs up to a small, house-like structure—it started to pour. We took shelter in a woodshed near it; once settled in, I said, 'Rol, you can never justify not telling me that Chain's boss, Martin Pitt, ran the Children's Garden—a prison you patronize. You must remember that.' Then I disclosed the crimes of the gamblers' headache, this Martin Pitt, and the complexities of his obsession with Chain. I detailed the strangulations at Pha Taem and Hollow Mountain, the biker assigned to terminate me in Pattaya, and the demise of the allegiance-switcher Nok, Chain's rival for Pitt and later Maitri's favor.

"Rollo stared directly at the pyramid while I talked, and stifled all comment. So I went on to depict, very tensely, how I roped Martin, strung *him* as he'd strung Cagney, returned the icon to its rightful guardian, and copped the reward.

"Rollo Y-z was appalled, chomped on his gums, quietly crazed, and consulted the webs of his fingers. Then muttered, almost privately (or evasively), 'Is there *no* lawbreaker's bed he fails to share? But I won't negate my judgment of Chain. Cory, you lack any proof that he arranged for Maitri to snap Nok's neck. That biker worked for Pom's cutthroat gamblers. And Nok did die in a bike crash.'

"'And Nok and Olie did steal their statue, which Olie then foisted on me,' I confirmed. 'It is a trans- or inter-world duplicity linking murders to freedom.'

"He darkened. 'Whatever it is, it's putting trigger-happy Maitri in *my* future.'

"I stenciled his fix on the pyramid. I said: 'Rollo, trust me, I will take care of this… The rain's stopped. Shall we climb the stairs?'

"'Those steps are slippery now, and cracked. Be no point, anyway.'

"'How so?'

"'Nothing is in that chapel on top. Maybe a pint-size altar and a lotta bird droppings. And pinfeathers.'

"'Then what're these steps for?'

"'To go down, not up: for Buddha to climb down. After his Enlightenment, the Gautama went to Mount Meru to visit his late mother and tutor. Then he descended from Meru to preach to humanity. That's what these stairs represent. Ever really look at a Walking Buddha?'

"'Well, yes, of course: the one in Hua Hin.'

"'The Walking Buddha's a distinct and *only* Thai conception. It's actually Buddha walking down, not striding along. Would have been hard to sculpt him stepping down: they had no dignified way to support that kind of balance.'

"'But he does walk, too, doesn't he—walk through Thailand?'

"'Um. Comes down, and walks through Thailand.'

"That night I forced a check on Rollo—'toward paying your income taxes,' I insisted. –He used my windfall to dent *Pom's* debts.

"Chain did not discover I was breaking my contract at the time that I was. He sensed my equipoise—and Pitt's craved 'thick skin,' but he hadn't the edginess, or insecurity, to investigate their cause. He thought I was working. Still, eighteen days were sufficient for that veteran to reverse my progress, so fusillade his wiles and vulnerable my breaches. So whilst he adhered, I'd visit Volker Altmuller and tell him there were no more Englishmen. I went to see Kambu-ja, my Cambodian, the diehard enemy of Pol Pot, at his railside shack and tell him that too.

"He'd learned, or second-sighted, it before I arrived.

"We sat by his hovel and stared at his ramshackle, entirely baronial world. I told him about incurable Pom and Rol's problem with Maitri. His craggy face did not stir; nor did he fuss with his infirmity. Kambu-ja was steeling himself for what he knew I thought was necessary. He'd find a new boss, or be his own.

"I might as well have been walloped in the gut. Kambu-ja could not hold what he wanted. But neither could I.

"Sometimes I'd go to the Afro's roof. A rotting sundeck was its draw, and a rosy face argued to defuse the gasp in my U.S. friends' first snap of me. I found a guzzling, fit Australian there named Holly, whom I'd see returning from Chula U. He was into endangered hornbills, an ecology project underway by then for circa two years in its Faculty of Science. Holly's job took him to eight isolated forests. He had tricks on the team in each forest, similar to salesmen at every satellite city. Such afforded him a tranquil, if cynical, outlook and the mild interest that rolling stones develop in people and places. I invited him to our room.

"We divided a ten-pack. Chain lay on the bed, a spectral punkah swaying atop his assurance. I asked Holly to speak indistinctly and slur his vowels, so that Chain would not understand us. He had no quarrel with this, and could even focus me while discussing Chain: a deceit that homebodies would have to practice.

"I mumbled, 'He has no notion that I'm leaving. I'll inform him when he can no longer alter that.'

"Holly said, '*I* don't dither wogs with my itinerary.'

"'I wouldn't normally, but this man says he loves me.'

"'You believe him, mate?'

"'Yes.'

"Holly couldn't resist glancing quickly at Chain. He tongued the foam on his red mustache and considered the situation. This bird-watcher was now the only disinterested person aware of our bond: I fancied his appraisal. He accepted I must know what I'm deserting and, with that noninterference the frequently hurt find wise, formulated none. He weakly lowered his eyes. I said, 'I'd still be anxious to learn how he fares after I leave. You're in and out of town, Holly: you're likely to run into him. Will you write and tell me if you do?'

"'Gotcha.'

"'You'll remember what he looks like?'

"'Shit-oath! Bloke's got surefire looks! You'll give me your address.'

"'Thank you. –A favor I could turn for you?'

"'That's a curly one,' Holly hiccupped. 'Don't get your knickers in a knot, but ask a lifer here to cremate me when I die. And take my ashes to the Twilight. When boys peel, he's to rub half the ashes into their thickest wombats, wombats with area; and to rub the other half onto the longest jackhammer.'

"Chain did not appear for the next three nights. I thrashed, intentionally awake those nights, and dozed for only an hour on the succeeding afternoons. On the fourth night he came in quietly at 5:50 a.m. He sat on the bed, undid the top stud of his designer jeans, and began counting his money.

"I snapped on the light and said, 'Where you sleep, you dream about me?'

"'What?'

"'You say me, always dream somebody before something important happen. With that person. And with you, too.'

299

"He twisted toward me in his gripping singlet and examined my face. 'No… I not dream about you.' He was tentative. 'Why?'

"'Have present, think like.' I opened the drawer of the bed table, took out Martin Pitt's glasses, and put them in his hand. He studied them for a suspenseful moment, then held them by the bulb with great care, as one would a talisman. His scrutiny moved from the injured wire to me, back and forth several times.

"He said, sidewise, 'He not need this?'

"'Not any more. You break this—look: bend the rim?'

"'For what *I* bend? Think *Campuchea*, have one leg.' He swallowed with difficulty, shadowed his gaze, and dissolved. 'Do this for me?'

"'Yes. And for me.'

"I could hear the clock ticking. Twenty seconds, thirty, forty… Then, to deflate his incredulity: 'Martin dead?'

"'Very dead. You free now.'

"He dropped the specs on the floor and worried his hands. I let a minute pass before asking him again, 'You sure you not dream about me?'

"'I tell you. I sure. …For what you ask two time?'

"'Because I am going home. In six days.'

"He was silent. Beyond alertness, nothing registered in his features. He was waiting for an explanation.

"'I buy airplane ticket. *One* way. I go home. I go back life America.'

"He grew stiff. Then jerked, sprang from the bed, and—in reflex, and as though prearranged and not suddenly invented—threatened: 'If I want stop you, I stop you!'

"I imagine this referred to the incrimination he'd avoided for any number of operatives, gunrunners, and traitors—that he'd always have over them, and the deficit they could be called upon to repay. So rather than go *there*, I pointed to the undeniable, 'You not safe with me now. See before, I try kill you.'

"'Not care!'

"'I do.'

"'Life *me!*' he shrieked. He stood against the wall: seeming torn between the frantic pacing I'd come to expect and pouncing on the sheets. Instead he about-faced, confronting me with his back and that slashed eagle tattoo steadily reappearing in the initial ray of false dawn. Hiding there, in this closed position, he solemnly intoned, '…And what about me?'

"'You?'

"'What happen now to me?'

"'You, Chain? –Whatever happens to prostitutes will happen to you.'"

I gasped: "Oh, no—Cory!—you didn't!"

"But I did," Cory calmly affirmed.

"How *could* you, man!"

"I could. I could. And I did."

I shot a foot forward. I felt naïve, confused—and too young.

Then a tremor rippled Cory's jawline, and he said: "I instantly recoiled at my words… Scalded with regret, I stammered, 'Chain! I—'

"He keened, 'Not know before Martin do that to Thompson! I love(d) Pridi…'

"He turned from the wall, moved to the bed, and slipped into it on one knee. A redoubtable, huge tear broke on the lash of his right eye and rode heavily over his cheek, coming to ledge in the corner of his mouth. Tasting its salt, he snapped his head and managed, 'Not talk, Cory. Not talk more. Have only six day. So for them, together. You, me, always together now. Day, night. No talk. Sleep.'

"This meant, outside the menial tasks related to my splitting, there should be no other reference to it. In the Thai manner, it must go unnamed: each day be just that day, in no wise enhanced. For in the harmony of decades my leaving him would, anyhow, never occur. And it has not, as yet—has it?

"Until, I'll grant, perhaps here and now, in you and this room. But for those next six days, Chain would not suffer an inch of divorce. We ate, slept, visited Khun Apirak and all his friends as a single body. Chain behaved as if nothing were afoot: he laughed, sorted the laundry, brewed teas, and rustled up spaghetti no. 9, my favorite. Only at moments, when we'd be sitting in a restaurant, sharing a whole sweet and sour bass, *his* favorite, did his gaze sometimes drift, empty and unguarded. He'd catch himself, smile, shift the condiment carousel closer to me, and find some minor oddity to comment on.

"He took me home with him several times. An Asian's family is himself: anomie's breakwater, a smudged blueprint necessary to function, so he wanted his sister, aunt, and niece to incorporate me as well. Mere steps from the river then, I proposed he accompany me there. 'Why?' he frowned. Any 'site' within sight of where we live is a painting that died on the wall; and he objected to being reminded of that one's mutability, with its symbolic blockades of kudzu and embattled debris. This swan-Naga, whose energy sidewinders swiftly in Bangkok, braved all routes on occasion and funneled, for Chain, to the cities of the falang where he secretly felt he'd spent his past lives; and where he faithfully, desperately, would always believe his redemption in this one waited.

"I said, 'Because is famous. Have something *belong* to Me-nam Chao Phya.'

"We admired the classic Old Customs House (now the Harbor Fire Brigade) at the bottom of Soi 36; and walked the historic pier, staring into the scintillant and softly chanting wash. The bowman of a klong buggy paddled us through the swelling caramel, and midway across I opened my backpack, still monopolized by the hemp rope.

"'See,' Chain sighed, indicating the piles of trash slapping at the buggy, 'Chao Phya nothing. Dirty.'

"'Then it won't mind taking this either,' I rejoined, letting the blood-stained rope slip into the jetsam. I watched a bowl-bellied rice ark smash the brackish eddies and a ferry make its short, direct run to Thonburi.

"My bench press, barbells, and much-resorted-to punching bag had to be disposed of. Chain didn't want them, observing that once you abandoned regular use, the calves, forearms, pecs, and biceps you developed would droop: then shrivel. Which God forfend! Rollo Y-z's son *was* eager to inherit my equipment, and his rushing over to pick it up would become my first and last chance to see Pom: that, ultimately, to-prove-fatal cardplayer. However, Pom hauled all with such alacrity, I hardly got an impression of him; he was in and gone in fast-mo: so I can't put a face on Y-z's good intention, with which he paved his road to hell.

"Funny not to have a clearer image of him—and so much else about Rollo." Cory Simon was yoked to a point over my left shoulder. "Pom was tall, broad in the neck, and wore glasses. Black horn-rims. A square, big head: common enough here. Taciturn. Not especially handsome, but don't quote me on that."

I said, "What are you looking at?"

"*Him*. Not Rollo's son. I have to tell you the ironic boil-down without reproaching either Chain or myself. To repeat, Chain never left my side during my last six days in Thailand. Yet it took only a few of them in his constant presence for me to register my full intrusion."

"Intrusion?"

"His were tasks outside the law, and mine had been tarred with the same brush—altogether too thickly for me. The recurrent is not dismissed by an appeal to coincidence: I'd paid as many dues on that turf as one could and still expect to live to write books. Though Chain abbreviated, was strained and sullen for years, and risked vigor now, was jocose—even chatty about inconsequentials—his alien best had the defeat of the *presently* inconsequential. He was mine alone for six days—and those six days excluded the man that was Chain."

Cory crushed his stub, lit two more smokes, and tilted mine on the ashtray.

I stalled: "After you feed pet boa constrictors, you have to let them be for a while. Because they like to think about it."

"Thinking constrictors!" His stare was so critical that I imagined some one or thing was really there. I said, "Over my shoulder—do you actually see him?"

"I do! –Not as the obtained, or ultimately unobtainable; or what we know and wouldn't want to; but as *when* we can want, and cannot want to know. Yet where's the sense in talking further? You've fallen a bit in love with him. That's why you're balking at how, in any outcome, I could have left him."

I said, "Chain is the lost primitive, your imprecise Uncas. When he takes on precision… And now may I hear the end of your sojourn, back then?"

Cory slouched on his side and addressed the door: downheartedly.

"My insomnia worsened. Besides Maitri, I was ripped by Chain's fortitude; and our dissolution. I took pills. Even so I'd sense Chain's vigil: wiping sweat from my beard, arms, and stomach.

"My plane had a midmorning takeoff. Rollo arrived while it was still dark with a carton of Pall Mall and a small stone elephant. Chain had trouble rousing me: I was already elsewhere. There I stayed during the dash to Don Muang, the procedure through tax clearance, currency-exchange, the airport fee, and customs. Non compos mentis, Rollo and Chain had to carry my luggage.'

"I slung a nylon bag onto the spools, quickly hugged the finally acquitted, and managed a '*Sawat-dee cap;* see you guys,' with clotted voice.

"Once beyond the gate, I realized I'd not had the diligence to wear on my sleeve the bitterness in this division: and turned to take my single, and indelible, trophy of our farewell. I saw the two of them, twenty yards off, leaning together, the ash-blond towered protectively over the Thai. Both were oval-mouthed, as if wailing in unrequited unison, 'Can you believe this? That man handcuffed us to him! And now he disappears, partisan to no one!' I passed out the moment I hit my window seat, remained out most of the flight, and lost the cigs and elephant, courtesy of an OD on yet more downs…

"What had gone unfelt was that I'd sprung a woody when I hugged Chain.

"And that was the last time I saw either of them."

"The last time?"

"Uh-huh. I am tired now. Could we—"

"Hey—stop—wait! What happened after that? To them, to you?"

"…I corresponded with them, of course, for years afterward. Five or six."

"And?"

"To be brief, I received a card from Chain eight or nine months later. It stated: 'I come to live in country of Spain. This my address. Your friend, Somboon.' Stapled to it was a nude portrait in cellophane. He was posed on a draped step-stool in classical profile, an elbow resting on the facet of his raised near knee, his scrotum and its long, sparse hairs made partially visible by the lifted thigh—that edible thigh! You see, I'd previously mailed a nude of myself to Soi 36. I'd been massaging a titian erection and was furtively snapped by my new lover when I'd the mistaken impression that he was bathing and that I, on his bed, was well out of sight. Steve was a Lao and Cambodian-battlefield photographer.

"And perhaps two years following that, another update. This said, 'I come back Thailand.' It enquired, pro forma, as to my family's health and mine, and furnished his old address. That was to be Chain's final attempt, so far as I know, to rekindle my—and reassure me of his own—priority.

"Holly-the-itinerant never wrote, but Khun Apirak did, twelve times. Tellingly, he included no telling details. For if Chain was all but away from Bangkok, and when there, face-bound, Apirak could not have dislodged any.

"With Rollo I'd communicate every six months. We used his latest toy, hour-cassettes. In reply to an inquiry re Oliver Littleton, Rollo said he'd not seen him since his visit to jail, and that if he were indentured in the Golden Triangle, he was only forgetting to water the poppies. To no inquiry at all, he stated obliquely that Kambu-ja was 'proving competent.' He hinted at concern over broadcasts (now anchored by Philip Bailey) rehashing that unchecked gay cancer. Otherwise Rol filled the sixty minutes with jumps in science and grammar and the innovative programs in his reassignment at Mahidol's west-bank extension.

"Then, a lengthy period in the late eighties when I heard nothing from him. After a barrage of badgering ones, he sent a cassette saying he was sorry for his laxity: he'd suffered a collapse at school one day and been rushed to hospital. He'd been in a coma for a time: and when he awoke was incapacitated, convinced he was dying. Now, thank goodness, he'd recovered; and felt, this trauma survived, ready to take on the globe and all its orphans. But in always choosing to rescue Pom instead of himself, I'm afraid that Pom would be his last orphan.

"He was in remission. Naturally Rollo Y-z wouldn't have known this. Except in constant replays, I was not to hear his voice ever again. In 1990, unable to abide his resumed and ominous silence, I took that new Minotaur by the horns and mailed a requested-signed-receipt letter to Sri Ayutthaya Road. It was returned to me unopened with—in the worst way to learn about it—the envelope stamped in red: '*DÉCÉDÉ.*'"

"Oh, man, that *is* rotten,' I agreed.

"Very. See, if a maypole, a jumbo, were in-house on his habitual forays to those bordellos in Patpong, he'd sit on it. You'll also remember that his lover was a war correspondent stationed above Chiang Rai, close to the Burmese border. NGOs presently in residence there have said they believe that entire sizeable city is HIV-positive: logical, since it is probably Burmese sex slaves who first infected Thailand. I told you that men up north, married or not, consider it a sign of their manhood to rent whores twice a month. With a lonely field-reporter..."

"And... Chain?"

"Listen, the majority of johns expect to penetrate a Thai hustler. The vamp is in his prettiness and presumed passivity, no? His *supposed* compliance. Chain, though he avoided anal sex if he could, certainly couldn't on all assignations; and that was when AIDS and how it's transmitted were still unknown."

I urged, "But with Chain—AIDS is an assumption, isn't it?"

"So what would *you* guess has become of him? That he found yet a third falang to take him back to Europe: and there he lives, happily ever after? He had—or has, today—the net of a rebel's élan; but not with the short fuse of *his* possessiveness, no, I shouldn't think so. Still, that's true: his falling victim to the plague is conjectural. It's correct to say his opalescence, which overrides time, does invite the possibility that he's endured to seem somehow more acceptable now than it did a decade ago. –Does that mitigation suffice?"

"You've searched for him here—recently?" I persisted.

"Of course. A lawyer restored and currently occupies his house. The older neighbors, typically, insist they never knew its previous inhabitants; and draw their gates. Again: the unnaming imperative, especially if the family's moving involved a death. His aunt and cousin in the Saladaeng shop are equally mute. Pavena got angry when I asked Somluck Khamsing, the country's close-to-worshiped and most recognizable kick-boxer, to do me a favor and pose questions just last week. If deceased, Chain's spirit would, anyhow, have already entered another body; and one not related to him.

"As for *my* welfare since then, in releasing Chain and the quasi control exercised by his reality, I predictably licensed a continuum with him to run amok. By day it took the form of imaginary immersion in drenching heat and humidity, by night a craving for the collar of his arm that was so relentless it prohibited sleeping alone. I spent years ducking the landlord. Then I naïvely went to work for a trade, based in Valdez, Alaska. Hiking in shirtsleeves or jogging in a tank top brought small relief; and aside from rewriting drafts on the breeding of wolves, the ennui and isolation did me in. After that, given that the climate meant diddly, I accepted assignments wherever my agent found them: urban planning in England or Ontario; and tropical locations, Kenya, the Caribbean, and the Celebes. One day, in a jungle on Irian Jaya, while trying to come up with a catalog for the two hundred and seventy-eight bird species there, I noticed that I did not feel hot. That night I slept. I'm here now to do an article on Prasat Khao Phra Viharn, the Parthenon of Asia, since the territorially disputed cliff on which it perches is temporarily open: it usually isn't."

"No, you aren't," I said. He finally looked at me. "You are here

307

now to write a bio of Parinya Kiatbusada."

"Excuse me?"

"Cory, I read *Pugilist*. It stuck with me. Its similarity to the boxer Parinya is obvious: and fated! So boxer and autobiographer Joshua Seabrooke, handed his Asian analogue, will also write up that boy's life. –It should be spanking."

Cory Simon squirmed: "Impressive speculation. Sneaky, very sneaky, young man! I'd no idea you'd done that much research. I'd no idea at the outset that I'd even allude to prizefighting, much less repatriate *that* alias. However, like I promised, the word is father to the idea. Everybody's idea."

"I detected your style." I nudged my box of tapes. "Hear these: Cory and Joshua are indistinguishable! It's your takes, pitch, rhythm, and phrasing. You wrote for *Architecture Digest*—you're big on Provençal and Greek Revival!"

"I once edited the last third of the *Digest*. Got sick of that too in time. How about Gustavo Rojo? You're not going to mention him?"

"Who?"

"The fellow who plays feature lead in *Tarzan and the Mermaids*. Folk who either go back a ways, or make it their business to, frequently claim I remind them of him. Born in Uruguay, 1927. Still does Latin soaps."

I said, "Ah, yes! Tico. In the film, he's called Tico. How did you know—?"

"Let's say a little bird told me—and the angle at which you scrutinized me a dozen times, his name was on the tip of your tongue. Pretty good for someone who never watches Tarzan movies… Still, you're wrong about Parinya: close, but wrong. It's Somluck, Somluck Khamsing I'm delving into. And I'm afraid he has *no* luck. Like at the Olympics. He gambles, to boot—poorly. He barfs when hit in the stomach. Yet he bankrolls his own training school for twenty boxers. You know, to toughen up those vulnerable spots, trainees, little kids, have to ram their shins and elbows against a tree until they skin. If they lose a bout, their coach will beat them within an inch of dying. So they dare not lose again... But enough, enough about work-in-progress! As for where I get my hoard right now, I still derive an income from my travel-takes on Central Africa and each of the Guianas. –*An East Coast Yank in Papa Doc's Court* straightened me out nicely for a while."

I said, "Made the bottom of best-seller lists, didn't it?"

"Yep. Invested those royalties wisely."

Cory glanced at his watch and smiled at me. He got us one-for-the-road, an Archa—"Horse": in the king's Thai. He emphatically toasted Khun Apirak. My tape had ten minutes to go. "Are you thinking of staying on here?"

"Do I give that impression? I shouldn't. Wild and gamey Loreleis await—on many another reef."

I wanted to ask what he planned to write after his book on *Muay Thai*. Like amateurs close. For a different way to wind up, his story of the food-taster for Hilton Hotels came to me. Not out of left field: since I had taken it to deride his teenage impulse to fly to Southeast Asia. It is about how "race" is a myth.

"There's a query slying on your lips," Cory noticed, downing half his Archa. "I see them moving. What is it?"

"I was working through that heavyweight, the guy who quit sumo wrestling to become a taster for Hilton Hotels."

"Who concluded that amongst its sugarcane walls and cane-leaf roofs, its dugongs, saltwater crocs, royal python, and megapode birds, *I* was the most exotic edit I'd find, in or outside of Jolly Boy? –So your question is?"

"If he were *really* now in this room, what would you like to say to Chain?"

"Good!" Cory responded. "–For a begged question, that is." He bit on his knuckles. Having already peeled off the label on his beer, he started to peel off the one on mine. He hummed to himself for a moment. "I think I should like to say to him, 'Thank you for sleeping with an American.'"

NORTHWEST'S CHECK-IN is at 4:00 a.m. I distrust wake-up calls at cut-rate joints. A midnight nap is tempting fate. My visa was due to expire that day. I reread my notes, could not concentrate, and hopped a shuttle out to the airport. The artery that runs there had no traffic at that hour (an elephant family and its mahouts caused a minor delay); I arrived at the international terminal with three hours to spare. I wheeled my baggage into a sitting area and slouched in front of a large TV. It was reviving Warner cartoons. I had fifty filled cassettes. I was confident about the other artists I pinned: with Cory, I felt my supervisor might say I crossed the limits of an ethical investigation.

A lot of time would pass before I decided to try to publish Cory's interviews in a separate volume. I needed to first get permission from what would then be a publicly reconciled Messrs. Simon and Seabrooke. I now had a vested stake in this disclosure. I would also feel accomplished to think I had a hand in it. Briefly, strengthening mental health and his sense of the inevitable or obligation won the day, and in less than a year I succeeded. As for Simon's claiming that I imitate him, he has a plethora of young, groupie imitators. I think that amuses him, and my becoming one tickles him even more. When I cell-phoned Cory, he went on and on about the circumference I planned to be, which creates a moral cosmos by defining what is good and what is not, and ended up by almost splitting my ears with: "Do what you want! The only thing we can't ask for on this earth is to be understood!" It was worth a stab. Though his rated sellers *are* Cory and Joshua's teamwork, I alone would capture the unruly and erratic in his stabilities.

The air-con at Don Muang is set for its awesome space when thousands of people assemble. With just me at 2:00 a.m., and an old woman pushing a broom, I felt chilly. I was too sleepy and uncoordinated by then to dig for a jacket under all those cassettes and bulky souvenirs. I also needed a cig, and every section I wandered over to was a nonsmoking area.

I stepped outside. I lit up there and regretted my lapse hours earlier, as I forever will, to confront Cory Simon—*and* Joshua Seabrooke—with my firm belief that if both personalities had elected to stay with Chain, Chain, assuming he is not, might still be alive today. I would have been able to see him. Then I gagged, and because my eyes had watered, saw the pea-soup pollution, like a cozy on top of, or a cataract spilling between, the deserted airport buildings. I felt the absolutely sauna-level humidity. And Bangkok's legendary, searing heat: so grave it could cinder the staunchest resolve.

CPSIA information can be obtained at www.ICGtesting.com
Printed in the USA
LVOW071229040512

280217LV00007B/3/P